ANGELS

of

HUMILITY

JACKIE MACGIRVIN

ANGELS

of

HUMILITY

A NOVEL

DESTINY IMAGE® PUBLISHERS, INC.

P.O. Box 310, Shippensburg, PA 17257-0310

"Speaking to the Purposes of God for This Generation and for the Generations to Come."

This book and all other Destiny Image, Revival Press, MercyPlace, Fresh Bread, Destiny Image Fiction, and Treasure House books are available at Christian bookstores and distributors worldwide.

For a U.S. bookstore nearest you, call 1-800-722-6774.

For more information on foreign distributors, call 717-532-3040.

Reach us on the Internet: www.destinyimage.com.

ISBN 13 TP: 978-0-7684-3625-9

ISBN 13 HC: 978-0-7684-3626-6

ISBN 13 LP: 978-0-7684-3627-3

ISBN 13 Ebook: 978-0-7684-9045-9

For Worldwide Distribution, Printed in the U.S.A.

1 2 3 4 5 6 7 8 9 10 / 14 13 12 11

ACKNOWLEDGMENTS

Thanks to Ronda Ranalli and the awesome team at Destiny Image. Thanks to my two friends and grammar consultants, Lori Garcia and Myrna Holmquist. I guess my strategy of using a comma after every twelfth word didn't work. To my writing buddy Jacalyn Mcleod. If I'd met you six months ago, this book would have been even better. To my wonderful friend Kathy Burris, to satisfy her desire to see her name in a book.

ENDORSEMENTS

You are going to love this book because you can apply these biblical, life-changing principles in your everyday life. Using real-life illustrations in a story form, Jackie Macgirvin brings to life a viable, easily understood example on the importance of intercession, humility, and living for the eternal realm. You cannot walk victoriously without observing these foundational truths.

Bobby Connor
Eagles View Ministries

Jackie Macgirvin's book *Angels of Humility* surpasses excellence. It is a glimpse beyond the veil into the realities of the spiritual realm. This excellent fiction makes your heart thrill and your hair stand on end as it explores the hardships of having faith while living in this world and the ecstasy waiting in the world beyond for those who have trusted Christ. Each page reverberates with the witness of the Spirit. *Angels of Humility* is for people of all ages who can read or be read to and who hope, believe, or dread that there is Someone or something more out there! Run, do not walk, to get yours and one for the people you care about.

Bonnie Chavda
Author, *Hidden Power of a Woman*

"And Satan trembles when he sees,
The weakest saint upon his knees." —William Cowper[1]

Foreword

If you're an intercessor or have a desire to be one, this book is for you. There are many excellent teaching books on intercession, humility, fervency, and eternal rewards; however, I am not aware of any fictional book that embraces these issues.

Through following the lives of two very different Christians, *Angels of Humility* gives an understanding of what one person, even a weak and unlikely one, can achieve for God. You'll understand the importance of your prayers and actions, now and in eternity.

The author's main goal is not to only entertain readers, but to impact their lifestyle in the following three areas:

1. The only way to be exalted is through the low door called humility. Anyone can be great in God's Kingdom—do small acts of kindness on a daily basis as unto Him. Unfortunately, dedicated Christians in the western Church are striving for prominence and position, the total opposite of Jesus' example and commands.

2. You really can pray without ceasing, even if you aren't called to be a full-time intercessor. Your prayers make a bigger impact than you can even imagine.

3. The only thing that matters about your life is the evaluation you receive from the Lord when you die. There are two kingdoms; the visible and the invisible—don't invest in the wrong one. You don't want to experience regret when your life is evaluated.

We know these things, but we are too easily distracted. As you read it will become clear that you do not want to suffer loss on that day! This book will strengthen your resolve to live a life wholly abandoned to Him.

This book is full of ideas for praying as you go, applicable for any person in any walk of life. With the nudging of her angels, Sarah, who is newly converted at age 71, discovers prayer walking, prayer driving, and praying for people who are pictured on billboards, magazine covers, or television. She prays for whoever is on the receiving end of any siren she hears. When she is waiting for a train, she prays for each of the drifters who painted the graffiti on the railway cars. She discovers that if she's not eating or talking, she can be praying in tongues and makes it her goal to do that constantly. She also prays everyday for the people who are going to die in the next 24 hours. Whew! If you implement half the intercessory ideas from this book, your prayer life will be radically impacted.

I recommend *Angels of Humility* to those who are hungry to grow in urgency, who want to be more disciplined in prayer, who want to increase in their understanding of how their daily choices make an eternal difference, and who want to begin or continue the life-long quest to be like our beautiful Savior who humbled Himself to take the form of a man, came to earth, and died on a cross.

Mike Bickle
Director, International House of Prayer
Kansas City, MO

INTRODUCTION

Angels of Humility is a call to radical commitment now. There will be a first time when our eyes will meet Jesus' as we stand before Him. I do not want my immediate response to be glancing at the ground in shame over the way I've lived. I do not want to waste the gifts and talents He has given me.

This story vividly portrays how the Lord values humility and prayer and how diligence can result in standing before His judgment throne and hearing Him say, "Well done, good and faithful servant." Surprisingly, this is within reach of every believer.

To be great in the sight of the world, one needs wealth, beauty, talent, a family name, and so forth. This excludes 99 percent of us. But God's Kingdom is the only kingdom where everyone can be great; one need only to be the servant of all, which is attainable by all.

I used to work in a medical complex where the office numbering system was quite confusing. Each morning as I went to get the mail, I would check for people who looked confused. Then I would help them find their way. I did this as a way of serving the Lord. According to Scripture, the Lord will reward me for each of these simple actions. I jokingly tell people that I think the Lord will give me a hot tub connected to my heavenly mansion for these miniscule actions and if I hadn't bragged about it here, He probably would have filled it with water, too!

People spend more time planning their earthly retirement than they do their spiritual eternity. Please don't let this happen to you. The blood of Jesus cleanses us from that which would keep us out of Heaven, but it does not eliminate our life's evaluation.

Whatever we build on that foundation will be tested by fire on the day of judgment. Then everyone will find out if we have used gold, silver, and precious stones, or wood, hay, and straw. We will be rewarded if our building is left standing. But if it is destroyed by the fire, we will lose everything. Yet we ourselves will be saved, like someone escaping from flames (1 Corinthians 3:12-15 CEV).

By examining the lives of Sarah and Pastor Paul, we see what can cause us to suffer loss or what can bring us incredible joy on that day. Please learn from them how to live well while you still have time. These 75 years are just the womb of life, but they affect how we spend eternity. Eternity is an incalculable concept for a finite brain, but it's a long, long time.

To him who overcomes, I will give the right to sit with Me on My throne, just as I overcame and sat down with My Father on His throne (Revelation 3:21).

So we make it our goal to please Him… (2 Corinthians 5:9).

The servant…said, "Sir, you gave me five thousand coins, and I have earned five thousand more." "Wonderful!" his master replied. "You are a good and faithful servant. I left you in charge of only a little, but now I will put you in charge of much more. Come and share in my happiness" (Matthew 25:20-21 CEV).

Suppose someone gives even a cup of cold water to a little one…. What I'm about to tell you is true. That one will certainly be rewarded (Matthew 10:42 NIRV).

I find this absolutely amazing that the God of the universe would give us a reward that will last for eternity for doing something so simple! This is within everyone's reach.

My prayer for you is that you will live in such a way that eternity will become a priority over this visible, temporal realm and that when you stand before the Lord you will truly share in His joy over your life.

Jackie Macgirvin

CHAPTER 1

"We are not human beings having a temporary spiritual experience; we are spiritual beings having a temporary human experience."

Pierre Teilhard De Chardin[1]

A death was in progress in Room 120 of Bradbury Manor, the town's nursing home. It is a wonderful, joyous death—a spiritual celebration in full swing. Two towering, ancient angels, clothed in dazzling garments of light, were singing, marching, and dancing around the figure of a frail, elderly lady, fetal and unconscious under a pink chenille bedspread. Sarah was unaware of the celestial celebration and the heavenly orders that would transition her into God's paradise—the eternal dwelling place for which she was created.

The angels paused from their celebration. "A stroke," whispered Malta, the worshiping angel smiling tenderly, as he gazed at Sarah's face. "The Lord is eagerly waiting, and I can hardly stand it myself."

"At sunrise this frail little intercessor, who was so dynamic a witness on earth, is finally going to rest in the Lord's arms," said Joel, the warrior angel, his two-edged sword by his side, his eyes ever vigilant.

It was a little before 5 A.M., and the angels glowed with anticipation of the swallowing up of her temporal, earthly life into an eternity of love and peace.

"Precious in the sight of the Lord is the death of His saints,"[2] shouted Joel. They resumed their marching, dancing, and praising around the bed. Sarah was wholly protected even in her vulnerable state.

Huddled together in the corner of the room, growling, were several yellow-eyed spirits. The largest one, Death, was busy formulating a final plan of attack with the low-ranking imps under his command. He despised them all. The feeling was mutual.

Just as they were ready to strike, Malta blew his shofar and the heavens opened. The atmosphere was energized with even more glory. Breathtaking sounds of celestial music wafted into the room, along with heavenly colors and fragrances. Angels carrying instruments surrounded Sarah's bed. This heavenly choir followed Malta's worship, and their joyful praise not only filled the room, but flowed back to the throne of grace like a tidal wave of pure joy.

"Great, more angels—that's just what we need," whined Discouragement.

"Make them stop singing," wailed Depression. "I can't take any more worship. I think I'm going to be sick!"

"Enough complaining!" barked Death. "We've got to attack now. When I give the word, charge. Maybe one of you can get to her pathetic, wrinkled body. She's barely holding to life by a thread."

"We couldn't even get to her when there were just two of them—I'm not going anywhere near that bed!" yelped Infirmity, ducking quickly to avoid a blow from Death.

Fear of Man emphatically agreed. "Do you see those angels walking back and forth with the swords? Do you see the impenetrable wall of protection and glory around her? You can charge if you want, but I'm staying right here!"

Chapter 1

"We've tried unsuccessfully to kill her for 16 months. Let's face it. We can't even steal one second from the life span appointed to her," said Intimidation.

Knowing it would indeed be impossible to penetrate the angelic worship, Death turned on these minion imps in anger.

"We had Sarah her whole life. How did you manage to lose her in the last year and a half?" he screamed. "Do you realize what she set in motion? This one wretched little old lady has started an avalanche of sal-sal-salvations around the world. You're all a bunch of incompetent idiots, and we'll be tortured for failing this mission!" The imps retaliated by hissing, cursing, scratching, and blaming each other for their failure.

Joel gazed intently at them with eyes like blazing fire. He unsheathed his flaming two-edged sword, and on his next pass by that side of the room, he slashed through the gnarled demonic mass. They vaporized into a harmless puff of yellow sulfurous smoke. Joel grinned as he resheathed his sword, "I love my job."

With the sun slightly below the horizon, the angels gathered around the bed in hushed excitement. Joel and Malta, always on the alert, bent over Sarah.

"Soooo—close," whispered Malta, stroking Sarah's forehead and smiling at Joel. They'd been her guardians for 16 months. Unbelievably, they felt even more love for Sarah welling inside them than before. "Get ready," said Joel, gazing into the opened Heaven, awaiting the final word. Malta lay his hand on Sarah's chest to feel her breathing, a little shallower each time.

"NOW!" shouted Joel, having received orders from the fiery throne. As her last breath escaped her frail, fleshly shell, the sun's first rays peeked over the horizon. Surges of light permeated the room as the heavenly corridor of glory touched earth. Sarah's spirit emerged into Malta's waiting arms. Glancing back at the bed, she caught a glimpse of her aged face, ashen-colored and wrinkled. She was whisked through the portal toward an unseen realm of eternity by a jubilant Malta, with Joel flying ahead. Escorted by her two triumphant angels, she was moving faster than the speed of light.

Liquid warmth enveloped Sarah. For the first time ever, she felt the complete absence of pain and the presence of total peace. She was leaving behind all sin and its damning results, with which she had lived since birth. Shielded by her two ecstatic angels, she moved rapidly toward a brilliant light in the remote distance.

CHAPTER 2

"Christ doesn't become precious to us until we are humble. When we preoccupy ourselves with our own wants and needs we can't see the matchless worth of Christ. Also, until we comprehend how lost we are we can't understand Christ's wondrous and redeeming love. Until we see our poverty we can't see His riches. No man enters the kingdom without understanding his own sinfulness and realizing his need to repent."

John MacArthur[1]

Sixteen months earlier:

Bradbury was a small, rural Missouri community of 8,000. Some still farmed their family's ground. Others commuted to Mt. Pielor 15 miles away, to work in the factories or stores that had sprung up there. These stores provided much needed jobs and less expensive goods and services, but also drew business away from Bradbury's town square.

Sarah was a widow who had lived her whole life in Bradbury. It had only been six months since cancer had stolen her beloved George away from her. The ache was no less intense; it still consumed her every waking minute and intruded on her dreams as well. Over the last two years of his declining health, she had gone from introvert to recluse, sitting by his bed, caring for him each day.

In the beginning stages of the disease, he was still talkative, but as he deteriorated, she spent hours just sitting beside him in silence. To pass the time she read books on raising orchids and taught herself to crochet. Now, six multicolored afghans were folded in Sarah's hall closet waiting to be donated to a good cause—the Elk's Club Raffle or maybe the High School's yearly fundraiser.

Sarah was shy and had many insecurities. Unable to have children, she had spent her life as a wife, doting on George. Her only contact with the outside world toward the end was the visiting nurses and Dr. Newbury. After George's death Sarah was totally alone, except for the demonic spirits who had flooded in to convince her that her life no longer had purpose. Agoraphobia kept her housebound except for necessary trips to the grocery store. At night, before she fell asleep, was the worst time of her whole dreadful day. The spirits clamored around, tormenting her, planting thoughts in her mind with their sticky voices:

"George is dead. You'll never see him again," shrieked Discouragement. "He's gone forever."

"No one else loves you," whispered Lying.

"You've got nothing to live for, no kids—no grandkids," growled Death.

When she managed to sleep, she slept fitfully. She woke frequently. Sarah eventually became afraid of sleep because she was besieged by terrifying dreams about George's death involving dismemberment and other gruesome images.

One night Suicide arrived at bedtime. "Since you idiots can't seem to carry out your orders to do away with one pathetic, elderly lady, I've been sent to take over. For some reason this is an urgent, priority assignment."

He slithered into Sarah's bedroom and whispered, "What a loser, you couldn't have kids. You've given your whole life to being a wife; now you're not. You've done what you were put here to do. Your purpose in life is over. You're just taking up space in your old age."

What's left for me? wondered Sarah. *It's all downhill from here.*

"Have you considered just ending your miserable, pathetic existence? The afterlife has got to be better than the present—the horrid grieving and the continual pity-party that consumes you."

When she finally dozed off from total exhaustion at 4:00 A.M., Suicide lay coiled around her, whispering wicked thoughts. She was barraged by scenes of taking her own life—using a razor blade, crashing her car, jumping off a bridge, overdosing on pills, even shooting herself. She awoke screaming at 4:15 and refused to go back to sleep.

Sarah was helpless as she felt her life spiral downward. Full-blown depression and exhaustion consumed her. Now she was too scared to leave the house even to grocery shop. There was no food, but it didn't matter; she had no appetite. Food no longer tasted good, and she began to drop weight from her already small frame.

"It's just a matter of weeks before she succumbs to me," said Depression, smiling. "She's lost her will to live."

"She should have been dead months ago," interrupted Suicide. "I'll get her before you do. She's highly vulnerable now. Her grief and exhaustion make her susceptible to taking her own life. I'm going to rub her nose in it that she never had kids." He sneered at Depression as he slithered next to Sarah and wrapped his scaly constricting body around hers.

"Well, one of us needs to take her out quickly," whispered Death. "I've heard rumors from the enemy's kingdom that she has a great destiny."

"At her age?" sniped Discouragement. "She's 71 years old and still as lost as a goose in a cloudburst. She's spent her whole life barely thinking about God. She's been ours all her pathetic life." His black lips curled into a smirk. "And she will be ours in death—for all eternity."

When Suicide replied, "The Godhead has worked miraculously through stranger people than her," a simultaneous chill penetrated the demonic horde.

Pastor Hall was sitting in his cluttered office reading his devotions. His radiant guardian angel, Aaron, full of wisdom and knowledge, waited until

Pastor Hall read the section about God's heart for the widows and orphans. When he saw the word *widows*, Aaron reminded him of something he was going to do six months ago.

He absent-mindedly ran his fingers through his silver gray hair. *Where would I have put that?* He rummaged through the bottom drawer of his old mahogany desk. The first layer was last month's bulletins, then the file with the church's electric bills and several candy bar wrappers, *I gotta get rid of the evidence,* he thought, resting his hand on his ample waist. He finally found what he was looking for at the bottom of "get-to-it-someday" papers— George's obituary from the Bradbury *Gazette.* Neither George nor Sarah had ever been to the church as far as he could remember, but Pastor Hall had made it a practice to visit all the community members who had hard times, whether they were church members or not. He'd done it for the last 18 years.

He closed his worn, leather-bound Bible with the dog-eared pages. *Maybe they'll get me a new one at my retirement party. This one is pretty much falling apart.* With a prayer on his lips he bounded to his car. Soon he pulled up in front of Sarah's small white bungalow with purple lilacs surrounding the front porch. His wife always commented on those lilac bushes, but he never knew who lived there.

He whistled all the way up the sidewalk. He loved sharing the Gospel. As near as he could figure, he'd been to almost half the homes in the whole town. He stopped to take a whiff of the fragrant lavender flowers before knocking on the screen door.

Although Pastor Hall had never seen Sarah, he was taken aback by the haggard figure with the sunken eyes staring at him suspiciously through the screen door. Her hair was unkempt, there were bags under her eyes, and her dress was just hanging on her frail body. "Send him away," growled Deception. "You've got no time for him." After his friendly introduction, though, Sarah overcame her distrust and invited him in.

Sarah was suddenly aware of how a new person would see her surroundings. She felt her face flush as she saw coffee cups half full, left scattered throughout the room. The vacuum cleaner was still plugged in from four weeks ago. Unwatered orchids were dying everywhere. She grabbed the plate with a half-eaten piece of moldy toast and tried to conceal it.

"Please, sit here," she pointed to an overstuffed floral chair by the fireplace; "I'll make us some coffee." She retreated to the kitchen. *What is wrong with me?* She threw the toast in the sink. *I'm losing it.* She cradled her face in her hands as she waited for the coffee. *I can't do anything right.*

"That's right sister," whispered Discouragement. *"You're just takin' up space."*

The spiritual atmosphere in the house was oppressive. While Sarah was in the kitchen Pastor Hall prayed and rebuked the demonic. He couldn't see them, but he could sense their evil presence by the revulsion he felt in his spirit, and he could see their obvious influence on Sarah.

In response to his prayer, two magnificent angels appeared in the room. Joel, a warrior angel, towered over nine feet tall; his chest was covered with a golden breastplate, and he carried a sharp two-edged sword on his hip in an ornately decorated golden sheath. He was fierce in holiness, constantly alert, and had eyes like flaming fire.

Malta, a worshiping angel, wore a brilliant white robe with a golden sash holding a shofar at the waist. In large pockets around his robe he carried a flute, lyre, and harp. Other pockets held scrolls of heavenly music tied up with ribbons. Glistening light reflected off his golden-blonde hair.

Alive with God's presence, they reflected the glory of Heaven and brought its fragrance with them wherever they went. Their heavenly bodies were strong and lean, but their real power was their constant lifeline with the Trinity. They were always aware of Father's orders. Joel and Malta had been ministering together since they were created, the warrior and the worshipper, each equally capable of defeating the enemy; together— unstoppable.

When Sarah came back from the kitchen, she felt her mood elevate slightly for the first time in months. Also, something told her she could trust the man sitting in front of her. After a few questions from Pastor Hall, she sobbed as she poured out her heart about how hard the last few years had been with George's cancer and then her depression.

After about 20 minutes she mostly composed herself and ended by saying, "Life's not worth living anymore. I'm just waiting to die. I'm embarrassed to say it," she looked away from his compassionate eyes and stared at the floor, "But I've even thought of taking my own life. I...I was never able to have children, and now my husband is dead. There's nothing left for me now."

"Oh, Sarah, I'm so sorry for all you've been through the last couple years." He leaned toward her. "But I can promise you that suicide is never the solution. It would be wrong for you to take your life because God gave it to you. Even though you're older, whether you're going to be around for one, five, or ten years, He still has a plan for you. He loves you so much, and He wants the rest of your life to be productive and joyful. You've been listening to the wrong voice, if that makes sense."

Sarah dabbed at her eyes with the tissue and shook her head no.

"Well, the devil hates you and he has a plan for your life—total destruction—misery and hopelessness on earth and an eternity in Hell after death..."

"*Woo hoo*," shouted Misery.

"...but God loves you, and He has a plan for your life on earth, and then for you to dwell in eternal Paradise with Him. He actually planned your life before He even created the world. You've been listening to the devil's lying voice, which will always lead to something evil. In this case, his lie says that you have no purpose for living and that you should take your own life.

"Don't listen," whispered Lying. "You don't have a purpose. You should be dead by now."

"Did you grow up in church?"

"No."

"In that case, I'm going to start with some basics. May I read a few things?"

She nodded. *Why has this kind man come to see me today?*

"Before I get to the good news, I'm going to share some bad news. The Bible tells us that all have sinned and fallen short of God's glory.[2] I don't know anyone who is perfect, do you?" Sarah shook her head in agreement.

"This next Scripture tells us that the wages, or the result, of sin is death.[3] Death is eternal separation from a loving God. But that's not what God wants; He wants relationship with all His children, including you. The Bible says that He's not willing that any should perish,[4] but that He came to give *everyone* eternal life.[5] Let me explain this a little more clearly."

"Nooooo. I can't take it," shrieked Depression, writhing.

"Because of God's holiness, He can't allow sin in His presence. Sin has to be paid for in order for us to be forgiven. Only then can we be in relationship with God."

"No, it's blasphemy. Don't listen. Don't listen," yelled Death.

"Only a person who is totally righteous can pay for sin. When a sinful human dies, his death doesn't pay for anything. Death is what he deserves. Remember, '*the wages of sin is death*'[6]? None of us has the ability to pay for our own sins. Because Jesus was sinless, when He voluntarily gave His life on the cross, it actually paid for everyone's sins.[7]

"Your sins are too bad to ever be forgiven," screeched Deception. "It's all a lie."

"Accept His sacrifice for your sin and then, in gratitude for the free gift of salvation, dedicate your life to following Him every day. Then He will show you His wonderful, life-giving plans. Isn't that wonderful news?" he asked with a big smile. "What an incredible gift! He is the God who sacrificed Himself for you."

"I always thought we had to earn our way to Heaven by being good enough," said Sarah.

"No, we can't cancel the bad by doing good. Remember, sin has to be paid for. And we don't live good lives to earn God's love or to get Him to save us; we live good lives out of gratitude that He saved us as a free gift. Plus, we now have His help to change those sinful habits that we used to be powerless over."

As Sarah struggled to understand what all that meant, Malta appeared behind her and repeated what Pastor Hall had just spoken. The angels' voices are not heard with earthly ears, but are apprehended by the human mind as a thought.

For the first time in her life, Sarah felt the weight of sin she was carrying. She realized that she needed forgiveness. Her strategy of trying to be a good person was woefully lacking compared to God's standard of holiness. *It hasn't worked for me so far.*

"Sarah, would you like to pray and acknowledge Jesus' death as paying for all your sins?" Sarah nodded her head.

"Nooo," screamed Depression. "She's ours!" Sarah's affirmation gave Joel the authority he needed to act on her behalf. With one slice of the double-edged sword, he freed Sarah from the demonic torment that was trying to take her life and rob her of her destiny. The demons fled in terror.

Softly, Sarah said, "Dear Jesus, thank You for dying for my sins so I wouldn't have to. I give You what's left of my life and ask You to show me what You want me to do."

When Sarah prayed, although she had no way of knowing it, in the spiritual realm she was clothed in a brilliant, glowing white robe of righteousness. Embroidered in glistening white on the sleeves were Sarah's spiritual gifts—prophecy (hearing from the Lord for other people) and intercession (fervent prayer).

"This is the same righteousness that Jesus has, as a free gift to you," said Joel. "Now when Father looks at you, He sees Jesus' righteousness, provided you continually ask forgiveness for your sins. It's the most incredible exchange in the world! Your filthy rags of sin[8] are traded for the most costly, most valuable robe of righteousness."

"And this," said Malta, "is the mantle of humility." He placed a drab brown-colored robe on her that totally covered her glowing white one.

"Next to the robe of righteousness, this is the most important garment. Don't ever take it off, Sarah, or you'll make yourself vulnerable to the enemy. Pride always goes before a fall,[9] but God gives grace to the humble."[10]

"Our Lord was cloaked in humility when He walked the earth. His indescribable glory was temporarily hidden, and humility and love were two of His distinguishing characteristics.[11] Most Christians never come close to accomplishing what the Lord has for them because they won't humble themselves," said Joel. "Humility doesn't get bestowed on you. It's a joint venture. God grants you faith and grace as you, through diligent prayer and practice, fight a spiritual battle against your innate prideful desires. God won't do your part, and you can't do His."

Pastor Hall continued, "Sarah, you have no idea how precious you are to the Lord. Did you know that the angels in Heaven are rejoicing right now over your decision?"[12]

"So are the angels right here," said Malta as he played a celebratory song on his flute. Joel looked into the open Heaven, raised his hands toward the sky, and worshiped the Lord. *"You are worthy...because You were slain, and with Your blood You purchased men for God from every tribe and language and people and nation."*[13]

These two angels would be with Sarah until her death. And although she was not aware of their presence, they would constantly guard and encourage her in the Lord.

Pastor Hall left and Sarah read the tract he had given her. One of the Scriptures was especially meaningful to her:

> *The LORD your God is with you, he is mighty to save. He will take great delight in you, he will quiet you with his love, he will rejoice over you with singing.*[14]

Sarah was more than a little confused about all that had happened, but she knew she felt immensely better. Her thoughts of suicide were totally gone, and she was able to sleep through the night. She left the house to grocery shop without fear, and she enjoyed eating again. Her strength was returning and she was able to revive most of her orchids.

She went to church that Sunday morning and made her public profession of faith, just like Pastor Hall had encouraged her to do. Two weeks later, she was baptized at age 71 and joined the over-60 Sunday school class. She gathered copies of all the free devotionals, tracts, and literature to take home and study.

Pastor Hall scheduled several meetings with Sarah to get her started on the right track. Sarah's primary spiritual gift, her true spiritual destiny, was intercession, which had lain dormant her entire life. Although Pastor Hall didn't realize this, the basic teachings that he gave her on prayer helped to get her started.

Sarah was seated across the mahogany desk with a pen and a notebook.

"Sarah, it's important that every Christian has a time of prayer with the Lord the first thing in the morning. Jesus is our model. The Scriptures tell us that He often withdrew by Himself to pray.[15] He never acted independently of the Father, but stayed until He received instruction and strength for His daily plans. That's why Scripture says that Jesus only did what He saw the Father doing.[16] If Jesus needed to meet with the Father each day, how much more important is it for us?"

This was all new to Sarah, but she nodded her agreement at this sobering thought.

"Now maybe you didn't know this, but the devil shows up at Christians' prayer times, too. He'll do everything he can to distract and accuse you. You can't let him derail you." He saw a look of confused horror spread across Sarah's face.

"Let me explain, Sarah. There's the visible, tangible world around us that we can all see, like the furniture here and the trees and grass. However, overlaying this natural realm is a spiritual realm that few people can actually see, but it's more real than the visible realm that is decaying and passing away. God is the creator of both realms. Remember the day I came to visit you? There were demons in the house that were assigned to take your life. When I walked in, my spirit sensed their presence. I started praying, and when you gave your life to the Lord they eventually left."

"I didn't exactly know they were demons," she said, "but I know my whole house feels lighter." She let out a deep sigh, "It sure feels like a burden has been lifted off me."

"You were being oppressed by the dark side of the spirit world. Ephesians 6:12 says, *'For our struggle is not against flesh and blood, but against…the spiritual forces of evil in the heavenly realms.'* That's just another way of saying that the visible, tangible world and the people in it aren't the real problem. It's the spirits motivating them who are the problem."

"Ephesians 6:12," said Sarah as she scribbled in her notebook.

"One way we fight back is through prayer. Your prayers release spiritual power to defeat the enemy in the spiritual realm. Then you see the breakthrough in the natural realm. First in the spiritual, then in the natural."

"Wow, I've got a lot to learn," said Sarah. "I'd never even heard the stories you read from the Bible on Sunday."

"Well, Sarah," said Pastor Hall standing up, "It's never too late to learn, and I commit that I will pray that you would grow exponentially in the things of the Lord and be a great hindrance to the devil's kingdom. Even after I move, I'll keep praying for you. And let me give you this book on humility. I give copies to every new believer. It's a great way to start your Christian life. The Bible says that God resists the proud, but gives grace to the humble.[17] I want grace and grace and more grace in my life. The thought of God actively resisting me is terrifying."

He shook her hand and Sarah managed to thank him, but she was so overwhelmed at his commitment to pray for her that she was crying by the time she got to her car. Just knowing that a seasoned Christian would be praying for her helped her feel less overwhelmed.

She read most of the book on humility that week and only missed having her prayer time one morning. The next week at their meeting, Sarah had more questions ready for Pastor Hall, especially about pride.

"Well," said Pastor Hall, "I'm glad you're interested. Most Christians don't fight against pride or understand enough about humility to earnestly desire it. That's a tragedy because if we humble ourselves, God promises to exalt us![18] Pride is one of the most deadly forces at Satan's disposal, and he uses it very effectively against us."

"That's exactly what the book said. It sounded like God takes these areas seriously," said Sarah with her eyes wide. Pastor Hall chuckled.

"Yes, He does—very seriously."

Sarah, flipped to one of the dog-eared pages. "It says that 'humility is the God-given confidence that does away with the need to prove to others how worthy you are, and the correctness of your actions. It gives the freedom to be who you were created by God to be, and to accomplish what God has for you to do—because you completely agree with Him.'"

"That's a great definition! I totally agree. We need to perform before an audience of One," he said pointing upward. Sarah nodded as that truth sunk in. "God has given each of us a different mix of spiritual and natural gifts. It's humility when we accept what we are given and use these giftings as God planned. Don't covet what other's have. It will throw you off of God's path for your life. You'll only be judged on what God gave you and the specific purposes that He called you to do."

"What do you mean, 'I'll be judged on what God gives me'?"

"When Christians die, their lives are judged and they are given rewards for their faithfulness or they '*suffer loss*' for their lack of obedience.[19] They all get to Heaven, but the Bible speaks many times about eternal rewards and being faithful with what we're given.[20] Develop your spiritual gifts. You entered the Kingdom late in life Sarah, so be diligent to give the Lord your time and your energy; make Him your priority above all distractions. When you get to Heaven and you really understand God's great love for you and the amazing sacrifice He made for you, you'll be grateful that you did."

"Do I really have spiritual gifts? I don't know what they are."

"Your spiritual gifts were picked especially for you by the Lord. You can understand your true destiny better when you function in your gifts. It helps you know who God created you to be and what He desires for you to do. There's a list in the last chapter of the book I gave you. Go home and read it. Pray and see if the Lord highlights anything to you."

At home Sarah read the descriptions of pastor/teacher, prophet, evangelist, apostle, administrator, leadership, faith, knowledge, wisdom, exhortation, discernment, ministering, service, giving, speaking in tongues, interpretation of tongues, miracles, healings, mercy, and hospitality.[21]

She faithfully prayed over the list. "I can't wait to meet with Pastor Hall next week. I've got so much to learn."

CHAPTER 3

"Do you wish to rise? Begin by descending. You plan a tower that will pierce the clouds? Lay first the foundation of humility."

Saint Augustine[1]

Pastor Hall retired two months after their last meeting, and he and his wife left Bradbury for Texas to care for his aged mother. But he was faithful to remember to pray for Sarah regularly.

The church board had called Paul Reynolds as interim to the little white chapel with the beautiful stained glass windows. With seminary graduation under his belt for less than a week, Paul had felt very grateful and relieved to be selected.

It was his first time preaching at Bradbury. Paul always started his sermons with a joke. "A woman calls her husband on his cell phone. He's driving in his car; 'Honey I want you to be very careful. I just heard on the radio that there's someone driving the wrong way down Old Highway 3.'

"'One?' the husband replies, 'There's *hundreds* of them!'"

The congregation roared with appreciative laughter. Paul let out a deep sigh of relief and ran his fingers through his perfectly coiffed, jet-black hair. At 6'2", with a natural athletic build—wearing his best and only suit—he presented a good first impression.

Maybe they'll like me. Maybe they'll call me as their pastor.

"Relax," said Saldu, to Paul's spirit. Paul's radiant guardian angel was standing in the pulpit directly behind him. "The service isn't about you. It's about glorifying your wonderful savior and Lord. Take your mind off your performance. Empty yourself and He'll fill you. Then you'll have truth and life to share."

Shifting his weight from his left to his right foot and back again, like he always did when he had too much nervous energy, he began again, "I'm happy to be here today serving as your interim pastor. I'd like to introduce my better half. Kathy, will you stand please?" A petite brunette with curly hair, wearing a denim jumper, stood from the second row and gave the crowd a big smile and a wave.

"Jordan is 2 years old, and he is in the nursery. I speak for all of us when I say we look forward to getting to know all of you and serving with you here at the Victory Church of Bradbury, Missouri."

At least I'll be employed until the search committee calls someone else. At the very least, he hoped they would be committee-typical and take six months making up their minds. That would give him time to get something else lined up. He had student loans up to his eyebrows, even though Kathy had worked until she was very pregnant with Jordan.

However, deep in his heart he was hoping to be the one, hoping to wow them with all the knowledge he'd gleaned from 89 graduate hours, not to mention his ability to read Hebrew and Greek. *God,* he silently prayed, *If this is Your will, I'd be so glad.*

At the back door shaking hands after the sermon, Paul tried every memory trick he knew to remember people's names. He pictured an outhouse floating in the ocean when he met John Seas. Angela Carver became an angel sculpting a big piece of cheese. Sarah Edwards was easy; her name was the same as the wife of his hero, the fiery evangelist, Jonathan Edwards.

For ten full minutes Paul basked in the adoration and compliments as the church members filed by shaking hands on the way to their Sunday dinners.

"Great sermon, pastor."

"I enjoyed that a lot."

"I never knew the meaning of that one word in Greek; that's very interesting."

If Kathy and Paul could have seen into the spirit world, they would have fainted at the sight of two tall, muscular angels with angular, chiseled features accompanying them to their small Toyota. Valoe had long blond hair and Saldu, brown. Their glistening white robes were girded at the waist with a belt of truth. Their enormous gossamer wings were folded behind them. After being in the throne room from eternity past, they literally glowed with celestial resurrection power. Hael, Jordan's plump, jovial guardian angel, was waiting to get in the back next to Jordan's car seat. Valoe and Saldu would fly along beside the small car. Even though these guardians had been with them for years, neither Paul nor Kathy were aware of their presence.

The minute Kathy and Paul were in their car, before the key was even in the ignition, Paul turned to Kathy and asked, "Well?"

"Well, what?"

"What do you mean 'well what'? How'd I do? What did you hear from the people?"

Kathy rolled her eyes, "Just the same things you did when we were standing together in the back."

"I know what they said, but what did they *really* think? Did they seem to like it? Did they follow along?"

"You did fine, honey. The sermon was very good; you know it's one of my favorites."

"Were they nodding? What did their body language tell you?"

"Honey, I was sitting on the second row. All I could see was you!" She patted his shoulder. "Take a deep breath and relax; you did fine."

"Kathy, I've got a good feeling about this," he said, as he eased the car onto the blacktop road and back toward town. "I think this might be God. I can see us settling here. I can see Jordan growing up here. I can see me taking this church from 60 members to 300, and I know you think the parsonage is charming."

"After the seminary dorm, living in a department store dressing room would be charming."

"No, I'm serious; I think we have a future here. I have a good feeling about this. It has potential. It feels like it might fit."

"Honey, I appreciate your enthusiasm, but you've got your cart way out before your horse. Relax and let God bring it about, if it's even Him. If it's not, He has something else. Just don't force it."

"Listen to your wife," said Saldu. "Realize the magnitude of your heavenly Father's love for you. If you humble yourself, you can get filled to overflowing with love and acceptance from Him every day. Now your insecurities cause you to crave affirmation from people. You're looking in the wrong place."

"Yes," said Valoe, "God's love truly satisfies. You could spill the excess over on Kathy and Jordan and the needy people around you. Instead you try to accumulate compliments to fill the bottomless dark pit in your soul. Without humility there can be no spiritual power, intimacy with God, or favor of God on your life."

Their 1993 Toyota stopped in the parsonage driveway. The engine dieseled for a few seconds after the key turned off and finally sputtered to a stop. Kathy shook her head.

"This car! It won't start when we want, and now it won't stop, either. Maybe it's demon possessed."

"Later this afternoon I'll get some anointing oil, or maybe some 10W40," said Paul chuckling, "and see if I can exorcise anything from the starter."

This caused Kathy to chuckle. She shook her head and then squeezed his arm.

Paul gathered Jordan out of the car seat and carried him up the cracked sidewalk, past the overgrown evergreen bushes, and to the front door of the small Tudor-style house. Brown paint was peeling off the wood trim and shutters.

"I can't get this lock to open. I'm jiggling it like Mike told me to," said Kathy.

"Here, honey, let me," he said, passing off Jordan to her arms. "Insert the key then pull it back just a little, then jiggle. See, it opens every time. Ah, home sweet home."

"Home sweet *temporary* home," she corrected. *Dear Lord, don't let him get his heart set on anything that isn't You. He's 26 years old, and his diploma isn't even framed yet. We're at the beginning of the beginning of our ministry, and we need Your guidance.*

She bent over to let Jordan down and scanned the living room. Boxes of all sizes were strewn from one end to the other. She shook her head. *Where to even start?* "I guess I'll heat lunch. Mike's wife, Jessica, brought lasagna and salad last night. What a blessing. We can get started unpacking after we eat."

After lunch, Kathy loaded the dirty dishes into the dishwasher and closed the harvest gold colored door. *I hope this works,* she thought. *Judging by the color, this dishwasher has to be at least 25 years old.*

After putting Jordan down for a nap she surveyed the mess: clothes, bedding, toys, pots, pans, and boxes of books. *How did we get so many books?* She moved a box off the couch and sighed the kind of deep sigh reserved for the challenges of moving. *It would have been nice,* she thought, *if the church had the money to move us. Poor Paul. He worked so hard; he must have made 20 trips with our little Toyota and didn't complain once. I guess that's the bright side to not owning a lot of worldly goods.*

"Paul, let's unpack while Jordan is napping." No answer. "Where are you?"

"I'm in my study, honey."

Kathy walked down the hall, peeked in the door, and saw him sitting cross-legged on the floor writing in a spiral notebook.

"What are you doing? Why don't you set up your desk?"

"Honey, I don't have time. I'm inspired. I'm writing out a five-year plan for the church."

"A five-year plan! You're the interim pastor," she said, throwing her arms in the air. "Besides, I need help unpacking."

"Honey, you can put away the towels and hang the clothes, you know, the light stuff. Trust me, I think this is God."

Kathy left the room shaking her head. In frustration she grabbed a towel and threw it toward the laundry basket. It passed through Valoe and hit its mark.

"She's got a wicked curve ball. I'd hate to have to try and hit off her," Valoe said as he grinned toward Saldu.

"You and me both," Saldu replied.

"It never ceases to amaze me," says Valoe, "why Father seems to call some of the most inconsiderate men to the ministry. They'll drive across town in the middle of the night to comfort a parishioner, but won't lift a finger to help their wives at home."

"I guess He wants them in the ministry so He can keep a close eye on them. Who knows what they'd do unchecked?"

"Yes, unfortunately we've seen that a few times."

"Well, Kathy's got her hands full with Paul. Right now, let's help her deal with the attitude that resulted in that wicked curve ball."

CHAPTER 4

"One day, The Holy Spirit said to Bartleman 'If you were only small enough, I could do anything with you.' A great desire to be little, yeah, to be nothing came into my head."

Frank Bartleman[1]

The telephone wires were on fire this Sunday afternoon. The trio of Wilma, Bernice, and Carol, three members from the lady's over-60 Sunday school class, plus the spirits of Gossip and Slander, made sure of that. Not even in seminary was one of Paul's sermons exposed to the scrutiny it received today.

Wilma pulled the handle that sent her recliner sprawling. "Getting a cell phone was the best thing I ever did," she said to Oreo, the big black and white cat grooming himself on the area rug. She arranged her ample frame, comfortably fitted in a pink bathrobe and matching slippers, in the recliner, and with her left hand, she pushed her first auto dial button. With her right hand she picked up a cup of coffee from the end table.

Her ten pre-programmed numbers were like a prayer chain in reverse, a destructive gossip network that spread rumors at the speed of light. It resembled a multilevel marketing pyramid of friends phoning friends. It was so fast and efficient that if it were Amway® Wilma would have been a billionaire by now.

Bernice set down her watering can beside her African violets displayed on her kitchen windowsill and grabbed the phone. "Hello."

"Hi Bernice. It's Wilma. What'd you think of the new interim today?" Before Bernice could answer, a thought popped in her head, *The mouths of fools are their ruin; their lips get them into trouble.*[2]

Bernice was so surprised by this thought that she didn't respond. *Is that a verse from Proverbs?* she wondered. After a few seconds, Wilma broke the silence.

"Well, frankly Bernice, I've heard better sermons. And what's with all that Greek mumbo jumbo?"

"Yes, the Greek, well that was, um, interesting."

"Interesting? I just thought that it was a big front he put up to try to impress us. He thinks we're all a bunch of small-town hicks and don't know anything."

The term "small-town hicks" was enough to play on Bernice's insecurities and suck her into the gossip session.

"I was pulling for him, Wilma, but I just don't think he's gonna make it. He's got awfully big shoes to fill, awfully big shoes to fill. Pastor Hall's retirement is just so hard to accept."

Twenty minutes later, Wilma sipped her coffee and punched speed-dial button number two as the spirits of Slander and Faultfinding perched on her shoulder. Across town, Carol hit the television remote's mute button, silencing the replay of her favorite soap opera. "Hello."

"Hi, Carol, it's Wilma. What'd you think of Pastor Paul today?"

Ardare, Wilma's guardian angel, stood behind the plush gray recliner— eight feet tall and radiating with celestial light.

As he listened, his countenance disintegrated. "Oh, I can feel Father's heart breaking even now." Tears rolled down his cheeks. "Wilma, you have no idea. If you only knew how grievous this is to Father, you would never spread your poison."

As Wilma hit the third number, a thought interrupted her, *As surely as a wind from the north brings rain, so a gossiping tongue causes anger!*[3] She shifted her weight uncomfortably in the recliner.

Joan put down her knitting and picked up the phone, "Hello."

Silence.

"Hello, hello, is anybody there?"

Wilma was distracted from Ardare's thoughts by Joan. "Hello, Joan, it's Wilma. How are you?"

"I'm fine Wilma. What'd you think of Pastor Paul today?"

Wilma haltingly began, "Um, well, I think, I think…"

"He's got awfully big shoes to fill," whispered Gossip.

"I think He's got awfully big shoes to fill," repeated Wilma, "and I don't know who he was trying to impress with all his high fallutin' Greek words…."

Ardare continued bringing conviction to Wilma, and each time she made an effort to resist. Finally, she threw off his conviction totally for the pleasure of gossiping with her friends. By the time Wilma had hit auto dial number ten, she had no memory of the verse from Ardare.

Number ten was Sarah Edwards; she was not a close friend, not even really a friend, after all, that's why she's number ten, but she was a new Sunday school member. Wilma was on a roll; the recliner felt comfy, and the phone had been charging all night.

The phone rang at Sarah's, but Sarah wasn't answering. She'd had a call from Bernice after Bernice hung up from Wilma. Carol called too after chatting with Wilma, and so did speed dial numbers five and seven. She'd enjoyed talking with Carol; it was just nice to feel included, but something happened when she was talking to Bernice. She couldn't get that verse out of her head:

Telling lies about others is as harmful as hitting them with an ax, wounding them with a sword, or shooting them with a sharp arrow.[4] *Those are all dangerous, destructive weapons,* she thought.

In her devotional yesterday she had read in the book of James that if a person can't control his tongue his religion is worthless.[5] She breathed a sigh of relief when the phone stopped ringing. She couldn't shake the sick feeling in her stomach. *Oh, God, help me. Help me to be a mature woman. I've got so much to learn. Please forgive me for gossiping just to fit in. Put a zipper on my big fat mouth.*

Malta looked at Joel and burst out laughing. Soon both angels were chuckling. "Prayers don't get any more sincere than that!" said Malta.

"Sarah," said Joel, "the Lord, in His mercy, is entrusting you with spiritual gifts, intercession for Pastor Paul and others. Instead of gossiping about him, now you'll be praying fervently. You'll even weep for him."

Sarah's gift of intercession was beginning with a burden for the new interim pastor and her local church, but before she departed for Heaven, it would encompass the world.

Sarah, still mulling over the meaning of the verse from Joel and Malta, repented again for her gossiping. *Forgive me, Lord. I've slandered Pastor Paul, and I don't know anything about him. He comes to our church the very first day, just out of seminary. The poor man; he must have been so nervous. I'm sure he wanted to do well. Lord bless Paul and his family. Bless his time here, whether short or long. Speak to him about his future and the church's.*

She continued praying, and when she glanced at the grandfather clock in the corner, 20 minutes had passed. *Maybe I am an intercessor,* she thought. She smiled as she remembered the last meeting she had with Pastor Hall before he left. Sarah had her dog-eared humility book marked up with questions. She was so grateful that she'd had Pastor Hall to go to for answers.

"I've been studying about prayer, and I do like to pray."

"You could very well have a gift of intercession."

"But it's not even on the list of gifts."

"My opinion is that it's not on the list because every Christian is sup-posed to do it. It's like tithing; it's not on the list, either." Sarah nodded. "My gift is as a pastor and a teacher; that's a very public gift. Intercession is a gift that comes with hiddenness. You'll be alone praying in your home for people you don't even know, and they will be touched by your prayers. You can pray for individuals; you can pray for war-torn nations. God is not limited by time or distance. Intercessors are the hidden workhorses of the Kingdom, but that's ok. God says He sees what we do in hiddenness, and He will reward us openly.[6]

"Can you explain something else about pride? The book said there is pride in my heart and that there is a demon of pride. That confused me."

"We get hit from the inside and the outside, don't we? We all struggle with certain internal areas; it could be temper, addiction, selfishness, pride, anything. These are in us and we are to actively fight against them. For instance, if I have greed in my heart I can bet that demon will be trying to take advantage of me and make me stumble because it's a place of weakness. Remember last week we said that we don't fight against people, but against evil spirits?"

Sarah shook her head but remained quiet. "What's going on?" asked Pas-tor Hall leaning toward her. "It's just that I lived 71 years thinking that demons were like werewolves and monsters. It makes me so sad. I guess it's better to know the truth late, than never."

"Sarah, it's no sin to be untaught, only unteachable. Remember, nobody can go back and start a new beginning, but anyone can start today and make a new ending."[7]

More revelation about prayer came the next day in the grocery store checkout line when she glanced at the cover of a woman's magazine. The model looked about 14 years old and wasn't wearing much more than a sul-try, come-hither look. *Dear Lord, what kind of parents would let their child pose like that?* She stopped; she hadn't really meant it as a prayer so much as just a comment, but Joel whispered to her, "Pray for her, she's anorexic. She's 15 years old, and the pressure she feels to look perfect and the shame from her anorexia causes her to cut herself."

Sarah realized right then that she didn't have to limit her prayers to people that she knew.

From then on, she prayed for every model and movie star on every magazine cover at the grocery store, for every person on billboards or in advertisements, to be saved. She also prayed for whoever was at the receiving end of any siren she heard. While waiting for a train to pass, she prayed for each of the drifters who painted the graffiti on the speeding railway cars. *And God, don't forget those who painted on the other side where I can't see.* Once she even tuned in to the baseball game just so she could pray for the players.

Pastor Hall had also helped Sarah understand that what she'd called "her premonition" all her life was really a gift from God called prophecy. He gave her some scriptural examples[8] and explained the difference between someone who is a prophet, which is rare, and someone who has a prophetic gifting, like Sarah, which is much more common.

"The Lord will put words or an impression in your mind about what He's thinking about another person. Prophetic ministry just means passing these words on to the person God intended to hear them at a particular time. These words are to strengthen, encourage, and comfort.[9] God can speak in many ways, but most of the time it's just an impression. A thought comes to you that isn't yours. The apostle Paul said that we should earnestly desire spiritual gifts, but especially prophecy."[10]

At first, Sarah was equally excited about her prophetic gifting, but after sharing some of her impressions with a few of her Sunday school class members and getting the cold shoulder, Sarah backed way off. She couldn't have known that they wouldn't receive a prophetic word from *anyone* who was a brand-new believer or a new member of their class. After all, many of them had attended that church for well over 30 years.

She continued getting impressions from the Lord about people, but after the chilly reception from her Sunday school classmates, and after reading in the Old Testament about how Joseph's family got angry with him for the same thing,[11] she decided that sharing her impressions would only get her in trouble. Joel and Malta encouraged Sarah to act on these words from the Lord, but with no results. They even tried to encourage receptivity among the members of the Sunday school class, but they had too much spiritual pride to listen to a new Christian.

CHAPTER 5

"Heaven. Don't miss it for the world."

Kenneth Cope[1]

"After John D. Rockefeller died someone asked his accountant, 'How much money did he leave?' The reply was classic: 'He left...all of it.'"[2]

Paul was in the church office every day the next week, going in early and leaving late. Kathy unpacked all the boxes, arranged as much of the furniture as she could, and with gifts of grace from Valoe, only let one sarcastic comment slip. As she was unloading the last box of books, she noticed a book on humility by Andrew Murray. *I always wanted to read this, and I never got around to it. I think I'll start this today.*

"Excellent choice," said Valoe with a huge smile. "Excellent choice." She plopped down on the couch, but before she could begin reading, Paul came through the front door. He looked around. "Wow, honey! What a job you've done. Look at the family pictures on the mantle." He pulled her off the couch and gave her a big hug. "I'm sorry I wasn't more help. I've been so busy getting settled in at the church. But you have done a great job, you really have!" Paul's apology released the resentment that had been building in Kathy and she hugged him back.

Now that everything was unpacked, the little brown Tudor-style house with the peeling paint was becoming a home, at least a temporary one. Fortunately, very little remodeling had been done over the years (probably for lack of finances), and much of the home's original charm was still intact. The rich oak trim had not been painted in the entry, living room, or dining room.

The living room was dominated by a gray stone fireplace and on both sides were glass front bookshelves which Kathy had carefully decorated with books and well-placed knick-knacks. Family photos and aromatic candles lined the dark-stained mantle.

There were three bedrooms, which allowed Paul to have an office. Jordan's bedroom, on the second floor, had a sloped ceiling which followed the roofline. His closet door was only about 4 feet tall. The roof continued to slant down inside the closet, forming a small, triangular shaped room—perfect for a little boy's hiding place.

Jordan was a generally happy, chubby toddler with his mother's brunette curly hair and his father's good looks. Although it was totally undeveloped, Jordan's prophetic gifting allowed him to sometimes sense the presence of his angel, Hael. This large, jovial guardian was constantly saving Jordan from scrapes, bumps, spills, and multiple boo-boos.

Kathy loved being a mother, and she constantly doted on Jordan. She frequently split her time between household responsibilities and imaginative games.

"Mommy, Mommy, you can't find me. I hiding again."

Kathy finished transferring the clothes from the washer to the dryer and prepared for an all-out search. They'd played the game dozens of times in the small dorm room. She headed down the hall toward Jordan's room, checking other rooms as she walked.

"I bet you're in the bathroom. No. I bet you're in the hall closet. No." She entered his bedroom. "You must be in the sock drawer," she exclaimed, pulling the drawer open to Jordan's delight. Muffled laughter escaped from under the closet door. "No, not in the sock drawer. You must be in the bookshelf. I know, you're on page seven of *Good Night Moon*," More laughter emanated from the closet. "Why didn't I think of it before? You're obviously under the bed. Well, there's no Jordan here. Where could he be? I know, the toy chest! I bet you're under all the toys, inside the hand puppet. NO!" she said, in mock frustration. "You're not in the hand puppet. Where could you be?" She sat on the floor and buried her face in her hands. "I think Jordan went away. I can't find him anywhere. That makes me so sad. Oh, boo hoo!"

The closet door flung open. "Mommy, I right here!" he shrieked as he ran and jumped on her lap. After plenty of tickles and hugs he chirped, "You go. I hide there again," as he headed for his closet with Hael, his smiling guardian angel, tip-toeing behind.

Sunday morning arrived. Paul had spent the week preparing the sermon-to-end-all-sermons. It had to top last week's, and last week's was one of his best. He'd used it for finals in his preaching class.

"This is your chance to shine," whispered Pride. "You've worked hard all week on this sermon. You know it backward and forward. Show 'em your stuff."

"Paul," said Saldu, "it's always about pointing people to Him; it's not about your reputation. If they leave talking about your great wisdom instead of what a great salvation they've been given, then pride has overtaken you, the people have been robbed, and the devil has won the day."

Paul felt conviction over his giddy anticipation of a stellar performance. Then he shrugged it off. *I've worked hard on this sermon all week; there's no reason I can't look good as well as give deep teaching about the Lord, too.*

Starting his sermons with a joke was something his favorite seminary professor had done, and Paul had carried on the tradition. It seemed to help form a bond with the audience. How can you not like someone if you just laughed at his joke? Paul had the perfect joke to go with his text; he'd even prayed for just the right one. But he couldn't have foreseen that the Lord was going to use that joke to truly change someone's life.

Paul grabbed the lectern with both hands. He shifted his weight from one foot to the other and scanned the congregation. *I think there's a few more this week; that's always a good sign. Lord help me.*

Joel and Malta were seated on either side of Sarah, who was sitting by herself toward the back on the left side of the church.

"A wealthy man strikes a deal with God. God agrees that when the man dies he can bring one suitcase, filled with anything he chooses, with him to Heaven."

"Oh, this is a good one," said Joel. "Have you heard it?"

"No," replied Malta, with a grin, "but, if you'll be quiet, I will."

"The man spends weeks pondering what he should take. Maybe diamonds and jewels; maybe money. After much thought and agony, he finally decides he will take his gold. One day he dies, and when he gets to Heaven he has his suitcase. St. Peter tries to take his bag, but he insists he has permission from God to bring the suitcase and its contents. St. Peter checks with God and then tells him, 'Yes, you can bring the suitcase into Heaven. This must be very special. What did you bring?' The man proudly opens his suitcase. St. Peter takes a step back in shock and says, 'You brought pavement?'"

All but two of the congregation roared. Wilma didn't laugh because she'd already made up her mind she didn't like Paul, and therefore, didn't approve of anything he said, funny joke or not. The other nonlaugher was Sarah. With the help of Joel and Malta, the joke pierced her spirit. She was being touched in such a powerful way that she didn't even hear the rest of Paul's sermon-to-end-all sermons. She could see his mouth moving, but was totally distracted by the punch line, "You brought pavement?"

"That's right Sarah," suggested Joel, "what must Heaven be like if God lines the streets with what humans consider their most valuable asset? Think of it this way, Fort Knox is crammed full of heavenly pavement. All the material possessions that you hold dear will eventually mean nothing, less than nothing; they are totally insignificant. When you die, you'll leave them all behind."

Her Bible was laying on her lap opened to Matthew 6:19-21. *"Do not store up for yourselves treasures on earth, where moth and rust destroy, and where thieves break in and steal; but store up for yourselves treasures in heaven....For where your treasure is, there your heart will be also."*

Malta whispered, "Life on earth is a vapor, Sarah. Everything here will pass away. Don't invest in the wrong kingdom. You *will* leave it *all* behind. You should be investing all you have, all your time, all your energy, everything for Him. Remember, you can't take it with you, but you can send it on ahead."[3]

Sarah had a spiritual paradigm shift: *I can see it now. All the possessions I collect here, they'll all be left here. But God's Kingdom—it lasts forever.* Tears welled in her eyes as she repented. *Jesus, please forgive me. I've spent my life so foolishly, worrying about things that will all end up in some garage sale when I die. I've worried about my bank balance and my house, clothes, furniture, how I look, and what people thought of me. I've wasted my life working for the wrong kingdom. Help me to value things that are lasting, the things that You say are valuable. Help me to live wholeheartedly for Your eternal Kingdom with the time I've got left. I know it's not much, but I want to give it all to You.*

Joel turned to Malta and smiled. "Father never lets a prayer like that go unanswered. We'll be very busy with Sarah."

CHAPTER 6

"The Only hope of a decreasing self is an increasing Christ."
F.B. Meyer[1]

"They that know God will be humble, and they that know themselves, cannot be proud."
John Flavel[2]

Sarah had never read the Bible growing up so she didn't even have a grid for God being active in anyone's life. She certainly didn't understand what the Lord was going to do in hers. The Lord, in His mercy, was helping her to redeem her wasted time, enabling her to spend the last of her life serving His Kingdom, and preparing her for a good death. She didn't fully understand the principle of heavenly rewards, and she certainly had no way of knowing that she would reap more eternal rewards than most people who are Christians all their lives.

She couldn't see Joel and Malta, who had taken up permanent residence with her. At night, they stood on either side of her bed, vigilant against the enemy's attacks. They needed no sleep and spent the night hours praying for Sarah and joining in the continuous heavenly worship around God's throne. In the spiritual realm, both angels glowed brightly with the Lord's glory, lighting Sarah's bedroom like a thousand candles. Since Sarah's natural eyes were unable to gaze into the spiritual realm, she could see only darkness.

"The Lord really enlightened her today through Paul's joke," said Malta. "I think she understands now that the Lord's Kingdom has nothing to do with status or possessions."

"Pride drives humans to fight for all those temporal things," replied Joel. "Satan's deception is so great. It's all a bankrupt system that is passing away. It's like fighting for a first class cabin on the *Titanic*. The whole thing is going down."

"His Kingdom is about being a servant to the least on earth and being exalted later. Humility fixes its eyes on God's Kingdom, and never wavers."

That night Sarah had a dream. She saw herself walking around her neighborhood. Her neighbors' houses were painted black; even the bushes, flowers, and grass were black. There were no lights on inside any of the houses, even though it was dusk. She walked around the block and arrived back at her house, which was painted its normal color, but a blindingly bright light was shining out from every window. It was so bright she almost couldn't look toward it. *It's like the sun has been captured and squeezed inside my house.* Then she woke up.

Sarah had the same dream the next night, too. Tuesday night before dozing off she prayed, *God am I going to have this dream every night? Please show me what it means.*

That night Sarah had the same dream, except this time she was pulling a child's red wagon filled with brightly burning, antique kerosene lanterns. She walked to each neighbor's house and left a burning lantern on each porch. She woke up with the following sentence in her mind. "Prayer walk—do this while you are able."

I just read about prayer walking in my women's missionary magazine. Now I understand. Thank You, Lord, for showing this to me. My neighbors are lost and I must help them. She wasted no time putting on her walking shoes, the broken-in brown loafers, grabbed her shawl, and headed outside.

The fall winds scattered dried leaves across the sidewalk, and her shuffling footsteps crunched them as she walked. She headed counter-clockwise around her block speaking out loud, "Lord, bless the Smith's, let them come to know You. Lord, bless the Stephens; let them come to know You. Lord, bless the new family who just moved in here. I don't know their names. I think they've got two toddlers; bless them Lord. Lord, bless the Bakers, especially their teenage daughter who's going through such a hard spell. Lord bless these people, I don't know who they are, but You do. Lord bless this family; they always keep their yard immaculate. I love their red gladiolas, Lord. Bless them today." Sarah walked completely around her block, then the next block.

She stopped in front of a small Victorian house with a new real-estate sign in the yard. For reasons she couldn't identify, she felt drawn to this house. "Lord, bless whoever just moved out and bless whoever will move in, too." She loitered a few minutes, finished that block and then moved on to the next block and ended up in front of the Reynolds' parsonage.

"And bless the Reynolds, Lord. You were so good to bring this family here. Thanks for the joke he told on Sunday that helped me to see things so differently. Help me to intercede faithfully for my pastor, his family, and my church."

Inside, Kathy watched Sarah outside. She recognized her from church. Sarah stood on the sidewalk facing the house, talking a mile a minute—to nobody. *How strange. I wonder what she wants?* Kathy headed for the front door, but by the time she unlocked it and stuck her head out, Sarah had turned the corner praying fervently for Kathy's neighbors. *I hope she's not a troublemaker,* thought Kathy. *I'll have to remember to ask Paul if he's heard anything about her.*

Sarah continued her prayer walks, usually in the morning, sometimes adding a second round at 4 P.M., too. She didn't see Joel and Malta walking to her left and right, blessing, praying, and agreeing with everything she said. Anyone looking with spiritual eyes would have surely been amused to see two, huge, strong angels in dazzling garments towering over a little 5'2" woman, wearing a brown robe of humility, who shuffled down the street—all three fervently praying for salvation to come to this neighborhood.

The Father sends Joel and Malta at the time of salvation to protect their charges from the enemy's attack, and to help them to become more humble and Christlike.

"Father is beautifully transforming Sarah's heart. It's a pleasure to serve one so willing to follow," said Malta.

"Yes, she will finish spiritually strong, even though her body will be very weak."

"Father is full of mercy to snatch her at the end of her life from the enemy's camp. You can bet Satan is spitting sulfur right now—"

"He's planning a counterattack," interrupted Joel, putting his hand on his sword. "We need to be especially vigilant."

Depression, Agoraphobia, Suicide, Discouragement, and Lying were arguing among themselves at that very moment. Demonic strategy sessions frequently deteriorated into vicious quarrels—there is no loyalty between demons, no cooperation, only hatred and vying for status.

Agoraphobia turned to Suicide, "You're worthless now. She's never going to take her own life."

"You had months and you couldn't take her out. I was only here for a few days," screeched Suicide. "If I'd had as much time as you—"

"Depression is right," hollered Discouragement, "we don't need you; you're of no value to us now."

"I've got better assignments available than with you losers." Suicide cursed and disappeared.

"If the truth is known, we're all pretty ineffective now that she's saved," grumbled Depression.

"I can't believe she slipped through our claws. We almost had her," whined Discouragement. "Can you believe those angels that are around her now? The whole miserable situation just got a million times harder."

"There's no hope. We have no weapons to overcome her."

"Yes we do," said Lying.

"Right," they both responded, "like we're going to believe you."

"Listen to me—for once," sneered Lying. "Since 'You Know Who' was raised from the dead carrying the keys to death and Hell, we are totally defeated."

"We know that," whined Depression, "I hate being reminded. Get on with it. What's your big secret weapon?"

"We have one weapon and only one weapon, but it is powerful—the ability and authority to exploit her ignorance. We can attack her in every area where she doesn't realize she has the victory. She's a new Christian; she doesn't understand that she's more than a conqueror."[3] They all shuddered at that phrase. "Since she's His daughter, a joint heir, she has all the power He does at her control, but she doesn't realize she has the power—"

"So she can't wield the power against us," interrupted Discouragement, his yellow pointed teeth showing behind his evil grin. "She's like Dorothy in *The Wizard of Oz*. She had the shoes that could take her home any time, but she didn't realize what they could do for her."

"That's right," said Lying. "The only weapons we've ever used in the last 2,000 years are deceit and bluff. But we've taken out many Christians because of their ignorance,[4] and we can still take her out, too."

≪≪≪

Most of the families on her street were gone during the day, so Sarah, with help from her unseen warring and worshiping angelic companions, grew bolder and progressed from merely asking blessings on her neighbors to declaring their salvations.

One day she stopped in front of the Reynolds' and paced back and forth praying. Kathy, who was hanging a picture in the living room, glanced out the window and saw Sarah pacing in front of the house, fists clenched, looking very intense and talking, talking, talking—to nobody.

Oh dear, this is getting worse all the time. She dialed the church. Paul wisely agreed to take her call, even though he was meeting with Mike Brooks, the head of the elders. He wanted Mike's opinion of phase one of his mega five-year church plan and was giddy with anticipation.

"Hi Hon, what's new? Again? No, I don't know anything about her, but I'll find out." He hung up the phone; his brow furrowed, and he leaned across the old mahogany desk toward Mike. "Tell me everything you know about Sarah Edwards; don't hold anything back."

"Why?"

"Well, it appears she's stalking my family. She comes to our house every day, sometimes twice a day, and paces up and down the sidewalk with her fists clenched, ranting and raving about who knows what."

"Are you talking about our Sarah Edwards?"

"Exactly. What do you know about her?"

"Not much, but I'd never peg her as a stalker, that's for sure. Does she knock at your door or look in your windows?"

"Well no. Stalking is probably too strong a word, but it's like she's got some weird obsession with our house."

"She was widowed about seven months ago. She'd never been to the church, and Reverend Hall led her to the Lord. She made her profession of faith, was baptized the following Sunday, and has been coming here ever since. That's about all I know. She seems sweet, sincere, and totally harmless to me."

"Has she caused any problems since she's been here?"

"Well," said Mike haltingly, "I don't know her personally, and I wasn't in on this so I hate to say anything, but there was one incidence shortly after she got saved; she was telling all her Sunday School class members that she heard from the Lord about them. It didn't go over too well. I can't say that they ostracized her, but they're not overly friendly. But I still don't think she's a stalker."

"She hears voices and thinks they're from God, and she stakes out the pastor's house?" said Paul, stroking his chin. "She's probably still experiencing heavy grief. I studied the stages of grief at seminary, you know. It sounds like she's not coping well. Is she still trying to tell people she hears from God for them?"

"I think that got nipped in the bud pretty quickly."

Paul leaned back in his well-worn office chair and let out a deep breath. "I think I'll let it go for a while then, if she's not causing problems in the church now. Maybe Jessica could sit by her this Sunday and get an idea about what's going on. If Sarah's got some kind of fixation or need to be recognized by us, I think Kathy and I should keep our distance for the time being. She probably needs grief counseling, but I sure shouldn't be the one to do it."

"I'll remember to ask Jessica when I get home," Mike said, but he forgot.

After Mike left, Paul had a counseling session scheduled with one of the college-aged church members, Luke. Paul had spent some time praying earlier in the week for Luke who was struggling with a call to missions. The Lord had showed Paul that it was His will for Luke to minister in India, but he knew better than to give a directional word.

Paul listened with compassion as Luke poured out his heart. He felt a strong call to India, but wondered where the finances would come from and if he should drop out of the community college and enroll in a mission's training program. Paul sympathized; he remembered struggling with his decision to enroll in seminary.

"Luke, I'm not going to give you an opinion one way or the other. I need to let the Lord bring you to the right conclusion; that way, if you go, when things get hard you won't doubt your call or blame me. I know that doesn't seem to help much," he said with a sympathetic grin.

"Here's what I'm going to recommend," he said as he stood from his desk and scanned his book shelf. "I'm suggesting you read these two books. One is about the life of William Carey and the other is about Amy Carmichael. She ministered 55 years in India without going on furlough! Also keep praying, and I'll pray for you, too. After you read the books, call me and we'll meet again." He gave Luke a big hug, looked at his watch, and then headed home.

Finding a balance between church and family is going to be harder than I thought.

CHAPTER 7

*"Depth under depth of self-love and self-admiration.
Pride! It was through Pride that the Devil became the
Devil; it is the complete anti-God state of mind. Pride
is essentially competitive in a way the other vices are
not. Pride is a spiritual cancer. It is my besetting sin."*

C.S. Lewis[1]

Kathy poured the boiling water into the kitchen sink, catching the spaghetti in a colander. She glanced at her watch for the third time and prayed another quick prayer asking for patience with her husband, who was late again. Valoe smiled and gave her a download of grace.

She strapped Jordan in his high chair just as Paul came into the kitchen with that "tail between his legs guilty dog look." He had decided he wasn't admitting to anything unless she brought it up, in spite of Saldu's encouragement that he should immediately apologize. Kathy bit her tongue and started portioning out the spaghetti.

"Alright, Kathy!" shouted Valoe, "way to not give it to him. Love is patient, kind, and doesn't keep track of wrongs."[2] Although Kathy's ears didn't hear Valoe's words, her spirit received their message.

As Paul ate, he shared what he had learned about Sarah. "It sounds like she's just real needy, real lonely, and still grieving. She's also been hearing voices and attributing them to God; then she went to her Sunday school class and tried to tell everyone what the Lord said about them."

"Maybe she has a prophetic gifting," said Kathy as she picked Jordan's garlic bread up off the floor and inspected it for dirt. Paul looked up from his plate at that moment and grabbed the bread from her hand. "Thanks hon, don't mind if I do." And before she could say anything, he'd taken a big bite.

"Maybe she's loony. Her *gifting* wasn't well received by the class so she must have been doing something wrong. The ladies in that class have been church members for hundreds of years!"

"Maybe she's not so much loony as she is lonely. I'll invite her in for a cup of tea the next time she comes by."

"I'd prefer you don't do that. She might be like a stray cat; if you feed her, she'll never go away."

"Then I'll speak to her at church and see if I can get a sense of what's going on."

"You've got a great heart, hon, but it's just not wise. If she's fixated on our family and has some desire for recognition, we shouldn't feed into that. Besides I don't want her around Jordan. Jessica is going to have a chat with Sarah. You can trust the situation to her."

The conversation quickly shifted to Paul's five-year plan for the church.

"Honey would you get me some coffee? I'd like to show you my completed plan. I finished it yesterday and ran it by Mike today, and he seemed impressed. He's not only the head of the elders, he's also head of the pulpit search committee, you know. I thought that was encouraging."

Kathy returned with two mugs of coffee and a washcloth. She handed Paul the mug that said, "Old preachers never die—they just go out to pastor." It was a graduation gift from his best friend in seminary. After cleaning applesauce from Jordan's hair, face, hands, T-shirt, jeans, and shoes, she released him from the confines of his high chair. He scampered into the living room to play with his collection of stuffed animals.

"Come around to this side of the table, honey, so you can see."

Saldu, who was standing behind Paul, glanced sadly toward Valoe, who was shaking his head. "Paul," said Saldu, "this isn't just about your plan. You're supposed to be pastoring Father's beloved children. You're supposed to be a servant-leader just like Jesus. If you want to tower over everyone in a grass root's movement, it probably means you're a weed."[3]

What Paul couldn't perceive was a spirit of Pride perched on his shoulder, influencing him. He opened a black leather folder to reveal 100 pages printed in multiple colors, complete with graphs and pie charts. "I've been working on this all week. I think this is God's plan for our church."

"Our church?" exclaimed Kathy, rolling her eyes and sloshing coffee over the side of her cup.

"Yes, *our* church. I think this is where we'll end up. I really do. Let me show you what I've done," he said, ignoring her obvious frustration. Valoe laid his hand on Kathy's shoulder, and she took a deep breath and vowed to compose herself.

"See, I've got a master goal of where the church should be in five years. Then I have subgoals for each of the individual five years and then smaller goals for every six months. If we break it down into six-month increments, it's very doable. See, that's 30 smaller goals, one on each page and the predicted timetable to start and accomplish it. If we're on track, three years from now we'll be starting a large building campaign. The church will be way too small. We'll need to buy land; I saw some last week. It's a little beyond the reservoir. It's about three miles out of town on the corner of JJ and Old Highway 3. Right there, at the northwest corner is, I'm guessing, about 40 acres. It would be perfect. Don't you think that sounds like God? I think He'll provide this land for the church, and I'm going to pray about it every day."

Saldu's face was sober. He looked at Malta and shook his head, "I'm doing everything I can to discourage it. He just wouldn't entertain the idea that his plan isn't also God's plan. It's all about what he thinks and feels. Humility results from laying down the right to be right, but pride is like a consuming fire. It's insatiable and, unless he repents, it will be his down-fall."

Kathy was reeling from Paul's discourse. "Don't you think you're getting a little ahead of yourself? You're the *interim*. You have no guarantee you'll be called as pastor. God might want us to take a church in downtown Harlem or Timbuktu—"

"But honey, you're not listening. I *do* think this is the Lord. The plan just flowed—" This caused Manipulation and Pride to burst into wicked laughter. "He can't tell the difference between our voices and God's?" Deception broke into a fangy grin, "I've outdone myself!"

"—all the information I learned in my church planting class was so applicable. See, my first goal," he said, flipping past the multicolored, multi-fonted title page, "is to start a prayer meeting, once a week. We have to ask the Lord to bless all this or it will fall flat on its face. I'm going to announce a prayer meeting. It's time to open the building on Wednesday nights. We can't just do Sunday morning and Sunday evening; we've got to stir the pot. This town needs to be saturated with the Gospel. Then after the prayer ministry is established, six months from now, we'll start a visitation program every Thursday night. We'll go out into the community in pairs and knock on every door." He flipped to the next page. "See, I've got the whole town marked in sections. We'll hit them one by one each Thursday night and keep going until every home in the community has had a visit from Victory Church of Bradbury."

"But honey—"

"In seminary I learned that on average, for every 11 houses you go to, one family will visit the church. Out of every five that visit, I think we should be able to maintain one. It's so simple. For every 55 homes we visit, we will gain a new family for the church. If you divide the number of households in our community by 55 I can predict—"

Paul's face was suddenly invaded by a lovingly worn, one-eared Winnie the Pooh with a small rip by its grinning mouth. "Daddy, sing to Pooh."

"Daddy's busy right now, sweetie. I'll sing to Pooh at bedtime."

"Sing now—for Pooh!"

"No, Daddy's busy I'll sing later. I promise. Go play."

Paul was too busy looking at his graph, showing the predicted attendance at the Victory Church of Bradbury, to notice the disappointed look
on Jordan's face as he shuffled back to the living room, dragging Pooh behind him. To Kathy, the disappointment was glaring. She glanced at Paul,
still absorbed in his charts, and excused herself to the living room where she
snuck up on Jordan and grabbed Pooh.

"My Pooh," she said cuddling the well-loved, tattered bear close, as she
sat cross legged on the floor. Jordan laughed.

"My Pooh," he said reaching his chubby arms to grab Pooh's one remaining ear. Kathy released her grasp. As Jordan snuggled on her lap, hugging
Pooh, she put her arms around them both and rocked back and forth as she
sang, "I love ice cream, I love candy, I love Tiggers aren't they dandy? I love
Piglet, I love Pooh. But most of all, I looovvve YOU!" She ended the song
with a rousing tummy poking, which sent Jordan into gales of laughter.

"Come on sport. I think it's Pooh's bedtime. Let's get ready and daddy
will be in to sing…." She finished the thought in her mind. …*Or I'll flog him
within an inch of his life with his stupid graphs.*

CHAPTER 8

"I used to think that God's gifts were on shelves—one above the other—and the taller we grow, the easier we can reach them. Now I find that God's gifts are on shelves—and the lower we stoop, the more we get."

F.B. Meyer[1]

"'Become nothing if you would become something.' In His rules of success, you must stoop to rise, go down to get up. And shrink to grow."

Unknown

The type for the headline on the *Bradbury Gazette* was bigger than it had ever been. The owner and editor, Clarence Harvey, had never felt the need to go bigger than a 63 font and had only used that once, when the robbery ring had been broken wide open by the sheriff. He only used it then because he was emotionally involved in the story—his home was one of the first ones hit, and they'd stolen his collection of antique fishing equipment, which was never recovered. Now he was equally stirred up and displayed the headline in all caps and size 82 font: "MINIMUM-SECURITY JAIL PROPOSED FOR BRADBURY!"

Emotions were running high all over the town that morning as residents opened their papers. The consensus was that no one wanted a jail anywhere close to their home or their hometown.

Sarah didn't read the paper that morning. She, Joel, and Malta had covered their regular prayer walk, and then she drove to her appointment with Dr. Newbury. He had been her family doctor for 20 years. Even though George had been treated by a cancer specialist in Mt. Pielor, Dr. Newbury continued to drop by the house to visit George until he passed away.

After exchanging pleasantries, he asked Sarah the reason for her visit.

"I'm just having a harder time getting around," she said uncomfortably, staring at the trashcan in the corner of the room. "I have a hard time getting out of bed and sometimes lifting my feet to take the next step; but then when I get going, it gets easier."

"How old are you, Sarah?" asked Dr. Newbury still perusing the chart.

"I'll be 72 next year."

"I hate to break it to you," he said with a sight grin, "but if you hadn't noticed, you're getting old. We both are!"

"Believe me, I know that. It just seems like it's more...." She shifted self-consciously and her voice trailed off. She decided not to tell him about the tremors that she sometimes had in her hands.

"Are you still taking your arthritis medicine regularly?"

"Yes. No. Sometimes. Well, mostly just when I need it."

"From now on I want you to take it every morning," He turned to face her for emphasis, "Even if you don't feel like you *need* it. Here's a new prescription. You're at five milligrams now; go to 10, and if you need to, you can increase to 15 at your discretion. If you don't see improvements in your mobility in a month, call me back and we'll do some testing."

Sarah thanked him and left. *Lord, let it just be arthritis*, she prayed as she walked across Main Street to Tully's drugstore.

Sarah handed the prescription to the pharmacist. He wasn't the regular. She wondered if he was the Jernstrom's son. His father was one of the deacons and had mentioned at church that his son finished his college and he'd returned to Bradbury.

He handed her the prescription.

"That'll be $20 even."

"Goodness, that's highway robbery! Last time I filled this it was $12."

"Well, maybe you can have me locked up in the new jail."

"Pardon?"

"The new jail. They want to build a jail in Bradbury." Sarah tried to refrain, but an audible gasp escaped her lips. She actually felt her heart racing. "A jail?"

"That's kind of everyone's response," said the pharmacist. "It was splashed across the front page of the *Gazette* today. It's already causing quite a controversy."

Sarah smiled weakly, fished $20 from her purse, and headed for the door. She had to go home and pray.

"A jail in Bradbury, that's not good," said Paul over his weekly lunch with Mike.

"Be careful," said Saldu. "You need to pray about this and not go off of assumptions."

"It's not a sure thing, but it's proposed," said Mike.

"If it's proposed, can it be opposed?"

"Sure, anything can be opposed. They already tried to build it in Leesville, but no one there would sell them land. That's why they're here. Mayor Forbes is all excited though because of the additional jobs it'll generate. But I think it's going to be a hard sell to the residents."

"Well, when we get the prayer meeting going on Wednesday we can spend time praying about this," said Paul wadding up the wrapper from his corned beef sandwich.

All the way home from the pharmacy, Sarah prayed about last night's dream, and she kept hearing Matthew 25:31. "God, was that dream from You?"

Last night's dream was unusually vivid and just plain unusual. She was visiting inmates, telling them about Jesus. It seemed very out of character for her and scary too. *God, I'm certainly the least likely candidate to ever do that!*

She pulled her old blue Chrysler into the driveway, bent slowly to pick up the *Gazette*, and went to the kitchen table with her Bible and a cup of coffee. She unrolled the *Gazette* and the headline made her gasp again. *It's like that television show where the kid gets tomorrow's headlines today.* She flipped in her Bible and started reading Matthew 25:31. She read about Jesus separating the sheep from the goats. She put down her coffee cup. *I don't know what that has to do with a jail.*

"Keep reading," said Joel.

Then the King will say to those on His right, "Come, you who are blessed by My Father; take your inheritance, the kingdom prepared for you since the foundation of the world. For I was hungry and you gave Me something to eat, I was thirsty and you gave Me something to drink, I was a stranger and you invited Me in, I needed clothes and you clothed Me, I was sick and you looked after Me, I was in prison and you came to visit Me."[2]

Sarah felt herself tearing up. *It's You, God—the dream was from You.*

"That's right, Sarah; you're learning to hear Father's voice. He speaks to you through the Bible, through words in your mind, and even through dreams. He's taking you through a season of letting you hear His voice very clearly so you'll learn to recognize it and believe it," said Joel.

"And," added Malta, "He's giving you His heart for the downtrodden, the rejected, and the prisoners. He wants you to know that He loves the widows, the orphans, and the outcasts. He wants you to know that no act of kindness is too small for Him to see and reward. God will never forget the deeds you do and the love you show.[3] Now read the rest of my friend Matthew's chapter."

Through her tears, Sarah continued reading,

*Then the righteous will answer Him, "Lord, when did we see You hungry and feed You, or thirsty and give You something to drink? When did we see You a stranger and invite You in, or needing clothes and clothe You? When did we see You sick or in prison and go to visit You?" The King will reply, "I tell you the truth, whatever you did for one of the least of these brothers of Mine, you did for Me."*⁴

"The Lord loves the unlovely—unfortunately His Church does not," Joel said. "Many who have professed to joyfully serve the Lord find it odious to serve people."

"Humble yourself, reach down to the outcasts, stoop to help the undesirables to their feet again," said Malta. "The lower you reach, the more the Lord can fill you, the more He can use you. He says three times in His Word that He gives grace to the humble. Without His grace, you can do nothing. His grace is everything. It makes all the difference in your life."

"That's right," said Joel. "Dead religion makes us exhausted workers; grace makes us lovers."

Malta ministered an increase of compassion to Sarah straight from the Lord's heart as he played the flute and then sang the Father's love over her. Joel raised his hands toward Heaven. Flames ignited on his palms, and he placed them over Sarah's heart.

Oh Lord, I'm sorry. I've ignored all the hurting people. I just didn't want to deal with them. I didn't know how. I was only concerned about my needs and those I loved. I'm sorry I've ranked people and placed higher value on certain ones. Help me to see people the way You do. Help me to look into their souls, to not to be distracted by how they look or swayed by their wealth or poverty. Help me to empty myself so You can fill me with Your compassion. Help me to love the things You love and hate the things You hate. Help me to use the rest of my time here on earth doing whatever You want. Amen.

Tears spotted the *Gazette*'s article.

Just as Sarah was pulling herself together, blowing her nose and dabbing her eyes, Joel suggested she turn to Hebrews 13:2. *"Do not forget to entertain strangers, for by so doing some have unwittingly entertained angels. Remember*

*the prisoners as if chained with them—those who are mistreated—since you your-
selves are in the body also."*

Now she cried again, the burden of the Lord resting heavily on her.

"Father loves Sarah very much. I'm curious what He will do next," said
Malta.

CHAPTER 9

"The Spirit builds confidence, the flesh builds arrogance."

Bobby Conner[1]

Driving to church on Sunday morning, Paul saw four signs and three banners in people's yards protesting the new jail. "It sure didn't take this town long to get organized against the jail, did it?"

"Apparently not," replied Kathy.

"Clarence Harvey, the *Gazette*'s editor, had posters printed and placed all over town. I hear he's going to rent space on a billboard. Financing it himself."

"Well, I can't blame them; jails have to be located somewhere, but I can understand why they don't want it in their town."

"Our town, dear," he corrected. "*Our* town. I'm announcing the beginning of the prayer meeting this morning. When that gets going, we'll put some time in on our knees about this jail." Although Paul didn't like himself very much for the next thought, he couldn't get it out of his mind: *If I can rally the church behind this movement, it could get me some communitywide exposure. And wouldn't the church members love me if I was instrumental in getting this jail thing canceled?*

"Paul," said Saldu, "walk in the Spirit and you won't fulfill the lust of the flesh.[2] The flesh always lusts; it's lusting now for recognition and accolades. But it's insatiable; it's never enough. If you don't learn to get your affirmation from the Lord, in your time together, you'll continue trying to manipulate praises from people, but they'll never satisfy. Only one opinion matters or satisfies. Seek the Lord on this jail issue and quit riding the wave of public opinion."

It was a rainy Sunday morning, so of course, attendance was down. That meant the offering was going to be down too. Paul sat in the front row tapping his foot to the special music. When it was over, he took his place behind the lectern and shifted his weight from his left to his right foot and back again. He took a deep breath and began.

"A mother skunk and two baby skunks were walking in the woods when they were startled by a hungry bobcat. The bobcat chased them and cornered them against a rocky cliff where there was no place to escape. The mother skunk was unbelievably calm. The baby skunks cried out, 'Mom, mom, what should we do?' She turned to the children and said, 'Children, let us spray.'"

"And we need to *spray* too. We need God's vision for this church and for the lives of each member: every mother, father, son, daughter, aunt, uncle, everyone!"

By the time Paul had finished, most of the church was in agreement that what they really needed was a Wednesday night prayer meeting. "We'll begin this Wednesday night at 7 sharp. Come and prepare to be blessed. Amen?"

"Amen," most of the congregation answered.

After shaking hands with everyone at the back door, Paul went to his office, opened his leather binder containing his five-year plan, and placed a big check mark in the empty box on page two. "Begin Wednesday prayer meeting—done."

"Paul," said Saldu, "you've barely prayed about your plan. You're just assuming it's also God's plan, and it's not. You're excited because you think it will bring you glory and honor. Don't make glory and fame your god and your goal. Humble yourself so He doesn't have to; it is by far the wiser of the two plans.

"Humans are blinded by their pride because they compare themselves to one another. If you stop and look at Jesus alone, you will get a true comparison. Looking at Jesus is the only way we can see where we truly stand. It is in Him we find our example of love and humility. If we look at those around us, we will not get a true measurement of what we are supposed to look like.[3] Trust me, Paul; no one in Heaven is impressed with your five-year plan."

≪≪≪

There was a good turnout Wednesday evening; even Wilma, Bernice, and Carol had come. It was about 6:45 and Paul was chatting with a group of people; the conversation was predictably about the jail.

"We need to pray, to pray that place right out of our town," said Wilma, shaking her fist. "Maybe we should pray and even *fast.*"

"Yes, I agree. Our town will never be safe. Our kids could never play safely outside," said John Seas, even though his main concern was really for his property's value. He and Lori had been planning to sell off part of their acreage to help finance some travel when he retired in eight months.

"What if, Heaven forbid, one of them escaped?" questioned Bernice.

"Maybe we could pass around a petition among the church members," added Carol. "The whole idea just gives me the creeps."

"I can see that this is a very important issue to all of us," said Paul. "I'll lead us in prayer about it tonight, and we'll see what comes out of this meeting."

Sarah arrived about the time the group was breaking up. She snuck into the back row and didn't wait for the meeting to start. She closed her eyes and prayed, *Lord, thank You for being good to me. Thank You for the way You've been talking to me lately. Help me to love the unlovely. Help me to pray more, especially for Pastor Paul and this congregation. Help me to love Your Word, and help me to hear Your voice in all the ways You speak to me—*

"It's 7," said Paul, adjusting the microphone, "Time to start. Thanks to each one of you who came to this prayer meeting tonight. We'll have an open mic so if you have something you want to pray about, I invite you to come forward. At 8 I'll close, providing the Spirit doesn't fall and keep us here all night," he said chuckling.

Joel looked at Malta. "No chance of that happening."

There was an uncomfortable five-minute period where no one went forward. All heads were bowed, praying that someone, anyone, would pray. Finally, Wilma decided that she would break the silence. As she walked to the microphone there was a collective, silent sigh of relief.

"Dear Lord, You know about the jail that they want to put in our town. I'd ask You to cancel these plans and send them back to the devil, where they came from." Amens resounded from all corners of the room. "You know that the town's children need to go to bed at night feeling safe, and we need to go to bed at night knowing our children are safe. That would just never happen again once they break ground on a jail."

Sarah sat in the back row in shock, her heart pounded. *Lord did I hear wrong? I was so sure it was You.*

Lying whispered, "Of course you heard wrong. These people have been Christians for years. Listen to the rest of the prayers and you'll get your answer as to who is right and *who* is wrong."

There were two prayers about finding the right pastor, and Michelle Bunkoff prayed for her husband to be saved and the gallbladder problems he had to be healed. Bernice prayed for the homebound members, and all the other 30 prayers were against the jail.

Two new demonic reinforcements also attended the prayer meeting that evening—Respectability and Intimidation were there to help sway Sarah. It was 7:50 and she was still wrestling with whether to go forward.

"You got ridiculed the last time you sincerely thought you heard the Lord," said Respectability.

"Remember how sure you were, and remember how no one in your Sunday school class appreciated what you had to say?"

"Who are you to think that you hear better than all these people? No one in this room except you—the brand new Christian—believes that this jail is from the Lord. Don't you think you're being a little arrogant? And we all know that arrogance is a sin," added Intimidation.

Confusion broke over her like waves; she felt like she was going crazy. Malta suggested she open her Bible to Matthew chapter 25. She half expected it not to be there. When she read verse 36, "*I was naked and You clothed Me; I was sick and You visited Me; I was in prison and You came to Me....*" she started to cry again. Malta gently whispered, "Yes Sarah, you heard from the Lord. See how the Holy Spirit rests on you when you read this verse? Do you feel how your heart grieves when you hear plans that go against Father's heart?"

"Intercede for Father's will, not the will of the people, to come to this town," said Joel. "Never stop standing for God's will, even if you *feel* like you're standing alone. You're never alone when you're standing for Father."

Malta was incensed from listening to 45 minutes of prayers that were addressed to God, but were contrary to His will, all begging Him to do something He had no intention of doing.

"Get up Sarah," encouraged Malta. "You're the only one here tonight who can pray God's will about the jail—the only one!"

With great physical and emotional effort, Sarah shuffled toward the microphone. Joel and Malta were providing invisible yet necessary support on her right and left. She was trembling as she bowed her head and closed her eyes.

"Lord," she began, her voice wavering, "I believe You've shown me that this jail is Your will. I know that's not a popular thing to say. I also believe that You showed me that I and other church members have the responsibility to visit the inmates and tell them about Your love for them. So I would just ask that You bring about Your will in our town on this matter." When she opened her eyes and looked up, the whole congregation was staring at her. She had planned to read Matthew 25, but realized she would break down sobbing if she tried. She felt far too vulnerable to cry in front of this group. She closed her Bible and with her two unseen helpers imparting strength to her fragile frame, she shuffled back to her seat. As she passed each pew, heads turned to watch her go by. The silence was loud.

I should have expected this from her, thought Paul. *Why am I not surprised? Now how do I close this meeting? Lord, how do I wrap this up nice and neat?*

"Why do you want things nice and neat Paul? Jesus stirred controversy everywhere He went," said Saldu. "Desire the truth, not the path of least resistance. You don't need a wish bone, you need a back bone."[4]

He walked slowly to the microphone. "Lord, thank You for the people who came out tonight to pray; bless them. Thank You that You see what lies ahead for our church and community. Bring Your will to pass. Amen."

Sarah didn't understand the impact that her prayers would have in Heaven, but she was pretty sure that between Paul and the church members, she'd just signed her social death warrant.

Lying immediately criticized Respectability and Intimidation for their failure at keeping Sarah from praying.

"Don't worry," said Respectability, "this is just round one. There'll be lots of other opportunities."

Driving home, Paul vented to Kathy.

"I can't believe it. I just can't believe it," He gestured wildly with his hand. "But yeah, I really can. If I'd expected anyone to stand in opposition, I'd pick Sarah."

"Be nice. She has a right to pray her conscience. Last I checked this was still America, you know."

"Very funny. You obviously don't understand the seriousness of the situation. Her actions are just going to cause division and strife. She's going to get everyone all riled up, even more than they are now, if that's possible."

"Well, maybe the Lord did speak to her."

"Are you crazy? She's clearly in the minority; her views oppose every other church member's and my own. Either she's deceived or I am. One of us sure needs to hear more clearly. We can't both be right."

"That's right, Paul," said Saldu. "The humble man can consider the possibility that he may be the one who is incorrect. Don't rationalize, don't cover up. Just admit your mistake, apologize, and go on; that's humility. Losing at something doesn't make you a loser, and failing at something doesn't make you a failure. The Lord is waiting with open arms to show you the real plans He has for your life and ministry. You must learn to seriously consider the possibility that you are wrong. Defensiveness is hidden pride."

The silence in the car the rest of the way home was as thick as the darkness outside.

Joel and Malta stood at the foot of Sarah's bed while she slept that evening, as they did every night.

"She's sleeping fitfully," said Joel.

"She knows she's a leper in the eyes of the church."

"Especially with Paul. He has a sincere heart, but he's just too ambitious for his own good—not for Father's good."

"He's filled with pride and wants the people's approval more than anything. More than he wants to hear from God, although he doesn't know that yet; more than he wants his marriage to work, and more than he wants a healthy relationship with his son," said Malta.

"He's paying way too high a price for things that don't satisfy. Father is trying hard to put him on the right path, but he's actively resisting. It's a shame the damage that will be done in the mean time."

"God always resists the proud. The only path to exaltation is through the small door called humility. You have to crawl through on your knees, and that is repulsive to Paul."

"I rejoiced when Sarah found the boldness to pray tonight, especially with Respectability and Intimidation whispering in her ear. What courage she has to go against the flow."

"That's exactly what Paul lacks," said Malta, shaking his head.

"Only in church could you pray for God's will to be done and stir up a hornet's nest!"

CHAPTER 10

"Q: What are the four virtues of the Christian life?" "A: Humility, humility, humility, humility."

Bernard of Clairvaux[1]

A hornet's nest was putting it mildly. Sarah was the hot topic with everyone who'd been at the prayer meeting. Wilma's auto dial numbers one to nine, got a workout. Frustrated, she deleted Sarah from number ten. That same verse about bearing false witness kept popping into her head, but with persistence she was able to throw it off again. This was just too juicy not to tell. By the time those who attended had called those who hadn't, practically the whole church had heard.

Ardare's heart was breaking as he watched the malevolent spirits of Gossip and Slander tighten their stronghold on Wilma's mind. His hand was on his sword, but he knew he could not draw it without her repentance and cry for help. He shook his head, "The tongue weighs mere ounces, but show me the man or woman who can hold it."

Oblivious to the supernatural realm or the spiritual warfare around her, Wilma dialed the phone again. The spirits taunted Ardare before turning their attention back to Wilma. Then they whispered destructive lies clothed as truth.

Joel and Malta were still there when Sarah woke in the morning. They hadn't slept, but weren't tired. They had never slept since they were created, not even a catnap, but they never grew weary. They were always watching, always alert, always diligent to carry out God's will. After Sarah had her prayer time, they watched as she struggled to sit up and position herself on the edge of the bed. She rocked back and forth, exerting great effort to make it to her feet. She shuffled off to the bathroom.

"Their temporal bodies always wear out from one affliction or another. Thank the Lord that their eternal spirits don't perish along with the flesh."

By the time Sarah got dressed and out of the bathroom, she was a little steadier on her feet. She made a pot of coffee, ate a bowl of cereal, and then started her prayer walk circuit. When she had the strength, she would prayer walk three blocks, on a really good day, four.

Sarah was forcing herself to come out of her shell. As she walked she made an effort to say "Hello" and introduce herself to her neighbors who were out in the yard. When she didn't know who lived in one of the houses on her four-block prayer route, she checked the mailbox so she could pray for the family by name.

Lord, let me make it four blocks today. I hear that Linda Sprague fell and broke her arm last week; I'd like to make it to her house. She started down her block, flanked on each side by her unseen intercessory companions. They protected her from hazards and demonic attacks she never knew existed. But, unbeknownst to her, one of the biggest foes she had was right inside the house at 1745 Cypress Drive, and his name was Pastor Paul.

Sarah stopped in front of his house and prayed, *Lord, let him see the truth about this jail. Show him the same way You showed me. Let him have compassion for the prisoners. Draw near to him and bless him; bless his wife and sweet son. Send guardian angels to protect them. Let them be healthy and have enough money. Lord, if it's Your will that Paul be called as full-time pastor, I pray You would show the committee in a clear, unmistakable way. Bless Paul today, let him hear Your voice and feel Your love for him. Amen.*

Thanks to Joel and Malta's assistance, she made it the full four blocks, arriving home in about 90 minutes. She poured a cup of coffee and perused the *Gazette*, which was still using all caps in 82 font to thwart the new jail. She shook her head. "Jesus, please bring Your will to our town. Don't let anyone, especially the church members, stop it." *It seems so strange*, she thought, *that the whole church could be standing in opposition to God's will. Lord, have mercy on our confusion.* She prayed fervently for the church for the next ten minutes.

Then a Scripture reference flitted across her mind, Joel 2:28-29. After a frustrating search for the book of Joel, she gave up and looked in the index, page 1245. She shook her head as she thought, *I wish I knew my Bible better; I wish I'd grown up reading it.*

And it shall come to pass afterward that I will pour out My Spirit on all flesh; your sons and your daughters shall prophesy, your old men shall dream dreams, your young men shall see visions. And also on My menservants and on My maidservants I will pour out My Spirit in those days.

She noticed the cross reference, and turned to Acts 2:17-18. She began reading, "'And it shall come to pass in the last days,' says God, 'that I will pour out My Spirit on all flesh....'" *How strange*, she thought. *It's the same verse in the Old and New Testament. It must be really important."*

"Sarah," said Joel, "praying in the Spirit is one manifestation of the Holy Spirit. It's a special prayer language, a spiritual gift from God. It's like a foreign language; you probably won't even understand what you're saying. But, it's your special, sacred love language with the Lord. It's your own unique, secret song that only you can sing to Him. Jesus says that those who believe in Him will 'speak in new tongues.'"[2]

She began to pray, *Lord, pour out Your Spirit on all flesh; pour out Your Spirit on me. I want to experience Your gift of speaking in tongues.*

Joel drew his brilliant, two-edged sword. The tip was ablaze. He touched the flame to her lips. "Be filled up and overflowing with the fullness of the Holy Spirit."

Malta played a melody on his flute that washed over Sarah, and she was hit with heavenly joy. She began to praise the Lord in English, and to her surprise, a flood of unintelligible words rolled out. It was as if her tongue had tripped or suddenly had a mind of its own. Sounds were still coming out, but she couldn't understand any of them.

For the longest time she prayed and sang in tongues, interspersed with laughter. She had read about speaking in tongues in Paul's writings[3] and in Acts.[4] She'd never heard teaching against it or knew it was considered controversial by some so she entered into the experience with wild abandon. Joel and Malta led a full-fledged worship service and Sarah followed along. She raised her hands, she cried, she paced, and she danced with unseen angels as much as her failing body would allow. These treasured petitions in Sarah's own prayer language were received with great joy by the Father and were echoed by multitudes of angels through His throne room.[5]

After 15 minutes she flopped down on the couch, physically exhausted.

"Get in the habit of praying in the Spirit all the time. Even if it doesn't feel anointed, it's powerful because the Holy Spirit is praying His prayers through you. He prays His perfect will. It's not tainted by your opinion, preference, or prejudice," said Malta.

"Also," said Joel, "since there is no time or distance barriers in the Spirit, you may be praying for people and situations on the other side of the world, things you'd have no way of knowing about. Praying in the Spirit shakes the devil's kingdom and thwarts his plans."

Joel turned to Malta, "Because of her obedience, Sarah will do many good works for the Lord. By the time He matures her as an intercessor, she will be armed and dangerous to the enemy's kingdom. She's halfway there already."

"This sweet little woman doesn't know the devil sees her as a dangerous warrior in the Spirit."

"Nor does she realize how badly he'd like to take her out."

In addition to taking their regular beating from Sarah's prayers during the next day's prayer walk, plotting against Sarah was more frustrating than ever for the demons.

Chapter 10

"Great, just great," moaned Depression, "She's got her prayer language. The Spirit of God prays through her now."

"Shut up! I know what that means. You don't have to talk about it," whined Discouragement.

"Can it get any worse?" asked Lying. "We have no weapons that can overcome that."

They tried several low-level physical attacks—placing twigs on her path or steering her toward cracks on the sidewalk that she could trip over, but these were not even challenges for Malta and Joel.

The three demons crouched behind a rose arbor in a neighbor's yard. "I just unlatched the gate," snickered Lying. "When Sarah rounds the corner that Rottweiller will be on her before she knows what hit her."

Joel sensed something wasn't right in his Spirit. He paused for a moment and then offered a prayer. "Father, send a spirit of slumber to Rex." Immediately, Rex trotted to the porch, turned around several times, laid down, and fell asleep. Discouragement and Depression prodded and yelled at him, but he would not be roused. Lying shook Rex's body violently up and down to no effect.

As Sarah and the angels strolled by the open gate, Joel nudged Malta and then called out with a big smile on his face, "You know what I always say, 'Let sleeping dogs lie.'"

CHAPTER 11

"God grant me a spirit of humility—but not weakness—in the face of the forces of evil."

St. Augustine[1]

After her walk, Sarah relaxed on her porch swing, thinking about her prayers.

I know that one reason we pray is to develop intimacy with the Lord Himself. I love those times each morning when I meet with Him, but I wonder why we have to pray for things that are God's will? Shouldn't those happen by themselves? I know the Bible says it's God's will for everyone to be saved.

"Don't fall for that old line from the enemy. He'd love to see you quit praying," said Joel. "God's plan is for everyone to be saved, but He has commanded believers to partner with Him in this redemptive process. He exhorts all Christians to pray for workers to be sent to the harvest field.[2] Prayer is a mighty weapon that He gives you from His armory to make sure His perfect will is accomplished. Intercessors are the stewards of God's promises to the lost, His Church, the nations, and the world. But if Christians fail to pray, God's full purposes won't be accomplished.

"Think of all the faithful people in the Bible who prayed until the answer manifested, even though they *knew* what they were praying for was God's will," said Malta. "For example, remember Elijah and the drought? God said it would rain, but instead of grabbing his umbrella and dancing home like Gene Kelley, Elijah prayed intensely. I was there! It took seven times before even a small cloud came in the sky. Only then did he quit praying."[3]

"And don't forget my friend Daniel," said Joel, jumping to his feet. "In response to his prayer, an angel was dispatched immediately to answer him. He was hindered by a powerful demon spirit. They fought for 21 days while Daniel continued to pray. Finally God dispatched our marvelous comrade, Michael, to help the angel break through."[4] Malta drew his sword, tossed it back and forth between his hands, and then sliced the air so quickly the blade seemed to disappear. "Your prayers are spiritual warfare that help defeat the enemy's kingdom by releasing warring angels. There is constant spiritual warfare going on against God's perfect will and plan."

"Sarah, there are even times when God stated He would do something and people's prayers changed His actions. King Hezekiah received a prophecy that he would die. He prayed and the same prophet returned and told him the Lord had granted him 15 more years.[5] Moses interceded for the children of Israel.[6] Abraham bargained with the Lord to not destroy Sodom and Gomorrah if there were only 10 righteous people there.[7]

Joel sheathed his sword and stepped aside as Wesley Kruger, the mailman, came up the stairs and startled Sarah.

"Here ya go, Sarah."

"Oh, goodness. I was totally preoccupied with my thoughts. Thank you, Wesley," she said, taking the mail. "You have a nice day."

"Oh, I plan to, the autumn and spring are always the best time of the year for me weather wise. I'm just enjoying the cool day."

Sarah flipped through her mail. *The phone bill and the water bill.* She sighed. George's pension wasn't that much, and the savings account was being depleted more quickly than she'd anticipated. *Lord, help me to trust You with my finances.*

The next letter was from Buchanan County Correctional Facilities Inc. *What's this about?* she wondered as she tore the letter open. It was the private company that wanted to build the jail. She took a deep breath. *Why would they be writing me?* Her heart pounded as she read:

> As you might have heard, we are interested in building a minimum security correctional facility on the outskirts of Bradbury and are interested in purchasing from you the 36-acre plot of land at the intersection of Old Highway 3 and JJ for a sum of $36,000. Please feel free to contact me.
>
> Sincerely,
> David Burris, President
> Buchanan County Correctional Facilities Inc.

Sarah didn't know whether to laugh or cry. She and George had farmed that land the first 23 years of their marriage. Then George had taken a job with the fire department and they had leased it to a local farmer. Sarah had no idea what the property was worth. She had always thought she'd just pass it on to her niece, since she had no children.

Oh, my goodness; I've got to pray. This seems to be straight from the hand of God, but I have to make sure. She went inside and sat on her couch, one of her designated prayer spots. Malta and Joel were right behind her. "Lord, show me what to do. I need to make sure that I hear from You." After praying for several minutes, she got up and poured a cup of coffee.

"Well, George, how would you feel if I sold our land, the land that we farmed for 23 years, the land that your father farmed practically all his life?" Her voice cracked and her hands began to shake. "Oh, George, I miss you so much. I'm so scared. I don't know if you ever accepted Jesus." She released the pent-up tears. How could she stand it if her beloved George was in Hell?

"Don't talk to George. Turn your anxieties into a prayer and give them to Father," whispered Malta. "The enemy's strategy is to run your emotions ragged. Pour out your emotions, hurts, and fears to Father. Then the Lord has room to fill you up with His peace and love."

"Give all your worries and stresses to Him because He cares about every area of your life,"[8] added Joel.

Oh Jesus, please show me whether George is in Heaven with You. I miss him so much. I'm tired of being alone. Now the whole church hates me, and if I sell the land, the whole town will hate me.

Clarence Harvey, the paper's editor, had been on the phone all morning, and he showed no sign of slowing. He'd been reminding everyone he could think of about the meeting tonight at the Elk's hall. "That's right, 7 sharp. We've got to stop this jail. See ya tonight. Bye." He scrolled to the next number on his cell and called again.

Between Clarence's persistence on the phone and the overwhelmingly strong feelings about the jail, the hall was packed. Everyone was milling around talking—no one lacked an opinion. Paul scanned the room for Sarah, but didn't see her. He breathed a sigh of relief. *That's just what I'd need is for crazy Sarah, one of my church members, to stand up and start in about God's will for the jail. This crowd would stone her before she got halfway to the door.*

Lying had been doing his best to distract Sarah. When she finally looked at the clock on the mantle, it was 6:55. She hurried to her car, drove to the Elk's club, and circled the block looking for a close parking space, a hard commodity to come by tonight.

"Just go back home," said Discouragement. "There's no parking within miles. By the time you found parking and walked your decrepit body to the meeting, it'd be over."

At 7:00, Clarence called the meeting to order. "First of all, I want to thank everyone for coming out tonight to deal with this important issue. We have a lot to get done so let's get on with it. I've been meeting with several men throughout the week, and I'd like to introduce them now. Eric Wilcox. You all know Eric owns the auto parts store just off the square. His brother Andrew retired from the fire department. Gary Carter, who's my assistant at the *Gazette*, and last, but not least, Paul Reynolds the new pastor at the Victory Church.

"Clarence," interrupted Paul, "I've got to correct what you just said. I'm the *interim* pastor. I'm not the new pastor yet." He flinched. He didn't mean to let that *yet* slip out, it just did. Selfish Ambition chuckled at Paul's mistake.

Clarence plunged on, "We've been meeting every day at noon to come up with a plan; and we're here to share it with you and then open it up to questions, suggestions, or comments.

"First, I'll give a recap. The company that wants to build this minimum-security jail is called Buchanan County Correctional Facilities Incorporated. They're a private company. They already have six jails operating in other Midwestern states. Since they are a private company, as long as they get appropriately zoned land, we cannot legally stop them from building, just like any other businessman who went through the right channels. But that doesn't mean we are giving up without one heck of a fight. Isn't that right?" he yelled, punching the air with his fist. The crowd's cheer nearly rattled the windows.

"Now I'd like to call Pastor Paul, the entering pastor. Paul, tell us what you're working on."

"Thanks Clarence. That's uh, the *interim* pastor. Well, I'm heading up a petition drive. My goal is to get as many signatures as we can by next Wednesday. We'll have tables set up at church this Sunday to get all the church members or any of you who'd like to visit. Service is at 10. Plus all this week, our deacons and I will be going door-to-door. The petitions will also be displayed at most stores around town. Everybody, please sign." Paul headed back to his seat; he and his demon Pride both enjoyed the round of applause elicited by his little speech.

Sarah was still looking for parking. Finally, in exasperation, she pulled into Edna's driveway one block from the Elk's club. She'd read in the *Gazette* that Edna and Clyde were visiting their grandkids in Atlanta for the week. Joel and Malta helped her out of the car and walked her up the steps. Lying, Discouragement, Intimidation, and Respectability followed at a distance.

ANGELS OF HUMILITY

By the time Sarah snuck in the back of the Elk's club and leaned up against the back wall, the other men had already spoken and Clarence was giving his spiel. "We can make our displeasure known to BCCF, but they don't have to do anything they don't want to. This isn't a government proposal; we don't get to vote on it. Once they buy land, we can't stop them. There are very few tracts of vacant land that are zoned for this. We need to be vigilant. Has anyone heard anything about a possible location?"

Sarah felt her face flush and her heart beating—pounding. She pressed her hands on her chest as if to manually slow it and tried to calm herself by breathing deeply. Respectability and Intimidation perched on her shoulder.

Lee Harms rose to his feet. "I got a letter yesterday; they were interested in some of my land south of town." He paused for effect. "I threw the darn thing in the trash." The crowd almost raised the roof. After the whoops and hollers died down, James Masters stood. "I got one, too; they were wanting the land I own by the park." There were gasps from all corners of the room. No one wanted a jail close to the lake. That's where half the town hung out during the summers. "They offered me a good price," he grinned, "but I'm turning 'em down." More cheering. Someone broke into, "For He's The Jolly Good Fellow" and everyone followed.

"Has anyone else heard from BCCF?" asked Clarence. There was silence.

"Shut up," whispered Intimidation in a gruff voice. "If you speak now, everyone will turn against you. This is your last chance to possibly have a friend."

"Aren't Christians supposed to be kind and loving?" asked Respectability. "Everywhere you go you cause problems. That can't be God."

"If you mention that you're even considering selling your land, everyone, and I mean everyone in this town will hate you. You'll die totally alone," hissed Intimidation.

Joel and Malta were holding Sarah up, literally supporting her weight. She felt lightheaded; beads of sweat clung to her upper lip and forehead. Over the internal sound of her heart pounding, she heard her own voice fill the hall. "Yes, I did." Then there was silence again.

"Well Sarah, what'd you tell them?" asked Clarence.

Sarah took a deep breath and scanned the audience. All eyes were looking back, silently pleading, anticipating her answer.

"Now's a good time to shut your mouth!" hissed Intimidation. "A very good time."

"I-I-I haven't told them anything yet. I just got the letter today."

"Well, you're surely gonna tell 'em 'No' aren't you? You wouldn't want the legacy of George's land to be a jail would you? George would never allow that if he was still here."

Paul buried his face in his hands thinking, *SHUT UP! SHUT UP! SHUT UP!*

Sarah felt sweat beading under her arms and trickling down to her bra. She took deep breaths and silently prayed, *Jesus, what do I say?* Then to her surprise she heard her voice throughout the room again.

"I'm praying about it, and when I hear from the Lord, then I'll know what to do." There was a stunned silence for three long seconds; then a dam of conversation burst. Everyone was talking to someone. Sarah stood in the back supported by her unseen helpers, watching the bedlam in slow motion. She scanned the crowd and heard her name everywhere. There were ugly looks, incredulous stares, fingers pointing, and tongues wagging. *Oh Jesus, I just want to please You; do I have to make everyone angry doing that?* She turned and pushed open the big oak door. The chilly evening wind blew across her warm body; she inhaled deeply. The tears came again, obscuring her view as she held the handrail and felt her way down the steps. Joel and Malta escorted her back to the car.

She pulled out of Edna's driveway and turned left. She'd go the extra three blocks out of the way to avoid driving past the Elks hall. Intimidation, Lying, and Despair were all attacking simultaneously. They were shouting about how foolish she was, how she hadn't heard from the Lord, and how she'd never have a friend the rest of her pathetic life.

When she was almost home, Joel suggested a drive out to the land. It didn't sound like an especially appealing idea, but neither did going home. She passed her street and headed for Old Highway 3.

CHAPTER 12

"Plenty of people wish to become devout, but no one wishes to be humble."

Joseph Addison[1]

Several additional spirits swarmed around Sarah, the result of the verbal curses that the town's people were unknowingly putting on her. The spirits' glowing yellow eyes peered from black scorpion-like bodies. Sarah suddenly felt nauseated, but attributed it to the horrendous experience she'd just had.

In just a few minutes she was there. As she turned off Old Highway 3 and onto the property, she heard the gravel crunching under her tires. A hundred yards from the intersection was an old cattle gate. She got out and with a groan and much effort pushed it open. She got back in the car, pulled through the entrance, and then got out again and closed the gate. The extra effort was worth it; she didn't want anyone to know she was here. She didn't want anyone to know she was anywhere. She just wanted to disappear off the face of the planet. Even with her angelic companions in the front seat, she'd never felt so alone in her whole life.

She sat in the car, scanned the land, and prayed in the Spirit, but this time there was no accompanying joy. The first field had been harvested. There were broken corn stalks everywhere. To the east she could see the remains of the house that was built by the original owners in the 1800s. The stone chimney rose eerily in the moonlight. The barn had been gone for years.

She hadn't been here for a long time, not since George died. Her loneliness, plus tonight's pressures and the demonic presence, overwhelmed her again as she crossed her arms over the steering wheel and sobbed. *What would George think about a jail? Can he see me now? Where is George anyway? Heaven?* She tried to encourage herself and refused to dwell on the alternative.

Delighting in their cruel assignments, the spirits swarmed around her. "Where's God in the midst of this?" growled Despair, gnashing his yellow teeth at her. "Why did He tell you to do something that makes everyone mad and then leave you alone and defenseless? Everyone hates you. You'll never be accepted by anyone in this town ever again."

"I thought knowing God was supposed to make you feel good and love everyone. It's only made you lonely," taunted Accusation as it burrowed its hooked talons into the side of her head.

"You probably heard wrong on this jail. If you don't sell the land, you could be the town's hero; then you could tell everyone about Je-Je-Je, God's son," stuttered Lying, breaking out in a sweat. "If you sell the land, you'll have to stay in your house hiding the rest of your life. You'll die a lonely recluse. What kind of a witness is that?"

"You could be dead for months and no one would even notice. They'd probably throw a party when you die!" whispered the raspy voice of a mocking spirit.

Malta began to sing, "When I survey the wondrous cross, on which the Prince of Glory died; my richest gain I count but loss, and pour contempt on all my pride."[2] The demons screeched and temporarily retreated to the back of the car where they huddled together, baring their fangs, snarling, and snapping at the two angels.

In desperation she cried out, "God, why does doing Your will have to make everyone mad? I need a friend. Is it too much to ask to have just one friend to confide in? Someone who doesn't think I'm crazy? This is too hard for me! I'm so lonely, and I miss George, and now the whole town hates me. You have to show me whether I should sell this land. Please speak to me, please. Please help me. I don't know what to do." She broke down sobbing again.

"Sarah," said Malta gently, "The Lord loves you, and in His wisdom He allows spiritual warfare to test and prove your faith. If you trust God, and don't accuse Him, He can use this hard time to work spiritual growth, humility, and authority into your character. He even tells us that we must endure hardship. The apostle Paul said, '*Endure suffering along with me, as a good soldier of Christ Jesus...do not let yourself become tied up in the affairs of this life, for then you cannot satisfy the one who has enlisted you in his army.*'"[3]

Sarah was in too much emotional pain to be very concerned about character growth that night. After crying out all her tears, she was physically exhausted and afraid that if she stayed there any longer she might not have the energy to push open the gate. *I don't want to sleep in the car all night.* After a little help from Joel, the gate swung open. She put the car in gear and headed home.

An evil presence flooded the car. The gargoyle-like spirit of Death had an assignment to carry out. "She must be stopped. The master grows impatient," he spewed angrily. "Get out of my way!" With his hooked talons he struck the black, low-ranking imps and sent them sprawling.

On the outskirts of the city, with no lampposts to help light the road and her eyesight still somewhat obscured by tears, the car drifted to the gravel shoulder on the right side of the road. In a panic, Sarah quickly overcorrected and shot across both lanes and through the ditch, where Malta brought the car to an abrupt stop. Sarah flew forward and banged her face on the steering wheel. Her emotions were on edge and her body was quaking.

"You don't have permission to take her life, you vile, deceptive spirit. I command you to leave by the blood of Jesus." Death didn't wait for Joel to draw his sword; the mention of the blood was sufficient. He departed cursing and vowing revenge. "We owned her for 71 years, and if she won't renounce God, we'll take her life."

Sarah felt something trickle into her left eye. She dabbed at her forehead. A cut across her eyebrow saturated the tissue with blood. She sobbed again, not as much from the pain as from the frustration of her situation.

Joel attended to Sarah, comforting, and encouraging her in the Lord's goodness and love for her.

"Even though you walk, or in this case, drive, through the valley of the shadow of death, you need not fear any evil. He is protecting you, even preparing a banquet for you to enjoy as He holds your enemies at bay."[4]

After she stopped shaking and the bleeding stopped, she looked outside for the first time. In front of her the headlights illuminated weeds that were as tall as the hood.

"Just pull ahead slowly Sarah," said Malta, motioning toward the hood. "Keep going and in just 10 feet it levels off and you can get back on the road."

Sarah put the car in drive and inched forward. She never looked out the left window to see where the ground dropped off sharply to the creek below. She was too busy obsessing about how she'd been abandoned by God. She didn't realize that if Malta hadn't stopped her car it would have rolled over several times, ended up in the creek bottom, and been obscured from view.

⋖⋖⋖

Kathy had stayed home with Jordan from tonight's meeting. Paul was pacing back and forth between the bookshelf and the tan corduroy recliner where Kathy was knitting. Saldu and Valoe were positioned by the front door, radiating their unseen heavenly glory into the room.

"And then she said that she didn't *know* if she'd sell the land to them or not. There was dead silence; no one said anything, and then the place came unglued, absolutely unglued. Sarah fled the building at that point, but it took five minutes for Clarence to wrestle the meeting back to order. People were livid," he said, raising his voice and gesturing with his arm.

"They wanted to know what they could do to keep Sarah from selling the land. Everyone felt betrayed, like one of their own was going to do them in, and of course she's one of *my* church members, so it makes me look bad, too!"

Kathy inhaled in preparation to speak, but Paul was too fast for her.

"I couldn't believe it when I found out that Sarah owns the land that I want for my new church. You can imagine how confused I felt, but then I thought this might all be from the Lord."

"How's that?" asked Kathy, tugging the yarn to undo a knot.

"Well, I want the land for the church, Sarah's church. BCCF wants the land for a jail. The Lord has provided a way of deliverance for Sarah that will bless the church, too. If she sells the land to the jail, everyone will hate her. If instead she sells the land to the church, she would be viewed as a saint—the town's rescuer. I can see a plaque in the foyer of the new church," said Paul pointing to the entryway of the house for effect, "a permanent tribute to Sarah. Why would she want to be the goat, when she could so easily be the hero?"

"OK, Paul," said Kathy, under Valoe's influence. "Really listen to this. It's time for a reality check. Number one, have you prayed about this plan? Are you sure you've heard from the Lord? Number two, the church isn't in any position financially to buy the land. Number three, you're still the interim, and number four, this is your grand and glorious five-year plan. The church doesn't even know about it."

"That's part of the beauty," he said with a smile as he leaned over her chair and took the knitting from her. "This jail could force the church to speed up the plan. I could meet with Sarah and ask her about the land and then, if she's willing, I'll propose it to the church to see if they are interested, which of course they will be. It's a win/win situation. The church will eventually get a new building and avoid a jail at the same time."

"But Paul, you don't even know—"

"Then we propose a monthly payment to Sarah for the land. Or maybe she would just donate it to *her* church. And, I might mention that the church members *and* the town's people would love me forever for solving this predicament." Kathy grabbed her knitting back and glared at him. *What's the use of even trying to express my opinion? He doesn't want to hear it, he just cuts me off.*

"I'm going to pray about this," he said over his shoulder as he walked toward his office accompanied by Pride and Self-Promotion. "I'd appreciate it if you'd pray too. Then I might go talk to Sarah in a few days." Saldu let out a sigh and followed Paul down the hall. "Keep her away from Paul with those needles," he said, leaving Valoe to help Kathy regain her composure.

In the office, Pride and Self-Promotion taunted Saldu with their shrieks and laughter. They knew he couldn't do anything to them unless Paul cried out for help, and he was a long way from there. Saldu stood across the desk from Paul. "Paul, you might impress people with your performance, but you'll never impress God. It's about your heart, and it's about loving and serving people; it's not about building a kingdom to glorify yourself. Even though the plan *seems* spiritual, it's not the Lord's. It's truly from the enemy. He knows that taking the wrong path is going to cost you time and pain. It will cost your family time and pain as well, and the same for the church. Spend time before the Lord renewing your intimacy and asking His opinion of the plan before you try to carry it out."

Paul shrugged off that nagging feeling that maybe the plan wasn't God's. He was too emotionally invested in it to even go there. *But Lord, help me to love better. Help me to love my family better, and help me to be sensitive to the needs of my church family. Help me to be a good shepherd for them all. Lord I do want to be a blessing and do Your will. Amen.*

CHAPTER 13

"Heroes will arise from the dust of obscure and despised circumstances whose names will be emblazoned on Heaven's eternal page of fame."

Frank Bartleman[1]

"Heroes aren't born...they're cornered."

Unknown

Though Intimidation, Respectability, Discouragement, and Despair were not making as much progress as they'd hoped battling against Sarah, the town's people, in their anger, gladly embraced the new demonic reinforcements with open arms—Accusation, Criticism, Gossip, Slander, Faultfinding, Impatience, Unforgiveness, Self-righteousness, Selfish Ambition, Unrighteous Judgment, Bitterness, and Treachery.

"It doesn't get any easier than this," said Unrighteous Judgment, with an evil sneer. "I've got more people calling to me than I have time."

"Gossip, Slander, and I will keep the people stirred up," said Faultfinding. "The rest of you will have plenty of time to work. This isn't going to go away quickly."

The talk around town about Sarah was rampant and unkind. Barbara, newly retired and a new resident, went to the post office to mail a letter, and all she heard was criticism and gossip. It was no better at the grocery store. At Nate's Hardware, where she stopped to buy a furnace filter, she even heard a threat.

"Dear Lord," she prayed, "the whole town is brimming over with hatred." Barbara had been at the meeting last night. Being unfamiliar with the town, she was late herself, and for that reason, ended up on the back row where she observed Sarah's discomfort at close range. She was close enough to see the sweat beaded on her upper lip, close enough to see Sarah's hands tremble and to observe the humiliation and fear spreading across Sarah's face just before she headed out the door.

Although Barbara understood why none of the residents wanted the jail, and she didn't want it, either, she did feel compassion for Sarah and wondered what made her take the unpopular stand she did. *Maybe she's desperate for the money. Maybe she lives on a fixed income.*

Barbara had almost followed Sarah out the door to comfort her, but she didn't want to risk being ostracized by association. She needed to meet people and make friends, and it was glaringly obvious that any association with Sarah would have been a social faux pas on a grand scale. Still, she was ashamed that she let what people might think of her prevent her from comforting someone who obviously needed it. *Forgive me, Lord. I could have helped someone, and I didn't.*

Her guardian angel Gadiel beamed, "And of course He totally forgives you." Gadiel looked about 30 years old in human age. He wore a shimmering multicolored cloak embellished with golden cord that went over his shoulders and around his waist, criss-crossing in the back and front. He carried an ancient spear with a carved wooden handle and a large silver spearhead. As Barbara drove home, Gadiel rode in the front seat, his large spear stuck through the top of the car.

Sooo much work to be done. Thank goodness the house wasn't a fixer upper. The previous owners had done a nice job of remodeling it before putting it on the market. She didn't even have to paint. But the boxes, the endless boxes, waited to be unpacked. *They're reproducing like rabbits,* she thought as she looked around. She'd been moving boxes a little at a time, trying to avoid getting overwhelmed; eventually it caught up to her. She collapsed on the couch and called her little pug dog, Hugo, who immediately jumped on her lap and began to lick her chin enthusiastically.

"Don't get too excited, Hugo," she said, "I don't even know where I packed the doggie biscuits!"

That next morning, when Sarah opened her eyes, her first sense of awareness was a splitting headache. She ran her hand across the cut on her eyebrow and the whole horrible experience came flooding back to her. She grimaced at the memory of last night's meeting. *Jesus, Jesus, Jesus, help me,* was all she could think.

Those words were enough for Joel to brandish his flaming sword and alleviate Sarah's headache by cutting off the cowering spirit of Infirmity clinging to the side of her head. Its stunned black form hit the floor with a thud. Righting itself in a hurry, Infirmity used its web-like black leathery wings to fly away.

Malta began to match the worship around the throne on his flute, and as wave after wave of "Holy, Holy, Holy," silently penetrated her soul, Sarah found the energy she needed to get out of bed. She shuffled by the mirror and let out a groan. She didn't even need to put on her glasses to see the black and blue welt surrounding her swollen left eye.

For the next two days, Sarah skipped her morning time with the Lord and her prayer walk and spent the time moping around the house. She was embarrassed at how her face looked, but even more, she was afraid to go outside. The spirit of Agoraphobia was back, convincing her that folks would point, call names, or even worse, attack her.

She sat down to have her cup of coffee. She broke her morning ritual by throwing the unopened *Gazette* into her trash after Discouragement whispered, "I'm sure you're the topic of every letter to the editor today." The paper landed with a thud. *No sense punishing myself.*

Sarah curled up on the couch. The days were getting chillier. She snuggled under the multicolored Angora blanket that George had given her as a Christmas present. As she ran her hand over the soft fleece, the loneliness swept over her again. She and George used to snuggle under the blanket as they watched nature documentaries or after they'd spent the evening dancing.

Dancing, thought Sarah; a smile crept across her face. She had developed a love for dancing as a little girl. About once a month, on a Friday night, her father would move the coffee table from the living room and start the big player piano. Then he would sweep Sarah up in his arms. She would carefully place each socked-foot on his black leather shoes, and they would laugh and dance to every song on the roller. These were some of her favorite childhood memories.

I was so excited when I found out George loved to dance. After we were married, we went to the lodge at Mt. Pielor almost every Friday night.

For a moment she was back on the dance floor in her black pumps. George looked dapper, as always, in his charcoal gray suit and red-striped tie. She could feel his arm around her waist. The orchestra was playing "Over There." She began to hum the music as she followed his lead around the large wooden floor. Even though the place was crowded, she never noticed the other couples. She and George were in their own world when they danced together. When the song finished in her mind, so did the cheerful recollection. She remembered how their dancing dates had ended when George became sick.

When he couldn't make the trip to Mt. Pielor, they began dancing in the living room together. She smiled at the memory of George shuffling around in his flannel pajamas and house slippers. As he continued to deteriorate, even one slow, slow dance with his feet hardly moving got to be too much. *What a change from the virile, dapper George I knew.* Toward the end, Sarah would just play the waltz music in the bedroom. It seemed to calm George. How she missed his arms around her when they danced.

Lord, talk to me. Is George there with You? Please, please answer me, Lord. I can't take this much longer. Give me courage. I feel like a prisoner in my own house. I'm too scared to go outside. I need to hear about the land. I'm lonely and desperate for a friend. She prayed in tongues for a while, but stopped when she didn't feel better.

Chapter 13

She heard the mailman on the porch. After waiting a few minutes to make sure he was gone, she went outside. The box was crammed with letters. Only occasionally was there a return address. *I guess the rest wanted to remain anonymous*, she thought. *Oh Lord, this is not what I need.*

CHAPTER 14

"Pride works frequently under a dense mask, and will often assume the garb of humility."
Adam Clarke[1]

"You can have anything in life if you will sacrifice everything else for it."
James M. Barrie[2]

A rusty blue Toyota pulled up in front of the house. When Sarah saw Pastor Paul get out, she breathed a sigh of relief. It was all she could do to keep from throwing herself into his arms when he came up the stairs. *Thank You, God, for bringing my pastor. Thank You. I need to talk to someone who is spiritually wiser than I.* She couldn't see the demons of Manipulation, Control, Judgment, Fear of Man, and Selfish Ambition that his actions had invited. They clung to his scalp and shoulders. The demons gloated and taunted Saldu, who followed along behind.

Joel looked at Malta, "Definitely not what Sarah needs now."

"Hello. Is this a good time?" asked Paul as he stepped onto the porch. He did a double take at Sarah's black eye, but chose not to mention it.

"Oh, yes. It's a very good time," said Sarah, concealing the handful of letters behind her back and looking slightly to the side to try to obscure her eye. "Please come in."

Sarah brewed a pot of coffee and they sat at the yellow Formica-topped kitchen table. Paul sat comfortably with the presence of these familiar spirits. He was making no effort to break free from their influence so the three mighty angels were unable to intervene on his behalf.

The biggest demon Manipulation whispered to Paul: "Thank you for allowing me to talk with you. I have some important things to share...."

"Thank you for allowing me to talk with you," repeated Paul. "I have some important things to share. Things that I think are from the Lord. Do you mind if we start with prayer?"

Sarah sighed in relief, "Yes, I'd like that." *Thanks, Lord, for sending me some spiritual guidance.* Joel and Malta stood behind her.

"Lord, please show us Your will and Your way. Help Sarah to make the right decisions during this difficult time for the town. Amen."

Difficult time for the town? thought Sarah, feeling exasperated, but she squelched a reply and the emotions that went with it.

"I assume you're feeling a lot of stress and pressure since the meeting the other night. Right?"

"Oh, yes," said Sarah feeling relief at having found a kindred spirit. "People are even sending me letters telling me what to do." She held up the pile of mail. "I just want to do what the Lord wants, but I need confirmation."

"I'm sure you do. I hope that I can help; that's why I'm here. I feel like I've heard a few things from Him about the land. It even started before there was talk of the jail, if that's helpful."

Sarah felt her clenched muscles relax. She exhaled deeply. Her tension was draining away. *Finally, Lord, You sent help.* "I'd really like some good spiritual guidance. This has been a confusing time for me, and I'm a new Christian—"

"I understand," said Paul cutting her off. "Well, ever since I got here, I felt like the Lord was going to grow our church. As you know, our present facility can only hold about 150 people. I've felt that the Lord is going to bless us with new members and we will need to build a new church building. This is where it gets really good—when I first arrived in town, I was driving around just seeing it all for the first time, taking it all in. When I got to the intersection of Old Highway 3 and JJ, that land just kind of jumped out at me, if you know what I mean. I had no way of knowing it was yours. I didn't know that until the meeting a few nights ago. I just know that the first time I laid eyes on it, I thought it was earmarked by the Lord for something special. Having a church on your land is a legacy I'm sure you'd be proud to leave, wouldn't you?"

He didn't slow down long enough for her to answer. "If you sold *or donated* the land to the church, it would be a win/win situation." The demons were heady over their success. Paul followed their lead exactly. "Everyone would be glad for the progress this would bring the town, not to mention soothing everyone's high-strung nerves."

He was careful never to mention the jail. He knew how she felt about that, but building a new church seemed holier than building a jail. Besides, there were people everywhere to minister to. You don't need a jail to find people in need.

Joel watched as three of Paul's black spirits swirled around Sarah. They had no legal right to land on her, but they could torment her.

Sarah felt troubled, confused. Even though neither of them had touched their coffee, she stood up and came back with the pot. What Paul was saying made sense. The first twisted spirit of Manipulation whispered to her: "It'd be great to have a new church on the ground. It would certainly calm everyone's ruffled feathers; more than that, it would probably make you the town hero."

"Remember," croaked Selfish Ambition, "how everyone sang, 'For He's The Jolly Good Fellow' at the meeting two nights ago?"

Sarah glanced at the pile of letters on the table. Seeing them made her heart race.

"That's right Sarah; you don't need any more hate mail, do you?" cooed the slimy voice of Fear of Man.

"Now we go in for the kill," said Manipulation. "Repeat after me, Paul, 'I never had the pleasure of meeting your late husband,'" Paul continued, "but I understand that this land was in his family for a long time."

"Yes, it was purchased by George's father when he was a young man. Then when we married, we farmed it for 23 years."

"Maybe the land is in your possession for such a time as this."[3] The demons all flinched at the passing mention of a Scripture passage. Sarah had never heard that phrase.

"What do you mean, 'for such a time as this'?"

"It's from the Book of Esther."

"I, I haven't read that book yet," said Sarah, somewhat embarrassed.

"I'll give you a brief overview. Esther was the queen. The prime minister named Haman hated the Jews and devised a plan, along with the king, to have all the Jews killed. The king didn't know Esther was a Jew. She had a choice to stay in the protection of the palace and watch her people perish outside or intervene by risking her life. God had moved her to the position as queen for 'such a time as this.' It was God's will for her to step forward. It was the time God had destined for her to bring deliverance to her people."

"For such a time as this," repeated Sarah.

"That's right," said Paul. "For such a time as this."

"I wish they would shut up," said Selfish Ambition. "It's like nails on a chalkboard every time they say that."

"Keep praying. I'm confident the Lord will show you His will," said Paul, standing to his feet. "I can tell that you want the Lord's heart on this. I'm sure you'll make the right, the rational decision," he said, shaking her hand vigorously.

"Please give me a call if you have any questions or want to talk. Once you come to a decision, we can announce the good news to the church." Paul was nodding his head. Before she knew it, Sarah was nodding, too.

Selfish Ambition and Fear of Man stayed with Sarah. The others left with Pastor Paul firmly in their destructive grip. They were so comfortable with him; they regarded him as their permanent residency.

Sarah walked him to the porch and watched as he drove away. She expected to feel better, but her muscles were tense again.

"Paul," said Saldu, looking stoic yet disappointed, "never measure others' worth or value by whether they agree with your opinion. What an arrogant standard. Let Sarah do what she wants with the land. It's hers. You just used every manipulative technique against her, including mentioning her dead husband. You never met him, yet suddenly you're invested in what he would think? You're a hypocrite. She's a valuable, living, breathing, blood-bought Christian standing right in front of you. All you can see is what you can get from her. Everything else is lost on you. You don't love people; you use people. If you don't cry out for help from the Lord to change that pattern, you'll never accomplish what the Lord has planned for your life, and it will bring you immeasurable pain."

"Paul, you've almost got her where you want her," whispered one of the clawed, leather-winged demons. "She teared up when you mentioned her husband. Did you see her nodding at the end? That Bible verse was a great touch. She's home looking at the Scripture now. I think you've got her."

"Pray about this land debate," said Saldu. "You could speak up for Sarah and give her the support she needs. You could be a spiritual buffer between her and the town's anger. Stand up and do what's right! Lead your church in the truth. What is politically correct is never heavenly correct. Remember, the Lord humbled Himself to live in a human body, die on the cross, and suffer for sins, none of which were His. In order to fulfill His plan for your life, you must lead the same humble, obedient lifestyle."

"Keep your eye on the prize, Paul," said Selfish Ambition. "Don't give up your goal. Think how many people will flock to your church if you solve this jail dilemma. You'd probably need to build right away. Don't let up; success is right around the corner."

Paul smiled.

Chapter 15

"Fear is an invitation to courage."

Bill Treasurer[1]

"Resentment is like taking poison and waiting for the other person to die."

Malachy McCourt[2]

In a few minutes Sarah was reading the book of Esther out loud. Joel and Malta enjoyed watching the demons cringe and retch. "God's Word is alive and active," whispered Malta. "The Word is a sword. It's powerful for warfare against the enemy."

"For if you remain completely silent at this time, relief and deliverance will arise for the Jews from another place, but you and your father's house will perish. Yet who knows whether you have come to the kingdom for such a time as this?" read Sarah.

"All Christians have at least one 'such a time as this' in their lives. Sometimes several," said Malta. "This is your time Sarah. It's your time right now."

A few days ago Sarah was convinced the jail was God's will. Now Paul and his demonically fueled logic had confused her, plus Fear of Man had her afraid of the consequences if she sold the ground to BCCF. *Things seemed so clear a few days ago.* Now Sarah was confused and distraught, almost to the point of being physically ill.

"The towns' people will never forgive you if you sell the ground," whispered the scorched voice of Selfish Ambition.

"You need to think about your future and your comfort these last years of your pathetic life," said Fear of Man. "You need to make some friends, and selling to the jail isn't the way to do it."

Some of the towns' people might even get violent. They feel really strongly about this jail," whispered Intimidation. "You are here all by yourself at night."

"You're not by yourself Sarah," said Joel. "The same Holy Spirit that raised Jesus from the dead lives inside you.[3] You are never alone. Don't give in to these spirits. The more you believe them, the more power they have over you."

"Right now you have more faith in your inability than in God's ability. Fear is really just faith in the devil. The demons only have power when you give them your worship."

I need clarity. I think I'll prayer walk. I just need to do it. Jesus, help me; I can't stay in this house forever. Before Malta even unsheathed his double-edged sword, the spirit of Agoraphobia was gone.

Sarah grabbed her denim jacket and pulled on her floppy garden hat. *Maybe this will conceal my identity and my black eye.* It seemed like a long time since she'd been out of the house even though it was just a few days. The leaves were mostly gone; the trees looked skeleton-like as they swayed in the breeze. There were many houses that had bales of hay, pumpkins, Jack O' Lanterns, or Indian corn out as decorations.

Sarah rounded the corner praying and thought how good it felt to be prayer walking again. When she turned onto the second block, she saw that the real-estate sign had been removed from the yard of the small Victorian house. A car was in the driveway, and there was a huge pile of empty boxes at the curb. "Let's stay a little longer here, Sarah," whispered Malta.

Lord help this person or family to get settled in quickly. Let them make friends and feel like they "fit." If they don't know You, bring them quickly to salvation. I pray Your favor and blessings on them.

Inside the house Barbara was still unpacking. She'd been at it all day. She had on her old blue sweat suit and had her salt and pepper colored hair pulled back. "You may as well get these out of the way," suggested her guardian angel, Gadiel. She grabbed the stack of empty boxes accumulating by the door and stepped out on the porch. Startled by seeing Sarah standing in front of her house, she jumped. *I'm a sweaty mess. I can't be meeting people, making first impressions looking like this.* She fought her first impulse, which was to drop the boxes and dart back inside.

Sarah was also startled by Barbara's sudden appearance. She ducked her head to hide her face and shuffled down the sidewalk. When Sarah was 20 feet away, Barbara worked up the courage to yell, "Wait, Sarah." Sarah hesitated, afraid she'd get an earful from a disgruntled citizen opposing her views. Slowly, tentatively, she walked back.

"You are Sarah, aren't you?"

"Yes, how do you know me?" she asked, still staring down to conceal her black eye.

"I was at the meeting the other night."

Sarah recoiled, as if preparing for a verbal kick to the gut.

"I'm new in town. My name's Barbara. I just wanted to meet you and say that what you did was very brave. We all need to do what God tells us, even if it goes against the flow. Do you understand?"

I can't believe what I'm hearing. The words were like a cool breeze blowing over her tattered soul. In her neediness, she blurted out, "Can I talk to you?"

Barbara was embarrassed by how she looked and the state of her house, but she felt this was a divine appointment. "Sure, if you can stomach the mess."

I'd go to the city's trash dump to have someone to talk to who understands, thought Sarah. "I don't mind at all," she said looking up for the first time.

"Oh my gosh! Did someone beat you up?"

"No. Just a car wreck. I hit my head. It looks worse than it is."

After clearing boxes off the couch and apologizing for not having anything to offer Sarah to drink, Barbara sat down.

"I was at the back of the meeting hall when you came in. What you did was very brave, very godly. You didn't back down; you didn't let your fear of what people thought stop you. I was going to come after you, um, but I was embarrassed. I'm new in town and didn't want to make enemies right off the bat. I'm really sorry."

"I understand," said Sarah, and she really did. "I'm the town's outcast. I got nine letters in the mail today, and I haven't had the nerve to even open them."

At Barbara's encouragement, Sarah shared about what had happened since her salvation.

"You've been through so much—both good and bad. It's exciting what the Lord is doing in your life. Some people are saved all their lives and don't seem to have that much supernatural activity going on."

"What do you mean?" asked Sarah.

"It seems like most Christians just go through the motions. Their lives aren't very different from their unsaved neighbors; they rarely pray for people, read their Bible, or take time to hear God's voice in any significant ways."

Until now, Sarah assumed that the Lord spoke to everyone like He did with her. "But doesn't He speak to them during their morning sessions with Him?"

"That's the problem; most Christians don't spend enough time with Him to learn to recognize His voice. Hearing from Him isn't a priority. But I believe the Lord has something special for you. I think He's going to do a lot with you before He takes you home. You're in the middle of one of those, 'for such a time as this' seasons."

"You have no idea what you just said." Sarah laughed for the first time in almost a week.

Sarah learned that Barbara had just retired from a secretarial position in a large city where she'd spent most of her life. She'd kept working at a job she had grown to dislike by promising herself that if she stayed on until retirement she'd treat herself by moving to a small town. She'd always liked Bradbury. A friend of hers from high school had lived there once. When her Realtor told her about this house, she came that day and made an offer. She went back home and gave the landlord her 30 days' notice.

After another hour, the conversation came to an end. "Thanks so much for listening to me tonight. You have no idea how good it feels to have a trusted confidant."

"Well, it was a God thing that I came on the porch when I did. Do you want me to drive you home? It's late."

"Thanks, but I'm fine walking. I just live one block over."

Sarah praised God all the way home, accompanied by Joel and Malta. Then she held tightly to the porch rail and slowly ascended the stairs. The big picture window behind the porch swing was shattered. The porch was covered with shards of glass. "Oh, Jesus, what does this mean?" she asked out loud.

She turned on the living room light and saw the brick. It had hit the coffee table, leaving a large gash and then bounced onto the floor. The couch and floor were also covered with glass. She felt the tears welling up again. She sat down in the floral chair opposite the couch and cried. Joel was at her front and Malta at her back, their ethereal wings encircled her, keeping away the spirits that wanted to buffet her.

After a while Malta began, "The enemy would like to see you paralyzed with fear again. He'd like nothing more than to bring your work for the Lord to a halt. But you need to know God's protecting you; don't ever doubt that. He loves you, and He has a plan for you to complete. Now here's the challenge. He wants you to pray for the person who did this."

Sarah recoiled at the thought.

Joel added, "I know it's hard; it can only be done with the Lord's help. Call out to Him for grace to bless your enemies."

I can't forgive them; look what they did to my home. They don't deserve to be forgiven. Two evil spirits were drawn to Sarah's unforgiveness, like flies to blood.

"That's right sister, preach it," shouted Bitterness and his gnarled cronies. "They don't deserve your forgiveness, just your revenge."

"Remember, forgiveness is God's provision for people who do wrong. People who haven't offended you don't need your forgiveness. Forgiveness is only for those who offend or hurt you," said Malta.

Sarah looked again at the brick and the gash on her coffee table and her anger was rekindled.

"Look at every trying circumstance that the Lord allows in your life as His way of purifying your spirit and attitude," said Joel. "You can remain bitter and head down Satan's path, or you can forgive and become more like Jesus."

Sarah sat for a while thinking, while a battle raged for control between her spirit and soul.

"Think of it like this, Sarah," said Malta. "Bitterness is like a snakebite. The snake that bit you, when it hurled that rock through your window, has already slithered away. But until you forgive, the poison is still circulating through your veins. It's only damaging you; your hatred has no effect on the snake."

"Whoever did this was scum," shouted Unforgiveness. "They deserve to go to jail, and that's all they deserve. Why would you even consider forgiving them?"

Malta continued, "Remember Jesus' parable about the king who forgives his servant 10,000 talents?"[4]

"Which is 20 billion dollars in today's money," said Joel with a grin. "That's *billion* with a "b.""

"Then that servant went out and found someone who owed him a mere 100 denarii." Malta paused and looked toward Joel.

"Twenty thousand dollars."

"His master had forgiven him an unpayable debt, but he choked his debtor and had him thrown into prison. When the king heard it, he was furious. 'You wicked servant! I forgave you all that debt because you begged me. Should you not also have had compassion on your fellow servant, just as I had pity on you?' Then he handed him to the torturers. Jesus said that we will not receive forgiveness from God unless we forgive others. No matter how badly you are treated, it is miniscule compared to what Jesus suffered to forgive your sins."

She still felt mad, and she still felt violated, but she realized the truth when she heard it. *Lord,* she began slowly and through somewhat gritted teeth, *You know who is responsible for this. I might never find out. I guess it's not important that I do. Will You help me not to hate and help me not to fear? I guess anyone who would throw a rock through an old lady's window is a pretty sad case. I pray that they would come to know You in a personal way and that You would change their hearts. Amen.*

With each word, the circle that Bitterness, Unforgiveness, Selfish Ambition, Agoraphobia, and Fear were flying around her grew wider. As little bits of glory fell from Heaven, the spirits became more frantic until they were jostling and scratching each other in the corner of the ceiling, trying to avoid the heavenly fragrance that invaded the room.

Sarah felt a little better after the prayer. She even had more energy. She picked up her dustpan and broom and slowly swept up the glass. After going over the couch with the attachments on her vacuum, she found a large piece of cardboard and with a black marker she wrote, "Jesus loves you." This was more than the demons could take; they cursed and fled to the kitchen. Sarah taped the cardboard over the window. Then she took the brick and set it on top of the television. *Every time I see it, I'll remember to pray for whoever did this.*

"Nooooo," came the voices shrieking in unison from the kitchen, "You must take revenge."

Rummaging through the closet she found a large crocheted doily. It was one she had made while sitting by George toward the end of his illness. She gently unfolded it and placed it over the dent on the coffee table. She placed the cranberry scented candle on it. "There. That's not so bad," she said, admiring her ingenuity. Then she went to bed. Joel and Malta stood beside her. "It's been a hard, hard week for Sarah," said Joel.

"Yes, just the kind of week the Father uses to build character into His children."

"And Sarah's learning fast."

CHAPTER 16

"Affliction is the wholesome soil of virtue, where patience, honor, sweet humility, and calm fortitude, take root and strongly flourish."

David Mallet[1]

"You can be pitiful or powerful, but you can't be both."

Joyce Meyer[2]

After her prayer time, Sarah crawled out of bed in the morning. The arthritis medicine certainly wasn't helping much, if at all, and she'd increased to 15 milligrams immediately after her doctor's appointment. As she shuffled to the bathroom, she made a mental note to call Dr. Newbury and make a follow-up visit.

"Look at your clothes basket," whispered Lying.

It was overflowing with dirty clothes. *I haven't done laundry for ten days. I'd better divide this into two loads.*

"Think how much time it will save if you just do it in one load," said Lying. "Only up and down the stairs twice instead of four times. You can do it all." She headed to the kitchen carrying the basket. She opened the basement door to go down the stairs, but paused.

"Be careful, Sarah," said Joel. "You need both hands on the rail." She'd never thought about going up and down the stairs with the basket before, but today there was an uneasy feeling. She looked at the steps for a long time then put the basket on the floor and pushed it with her foot. Halfway it over-turned, spilling dirty clothes at the foot of the stairs. She grasped the rail as she cautiously made her way down each step, assisted by Joel and Malta.

She checked the washing instructions on a new, brightly colored blouse she had just purchased. The first tag said "Made in India."

"Watch this," said Joel. "Here's a great prayer opportunity." Malta nodded. "Sarah, the woman who sewed this blouse lives in Bangalore. A mission organization taught her and many other women marketable skills so they can support their children. Many of the husbands are alcoholics and unfortunately their paychecks are rarely spent on food. This sewing group of 30 women is now able to provide for their children while they are being taught the Gospel. Whenever you wear this blouse, remember to pray that these ladies would prosper spiritually and financially."

After loading the washer and praying, she turned around and noticed a box on the gray storage shelves that Malta was pointing at. It was marked "OLD DOCUMENTS," in George's writing. It had been there for years, but today, for some reason, she decided to see what was inside.

She dragged the trashcan over to the shelves, gave the box a big tug, and it fell to the floor, stirring up so much dust that it gave her a sneezing fit.

"God bless you," said Joel and Malta as she slowly sat down on the area rug. The first document was their taxes from 1949. She smiled. *George was nothing if not organized. That was such a hard year for us. President Truman signed to raise the minimum wage to 75 cents an hour. We had to cut the amount of help we could use during harvest season.* She smiled, looked at the taxes again and with slight hesitation threw them in the trashcan. *I guess I'll clean these out so no one has to do it after I'm gone.*

The next six stacks were the next six year's taxes. Then came the utility bills from 1948. *What was that man thinking?* Next was a yellowed newspaper. She opened it carefully. It was the *Gazette*. On the front were George's picture and the headline, "Local Fireman Saves Twins In House Fire." She remembered the incident well. It was the first year he'd been with the department. It wasn't until George came home for dinner that she found out what a hero he was, and then not until dessert when she inquired about his day. She smiled as she read. Then she flipped through the paper and scanned the weekly grocery ad. Eggs five cents a dozen. She smiled again and set the paper aside. After a few more inches of old taxes and old insurance papers, she pulled out a hand full of letters. She recognized her writing at once. It was her old love letters to George. She clutched them to her heart. *I never knew he saved these.*

After considerable effort, she got to her feet, still holding the precious letters, and headed slowly upstairs. Entering the kitchen she saw yesterday's stack of mail. She looked at the letters in her hand and picked up the letters on the counter. She pulled out a letter from her niece and one from Buchanan County Correctional Facilities and threw the rest in the trash. *That felt liberating,* she thought. She poured a cup of coffee and sat down at the yellow table with her old love letters.

The top letter was one that she had written to George when he was away that first year at college. *I missed him so much I literally didn't think I could stand being apart.* Then she realized that these feelings from many years ago were the same she had been forced to endure since his death. Only her love now was more mature, more intense; and he wouldn't ever be coming home to visit for spring break.

There were 64 letters. She'd written them over a period of two years until they'd decided to get married when George started his junior year. Although Sarah wanted to read them all in one setting, she decided to ration them. *I'll read one a day, and then I'll start over.* It seemed like a healing thing to do. Reading them all at once seemed gluttonous, like she'd use up something precious that she could never replace.

She started putting them in chronological order according to the postmarks. The last letter in the stack was not her handwriting, nor was it George's. It was postmarked from Bradbury and the year was 1926. It was addressed to Lorna McHone. *That was George's mother's maiden name. I think I'll read two today.* She carefully opened the yellowed pages. It was from George's dad before he and Lorna were married.

Dearest,

I miss you such that at times I can think of nothing else. I am making a way for us to be together forever. Something so exciting has happened. I am the proud owner of 36 acres of rich farmland, which has a house and barn. It was a full-fledged miracle that I have gotten this land. Who would have thought that an 18-year-old would ever be a landowner?

For the last three months I've been working as a farm hand for Reverend Templeton. He farms and on the weekend he rides the circuit preaching to several different churches. Then he's back working hard on the farm through the week. When I started the job he told me it would just be temporary because he felt God was telling him to sell the farm to spend more time on the circuit. He was all ready to sell the land to the neighbor who had offered him a price of $450. I had started looking for other work when Reverend Templeton came to me and asked me if I'd be interested in the farm. I told him "Yes," but I'm the last person who would have means to acquire $450. He looked me straight in the eyes and said, "The Lord told me He wants you to have this land. I'm prepared to take $100 a year for four and a half years, with no interest."

You know, Lorna, that I am not a religious man, but I got down on my knees and thanked God for this gift. I'm putting in the first crop and after the fall harvest, I will send money for you to come to Bradbury.

Respectfully,
Vernon Edwards

Sarah laid the letter on the table; her hands were shaking. *I never knew how he got the farm.* She hurried to her car and drove out of town on Old Highway 3 and past the land. She turned left on Old Cemetery Road and pulled onto the dirt drive. She stepped carefully through the weeds. This old cemetery, in need of mowing and repair, was where most of the town's settlers were buried. The largest tombstone was William Bradbury's, the town's namesake; next to him were his wife, an infant daughter, and two adult daughters and their husbands. After looking for five minutes Sarah found a small flat headstone, off in the corner, more like a large brick. On it was carved:

Reverend Arthur Templeton

May 19, 1855 - July 28, 1933

He preached Jesus

She slowly sat down beside the small headstone and ran her fingers over the letters. "You see, Sarah, the Lord has had plans for this land from before the foundation of the world," whispered Malta. "He was orchestrating them before you were born. You're one link in those plans. Reverend Templeton was another link, and he was faithful. He heard the Lord's voice and sold the land to George's father so you could own it today. It's your turn to be faithful." Malta laid his large gleaming hands on Sarah's shoulder and she began to weep.

"Remember the dream you had about the jail before it was announced? Remember the Scriptures and how they undid you emotionally? That was Father talking to you. Don't be thrown off track by anyone or anything," said Joel. "All of the confusion is from the enemy to keep you from following through with Father's plans."

"It will be hard to go against what the town wants," said Malta. "There will definitely be a high price to pay. You will suffer, but one place that you can go deeper with the Lord in intimacy is in your sufferings. Instead of fleeing from the pain, feel it and meet Him in your pain. Realize that this very pain is part of what He suffered for you when He was on this earth. Remember that He was despised, and rejected.[3] Then take your focus off yourself and thank Him that He loved you enough to suffer like that for you. Remember, no injustice you'll ever suffer will come close to what He suffered for you."

"You see Sarah, in addition to suffering everything we suffered, He also carried all your sorrows and griefs just like He carried all your sins.[4] He understands every physical and emotional pain, and He will give you the grace you need. You can go to Him and find relief and healing there," said Joel.

Sarah's shoulders heaved up and down under Malta's hands as she continued to sob.

"Even in your seemingly darkest hours, He's a good God, and you can trust Him. He not only moved Barbara here in answer to your request for a friend, but also as an intercessor for you. Pastor Hall is still praying for you, too. Did you know that intercessors need people to intercede for them? They're high on Satan's target list," said Malta.

She thought about the two people praying for her and took several deep breaths to try to bring her sobbing under control.

"Sarah," asked Joel, "when you face eternal judgment and it is too late to do anything more about this situation with the land, what will you wish then, with all your heart, that you would have done at this critical time as you are actually dealing with it?"[5] Sarah breathed a desperate prayer and ran her hand again over Reverend Templeton's headstone as a kind of connection with his obedience.

After several minutes, a new determination welled up inside of Sarah. She understood that she was a conduit for the Lord's plans. She wiped her eyes, cleared her throat, and spoke. "I have come into the Kingdom for such a time as this," she said with great resolve. If the Lord suffered so dreadfully for me, then I can surely suffer some because of Him." Sarah made a vow, "Lord, I want to be the next faithful link in Your destiny for this ground. Thank You for Reverend Templeton's faithfulness and thanks for showing me Your will. I'll sell to BCCF. Amen."

The manipulative spirits that had formerly been taunting Sarah began wailing. Black fur and accusations flew as each one turned on the other. "You heard her boys," said Joel with a broad smile. The demons stopped bickering and looked up, but before they had a chance to leave his flashing sword sent their wretched bodies flying. Oh, yeah. He loved his job!

CHAPTER 17

*"I am sure there are many Christians who will
confess that their experience has been very much like
my own in this, that we had long known the Lord
without realizing that meekness and lowliness of heart
are to be the distinguishing feature of the disciple as
they were of the Master. And further, that this
humility is not a thing that will come of itself, but
that it must be made the object of special desire and
prayer and faith and practice."*

Andrew Murray[1]

She took the letter from BCCF and sat on the sofa. As she opened it, her hands were shaking, but her spirit was totally at peace.

Dear Ms. Edwards,

We've not received a response from our last letter. We wish you to know that we are still interested in purchasing your land. We would like you to consider selling it to us for the sum of $50,000. I have enclosed a contract for you to look over. I will contact you in a few days if I don't hear from you.

Sincerely,
David Burris,
President Buchanan County Correctional Facilities, Inc.

"Fifty thousand dollars? They're offering me $50,000. Lord, what will I do with that kind of money?"

Her thoughts were interrupted by Pastor Paul knocking on the door. Of course he never went anywhere without his little black cohorts surrounding him. The first thing he saw was the hand-lettered "Jesus Loves You" sign over the window. He shook his head. It reminded him of the guy at the sports arena with the rainbow-colored wig and the John 3:16 sign.

She invited him in.

"What happened to your window?"

"Someone's not too happy with me right now, lots of someones, actually."

"That's terrible. It just shows how emotional some people can become over these sticky issues. Everyone has strong feelings about your land, that's for sure."

"Please sit down, Pastor. I'll get some coffee," she motioned toward the couch and went to the kitchen. Paul didn't set out to read the letter, but it was laying face up on the coffee table. He could read it without even leaning forward. *Fifty thousand dollars! Unbelievable, no wonder she wants to sell to the jail.* Sarah returned and handed Paul the cup.

"I assume you're here to follow up on our conversation a few days ago. The Lord has just showed me specifically that I'm supposed to sell to BCCF. Just today."

Right, Paul thought, *and I bet He had fifty thousand reasons.* "Well, I'm sorry to hear that. The potential for good for God's Kingdom that a new and larger church facility could produce is incalculable."

"Oh, but the Lord has a plan for this land, and I'm just following it. I really have no say in the matter if I want to be obedient. It's like you said, 'For such a time as this.'"

He set the cup on the coffee table next to the letter. Sarah didn't see him roll his eyes as he let out a sigh. "Well, I'd encourage you to continue to pray about it," he said, trying to conceal his growing aggravation.

"Oh, I have. A lot. And the Lord answered just today."

"Sarah, I don't mean to offend you, but you are a new believer. I don't doubt your sincerity, but many times people *think* they've heard the Lord and it's not the Lord, especially if they have strong feelings about one particular option. It's easy to believe that option is from the Lord because we want it so badly." This statement caused the demons to snicker wildly among themselves. "All I'm saying is, maybe you could keep praying and some of the ladies from the church could drop by and talk to you about it."

"Oh, no. I don't need to keep praying. I *know* I heard from the Lord."

Paul sat silently in the chair. When he could think of nothing else to say, he stood to his feet. "Well, have a good day," he said curtly and headed for the door.

Sarah signed the contract and walked to the post office box whistling. *Lord, bless this endeavor,* she prayed as she dropped in the letter. A wave of peace swept over her as she heard it clunk on the bottom. She reveled in the feeling for a few moments, then headed for Barbara's house.

Joel gave Malta a high five.

CHAPTER 18

"We must overcome the impulse to attempt to finish in the flesh what God has begun in the Spirit. This is a great offence to God—our attempting to substitute human zeal for Heaven's anointing."

Bobby Conner[1]

"Character is the hardest thing to gain and the easiest thing to lose."

John Paul Jackson[2]

Paul was fuming when he left Sarah's. Saldu tried to calm him. "Paul, Father brought you to this church for a purpose, and the enemy has distracted you. Your five-year plan isn't the Lord's five-year plan. And you shouldn't be fighting this jail, either. You're not in Bradbury to win a popularity contest; you're here to do the will of God. You've compromised His truth because of your need for love and acceptance, not just with the church people, but the whole town.

"Think of your life this way. God is looking down at you from Heaven. You're at the top of a ski slope and there's a mile of virgin snow beneath you. You shove off and with the Lord's help you ski successfully to the bottom. Not only are your tracks visible from Heaven, but you leave a trail for others coming behind you to follow. Because of you, they find their way, too. This speaks of the potential for your life to have Heavenly and earthly impact.[3]

"Paul, the Lord has made you a leader and He has great plans for your life. You're very charismatic and people will follow you, but your challenge is to step out of the way and point them to Jesus, not to keep them huddled around you like a fan club. Give up all honor like Jesus did; seek honor from God only, empty yourself, count yourself as nothing so that God may be exalted and may be all. There is an irrefutable rule in God's Kingdom: Those who seek exaltation never receive it."

When Saldu stopped, Paul's little black soulmates immediately helped him key in on the part of Saldu's message about leadership.

"You're a leader, Paul, and your five-year plan is nothing short of brilliant," whispered Deception. "It's like God dropped a heavenly blueprint in your lap to teach you how to grow the church for maximum eternal impact."

"Forget the plan," urged Saldu. "To be truly great in the Kingdom of God, you must be humble and passionately in love with the King. Like Mary at Jesus' feet, you need to be content to sit and wait on Him.[4] You should hang on His every word. You must be willing to look foolish in the eyes of your peers as you proclaim boldly what God has told you to say and do."[5]

"Now about that jail, Paul," said Manipulation, sidestepping Saldu's comments, "I've got an idea to thwart that thing that can literally make you the town's savior. You'll have hundreds of people skiing behind you, following your godly example."

Paul bit: hook, line, and sinker. He drove straight to Clarence Harvey. "That's right. I saw the letter. They're offering her $50,000 for the land."

"Fifty thousand dollars?" Clarence cursed under his breath. "That's more than twice as much per acre as most property around here is bringing. Of course she'll sell. She'll never get that price again, not in her lifetime."

"Maybe she could," whispered Deception. "Maybe she could," repeated Paul.

"What are you talking about?"

"Maybe we, the town, could do a fundraiser. If we raised $50,000, she'd have no reason not to sell to us."

Clarence paused; his business mind evaluated the feasibility of the idea. A big smile spread across his face. He slapped Paul on the shoulder. "I like your style. That's a great idea, buddy!" Paul smiled and reveled in the affirmation of an older father figure.

"I'll get on the phone with some businessmen who have fairly deep pockets. I'll get Gary to print some posters and flyers, and maybe I'll do another billboard."

"We can take a special offering at church this Sunday. I'll swing by Sarah's house and tell her the good news."

"Great, give me three hours, and I'll have this campaign in full swing."

"I'm on my way to Sarah's."

Paul knocked and knocked, but Sarah wasn't there. He went back to the church and tried to call several more times. *She doesn't even have an answering machine. I'll have to call later in the evening.*

Sarah was at Barbara's recounting the story with great excitement. "And then I found the letter yesterday in the bottom of a box that had been in the basement for who knows how long. George's father was practically given the land by a minister. And George's father wasn't even a believer, as far as I know. George had one brother, but he was killed in the war, so the farm passed on to George. Now it's mine, or it was until about an hour ago when I mailed the contract. And when I dropped the letter in the mailbox, I felt such a peace inside, like a warmth. It's hard to explain. All I know is that I was desperate. I couldn't take much more stress. I still can't believe how it all worked out."

"That's an unbelievable story. God is so creative. You did the right thing, but…." Barbara hesitated. "It was really ugly at church this Sunday. You know how the people around here are gonna feel. Even if they heard your story, the spiritual significance would be lost on most of them. They'll just think you're looking out for your own interests, you money-hungry old coot," said Barbara, assuming a different voice and shaking her finger at Sarah. They both laughed; then Sarah turned serious again.

"Well, I don't know how bad it will get, but I have God, and I've got you, my friend, and I have the unwavering belief that I was following God's will. Surely that will be enough."

"It will be, but still no guarantees it will be easy."

Sarah convinced Barbara to let her help unpack as they talked. First they unwrapped dishes for the china cabinet. Then they finished unpacking the guest bedroom as they chatted and learned more about each other's pasts. Much to Hugo's delight, they even found the doggie biscuits. Barbara helped Sarah up and rubbed her back. "Oh, it's 11! That's way past my bedtime. I've got to go."

At home her phone had been ringing all evening. Pastor Paul finally gave up and went to bed at 10:45. *I'll call first thing in the morning,* he thought.

The ringing woke him the next morning. *Why did I set the alarm so early?* After a few seconds he realized it was the phone.

"This is one of your church members, Alicia Moore. My husband, Jim, he doesn't go to the church, but, well, he's been rushed to the hospital with a heart attack...." Her voice cracked. "Would you come to the hospital now? I'd be very grateful." Paul glanced at the clock 6:35.

"Sure, I'll be right there." He started praying silently for Jim as he dressed and ran to his Toyota.

Jim was in surgery when Paul arrived. He spent the next few anxious hours with Alicia and the kids in the waiting room. His prayers were a great comfort to Alicia, and he was unaware that they had helped her husband to survive his operation. Then she told the whole story of the heart attack. He even continued listening attentively when she told the story of their courtship—they had started dating at the senior prom. When he glanced at the clock on the wall, it was 10 A.M. *Oh my gosh, I need to call Sarah.* He excused himself and stepped into the hall.

Sarah had just completed her prayer walk and arrived on her porch when she heard the phone ringing. By the time she unlocked the door, it was silent.

Paul tried again in an hour, but Sarah was finishing yesterday's laundry in the basement and didn't hear the phone over the dryer.

When Paul finally left the hospital, he swung through downtown. Clarence and his assistant had been busy. It was less than 24 hours since he'd conceived the fundraising idea, and already there were posters on every utility pole and in every store window, and several kids were at the intersection with cans collecting change from passing motorists.

A sick feeling welled up from his gut. He needed to talk to Sarah right away. He turned his car around and headed toward her house, praying all the way.

CHAPTER 19

"Accept every humiliation, look upon every fellow-man who tries or vexes you, as a means of grace to humble you. Use every opportunity of humbling yourself before your fellow-man as a help to abide humble before God."

Andrew Murray[1]

"Spite is never lonely; envy always tags along."

Mignon McLaughlin[2]

As Paul stood on the porch and knocked, he felt himself sweating. *Please God, she can't have already sold the land. It's been less than 24 hours.*

Sarah opened the door. He tried to read her face when she saw who it was. He sat down at her invitation. Where to begin?

"Sarah, I know you feel like you've heard from the Lord to sell the land to BCCF, but—"

"Oh, I did hear from the Lord, and it was in the most wonderful way, pastor. Let me tell you what happened."

"Maybe in a minute; right now I need to know if you've actually *already* sold the land." He closed his eyes and braced himself for the answer he didn't want to hear.

"Why yes, I did. Right after you left yesterday I signed the contract and walked straight to the post office box. It all started with that verse you gave me, 'For such a time as this,' and—"

He sighed deeply and looked at the floor. His heart raced. The deal was already done as he was pitching his fund-raising scheme to Clarence. He longed to be the hero; why was he always the goat? As he stood up a feeling of dread washed over his entire body. His demons were amused, laughing, celebrating their success of Paul's failure.

"You look a little pale. Are you all right?"

"I just have to go take care of some business," he mumbled numbly.

"Can I finish telling you the story?"

"No, not now." He headed out the door.

"Well, drop by when you can stay longer. I'd like you to hear it. It really is quite the story," she called to him, but he was already gone.

He shoved his key in the ignition and smacked the steering wheel with the palm of his left hand. *How can one woman cause me so much trouble? Every time I turn around, she's causing stress in my life.*

"That's right, Paul. It's Sarah. She's like a thorn in your flesh," Self Pity's sticky voice flooded his mind.

Even though he told himself there was no sense postponing the inevitable, he still drove around the block three times before parking in front of the *Gazette*. There on the plate glass window was a multicolored, canvas banner three feet by four feet, promoting the fund-raising campaign. He held his head in his hands. It had been years since he'd felt this scared. *Oh God, do I feel sick. How can I work this out?*

He walked in the front door. Clarence's face brightened. Paul shoved his hands into his pockets to conceal their shaking.

"Paul, buddy, come here, I want to share the progress we're making with you," he said wrapping his arm around Paul's shoulder. "We're up to $15,000 already, and I still have three potentially large donors who haven't gotten back to me yet." He stopped long enough to look at Paul's ashen face.

"What's wrong?"

"I-I tried to get a hold of Sarah yesterday and this morning, but she's been gone. I just talked to her, and she's already sold the land."

"When?"

"Yesterday, after I left her house." All Clarence's frustration over not being able to stop the jail spilled out on Paul. He withdrew his arm from Paul's shoulder and gave him a shove. Paul took several steps back to retain his balance.

"WHY DIDN'T YOU TELL ME SOONER? I'VE GOT A FULL-FLEDGED CAMPAIGN GOING, AND I'M TAKING PEOPLE'S MONEY FOR A CAUSE THAT'S NONEXISTENT! THAT'S FRAUD. HOW COULD YOU DO THIS TO ME? IT WAS SO STUPID…."

Paul felt his face flush; he glanced at the other employees who were watching him and then stared at the floor until Clarence was done with his verbal assault. "Sorry," Paul mumbled. "I tried to contact her…." His voice trailed off. As he walked toward the door, he heard Clarence's continued rant about him to the office staff. "How can anyone be so incompetent? I've printed $500 worth of publicity…."

All the spirits saw Paul's vulnerability as their opportunity to torture him. Humiliation and Self-Pity hovered over him.

"You can't do anything right," snarled Guilt. "Man, I can't do anything right," repeated Paul. He listened to the little car whine and shoved the gearshift forward. He headed out Old Highway 3, turned onto JJ, and parked. Leaning against the fence he looked out over the land. Saldu appeared behind him, laying a hand on each shoulder. This caused the gnarled demons to gnash their fangs and watch from a safer distance.

Clarence's tirade had made Paul feel small, stupid, and totally incompetent—the same way he felt when he was young and his father would rage at him. *Sometimes I deserved it*, he thought, *but lots of times…well, I guess Dad had his reasons.*

"Paul," Saldu said, "go back to your childhood, and think about your dad. God can heal the past wounds so you can minister powerfully from them out of a place of strength." Suddenly Paul remembered the one summer he had played baseball.

"I worked so hard. He would never even help me practice. The answer was always the same. 'Dad would you pitch to me? Dad would you hit me some grounders?'"

"Not now son, I'm busy," said Paul, rolling his eyes. "Geeze, you missed the first six games of the season. Finally you made it; Coach started me on shortstop. I caught every grounder except one fast line drive. At bat I walked twice, got two singles and a double. When the game was over Coach went out of his way to tell you what a good game I had played and your first and only comment to me was, 'Why'd you let that grounder go by? You know they scored on that.'" Paul had raised his voice, shouting his painful memories to no one. "Uncle Emery was closer to me than you were, then that relationship ended," his voice cracked as his shoulders slumped.

His mind flashed to the terrifying times his dad came home drunk. Everyone would scatter. He still experienced those memories from the perspective of a little boy, and they were still too threatening to deal with. He forced them from his mind.

It would have made such a good location for our church. God, why don't things seem to go my way?

Saldu said, "You're not a failure in your heavenly Father's eyes. He has great plans for you if you submit to *His will*. He has plans that exceed your highest expectations. Right now you think you want self-promotion and the approval of men, but what you really long for is to do work that will last for all eternity. You want fruit that remains.[3] You want the earth to be different because you were here. Remember your favorite verse? Jeremiah 29:11-13, "*'I know the plans I have for you,' says the Lord, 'plans to prosper you and not to harm you, plans to give you hope and a future. Then you will call upon Me and come and pray to Me, and I will listen to you. You will seek Me and find Me when you seek Me with all your heart.'"*

Paul quoted the verse along with Saldu and then smiled briefly. He used to pray it all the time at seminary until he got the position as interim and busyness took over.

"Remember, Paul, His yoke is supposed to be easy and his burden light,[4] but you're creating a heavy load where it isn't needed. You're still knocking yourself out trying to get approval because you never got it from your dad. You've done it all your life. Let's get your heart healed. The Lord is big enough to fill the gaping wound that your dad left. Then you won't have to keep up a false persona of perfection and go chasing after approval from Clarence or anyone else."

God, why is it so hard for me to trust You? I want to believe Your Word. I want to do Your will. I'm messed up. What's wrong with me? I really need help. Paul felt a little better after his honest confession.

"All your life you've believed a lie. Your heavenly Father is not like your earthly father. He is trustworthy. You can just crawl up into His lap and relax. Just enjoy Him and let Him enjoy you. You don't have to earn anything. He loves you unconditionally. Remember, even the best earthly dads can't meet all their son's needs. Only the Lord can do that. Quit knocking yourself out trying to look perfect. On your own, you'll never measure up. Accept your weaknesses. Remember, His strength is perfected in weak people."[5]

I'm trying so hard, and it's wearing me out.

"You're being driven by your insecurities. Don't run ahead of God. You plant and God will harvest. It's a partnership. He wants to be with you. He wants intimacy with you. He wants to play with you. He wants to work with you and pour His blessings out on you. It grieves Him when He sees you working so hard in your own strength on your own plans because you can't accomplish anything of eternal value on your own."

I'm physically and mentally exhausted. I've got to slow down, Paul thought, shaking his head.

"Do only what the Lord has called you to do. Forget the rest. Jesus only did what He saw the Father doing."[6]

"That's right," said Paul out loud, "I don't have to do everything. I can never do everything."

Shame perched on the fence beside Paul and joined the conversation, "Remember how Clarence was your pal? Then you couldn't deliver, and he blew up. People eventually see right through you, Paul. If anyone gets too close, they'll eventually decide they don't like you. You just need to accept that in spite of all your efforts you're just not good enough. You'll never measure up." Paul's face flushed as he relived Clarence's tirade.

"Wait, Paul, whose fault was that whole fiasco, really?" whispered Blame. Then Paul thought of Sarah. *This is all her fault. I wouldn't be in this mess if it weren't for her.*

"You're entering dangerous water, Paul. Don't hold on to bitterness. Confess it to Father now," encouraged Saldu. The thought hit Paul's mind, but angry images of Sarah pushed it aside.

"Paul, don't give in to the enemy. Blessed are the peacemakers."[7] After a brief battle for control of his mind, Paul gave in to Unforgiveness and began entertaining fantasies of revenge.

This is going from bad to worse, thought Saldu. He took a step backward. Before he even saw them with his acute spiritual eyes, he could smell their ghastly stench. The additional winged creatures flocked around Paul, feeding on his wounded spirit with great delight. Tormenting spirits of Self-Hatred, Condemnation, Accusation, Faultfinding, and Impatience taunted him with flashbacks of past failures, from Clarence all the way back to his childhood. Paul was overwhelmed with feelings of inadequacies and failure. "WHY CAN'T I DO ANYTHING RIGHT?" he yelled as he kicked the fence.

"Unmet expectations lead to disappointment, unforgiveness, and then bitterness," said Saldu. "Cry out to Him to heal the lack and disappointment you experienced in others; that is where you'll find peace. Once you learn how to receive unconditional love from Him, all the grudges from the failures of others will just fall away. Then turn your energy into looking at what you can learn from past actions. Purpose to react differently to disappointment next time. You are the only one you can change, and only then with God's help."

To complete his tests Dr. Newbury asked Sarah to spread her fingers and hold her hands out. They both watched as her hands trembled.

"Can you hold them still?"

"I'm trying."

"Anything else different?"

"Well my handwriting has changed; it gets smaller as I write."

"Sarah, I'm referring you to a neurologist, Dr. Schumacher, at Mt. Peilor. She can do a full battery of neurological tests."

"Tell me what you're thinking—worst-case scenario."

"I don't want to jump to conclusions, but since you asked, worst-case scenario I think would be Parkinson's."

"What exactly is Parkinson's?"

"Parkinson's disease is caused by the death of brain cells that produce the chemical dopamine. Dopamine helps control physical movement. That could be why you can't control the movement in your hands and it's harder for you to get around."

Sarah felt numb as she drove out of the parking lot. That she could have Parkinson's was not a new thought for her. She'd thought it every day for the last three months. But hearing a doctor say it gave it more weight—it crushed in on her like a heavy rock on her chest.

Despair whispered, "You'll have to leave your house. This seals it; you'll have to move to a nursing home."

"Maybe," said Accusation, "If you'd fed George healthier food, he'd still be here to help take care of you now that your health is failing."

I've never been helpless before... thought Sarah as a tear rolled down her cheek.

"Sarah," said Malta, "your life is secure in the Lord's hands. Your days were numbered before the foundation of the world. Every day of your life is already written in His book. He will walk you through each day and will be waiting to meet you when you've lived the last page and the back cover closes on your life." She tried to cling to these thoughts and found a small measure of comfort.

She made an appointment to see Dr. Schumacher in six days and called Barbara to see if she'd go along.

≪ ≪ ≪

Sarah's phone rang that evening; the raspy voice whispered, "Get ready for another brick through the window." Click.

"Oh, Jesus, help me. I can't take this again. Please protect me." Her prayer stunned an infiltrating spirit of Fear, and Joel easily sent the black-winged beast retreating with a slap from the back of his hand.

"Keep praying. Pray for your enemy. They *hate* that," said Malta. "You have no idea how powerful those prayers are." Sarah turned on the porch light and all the inside lights. *I'm here by myself. What if they break in?* Her heart began to race.

"Sarah," said Joel, "don't let the enemy run wild with your thoughts. Once he gets a foothold with worry in your mind, he can literally control you. Second Corinthians says, *'We demolish arguments and every pretension that sets itself up against the knowledge of God, and we take captive every thought to make it obedient to Christ.'*[8] Taking your thoughts captive is an action you have to constantly repeat. It's not something you do once or something that will be done for you."

Sarah picked up the brick from the television and went to her bedroom and locked the door. She didn't want to be in the living room in case another one came hurtling through the window.

"Remember what the apostle Paul said?" asked Malta. "Fix your thoughts on what is true and honorable and right and pure and lovely and admirable. Think about things that are excellent and worthy of praise.[9] He certainly had enough to worry and stress about. His life was constantly in danger, but if he had let the devil control his thoughts with fear, we wouldn't be reading the story of his incredible ministry in the Bible today."

My life was filled with fear and it almost killed me. I've got to resist these thoughts. Painstakingly, she knelt by her bed. She set the brick on the floor and opened her Bible to Psalm 140:1-3, *"O Lord, rescue me from evil people. Protect me from those who are violent, those who plot evil in their hearts and stir up trouble all day long. Their tongues sting like a snake; the venom of a viper drips from their lips....*"[10] She prayed. *"Father, please protect me from harm. Please send angels to surround my home."* Then she prayed for the person who threw the brick. She didn't know what else to do so she just kept praying so her mind wouldn't wander.

"Sarah, you are totally safe," whispered Joel. "The eyes of the Lord run to and fro throughout the whole earth to show Himself strong on behalf of those whose hearts are loyal to Him."[11] Malta and Joel stayed with her, encouraging her that nothing could separate her from God's love—not death, nor life, nor angels, nor principalities, nor things present, nor things to come, nor powers, nor height, nor depth, nor any other created thing.[12]

Outside, six other angels appeared. One stood guard at each corner of the house. Their golden wings were spread wide, and they were armed for battle. Each one held an ornate silver shield and a flaming sword. The other two sat on the porch swing, visible to all, their heavenly glory restrained, but disguised as men wearing sweatsuits and built like professional wrestlers.

A car turned the corner, cut its headlights, and pulled slowly toward the curb. The passenger, holding a large rock on his lap and a can of spray paint said, "There's two guys on the porch. Keep driving. Go, go." They disappeared into the night and never came back.

When all the citizens of Bradbury found out that Sarah had indeed sold the land, a rage spread through the town. At first Clarence got people riled toward Paul, but Paul and his dark friend Manipulation were able to help them vent toward the real guilty party—Sarah. This animosity was in full swing. It would eventually run its course and end up as a stronghold of Anger and Depression hovering over the town.

The check for $50,000 arrived by registered mail. Sarah sat on her couch staring in disbelief. *Of course I'll send $5,000 to my church. She bit her lip. Nursing homes are really expensive, Lord what do You want me to do with the rest?*

The $5,000 check that Barbara dropped in the offering for Sarah was enough to temporarily lift Pastor Paul's mood. *Finally, something good came from the sale of her ground.* He shook his head. *If Missouri ever has a hurricane I'm going to suggest they name it Sarah.*

Chapter 20

Humility Prayer

*"God, I am far too often influenced by what others
think of me. I am always pretending to be either
richer or smarter or nicer than I really am. Please
prevent me from trying to attract attention. Don't let
me gloat over praise on one hand or be discouraged
by criticism on the other. Nor let me waste time
weaving imaginary situations in which the most
heroic, charming, witty person present is myself.
Show me how to be humble of heart, like you."*

Alpha Omega[1]

Six months came and went in Bradbury. Winter was pushed back by
the invading spring. The trees were leafing out and daffodil bulbs began
poking through the ground in response to the sun's rays. As good weather
returned, garage doors went up and lawn equipment spilled out onto drive-
ways. Neighbors chatted, renewing their friendships after the long winter.

The church had voted to call Pastor Paul, much to his relief. He'd immediately unveiled his grand and glorious five-year plan. A visitation program
on Thursday nights was in the works.

Kathy was still enjoying full-time motherhood with Jordan and had
made some good friends. She had also taken over as the adult Sunday school
director. But she was concerned about Paul and their lack of unity. She

prayed in earnest for him. She knew in her spirit that things weren't going well. She was especially uneasy about his five-year plan. Her concerned questions to Paul brought frustratingly vague and frequently snippy answers. When she tried to share what she was learning from the book on humility, he would listen somewhat patronizingly, but she never saw any attempts at change. Even with encouragement from Valoe, she felt resentment creeping in, especially when Paul consistently worked 70-hour weeks.

The jail was on the way to completion. The residents of Bradbury had reached a resentful resignation over its presence. Twenty men had even taken construction jobs and were getting paid a good wage. There was talk about more good-paying jobs once the jail opened, which was scheduled for two months if it wasn't a wet spring.

Clarence was still fuming over the jail, but everyone was tired of hearing about it—it was fast becoming a reality. So the proposed 1½-cent sales tax increase to rebuild the bridge over the Platte River became the new cause to pour all his energy into.

Wilma, Bernice, and Carol were still enmeshed in their gossip hotline. Nothing Ardare or the other angels did could permanently penetrate their hearts. They'd feel conviction, but the ringing of the telephone made it disappear. Ardare and his friends cried many tears from the Father over these ladies.

Barbara was enjoying her new home and had it decorated with the antiques she had collected over the years. She had big plans for the yard. She'd never had the time or enough land to have a garden or grow flowers. Her dog-eared seed catalogs were spread over the dining room table. She and Sarah were closer than ever, and she continued to encourage Sarah in the things of the Lord. She remained God's merciful answer to Sarah's desperate prayer.

Sarah had been given a slow death sentence. Doctor Schumacher had diagnosed her with Parkinson's. Even though she was taking several medicines, she was very aware of her decreasing mobility and ever-increasing tremors. Sarah had stayed inside for months, but not because of Agoraphobia. That spirit had been defeated. She just couldn't risk falling on the ice. Barbara had faithfully grocery shopped for her.

Every day that Sarah had been trapped by the weather, she, Joel, and Malta sat on the couch together. A cup of hot chocolate, coffee, or tea sat on the side table, depending on her mood. She closed her eyes and mentally "walked" the blocks, picturing every house and praying for its inhabitants. She surprised herself; she was able to imagine every house on all four blocks.

Sarah's times of intimacy with the Lord had increased her desire to surrender totally to Him and had allowed Him to grow her into a powerful intercessor—His life's plan for her. At home she listened to religious television programs and radio shows. She read her Bible and prayed for missionaries, the visitation program, the church, Pastor Paul, her niece in Tallahassee, and the requests from a magazine called *The Voice of the Martyrs*,[2] which told of Christians being persecuted and executed all around the world.

I knew that people got martyred in the Bible, but I never dreamed that thousands of Christians are martyred now.

Sometimes the Lord gave her a glimpse of an emaciated man or woman being held in a cramped, dank cell. When this happened, she would pace or curl up on the couch under a blanket and sob and pray until the burden lifted off of her.

She also dedicated a special prayer time for "The 10-40 Window."

Sarah fluctuated between grief and incredulity when she discovered that it contains over 70 percent of the world's people, but only 8 percent of all missionaries. Less than half of 1 percent of church budgets reach the window. Ninety-seven percent of the poorest of the poor dwell there, trying to survive on less than $1.40 per day. Of the world's 50 least evangelized countries, 37 are within the window.[3]

Each day she cried out to God for these requests, sometimes multiple times. Her life was becoming a living prayer.

"She thinks she's a candle shining a little light into the darkness," said Joel. "She's really an inferno for God's Kingdom, consuming the enemy's plans and burning up his territory."

Sarah put on her jacket and stepped on her front porch, eager to start her prayer walks again. *I feel like a bird released from a cage*, she said, flapping her arms for emphasis and chuckling. Malta and Joel spread their huge, gossamer wings and flapped along with her, joining in her laughter.

As they began their walk, Malta reminded her that she used to be the woman who almost starved to death because she was so terrified to leave her house.

When she thought back on her life after George's death and before she accepted the Lord, she couldn't identify with that Sarah at all. *I can't believe I even contemplated taking my own life. I'm a totally different person.*

"You are a totally different person, Sarah; you have been delivered from the powers of darkness and translated into the Kingdom of God's son.[4] You are new in Christ."[5]

"Thank You for making me Your daughter and delivering me from that awful spirit. Thank You, Jesus; it's so nice to be outside again," she said out loud.

She took a deep breath of the brisk, outside air. It was still nippy, but she didn't care. The snow was off the sidewalks so she could safely shuffle along. The medicine didn't seem to be working, at least not to her satisfaction. The doctor said she was doing fine, but she felt the disease gaining on her. As she rounded the corner, she looked up in the sky and saw a commercial airliner heading west. "I wonder how many people are on that plane?" asked Malta.

"Two hundred and thirty seven including crew, and there are seven dogs down below," said Joel with a grin.

"I wasn't asking for your benefit." Malta rolled his eyes. "So, SARAH, how many people do you think are on that plane?"

I wonder how many people are on that plane, thought Sarah. *I wonder how many are saved?* She stood until the plane was out of sight and prayed for the passengers' salvation, that they would all fulfill their destinies and that the enemy's plans against them would be defeated.

After she finished her prayer walk she had a snack. Then she gathered her Bible and got in the car. She followed Old Highway 3 out of town and pulled across the street to look at the jail. Because of the cold weather, it had been several months since she'd been there. Most of what she was used to seeing had been bulldozed. The old wood fence surrounding the property was gone. She remembered how she and George had labored to keep it repaired. *And then there was the time we had to paint it. Oh, my goodness!* She smiled at the memory now, but it wasn't amusing then.

The jail's huge. I guess it has to be to hold over 100 inmates, she thought. The four exterior walls were up and the roof was on. She felt a deep satisfaction for the part she had played, her small link in God's plan for "such a time as this."

She left the jail and parked at the cemetery. She sat by Reverend Templeton's grave. As she touched the head stone she repeated a quote she'd read in her devotional guide last week. It had stuck with her. "He is no fool who gives up what he cannot keep to gain what he cannot lose."[6] *Reverend Templeton, I feel like we are kindred spirits, drawn together by God's plan for a plot of land. I look forward to meeting you when I get to Heaven. By the way, I know you know this since you're with Jesus, but the plan for our land is progressing well.*

When she got home she took four pieces of typing paper and in her best penmanship she painstakingly printed copies of the phrase from her devotional guide. The tremor in her right hand had worsened, interfering with her writing and crocheting. *This looks like a first grader did it,* she thought, somewhat disgusted by her best efforts. Nevertheless, she taped one on the wall at the foot of her bed, one on the bathroom mirror, and one in the living room. *Now for the one location that will really get the most traffic—my refrigerator door.* In order to make room she had to rearrange all the pictures and newsletters from missionaries whom she prayed for daily. She called it her "devotional refrigerator." She never got something to eat without praying for someone who was ministering in another country.

"Sarah, you need to add another daily prayer ritual," prompted Joel as she read the obituary page from Mt. Pielor's Sunday paper. As she scanned the pictures, she wondered what kind of lives these people had lived and if they had known the Lord. She was saddened by the finality of the situation. No more chances; they had made their choice—destiny was sealed. *I hope they chose wisely,* she thought. *Life is so fleeting. I wonder how many people last week thought they'd end up in the obituaries this week?*

"Pray each day," said Joel, "for the people all around the world, who are going to die in the next 24 hours. Pray that the Lord would give them repeated chances to be saved and that the enemy's deception that clouds their judgment would be supernaturally removed. No one who even catches a fleeting glimpse of our Lord's great love would ever reject Him."

"The Lord is not willing that any should perish. Even if someone has spent his whole life cursing God, He still longs to snatch them from the enemy's kingdom on their last day on earth.

Joel added, "When Christians get to Heaven, they receive a full understanding of the incredible price that Jesus paid to obtain their salvation. They will worship around the throne day and night crying out in thankfulness, "Holy, Holy, Holy." However, those whose hearts are overflowing with the most gratitude are those who were snatched from Hell on their last day on earth, possibly at the moment of their last breath. Those are the very best worshipers."

"My friend, C.T. Studd was a missionary to China, India, and Africa during the early 1900s," said Malta. "While he was on earth he said, 'Some want to live within the sound of church or chapel bell; I want to run a rescue shop within a yard of Hell.'[7] The Lord wants you, through intercession, to work at that rescue shop."

With a tear in his eye, Joel said, "There are about 100,000 a day who die without our Lord, and He has already paid the full price for their salvation."

Sarah prayed this for a few days in a row and then it slipped her mind. Later in the week she turned on the evening news and was horrified at what she heard and saw. A major earthquake had hit Afghanistan.

"More than 5,000 people may have died in a powerful 7.6-magnitude quake," said the announcer. "Several villages have been completely wiped out. As you can see here, people rushed to dig with bare hands, trying to rescue children trapped beneath the rubble of their school."

Sarah quickly turned the television off and began sobbing and praying. "Oh Jesus, please, please forgive me for not taking Your command seriously to pray each day for the people who are going to die.

"Lord, I know there are many people still alive and trapped beneath the rubble and that many others will die in the next few days. Lord, please have mercy. You are the God who is not willing that *any* should perish. Would you make Yourself real to every person crying out in prayer, even if they aren't crying out to You? Lord, You are the true God; would You answer them?

"Lord tear down deceptions and strongholds that would keep them from accepting You. Would You let them see Your eyes of love looking into theirs, longing for them to turn to You, and longing to take them to Your Kingdom of life? Lord, would You snatch them from the enemy's kingdom even during the last seconds of their lives?

"Send Your angels to minister to every injured person. Please supernaturally guide the rescue workers. Let them get to the people who are still alive. I pray for the people who have lost loved ones and are homeless and traumatized. Lord, in some tangible way will You make Yourself real to them?"

Sarah continued to pray most of the rest of the evening and fell asleep with a plea on her lips for salvations in Afghanistan.

Sarah hadn't been to church all winter, partly because of the weather, but also because Fear of Man had convinced her she would not be well received. Now that the weather was nicer, Barbara encouraged her by saying that most people at Victory Church were over it by now, but Sarah was unconvinced.

Thursday came and Sarah thought about attending the new visitation program, but in the end decided it might not be wise. *I'll just slow down whatever group I go with*, was her rationalization. But she still struggled with fear of rejection. The memories of the first prayer meeting and the town meeting at the Elk's lodge were still an open wound. If she imagined them for any length of time, she felt a knot in the pit of her stomach. She decided that her contribution would be to pray for one hour every Thursday night, starting at 7, for those who were visiting. *Lord, I commit to do this as long as the program continues, provided You give me the grace I'll need.*

Pastor Paul, wanting good attendance the first night of the visitation program, and being nobody's fool, scheduled a potluck dinner to kick it off.

Forty-three people attended. Wilma brought her homemade peach cobbler (although she went home immediately after the potluck). *It doesn't get any better than this*, thought Paul, scooping seconds out of the baking dish.

Each Thursday evening, Sarah was on her knees praying, and each week someone was saved. People started visiting and joining the church. Sarah also spent another hour each week praying for Pastor Paul and the church. God was honoring her prayers. They thwarted some of the traps the enemy laid for Paul.

Pastor Paul, on the other hand, had let his prayer time slide to mostly the Wednesday night meeting. The rest of the time he was just too busy. He had great intentions, but when he went to bed at night and reviewed his day, he just couldn't fit it in. He had to prepare a killer sermon each week. *I don't want the church to regret their decision to call me as pastor.* He'd also started doing counseling—marital and individual. At least three evenings a week were tied up at the church. He was trying to get a cross-denominational prayer breakfast going for all the pastors in town. There were occasional hospital visits, and he at least tried to squeeze Kathy and Jordan in somewhere for some quality family time.

Deception perched on his shoulder and dug in his gnarled claws. His red eyes flashed as he whispered, "The Lord is really blessing your efforts. You've added four new families recently. If this keeps up you'll be ahead of schedule for your building campaign." Paul was sure he could feel the smile of God over his life because so much was getting done. Productivity always came with a sense of satisfaction, along with an intense, but short lived, boost in self-esteem. Then he was back on the treadmill chasing his next affirmation fix.

Saldu had repeatedly told him that his priorities were backward. He told Paul about the church at Ephesus,[8] whom the Lord commended for not growing weary in their many good works, but then rebuked for leaving their first love.

"Paul, all the busyness in the world means nothing if you've lost your passion and intimacy with the Lord. Start slashing items off your calendar to clear time to spend with Him, for prayer and Bible study. The Lord longs to hear from you. Prayer isn't a last resort in a desperate situation; it's a preemptive strike against the enemy."

CHAPTER 21

"We judge ourselves unworthy servants, and that judgment becomes a self-fulfilling prophecy. We deem ourselves too inconsiderable to be used even by a God capable of miracles with no more than mud and spit. And thus our false humility shackles an otherwise omnipotent God."

John Eagan[1]

"Give God what you are and what you're not. Then He'll get the glory when He changes you."

Joyce Meyer[2]

Joel smiled at Malta as Sarah picked up her daily devotional guide. He reached for his sword; the tip was on fire. Malta smiled, "Father's increasing her prayer anointing today." Sarah prayed that the Lord would bless her time in the Word, as she always did, and opened the pamphlet. The first verse was Colossians 4:2. She read out loud, *"Devote yourselves to prayer, being watchful and thankful."* Lord, help me to devote more of my time to prayer. I'm so limited in what I can do, but I can pray. Show me how to devote myself to prayer and give me a special grace to pray without ceasing.

Next was Ephesians 6:18, *"And pray in the Spirit on all occasions with all kinds of prayers and requests...."*

"Sarah," said Malta, "First Corinthians 14:15 says that if you pray in tongues, your spirit prays, but your mind, or understanding, is unfruitful. When you pray in the Spirit, the Spirit prays through you. You only give breath and enunciation with your mouth. Since this type of praying by-passes your mind, you can pray in the Spirit even when you're reading a book, watching television, or reliving a nice memory. Get in the habit of praying in the Spirit all the time. Even if it doesn't feel anointed, it's power-ful because the Holy Spirit of God is praying His prayers, His perfect will, through you."

"If you're not eating or talking, you can be praying in the Spirit," added Joel, touching the tip of his sword to her lips. "Increase in your ability to pray in the Spirit. Increase now."

Sarah felt nothing special or supernatural, but had a dogged determina-tion that she would get in the habit of praying in the Spirit as much as she could—starting now. To test this, she began praying in the Spirit silently and picked up her devotional guide and read the rest of the page with her mind. *It really works. Whenever I'm not talking or eating, I can pray in the Spirit, no matter what I'm doing.* She decided that to develop this habit she'd always pray in tongues during certain activities; once these became a habit, she'd add more.

Lord, help me to remember to pray in tongues when I'm watching television, reading, driving, or taking a shower. Help me to remember other times, too. Ev-ery time she went through a doorway, she cultivated the habit of checking herself to see if she was praying.

After having a snack, she turned on the news and prayed in the Spirit. *My goal is to pray in tongues all the way through this program.* She settled back and listened to the anchorman talking about a foiled purse snatching in Mt. Peilor.

The first 15 minutes the Spirit prayed through Sarah for the Christians among the Ibo people in Gambia, an Islam country in Africa. Sarah knew nothing of Gambia, let alone the Ibo people, but the Spirit knew them inti-mately, their every need, and her prayers for them were answered.

The next ten minutes Sarah prayed for the crew of a fishing vessel that had been overturned three miles off Japan's coast. When they were plucked from the water by a passing ship, the Spirit prayed on for a young Vietnam-ese believer. His parents had disowned him because he refused to participate in the Tam Giao, a mixture of ancestor and spirit worship. Sarah would not see him until Heaven, but her five minutes of prayer helped sustain him during this difficult time of family rejection for the sake of the Gospel.

The local news was over. The main thing on Sarah's mind now was tomorrow's weather. She had no idea she had ministered all around the world, touching needy lives from the comfort of her couch.

"Let's go for a ride and see what's going on over at your jail," suggested Joel. "And don't forget to pray in tongues while you drive."

She prayed in tongues all the way there. She parked across from the jail and prayed for the construction workers' safety and the jail's timely opening. She especially prayed for the chaplain, whoever he would be. She prayed for the future inmates and for their families who would be affected by their incarceration.

"I can start praying now, laying the groundwork for the inmates who will hear the Gospel." Then she thought of Reverend Templeton and prayed for his current-day descendants, whoever and wherever they were, that they would all know the Lord and be as obedient as he had been.

Sarah had embraced the phrase on her refrigerator, "He is no fool who gives up what he cannot keep to gain what he cannot lose." She would do all she could for God's Kingdom with the time she had left on earth. The things that used to hold her attention just didn't seem as important anymore. She frequently thought of her favorite punch line: *"You brought pavement?"* It made her chuckle, just as often it made her cry.

≪≪≪

The spirit of Fear of Man was still keeping her from going back to church, and no one from the church had called to say they missed her. But fueled by her prayers, the church was growing weekly. Pastor Paul was almost beside himself. He felt a deep satisfaction that for once he was finally doing something right.

"Way to go, pastor! You're the man with the plan," snickered Deception, digging his claws in deeper.

When Buchanan County Correctional Facilities called, offering him the job of part-time chaplain, his demon acquaintances flew into a frenzy. "You hardly have the time to keep up with all the good things going on at your church. Your church and your family would suffer if you said "Yes." God couldn't be in favor of that," said Respectability.

In addition to that bit of rational thought, deep inside, Paul was still irked that BCCF had built on the church's land and that he had been humiliated through the whole process. "Of course Sarah was to blame for that," added Bitterness.

He didn't even pray about taking the position, but he felt a sense of smug satisfaction as, "No, not at all interested," rolled off his tongue before he slammed down the phone.

Where was Sarah? He hadn't seen her at church for the longest time. *Maybe she switched to the Baptist church. Oh well, wherever she was, she was no doubt causing problems for some poor pastor. Good riddance to bad rubbish.* He flinched, feeling conviction from Saldu. *"Sorry God, I didn't mean to be that harsh."* But still, he was glad for wherever she'd disappeared to.

The jobs at the jail were filled with folks from Bradbury, and some men even drove in from Mt. Pielor. As the time for the jail to open neared, Sarah went to investigate. When she walked through the front door and looked around, she was overwhelmed with a sense of destiny. *"I can't believe it's here Lord, on my land, according to Your eternal plan. I almost feel like I'm on holy ground."*

"I'm here to see the chaplain," she explained to an employee wheeling a cart stacked with boxes.

"There is no chaplain yet." Sarah's heart sank. She had planned on following the chaplain's guidance as to how to get involved. "Is it OK if I look around?"

"Fine with me. Just be careful. People are moving furniture and stuff everywhere."

By "look around," Sarah of course meant prayer walk. She shuffled up and down every corridor, prayed over every cell, every employee's office and locker, even the kitchen, laundry facilities, loading dock, and mechanical room. She backtracked, wanting to spend more time praying in the chaplain's office. It was a small room painted institutional beige like everything else. The mini blinds were hung and there were several bookshelves, but that was all. As she raised her hands to pray, flanked by Joel and Malta, she heard the Lord's voice, "I am the God of the second chance. My unfailing love never ends! By My mercies you have been kept from complete destruction. My faithfulness is great, and My mercies begin afresh each day."[3]

"When He was on earth," said Joel, "Our Lord spent His time with tax collectors, prostitutes, and the demonized, those who were truly down and out. He left the 99 and went out after the one who was lost."[4]

Sarah gasped, "Lord, if You were on earth today, You'd be at this jail ministering."

Again Sarah heard the Lord speak to her, "My precious daughter, I am so pleased with you. You took an unpopular stand, and you felt like you were standing alone, but I was with you every second. I never left you. I will never leave you. I am pleased that you will be My ambassador to these broken men who will soon be arriving."

Ten days later, on a gray, drizzly day, the jail opened quietly. There was no ribbon-cutting ceremony, and Clarence refused to run an article about it in the *Gazette*.

Sarah was especially excited that the jail was opened. At the same time, she knew it meant that if she was going to be obedient she was going to have to move way out of her comfort zone.

I am absolutely the least qualified person on the face of the planet to minister to these inmates.

"No Sarah," said Joel, "you are the most qualified because you are the only one who is willing. Your availability to God's use alone qualifies you above everyone else. Besides, I promise you, Jesus never said to anyone, 'Well done my good and qualified servant.'"[5]

"Don't look at your perceived lack of abilities," said Malta. "Look to God's abilities. He has always used weak people.[6] That's the only kind there are."

"When you enter Heaven and talk to King David, the adulterous murderer,[7] or the apostle Paul, the former persecutor of the church,[8] or the miracle-working deliverer of God's people, Moses, who ran and hid for decades in the desert[9] you will find they all say the same thing. 'I still find it hard to believe that God worked through me with all my flaws and sins. His mercy was there for me every step of the way, and I was in need of it every step of the way. He forgave my horrendous sins, and His power is responsible for anything I accomplished for His Kingdom. Even my ability to say yes to Him was His grace in my life.'"

"Sarah, if you say yes to God, you have no limitations because He has no limitations. If what you're grasping for and planning on doing for the Kingdom isn't way beyond your ability, you're probably not doing the right thing."

CHAPTER 22

*"I believe that if God finds a person more useless
than me, He will do even greater things through her
because this work is His."*

Mother Teresa[1]

*"Let us touch the dying, the poor, the lonely and
the unwanted according to the graces we have
received and let us not be ashamed or slow to do
the humble work."*

Mother Teresa[2]

Sarah had an especially hard time getting out of bed that morning. She couldn't get her legs to cooperate with her body. After much struggling and prayer, she finally sat up on the edge of the bed. She knew what the doctor had said, *But canes are for old people.* She grudgingly reached in the closet and grabbed the silver quad-cane with the four little legs at the bottom. As she stared at it, she thought that it seemed like just yesterday that she and George had been married. *Where has my life gone? Why did I waste 71 years? How could I have been so foolish? Lord, help me to use the short time I have left to bring glory to Your name.* She could almost feel the pages turning on the book of her life.

Sarah managed to drive to the jail. She had to admit the cane made her steadier on her feet, but she felt like it couldn't have been more conspicuous if it was plugged into an orange extension cord and was flashing a fuchsia neon light. In her free hand she carried a clear plastic container packed with homemade cookies. She thought they might open some doors. She showed her driver's license and signed in at the checkpoint and turned left down the main corridor of cells. Since she knew the layout, she shuffled on. Joel and Malta accompanied her. She had no idea what to do or say. *Help me Lord. Give me Your heart for these inmates. I need Your compassion, and I certainly need boldness. Lord, release Your mighty angels to touch these prisoners so the Sauls can become Pauls.*

She felt her rapidly beating heart. Several of the inmates looked up at her. A guard stopped her rather abruptly. "Your business here, ma'am?"

"I'm just here to visit."

"Which inmate?"

"Umm, well, all of them."

"What's your purpose here ma'am?"

"Well, I, I," she felt like she had at the first Wednesday prayer time. Her face flushed but she managed to straighten up and say, "I think God told me to visit and pray for these inmates."

"You have to visit a specific one. I can't just let you wander up and down the halls. Unless you have someone specific, I'm afraid you'll have to leave."

Anxiety washed over her. *"I can't believe I've come this far to get thrown out of a jail built on my own land. Jesus, help me. I need wisdom, and I need it quickly."* She stared up at the guard not knowing what to do. Behind her an inmate from a close cell called out, "Did you bring me cookies...Mom?"

"Why yes, son, I did. And they're your favorite," she said as she turned around. Then she burst out laughing. The inmate was an African American. A voice from the next cell called out, "Mom, did you bring me cookies, too?" In just a second most of the inmates were calling out to "Mom" for their share of the cookies. Sarah laughed and turned back to the guard, who knew when to give up.

"I must have been a terrible mother," she said. "All my sons are in jail."

She slowly peeled the lid off the clear plastic container and walked to each cell offering her chocolate chip cookies. "Thanks, Mom," they said. "Bless you, son," she replied.

There were only 15 inmates now, but it would fill up as jails in different counties sent their overflow to Bradbury. There were two cookies left, which Sarah offered to the guard. "Thanks, Mom," he said, rolling his eyes.

"I'll be back tomorrow with more cookies," she said. Several inmates waved or shouted, "Bye, Mom."

She made it back to her car and sat down. The armpits of her blouse were saturated and her heart was still pounding. *Well, contact is established. What do I do next, Lord? Yes, that's a good idea.* She pulled up in front of Wilhelm's grocery store, went inside and asked the stock boy to please bring all the Slice 'N Bake cookies to the register for her. Cookies from scratch were very time consuming for her now. If any of the inmates noticed the difference, they never complained.

She, her cane, her cookies, and Joel and Malta were at the jail every day for the next six days. Most of the inmates were quickly conditioned like Pavlov's dogs. "Hi, Mom. Got cookies?" they said when they caught a glimpse of her. Some were only interested in the treats of course, but others felt comfortable chatting with and even confiding in Sarah. As she felt more acceptance, she also became bolder, asking certain inmates if she could pray for them, telling them the story of her land and how the jail got here, and presenting the plan of salvation, which she read from Gospel tracts she carried in her pockets.

The Lord highlighted a specific inmate named Will. His arms were covered with tattoos of dragons and other angry looking beings. He wasn't very friendly to Sarah, or anybody, for that matter. When Sarah visited with his cellmate, Stan, Will turned away. When she spoke of religious things, he would sneer or make derisive, profane comments. The Lord told Sarah to pray for him, which she did daily. One evening, she was fed up with his abrasive comments to her. She began praying *about* Will, not *for* him. "*Lord, I don't think I can tolerate him anymore. He's rude and crass. He needs to learn some manners.*"

"Time for a lesson in compassion," said Joel. Malta nodded.

The Lord showed Sarah an image of William when he was about 3-years-old; he dropped a glass of milk in the kitchen. The glass shattered. His father turned, took several quick steps, swooped down on his son, and beat him. It was horrible for Sarah to watch, and she cried out, "Stop, make him stop."

When the image was finally over, Joel began, "The Lord looks on all His children with great love and compassion, even those who curse His name. William is lost, but he's no more lost than you were when He had compassion and saved you. You were a criminal, found guilty in the Heavenly courts. Sarah, you were dead in your trespasses and sins[3] and a child of disobedience. You were God's enemy. Don't ever forget; you did not choose Him. In His great mercy, He chose you. Each of William's sins can be completely forgiven by the blood of Jesus, just as your sins also needed to be covered—and still do. To the Lord, William's status is no different than yours was a year ago. God just saved you first."

"Remember, the vilest sinner is just one revelation from the Kingdom of God," added Malta. "The Lord is grieved that in spite of His willingness to forgive, William still identifies himself by the worst moment of his life."

Joel drew his sword. It ignited as he pulled it out of the engraved golden sheath. Without hesitation he plunged it into Sarah's chest, piercing her spirit. She wept, grieving over the ugliness of her judgmental attitude. In her spirit she saw God's great love for William and for all the inmates who had been victimized and, in their brokenness, had victimized others.

"Don't ever forget, Sarah, that pride comes before a fall.[4] The Lord requires humility from His followers. Pride has crept in over the works you've done for Father. You can never repay the gift He's given you nor can you impress Him with your attempts at holiness. Repent of your attitude and ask the Lord to cleanse you. The Lord says if *you* humble yourself, He will exalt you. If *He* has to humble you, He doesn't promise you anything."

When that truth pierced Sarah's heart, she couldn't repent fast enough. Through her tears she prayed, *God, I repent for the pride I feel for the things I've done. Instead I offer them to You as a sacrifice of praise, not trying to impress You or use them as leverage. I'm sorry I judge people so quickly. Help me to see all people as You see them.* Joel replaced the dull, drab mantle of humility that pride had caused her to shed. Malta played a melody on his lyre; the music washed over her like waves of the Father's love. She felt it go through her again and again—the Lord's great love for the lost—the Lord's great love for her.

From then on, she prayed daily that the Lord would help *her* to humble herself. *It doesn't take a rocket scientist to see which of those two choices is best.*

CHAPTER 23

"Our love to God will be found to be a delusion,
except as its truth is proved in standing the test of daily
life with our fellow-men. It is even so with humility. It
is easy to think we humble ourselves before God. Yet,
humility toward men will be the only sufficient proof
that our humility before God is real."

Andrew Murray[1]

"No peas," said Jordan.

"Yes peas," replied Paul.

"NO PEAS!"

"YES PEAS!" said Paul, raising his voice to match Jordan's increased volume.

"Honey," said Kathy, touching Paul on the hand. Then she turned to Jordan. "Jordan, eat your peas, like the good boy you are. Peas pleeeease," she said, exaggerating her enunciation.

"Peas please, peas please, peas please," he repeated giggling. Then he made a face, took two big bites, and declared, "Done."

"Yes, you are. And I thank you." Let me wipe off your hands and you may get down and play."

"Honey, have I told you you're amazing?" said Paul, putting his arms around her.

"Yes, but I like to hear it frequently. You can't say that too much to a woman!"

"OK, you're amazing, you're amazing, you're amazing," he said kissing her between compliments.

"Thank you."

As Kathy was reveling in his kind words, the topic changed to church, which it frequently and predictably did. Fueled by Sarah's prayers and the prayers of other members, the church's growth continued. There were visitors at almost every service. The Wednesday evening prayer meetings were well attended, as were the Thursday visitations. And of course, every pastor's dream, the offering was up.

"Kathy, I was talking to Mike today, and we're thinking that with the growth that we're seeing, maybe we should jump ahead with the building campaign. If the growth we're experiencing now keeps up, we're going to have to go to two Sunday services. Wouldn't that be great? We're almost the biggest church in town, numerically. I think the Catholic Church is still ahead of us by about 30."

Kathy didn't say anything, but a sick feeling rose in her gut. Paul always seemed so proud of what was going on at the church, but in a bad way, like he was solely responsible. It seemed like he was manifesting all the signs of pride that she had been reading about.

"Honey, why don't you take a week off and we could get away? You've been working six, sometimes seven days a week, and you never get home before 7:00."

"I can't take time off—things are really moving."

"But I really need some time with you." She put her arms around his shoulders and stared into his eyes. "I feel so disconnected. We used to be partners back in seminary when we'd talk about what ministry would be like. You used to ask my opinions and you valued my prayers. Maybe we can just go away for a weekend. Mary could watch Jordan, and we could just spend some time alone."

Paul pulled away from her and stated incredulously, "A weekend? I can't be gone on a *Sunday*. I need to be here to preach. What are you thinking?"

She was thinking that he was so insecure that he didn't want anyone in "his" pulpit for fear they would preach a better sermon, but she refrained from saying it. "Sorry," she mumbled and turned away to hide her tears. She'd initially been attracted to Paul for his ambition; now that trait had come back to bite her.

"We used to pray together, but now you've pushed me to the outside. Now you're making all these ministry decisions and all you want me to do is blindly follow you," she finished the rest of the sentence in her mind, *even when I feel you're wrong.*

He rolled his eyes and went to his office. *Things are going so well at the church. Why are they so hard at home?* He picked up a piece of paper off his desk and perused it. He hadn't told anyone yet, but he'd called the radio station at Mt. Peilor to get their rates. *Airtime is really reasonable. Maybe in a few months we can start broadcasting Sunday's message.*

"Paul," suggested Saldu, "It's better to be a well-done, good, and faithful servant than a half-baked famous preacher."[2]

In her bed that night Kathy prayed, through silent tears, as she had for the past several months. *Lord, please, I need a husband, and Jordan needs a dad. Don't let our marriage become a casualty of his ministry. Help him to find a balance. We used to be a team. He'd confide in me, and he valued my prayers. He respected my input. Now it's like a big door has slammed shut in my face. He won't even let me inside his thoughts, much less his heart.* Valoe stood watching over her, echoing her prayers, as he did every night.

She fell asleep and dreamed that she was on the roof hammering away at hundreds of loose shingles. It seemed like for every one she would hammer down, two would pop loose. She was exhausted, sweaty, and frustrated. In spite of the fact that she was actually losing ground, her determination kept her at it.

Valoe appeared in her dream. "Kathy," he said reaching for the hammer from her aching hands, "you need a rest."

"No, I can't stop," she said refusing to let go. "I have to get these shingles fixed before it rains. I have to save our house. It's all up to me."

"No Kathy, it's not all up to you," said Valoe, taking the hammer and holding her blistered hands in his. "You're in danger of falling into the same trap that Paul has. 'It's all up to me. Work, work, work.' I know that Paul's preoccupied, but don't look to yourself; look to the Lord. By yourself you can never be enough or do enough. You can't change Paul; you can only pray for him. You need to push into the Lord even more. He'll help you find that place of rest in the middle of the storm. He's the only one who can. The storm might not abate, but He wants to give you grace to dance in the rain. You must learn to cast your burdens on Him. He wants to comfort you and has sent a Scripture for you, Psalm 127:1-2."

Kathy woke up and wondered, *That was bizarre. Roof repair? An angel? Was that from the Lord? It sounds like a pizza dream. I guess there's one way to tell.* She grabbed her Bible and book light off the nightstand and read, *"Unless the Lord builds the house, those who build it labor in vain. Unless the Lord guards the city, the guard keeps watch in vain. It is in vain that you rise up early and go late to rest, eating the bread of anxious toil; for He gives sleep to His beloved."*

For the first time in a very long time, Kathy felt the peace of God rest on her. *Lord, it was You. You know my situation and see my frustrations. Thank You for listening to my prayers. Lord, I can't do anything in my own efforts. Help me to remember that when I get frustrated, especially with Paul. God, will You build my house?* Kathy fell asleep meditating on those verses. She would faithfully cling to them each day and they would bring a measure of peace to the disappointment and loneliness she felt.

CHAPTER 24

"Not the fastest horse can catch a word spoken in anger."

Chinese Proverb

"He who angers you conquers you."

Elizabeth Kenny[1]

Sarah was succeeding in her goal of praying in tongues whenever she drove. She usually visited the jail at least three times a week, sometimes more, depending on her mobility each day. As she drove she prayed out loud in tongues so she would know if she got distracted and stopped.

"Sarah," said Joel, "Today I'll teach you how to become even more of a threat to Satan's kingdom through intercession—"

"That's right," interrupted Malta, who was too excited to wait. "Begin by praying in tongues silently and then pray with your mind at the same time. You're praying with your spirit and your mind. You're praying two prayers at once."

"You might be praying about the same thing or each prayer might be totally different, but twice as much prayer is ascending before the Lord's throne as a fragrant offering to Him."

Sarah switched to praying silently in tongues and in her mind she prayed for the other drivers to get saved. Then she prayed for each inmate by name. *Wow, I can do it,* she thought, as she pulled into the parking lot. *I just doubled the amount of prayers I prayed in the same amount of time. This is even better than praying in tongues when I read or watch television. This is praying in tongues while I pray! God, You are so awesome. I'll call this type of prayer "double dipping" because it's getting twice as much accomplished!* Oh, and Lord, I need Your grace to develop this new habit.

The jail was about half full now, with almost 50 inmates. Although they all had varying levels of responsiveness to her, they all knew two things about "Momma Sarah." She always brought cookies, and she sure loved to talk about Jesus.

She had continued praying for Will with little visible response. But she was not about to give up. The glimpse of his father beating the helpless little boy always brought compassion. One day when he cursed at her, all she could see was the little, terrified boy behind the hulking, angry tattooed man. "Bless you, Will," she responded as she moved on.

≺≺≺

The next time Sarah came to the jail, she had traded her cane in for a walker. She'd bought the deluxe model that had a basket on the front to hold the cookies and pouches on the side to hold her Bible and multiple tracts. As she entered, one of the guards said, "Sarah, the director wants to see you in his office." That made her heart beat a little faster, and she prayed a little harder as she shuffled down the long beige hall. She had met the director once before, and he seemed like a nice young man. Everyone seemed young to her these days.

The director, Richard Walker, welcomed her into his office and even helped hold her chair as she sat down. After some chatty small talk he said, "As you know, we have no chaplain. We just haven't been able to fill the position. I know you've been visiting here regularly, and I wanted to know if you are interested in the position; part-time is all that's budgeted for now."

"Me, a chaplain?" Sarah tossed back her head and laughed. "I'm very flattered, but I don't think I'm official chaplain material. Maybe I could be an honorary chaplain until the position gets filled. Now I'm just having a good time getting to know these inmates. But I'll pray that the Lord would bring the right person to fill the position."

At home she followed through on her promise. As she prayed, the Lord showed her a picture of the man he wanted as part-time chaplain. He was limping toward the jail entrance, and from Sarah's vantage point, all she could see was his back. He knelt at the door and cried out to God. She knew he was repenting, and it had something to do with the jail. She couldn't make out his words, but she could feel the heaviness of his great burden. Then God's mercy spilled down on him like refreshing rain. As he stood to his feet, his new posture was confident, assured. He walked steadily through the big double doors, and once inside, the jail roof exploded in a fireball of heavenly activity.

Sarah was enthralled with the scene the Lord was showing her. "Yes, Lord, Yes, Lord," she was yelling. "Bring Your servant here." Then she was inside the jail looking at this man, still with his back toward her, ministering to the inmates with power and authority. When he moved to Will's cell, he went in and touched him and spoke, "William, you are a man like me. We both had unloving, abusive fathers. However there is a heavenly Father who loves you like you've always wanted to be loved, like you need to be loved. The good news is you don't have to earn it, and you can never lose it." As Sarah watched the ministry continue, William broke. *Whoever this new chaplain is, he's certainly anointed for this work*, thought Sarah. *Lord, please show me who this is.* When he finally turned, Sarah smiled and let out a shout of delight, "It's Pastor Paul!"

The Lord went on to show Sarah that she was supposed to minister with Paul under his authority at the jail. He showed her that He had another pastor slated to take the church to its next level. Paul's position at the jail would almost immediately transition into full-time work. "Praise the Lord," Sarah shouted. "Thank You, God! Thank You for answering my prayers."

Then she thought, *That's why Will isn't responding to me. The Lord's arranged it so Pastor Paul will touch his heart.* She decided she'd be no less dedicated in her prayers for him, but she was able to let go of some feelings of failure that had been attacking her. *Thank You, Lord, that Will's salvation is in Your hands and doesn't rest on my minuscule capabilities.*

The next day at the jail Sarah went straight to the director's office. She was moving so fast the janitor commented, "Slow down Sarah or the wheels on your walker are gonna ignite."

"I can't slow down. I'll just have to take that chance," she replied, laughing.

In the director's office, she didn't even sit, she just blurted out, "I know who your part-time chaplain is."

"Well Sarah, let me in on the secret so we can both know."

"It's Pastor Paul from the Victory Church."

"Nope, it's not him."

Sarah was taken aback. She almost felt slapped. After yesterday's revelation she thought everything would fall smoothly into place.

"W-what do you mean it's not him?"

"Sarah, he was my first choice. For some reason, I thought he'd be the one, but when I asked him, he told me an immediate, 'No.' Didn't even want to pray about it like I thought pastors do. "

"You asked him and he told you no?"

"He sure did. Said he wasn't the least bit interested; then he hung up on me."

"Well, I'll talk to him. I know he's supposed to be here."

"I hope you have better luck than I did."

Sarah prayed all the way to the church. As she pulled into the drive, the first time since that fateful Wednesday night prayer meeting, she felt the emotional turmoil churning again. She was toying with the idea of going home and making a phone call, but pressed through when she saw Paul's Toyota in the parking lot.

Pushing her walker down the hall, she breathed a prayer for the Lord to bring about His will in their lives, especially as partners in ministry. Then she took several deep breaths and knocked on the large oak door with Paul's gold nameplate prominently displayed.

"Yes?"

"Pastor, it's me, Sarah." Paul shook his head. *Just what I need, an unexpected visit from Typhoid Sarah.* "Come in," he said in his most cheerful voice.

Sarah had barely sat down before she, in her exuberant naiveté, tactlessly blasted him with the verbal tidal wave she was so excited about. "Pastor, I heard from the Lord that you're supposed to take the part-time position as chaplain. I'm supposed to work with you. Then, I don't know when, but you'll eventually work there full-time. The Lord has someone already picked to succeed you here. And there's an inmate there named Will. I can't get through to him, but I know you can because you both were abused by your fathers—"

Saldu had started talking to Paul even before Sarah did, in an attempt to prepare him, "Let go of your selfish ambition and conceit; humble yourself and see others as better than you are. Don't continually look out for your own interests, but take an interest in others."[2] Paul totally disregarded the conviction. He leapt to his feet and leaned far over his mahogany desk. "HOW DARE YOU barge into my office like this." Sarah had unknowingly hit both of Paul's most vulnerable sensitivities: his abusive father and his fear of being replaced at the church. This church was where he sucked up what little self-esteem he had. Of course, the idea of having to be around Sarah regularly was also repulsive to him.

Sarah was taken aback at the hostile reaction to what she considered extraordinarily good news. "Oh, I-I'm sorry. I was so excited. I saw it in the Spirit. I saw that we're going to be ministering together—"

"Sarah, take your craziness and get out. Just leave me alone," he yelled, pointing toward his door. "I don't want anything to do with that jail, and I certainly don't want to minister with you!" He could feel his heart beating in his neck. He knew his voice was elevated, but he couldn't help himself.

"B-b-but don't you see," stammered Sarah as she struggled to get out of her chair, "You were attracted to my land. You thought it was to build a church there, but you were attracted to the land because you're supposed to minister at the jail—"

Paul marched around his desk and flung open his door. It slammed into the doorstop with a loud thud. Pointing toward the hallway he screamed, "I said, GET OUT."

CHAPTER 25

"And I sought for a man among them who should build up the wall and stand in the breach before Me for the land, that I should not destroy it; but I found none"

(Ezekiel 22:30).

Sarah was still shaking when she pulled into her driveway. She'd had a good cry—all the way home. *I sure didn't mean to make him mad. I thought he'd be excited to know what wonderful plans God has for his life.*

When Sarah got inside, she called Barbara, who came right over. She listened for a long time and then prayed over Sarah's wounds. "Sarah, can I give you some advice?"

"Sure."

"The next time you hear from the Lord and it involves someone else, ask the Lord what to do. Are you supposed to pray and tell them at a later time? Are you just supposed to pray about it and not share it at all? But if you feel like you're supposed to share what the Lord has shown you, do it in a gentle way. Don't try to be their personal Holy Spirit. It's your job to pray and His job to intervene. If you are supposed to share, you could say something like: 'I think I heard this from the Lord, but I'd encourage you to pray about it and see if you get confirmation.' If you say that you heard it from God, what can they say? It puts them on the spot."

"Yes, I see that's a better way; I guess I was pretty abrupt," said Sarah as her face flushed. "I made that same mistake with my Sunday school class when I first got saved. They didn't respond well, either. Now I see what I did that angered Pastor Paul. Maybe I should call him and apologize."

"Why don't you hold off on that, at least for a while?" said Barbara with a grin.

After Barbara left, the spirit of Despair settled back over Sarah. *Lord, I could use a boost. I really feel bad now.* She got her humility book and read the underlined passage about Jesus, "*...I am among you as one who serves.*"[1]

She felt an urge to sort through the boxes that Barbara had brought up from the basement for her. *That doesn't sound like much of a pick-me-up. That sounds like a lot of work, but I guess I don't have anything better to do. I'll meditate on this quote while I work.* The first two boxes were uneventful; the contents went straight to the black trash bags. The fourth box was marked "Misc." When she opened it, she let out a shout. It was more of George's love letters to her. *I thought these had been lost years ago.*

She'd read all the old letters in one setting. The letters were always an exercise in happiness and grief. Tears always flowed, but in the end she felt better. She pulled the top letter off the stack and gingerly opened it. It was from George when he was at college. It started with the same familiar salutation that they both had used. She closed her eyes and pictured George speaking those words, "My Beloved." She still couldn't believe he was gone.

Halfway down the page she read the following:

> One of the fellows down the hall invited me to visit his church last night. I don't even know why I agreed to go. There was a revival going on. Lots of singing and preaching. I was thinking what a waste of my time it was when I could have been home studying. Then all of a sudden I was

crying. No matter how hard I tried I could not stop. Suddenly I remembered having that same feeling once before, when I was very young. Grandma had taken me to church and the same thing had happened. I was crying and before I knew what I was doing, I went to the altar and prayed. When I got up, I felt different; grandma told me I was "born again." I had forgotten about the whole experience until I had that compelling feeling again tonight. I went forward again and prayed like I did as a child and gave my life to Jesus. My emotions were so intense and I am thoroughly confused by the whole experience. Maybe someone will come alongside me and help me understand what I did.

She had no memory of this letter. *It wouldn't have made sense to me then anyway. Why didn't he follow through with his commitment? How could he give his life to Jesus and then never mention Him again?* Sarah felt like the life was being squeezed out of her. She was stuck between agony and ecstasy and didn't know which was the truth. She cried out, "Help me Jesus. Please show me if George is with You." Her hands were trembling as adrenalin rushed through her system. She dropped the letter like it was poisoned.

"Sarah," whispered Joel gently, "George had two very real encounters with the Lord, but he was like the hard path in the parable of the sower.[2] The seed fell into his heart, but he did not understand it. The enemy came and snatched it away before it took root. However, he did have a praying grandmother. Even though she was with the Lord long before George died, the Lord honored her unceasing prayers."

"The last three days of his life, when he was on the morphine drip and in a coma, the Lord appeared to him because of those prayers. The Lord rebuked the deception that had kept George from seeing Jesus' love for Him and gave him one final choice. Of course no one who sees Jesus in His beauty would ever say no. George made it to Heaven at the last hour. He had nothing to give the Lord and had earned no eternal rewards. His gratitude is so great that he has not left the throne room to explore the vast beauty and mysteries of Heaven since he arrived. He praises God day and night with the cherubim, elders, and millions of others.

"And," said Joel with a huge smile, "He also intercedes for you."

A huge weight rolled off of her though she continued to sob out her thanksgiving to the Lord for what seemed like hours. *Thank You, Lord. Thank You, Lord. Thank you for rescuing him from Hell at the last minute. I'll get to see him again. He's in eternity with You! Thank you for snatching him at the end of his life.*

She regretted that she hadn't been in a place to encourage him to follow through on his commitment. But God was merciful, hallelujah! *Thank You, Jesus, for getting us both.*

She had run the full spectrum of emotions today. *I forgot to eat dinner. I'm starving.* She prayed for a missionary in the Philippines when she got the sandwich ingredients out of her devotional refrigerator and prayed for a couple ministering in Romania when she put the roast beef back.

Leaving the kitchen to enter the living room, she passed through a door. *OOPS, I'm not praying in the Spirit.* It wasn't happening immediately, but she was cultivating the habit of continual prayer.

"Great job Sarah," said Malta. "Remember Ezekiel 22:30 where the Lord looked for someone to stand in the gap in prayer so He would not have to bring judgment, but He found no one? Remember George's grandmother? She was an intercessor, and intercession is spiritual warfare. Stand in the gap praying, and stay in the gap praying until the Lord repairs the breach in the wall. God has bestowed on humans an incredible dignity by allowing them to partner with Him. You be that one who is always praying, Sarah. Never let it be said again as long as you dwell on this earth that the Lord looked and found no one. Your prayers make a difference. You won't know how much until you get to Heaven, but, by faith, diligently stand in the gap each day. Many people's lives depend on it."

Sarah felt a mixture of emotions—the privilege of a destiny call on her life, but also the seeds of doubt that her prayers could really matter that much. However, the example of George's grandmother made Sarah recommit herself to prayer.

"Sarah, when you were born on the earth, you were born into a spiritual battle that you didn't ask to be a part of; no one does. The enemy is just there like a roaring lion waiting to devour every human being.[3] When you were born again, it upped the ante in a way that you can't understand. You went from being a member of the devil's kingdom and being absolutely no threat to him to being his archenemy and a huge threat to his kingdom—"

"Actually," interrupted Joel, "all believers are a huge threat, but they don't believe it because they look at their limitations instead of looking at God's limitless power that can work through them—"

"So now you're a Christian with all Jesus' power at your control and the devil is enraged. You're a terrible threat, and he declared a full-scale war on you and your life. You didn't ask to be caught up in this spiritual battle, but you only have two options—fight back or take a break and be devoured. Backing off or letting your guard down is suicide in your battle against the raging powers of darkness that seek to destroy you and your spiritual inheritance. The devil doesn't back off just because you become weary; that's his opportunity, and he'll take it every time. There is no neutral zone where you can time out and take a break."

Lord, help me to understand the seriousness of being an intercessor. Please, please give me the grace to carry it out.

That night Sarah had a dream. She was living in an ancient city with a massive wall surrounding it. The wall was in terrible disrepair. Crumbled mortar and fallen stones had left huge gaps. In spite of the damage, life was progressing as normal among the city's inhabitants.

One day Sarah heard a sound in the distance. It was almost unperceivable so she ignored it. It became louder, but still she and everyone else disregarded it. Finally, it grew so deafening that she climbed onto the broken wall. Her heart almost failed her when she saw an evil horde of huge soldiers in full armor. *There are hundreds of thousands of them!* An evil swarm, as far as she could see from the east to the west and from the south.

Each of them must be nine feet tall! They're giants.

They marched almost mechanically, in perfect unison, on their way to fulfill their goal of total annihilation of her city. As the first companies neared the wall, there were still thousands of soldiers marching over the far horizon.

They were clad in silver armor from head to toe, and carried awesome and terrifying weapons—jewel-encrusted shields and massive swords. Other companies carried spears or bows and arrows to accomplish their deadly work. The leaders of each troop rode on horseback and carried colorful war banners that whipped in the wind. This threatening army seemed undefeatable. *I have no weapons. We have no weapons. We're doomed.* Sarah turned to run, but realized that with the breaches in the walls they all would soon be dead.

From her place on the wall, she yelled to be heard over the tremendous din. "There's an army marching! They're going to slaughter us. They're almost here. *Everyone* needs to stand in the gap. NOW!"

Then Pastor Paul, the highly educated and well respected religious leader of this town spoke to the crowd, "Don't listen to her. What does she know? Who would attack us? We're right in the middle of God's will," His soothing voice calmed the agitated people. Kathy was there standing by his side.

"This is no time for a debate," screamed Sarah. "Listen. You can hear them! They're almost here! We can't let them breach the walls. Everyone climb up; take your place."

Though most ignored her, in spite of the deafening sound of the marching foot soldiers, about 50 people discerned the impending calamity—commoners, merchants, teenagers, even mothers with their children, some of the elderly, and Kathy. Each one purposefully climbed the city wall and took his or her place standing in its gaps.

It's hopeless, thought Sarah as she scanned the horizon; *we can never stand against their destructive power.* But she screamed out, nevertheless, trying to be heard over the chaos, *"PRAY! EVERYBODY, PRAY!"*

The front line of the attacking army was at the wall. The archers were taking aim, their bows drawn back at the intercessors.

The Holy Spirit reminded Sarah of Ephesians 6:12: *"For our struggle is not against flesh and blood, but against the rulers, against the authorities, against the powers of this dark world and against the spiritual forces of evil in the heavenly realms."* As the 50 began praying, Sarah cried out, "I REBUKE THE POWERS OF EVIL IN JESUS' NAME!" She simultaneously flung her arms across her face and turned sideways for protection. She fully expected to be impaled by a shower of arrows but nothing happened. Then she heard the sharp clanging of steel. Slowly, she turned to see the first third of the army laying dead on the ground. The remaining two thirds kept marching resolutely toward the wall, stepping on and over their dead cohorts.

Stunned, but encouraged, the intercessors all shouted as one voice, "I rebuke the powers of evil in Jesus' name!" To their amazement, puffs of black sulfuric smoke wafted from the armor of the middle third and the empty armor toppled! Spears and shields clattered. The hillside was littered with empty armor and useless weapons.

Suddenly, the verse made sense to Sarah. "It's a demonic army. It's just little demons wearing big armor," shouted Sarah. "The enemy really is defeated through Christ's death on the cross. They fight us through deceit and bluff. If we are in bondage to them, it is because we don't know that we are in Christ and share His victory over Satan. They only have the power over us that we give them. The demons must flee at our command! When Jesus retrieved the keys to death and Hell, we were participants in that victory. Because Satan is beneath Jesus' feet, he is also beneath ours."[4]

The intercessors erupted into praise.

"RETREAT! RETREAT!" screeched the head spirits. The last third of the demons retreated into the second heavens, not even waiting for the next verbal deathblow. Their armor and weapons dropped, clanging impotently to the ground. They were well aware that on the back of Satan's neck is a nail-scarred footprint.

All Sarah could see was the glint of the sun shining off of hundreds of thousands of suits of armor lying in disarray. Just a few minutes ago she had been terrified—sure that they would be slaughtered, totally annihilated. But at the Word of God, there was no violence, no disaster, no destruction to the city. God had delivered them.

"Submit to God and resist the enemy. Then he will flee!"[5] shouted one of the other intercessors. They all worshiped and celebrated Jesus' victory over the powers of darkness and rejoiced that the same authority had been imparted to them—Satan's dominion ended at Calvary.

As they left their places on the wall and climbed down, the city's residents met them. "Where are all the soldiers you said you saw? We told you there was no reason for concern."

Chapter 26

"Contrary to popular and false belief, it's not 'those who help themselves' whom God helps; it's those who humble themselves. This is the promise of humility. God is personally and providenally supportive of the humble. And the grace He extends to the humble is indescribably rich."

C.J. Mahaney[1]

"You will choose between two teachers in life: Wisdom or consequences."

Wayne Cordeiro[2]

Pastor Paul had been shaken to his core by the word Sarah gave him. How could she know he'd had an abusive father? He hadn't even told Kathy. His father had died when he was a freshman in college, and he hadn't met Kathy until the following year. He'd been careful to always talk about his dad's good side and then change the subject. He sure wasn't going to tell Kathy what Sarah had said.

Deception immediately appeared and perched on his shoulder. *"Leave the church? Why should you leave the church? The Lord is obviously blessing everything. Every time you turn around, new members are joining."* It was like a dream come true for any pastor, but especially one so fresh out of seminary and still wet behind the ears.

"Paul, use your discernment," pleaded Saldu. At the word *discernment*, Deception let out a squeal, as if impaled.

"How," continued Saldu, "could Sarah know about your dad being abusive? She could only know that if the Lord told her. And if she heard it from the Lord, then that gives credibility to the other part of the message about taking the jail's director up on his job offer. You need to set aside your own earthly gratification, which, trust me on this, in eternity will only shame you, and love the Lord enough to be obedient to His plans for you. You felt the Lord drawing you to the land. That's good, but you didn't pray to find out why. When the opportunity to thwart the jail came, you inserted your own desires and called it God's plan. You misinterpreted His will. People conceive of plans and label them as being directly from God all the time. Then when their plan fails, they're mad at God and at everyone else for letting them down."

"But," screeched Deception, "that part-time job would eventually lead to you leaving your church. You don't want that. Most pastors never experience the type of success you're seeing now, and this is your first church. You'd be a fool to leave."

Saldu stood with his arms folded across his chest and a somber look on his radiant face. He was steadfast in obedience to the Lord and knew that this was also what Paul needed. His voice was stern. He pointed his unseen sword at Paul's heart. "Paul, you need to follow the Lord's plan for your life, not your plan. This is not a game. There are eternal consequences at stake. There's a way that seems right to a man, but the end is death.[3] Do you understand? Disobedience leads to death."

Paul wrestled with the situation, flipping back and forth between Sarah hearing from the Lord or possibly knowing the information some other way. He finally dismissed it. The prospect that it was true was entirely too scary to entertain. What if the Lord really spoke to Sarah and she wasn't nuts? Then he'd be the one on the outside looking in. *No, it absolutely couldn't be.* He didn't know where Sarah got her information; maybe it was just a good guess. But he wasn't going to become a chaplain at *that* jail, especially if it meant ministering with Sarah. Deception rubbed up against Paul's face like an affectionate cat then turned and sunk his jagged talons into Paul's skull.

Saldu sighed, sheathed his sword, and interceded for Paul.

Barbara gave Sarah a book on healing. Sarah devoured it. She'd heard people at prayer meetings praying for God to heal, but she never knew the outcomes. Now she delved into the topic. Hope rose in her spirit, and she posted verses around the house. "He personally carried away my sins in His own body on the cross, so I can be dead to sin and live for what is right. I have been healed by His wounds,"[4] she would say over and over. She had already figured out that when she got healed she would donate her cane and walker to the Bradbury Manor. Every night before she went to bed she expected to wake up in the morning with full mobility, and every morning so far, she was disappointed.

The idea of being healed and the revelation that George had accepted the Lord elevated Sarah's spirits, even though her body continued to be uncooperative. She was only going to the jail twice a week now. It was just too laborious to make the trip. On the days that she couldn't go, she prayed for all the inmates and looked forward to the next trip.

The next day, armed with her cookies and her walker, Sarah went out visiting prisoners. When the most responsive inmates heard her walker squeaking from around the corner, they began crying out, "Momma Sarah, Momma Sarah. Did you bring me cookies?" It always lifted her spirit no matter how tired her body was from the increased effort it took to get there.

As she made her cookie rounds this day, one of the inmates, an older prisoner nicknamed Skinner, wanted to speak to her. He let down his macho demeanor and confided that he was having recurrent nightmares that terrified him. "I even stayed awake last night 'cause I couldn't face 'em again. When I sleep, this black, snake-like, evil thing comes to me and flashes all the bad stuff I ever done in front of me, startin' when I was a little kid. It's like a movie. It goes really fast in front of my eyes. While it's playing, this thing is laughin' this sick laugh. When it's done it makes fun of me by sayin' stuff like, 'See all the evil in your life? You belong to me. I'm waitin' for you. You can't escape. Why don't you kill yourself and we'll go easy on you?' Then I wake up and I'm sweatin' and my heart is poundin'. I need help, bad."

Sarah knew it was demonic and that the first step was salvation. "You might not believe this, Skinner, but I think you have a demon that torments you. And that demon is right about one thing. At this point the devil owns your soul for eternity because of all the bad things you've done." Skinner dropped his eyes in shame. "But the great news is that God loves you so much that He provided a way to save you from the enemy." Joel and Malta watched Sarah, both of them beaming like proud parents. "You see, the Bible says that all have sinned and fallen short of God's requirements.[5] We all belonged to Satan's kingdom. But God sent Jesus to pay for our sins. If we believe that He died for us, our sins are all forgiven. Then He even gives us His goodness as a gift. When we die and we stand before God, our sin is forgiven and all He sees is righteousness, so He lets us into Heaven. It's like God looks at us through "Jesus-colored glasses" from here on out. And it's all a gift; you can't earn it, and you can't undo it. Have you heard the verse John 3:16?"

"Yeah, everyone knows that. Learned it as a kid."

"Can you say it?"

"Sure. 'For God so loved the world that He gave His only begotten son that whosoever believes on Him will not perish but have everlasting life.' Hey, that's exactly what you just told me."

"Right. Would you like to pray now to accept Jesus?" Sarah was trying not to let her voice quaver, but she was gripped with equal parts of anticipation that Skinner would say yes and apprehension that he would say no. After a moment's hesitation, he nodded yes.

Sarah realized she'd been holding her breath and slowly exhaled. "OK, repeat after me. 'Dear Jesus, thank You for dying on the cross for my sins. I ask You to come into my heart and be my savior and forgive me of my sins. I give my life to you to do with what You will. Amen.'"

Skinner finished praying, and Sarah was the one crying. "Now Skinner, God isn't keeping track of your wrongs any more. He's keeping track of Jesus' rights. Do you understand?" Skinner nodded his head.

"Cast out the spirit, Sarah," said Malta. "Your faith cripples the enemy's power." A spirit of Boldness, which she had never felt before, came over Sarah. "By the power of the blood of Jesus, I command you evil spirit to leave, now."

Joel and Malta watched as a large warrior angel appeared behind Skinner. Stunned by Sarah's prayers, the demon Suicide that was coiled around Skinner's torso and neck, fell to the floor. The angel brought his sandaled foot down on the serpent's throat, pulled a silver knife from his sheath and sliced off its head. It howled mournfully and disappeared, leaving a black puff of putrid smoke.

The three angels rejoiced together. "Remember the first time we saw Sarah?" asked Joel. That same foul spirit was about to take her life. She was totally in its clutches. Now she's in authority over it. She sent it fleeing!"

"Hallelujah," shouted Malta.

"Now I don't think you'll have problems anymore with that dream, Skinner," said Sarah. "But if you do, you just tell your little tormentor that those are no longer *your* sins. God is not holding them against you.[6] They've all been forgiven, and you are owned by no one but Jesus," said Sarah as she leaned forward to give Skinner a big hug through the bars. "You may be incarcerated, but for the first time in your life, you are truly free."

Skinner's angel began to sing a hymn he had heard as a youngster in church. Without even realizing it, Skinner hummed along.

Sarah left the jail that day feeling great. It was the first time that she'd ever led someone to the Lord. She and her angels sang and praised all the way home, allowing her to temporarily forget her physical infirmities.

Later that night while she was sitting on the couch, Malta played the flute and led Sarah into a time of intercession for the inmates and Pastor Paul. *Oh God I'm so grieved that there's no chaplain at the jail to disciple the inmates, no one to hold services or a Bible study. How will they grow and mature? Lord, please touch Pastor Paul's heart. Have mercy on him in his disobedience. Please don't hold his sin against him, but put his feet on the right path. Lord, deal with whatever attitudes prevent him from doing Your will. How will Will get saved if Pastor Paul's not there ministering? Lord, unless You heal me, I won't be able to go there much longer.* She travailed in prayer for an hour and a half. She was too drained to make the slow journey to her bed so she spent the night curled under the alpaca blanket on the couch.

The ringing phone woke her the next morning. Her back was stiff from sleeping on the couch, which slowed her movement even more. She picked up the phone on what was going to be the last ring. It was Barbara's cheery voice on the other end. "How are you doing today?"

The Lord had spoken to Barbara, telling her to help Sarah more. Barbara was glad to oblige. She could feel the Lord's pleasure over these acts of kindness. *The Lord is jealous for the well-being of the widows and orphans,*[7] Barbara thought. She enjoyed tending her garden and her flowers, but there was never anything pressing on her schedule. Barbara's time was totally her own, and she was happy to lavish it on Sarah.

Later in the week Barbara drove Sarah to the neurologist in Mt. Pielor. After the exam Dr. Schumacher floored Sarah by suggesting it might be time to think of leaving her home. "We don't want you to fall and hurt yourself. It's not good for you to live alone. Have you considered the Manor?"

When the conversation ended, Sarah was staying in her home by herself, but would compromise. She agreed to wear a special necklace; if she needed assistance she would merely press the button on the necklace to summon immediate help. At the end of the visit, Dr. Schumacher looked sternly at Barbara, "Sometime in the next few weeks, I want you to take her by the Manor just to look around. Do you understand"? Barbara nodded.

The ride home was somber. "Why isn't the Lord healing me?"

"I don't know. I just know that He has His own perfect timing. Don't give up and lose faith. Remember, faith precedes everything God does for us. Without faith it's impossible to please Him. And you must believe that He rewards those who diligently seek Him."[8]

"I was sure I'd be healed by now. The book I read says it's God's will to heal everyone—that's in the Bible. He healed them all."[9]

After a long pause, Barbara said sadly, "I don't have any easy answers, but I promise to keep praying for the Lord to touch you."

I must not have enough faith, Sarah thought. *How do I increase my faith?* She remembered the Bible says that faith comes from what is heard through God's Word.[10]

Maybe I'll read my Bible more and increase my faith that way.

Sarah was a woman with a mission, spending all her spare time in the Word. However, her health didn't improve. *What can I do to show the Lord that I have faith? I just need a mustard seed's worth.* Sarah decided that she would stop taking her medicine. *That will prove that I have faith. If I didn't believe I would be healed, I certainly wouldn't do that.* She skipped her bedtime dose of her Parkinson's medicines. In the middle of the night, she woke up and tried to turn over in bed. She couldn't roll over! A wave of panic and adrenalin swept through her as she struggled. *It feels like my legs are made of cement!* She didn't know what to do except pray. After praying for 30 minutes with no results, she reluctantly admitted she needed help. She was too embarrassed to press the button on her necklace. They would send the police or firemen or an ambulance, and the sirens would wake up the whole neighborhood. *They'd probably cart me off to the hospital and tell me to go to the nursing home.* She finally decided that she would call Barbara. She reached for the nightstand. It was 3:30 A.M. when Barbara groped for her phone.

"Hello."

"Barbara, I'm so sorry to wake you—"

"Sarah, are you all right? Did you fall?"

"No, I didn't fall and I'm embarrassed to call you, but I need your help. Can you come to my house and get me some medicine?"

"I'll be right there. Are you hurt? Are you sure you're OK?"

"I'll explain it when you get here."

An embarrassed Sarah explained it all, and Barbara gave her the missed dose of her medicines. "I still think we should call the doctor."

"I'm not waking anyone else up. I'm adamant about that. I'll call in the morning if I haven't improved."

In spite of Sarah's protests, Barbara spent the night on the couch. In the morning Sarah's mobility was back to "normal." Barbara had the coffee made when Sarah woke. Sarah was very embarrassed and apologetic, although Barbara threw the whole thing off as nothing. But she did extract a promise from Sarah to always take all her medicine.

"I had no idea how bad I was without my medicines. I thought I was bad when I was taking them. I just missed one dose and my legs quit working."

Sarah was tearing up and Barbara looked at the floor. She felt impotent. She felt worse than impotent; she felt responsible. She was the one who gave Sarah the book on healing.

Barbara crawled into bed that night with a heavy heart. She silently prayed, *God, You're going to heal Sarah, aren't You?*

The next morning Barbara pulled into Sarah's drive at 10 A.M. sharp. Sarah was waiting on the porch swing. Barbara helped her down the front steps and into the car. They drove in silence for several minutes. "I'm sorry we have to do this," said Barbara. "But it's doctor's orders. It's just good to have a back-up plan." She turned the car into Bradbury Manor, the town's nursing home, parked, and came around to help Sarah up. Sarah never went anywhere without her walker now.

Later that night in her bed, Sarah wept. She hadn't told anyone, but her tremors had gotten so bad she'd had to change her eating habits. Eating with silverware was too difficult now. Soup or salad was out of the question. Sandwiches, apples, bananas, a muffin, anything big she could pick up with both hands was all she could manage. If she filled a glass more than half full, the beverage sloshed over the side. She would put a glass on the table and drink with a straw so she didn't have to hold it and splash the liquid down the front of her blouse.

The spirit of Fear invaded her room and tormented her with images of the most infirm, helpless patients—half conscious, unable to hold their heads up, drooling out of the sides of their mouths. She could even smell the stench of urine that had assaulted her as she shuffled down the hall with Barbara.

"Jesus, Jesus, please help me." She wept until she fell asleep.

The next morning, she called the local handyman, Herald Ray, to make her home safer. He moved her washer and dryer from the basement to the pantry, between the kitchen and the back porch. She also had him install grab bars in the bathtub and bring the rest of the boxes upstairs. Now there was no need to go down those basement stairs, ever. *I can stay in the house longer. What do doctors know, anyway?*

She also spent time the next ten days sorting through her closets, under her bed, and through her dressers. Then she called the local charity to come cart it away. It felt good to unclutter her house, and she didn't want to be a burden to anyone when she passed on.

CHAPTER 27

"The moment humility announces herself she is already out the door."

Walter Buettler[1]

"He that is down need fear no fall."

John Bunyan[2]

"Three men were taking a tour of the White House," said Pastor Paul to the congregation. "It turned out that all three of them were contractors. 'This must be my lucky day,' replied the guide. 'The security door that the president uses is broken. Maybe you can all bid it for me.' The contractor from Missouri took some measurements and said, 'I can fix it for $400. That's $200 for parts and $200 for labor.' The contractor from California examined the door and said, 'I can fix it for $500. That's $250 for parts and $250 for labor.' The contractor from New York said, 'I can fix it for $2,400.'

'Twenty four hundred dollars? That's outrageous. You didn't even measure it. How do you get $2,400?' asked the incredulous tour guide.

'A thousand for you, a thousand for me, and we hire the guy from Missouri.'"

Paul loved their laughter almost more than anything. It was like the congregation was saying he was just one of them; he fit right in.

"I have a very exciting reason to be talking about contractors today. The elders and I have been discussing the rapid growth going on in our fellowship, and we are proposing that the church begin a fundraising drive in preparation to buy land and build larger facilities projected for completion in two years. This plan has been divided into very attainable smaller goals, and we won't go on to another until we reach the one directly in front of us."

Paul spent the whole time that morning explaining the details and extolling the virtues of the plan. After the service, the feedback was mixed. A lot of the members, mostly the newer or younger ones, were very excited about the church being taken to the next level. Then came the, "We've-never-done-it-this-way-before," group who would fight any change as if their lives depended on it. They rallied informally to do just that, with Wilma leading the deadly phone brigade under the influence of several destructive spirits intent on breeding division.

Paul wasn't aware of them as his family ate lunch, however. He was still high on the idea of bigger, better, and more prestigious, even as the phone network snaked through the older members of the congregation. Wilma picked up the phone and Ardare said to her: *"They sharpen their tongues like swords and aim their bitter words like arrows. They shoot from ambush at the innocent, attacking suddenly and fearlessly. They encourage each other to do evil and plan how to set their traps in secret.'"*[3]

"No, No," shrieked Gossip, "this young pastor just gets voted in, and he has the audacity to make plans to abandon your church and build a new one, who knows where. This is the church where you've grown up, Wilma. You were married in this church, and all your kids were baptized here. If Paul thinks he can just close it down and build another one just because of some vote of the elders—well you just can't let that happen! It's your responsibility to do something."

From her comfy recliner, Wilma rallied the troops and formed a battle plan, much to Ardare's dismay.

Bernice thought they should all make their voices known by withholding their tithes, and Carol proposed a petition they could circulate. Wilma felt maybe the group who wanted to build should leave with Pastor Paul and go build. The rest of them could stay right where they were and find a pastor who thought more like they did. Then everyone could be happy.

Although Sarah hadn't been there since that first Wednesday prayer meeting, her name was on the list of older adults. Later in the week, when the phone tree got more organized, she received a call from someone she couldn't even remember.

"Sarah, my name is Katherine Plumb, and I'm helping with the committee against the building campaign at the Victory Church." Sarah felt her heart skip a beat at the mention of the church's name.

"You go there, don't you?" Rather than explain the "unique" circumstances, Sarah just said, "It's my church." She was immediately hit with a barrage of gossip organized into a plan to squash the new building campaign.

"Pastor Paul wants to start a building campaign for the church?" asked Sarah.

"Yes, and if successful, we would be forced to leave our beloved church and move to a new facility, who knows where?"

"Well, that's not good," said Sarah, thinking of Paul's forward drive with the church when he was supposed to be gravitating toward the jail.

"Good, I'm glad we can count on your support. Now, here's what we're asking: withhold your tithe, sign the petition that Carol is circulating, and boycott Thursday visitation. If we didn't keep getting so many new members, we wouldn't be outgrowing our facilities. These are our first efforts. If they don't work, you can be sure we'll try something else." Before Sarah could think what to say, Katherine concluded, "Thanks for your support; look for Carol; she'll be set up in the Sunday school room with the petitions. Bye."

Sarah was stunned by the divisiveness and evil that she felt from the plan to usurp the building campaign. At the same time, she knew that Pastor Paul was not supposed to be pursuing a secure future at this church. *Both sides are wrong. I guess two wrongs will never make a right.*

She opened her Bible to James chapter three to look for the verses on controlling the tongue, but her eyes fell on verse one of chapter three. *"Not many of you should presume to be teachers, my brothers, because you know that we who teach will be judged more strictly."*

That's Pastor Paul; he will be judged more strictly as a leader. He's not where he is supposed to be, and he is leading this group of people where they shouldn't go. I wonder if I should share this with him? She smiled, remembering Barbara's advice. *I better pray about it a lot before I decide. I sure don't want to go shooting my tongue off and causing more problems.*

She put her feet up on the coffee table and relaxed while she prayed in tongues silently, and with her mind she interceded for the church and Pastor Paul.

CHAPTER 28

"The only humility that is really ours is not that which we try to show before God in prayer, but that which we carry with us....It is in our most unguarded moments that we really show and see what we are."

Andrew Murray[1]

"If you are looking for an example of humility, look at the cross."

Thomas Aquinas[2]

Paul was in his office meeting with his trusted confidant, Mike. Mike had heard from Jessica, his wife, who heard from an older member of the church who sometimes babysat for them, who had received a phone call that there was an organized movement against the building campaign.

"Can't they see, can't they just see what a good thing this is for the church? I swear, every time I try to accomplish something, there's someone to oppose it," said Paul, slamming his palm down on his desk.

"Kind of like Jesus?" said Mike, smiling.

Paul looked a little less intense and then laughed, "Yea, kinda like Jesus."

"I'm not sure how to deal with this, are you?"

"No," said Paul, suddenly serious again, "they didn't have a class on preventing church splits in seminary."

"Apparently they should have."

"Maybe if we can find out who the informal leader is, we can talk to him. If we succeed in changing his mind, the opposing structure will naturally deteriorate."

"I don't think it will be quite that easy. From the sound of it, most of the older adults feel strongly enough to sign a petition, withhold their tithe, and boycott Thursday nights," said Mike.

"I could care less about their petition and few of them visit on Thursdays anyway, but if the majority withholds their tithe, it could be serious. The over 60 group gives nearly 65 percent of the budget. How long could we last with that kind of a reduction?"

"Well, the group health insurance for the staff just went up, and the parking lot is going to have to be repaved. I'm afraid someone is going to fall and get hurt. We're also looking at a new roof pretty quickly; the old one is leaking in the women's bathroom, third stall—"

"All right, I get the picture."

"I've got to get home. I'm late for dinner," said Mike.

"Me too. If you come up with anything, give me a call."

In a special effort to bless Paul, Kathy had cooked all day making his favorite food, her homemade enchiladas. But Paul was preoccupied; he wasn't so much eating as he was shoveling his food around the blue floral plate.

"Honey, are you OK?"

"Yea, just discouraged. I just talked with Mike, and apparently most of the members over 60 don't want the building campaign and are threatening to withhold their tithe."

"That's terrible," said Kathy.

"Terrible," mimicked Jordan, who had stirred a bite of enchilada into his milk and taken a big swig, causing Hael to laugh.

"You're telling me," he said shoving his plate across the table. "How could they oppose this plan? It's best for the whole church's future."

"That's not exactly what I meant," said Kathy. "I meant it's terrible that they're choosing such an ungodly way to protest. The tithe is holy and paid to God. You don't withhold it if you don't get what you want. It's not leverage or a bargaining chip."

"That's right, too, and the Lord isn't going to bless their crappy little efforts," said Paul with a scowl.

After a slight hesitation Kathy spoke, "I know someone else whose attitude He isn't going to bless. I know this is hard, Honey. I know you've been formulating this plan since the minute you walked in the door. I know that, but you have to respond appropriately. You have to respond in a godly way even though you're being opposed. It's really not even you, personally. It's just your plan."

"Godly way," mimicked Jordan.

"See, out of the mouth of babes," she said chuckling at Jordan, but turned serious again when Paul threw down his napkin. "You always side with other people, and you always belittle my ideas. I can't tell you anything."

"That's not true. I want to be more involved, but you're shutting me out. Paul, you just don't want to entertain any opinion but your own. It's like you're afraid that if I have any ideas or thoughts that I'll hijack your authority, but I just want to work together as a team."

"You're not the pastor. You don't carry that responsibility. The buck stops with me."

"No, but I'm your wife, and you really should consider my input before you immediately discard it, on any topic, church related or not."

"If you come up with any wonderful words of wisdom to deliver me from this situation, I'll be in my office." Kathy didn't speak what she was thinking, *I suggest you come up with a plan and then do the total opposite.*

Paul's manipulative spirits were circling around him, hissing, spitting, and generally working themselves into a froth at the rich opportunities that lay ahead.

"As long as he's filled with anger, he's in our clutches."

"We can take him down and his marriage, too."

Sarah had her own secret resentment with God. She was growing impatient for the healing she knew should come. Physically, each day was harder than the next. *Lord, who's going to minister at the jail if I'm not there? I know it's Your will that I be there so why are You withholding my healing? It says that if You made the ultimate sacrifice of Your Son that You will freely give us all things,*[3] *that if we ask for bread, You won't give us a stone,*[4] *that You had compassion on the multitudes and that You healed them all.*[5] She thought of withholding her medicine again to call God's attention to her faith, but remembered the embarrassment it caused and her promise to Barbara. She tried to get off the couch without her walker. After a few ineffective attempts, she gave up and grabbed for the dreaded contraption. *I hate, hate, hate this thing,* she thought. In her honest moments, she knew she could not stay by herself very much longer. The thought of leaving her home and moving into the Manor felt like death.

God, where are You?

Joel, radiating with divine light, spoke firmly to Sarah, *"You are not a victim, but an overcomer. Put on the whole armor of God to resist the enemy's attack. He is already defeated, but you must fight. If you let down your shield, he will seize that opportunity to advance against you and bring destruction. Don't give in to Anger or Self Pity."*

Malta played on his flute to comfort Sarah. The notes were swirling around her, but she couldn't receive the soothing music. Joel drew his sword to plunge it deep within her heart and spirit, but the sharp tip would not penetrate. "She's built a wall. She's angry at Father," said Joel as tears welled in his eyes.

"This might just be the toughest thing Sarah has to face in the rest of her time on earth. This is a deception that will lead her astray in every area of her life. Unknowingly, she has opened a door to the demonic, and she needs to confess her anger quickly," replied Malta.

"No one should ever doubt Father's goodness, regardless of how bad the circumstances appear."

Though Sarah couldn't see or feel it, Joel and Malta watched as a high-ranking, black spirit of Accusation flapped into the room, circled Sarah, and came to rest on her shoulder. Delighting in its malicious assignment, it dug its gnarled talons into the tender flesh of her neck and sneered at the angels. Joel and Malta grimaced, revolted by its evil and arrogance. But without permission to act against it, their weapons and worship would help Sarah very little as long as she clung to her bitterness against the Lord. They didn't speak; they didn't want the demon to derive great pleasure from hearing it, but they were both thinking it: *She had invited the spirit and it had come.*

Joel and Malta stood by Sarah's bed as they did every night. Accusation was beside her in the bed, feeding her its lies and poisoning her mind. Joel and Malta were grieved to tears, but knew they were not allowed to intervene until Sarah changed her attitude and repented.

"Where is God now?" Accusation's slippery, beguiling voice whispered. "If God is so good, why did He let George die, and why is He letting you die, slowly, a little each day? If He loved you, He would have healed you by now. He's not going to heal you; you're going to die in that nursing home, old and alone."

"Can't you just picture it?" whispered the spirit of Fear. "Imagine yourself fetal in the bed, unable to move or even swallow, an IV tube pumps liquids in and a catheter takes them out."

Laying in the dark, Sarah succumbed to the demonic suggestions. Her heart raced, her blood pressure shot up, and she was starting to breathe heavily. She pictured the terrifying scene in great detail. She'd be trapped inside her uncooperative body, a prisoner, possibly even unable to communicate her wants and wishes. How long would she hang on like this? Weeks, months, years? The tormenting spirits continued their taunting images.

Joel and Malta were enraged that Sarah was terrified, that her mind was being violated by these demons sent to destroy her. The yellow eyes flashed at them, the raspy voice of Accusation taunted, "I'll undo in one day what it's taken you a year to do."

"Your power is not as great as you pretend. You're nothing but defeated cowards," said Joel. "Your only weapons are bluff and deceit. Sarah doesn't even have to entertain you, much less be influenced by you. She has complete and total authority over you."

"But she doesn't believe that, does she?" said Accusation, smirking as he shielded himself from the glory radiating from the angels. "She doesn't really believe that at all, and I'll exploit that weakness to its fullest extent—all the way to the nursing home."

Sarah didn't visit the jail the next day like she'd planned, or the day after. She was slowly being drawn into a black vortex of depression. She lay on the couch. She wasn't hungry. She was restless and agitated. She tried reading the old love letters, but they only made her cry and feel sorry for herself because she missed George so much. For some reason, they weren't therapeutic anymore.

The demon voices seldom rested. "If God loved you, He would have healed you. He's all-powerful; He could do it in a moment. What other explanation is there? Why would God love you? You spent 70 years living for yourself without giving Him a thought."

She became more despondent as she entertained their vile demonic lies. The more negative and critical ideas polluted Sarah's mind, the more debilitated her body became. Sarah was already imagining how it would feel to be totally incapacitated.

"*A cheerful heart is good medicine…*"[6] said Joel to Malta, "Unfortunately, the opposite is also true."

Barbara was out of town at a church conference and unaware of the situation. The jail's director noticed her absence and called, but by the time she got up from the couch the phone had stopped ringing.

CHAPTER 29

"We will never be satisfied in the pursuit of false and temporary fulfillments. Only when we begin to touch and experience some of these eternal satisfactions will we be empowered to let go of the inferior ones."

Mike Bickle[1]

Sarah was depressed. She passed the next several days laying on the couch weeping off and on. When she became overcome by boredom, she'd turn on the television. "I can't believe I've stooped to watching daytime talk shows and soap operas. Even when I wasn't saved I didn't do that." She turned off the television and read her Bible, but it seemed dry and irrelevant. After awhile she turned the television back on. She tried to pray for the actors, but gave up.

Lying on the couch she remembered that the pilot light was still lit on the furnace. *George used to turn it off each year to save money when the weather warmed. I think I'll do that.*

Immediately Malta whispered, "Sarah, it's not wise. You can get a neighbor to do it for you."

She lifted herself slowly off the couch and with the aid of her walker headed toward the basement door, grabbing her cane on the way. When she passed through the door to the kitchen, she automatically started praying.

She threw off additional warnings from Joel and Malta, which manifested as that nagging feeling that what she was contemplating wasn't wise. She slowly opened the basement door and transferred her first hand from the walker to the handrail.

"This is great," snickered Depression, in an uncharacteristic burst of pleasure. "We don't have to do anything except stand back and watch."

"After all our failed efforts, she's doing it to herself," laughed Intimidation.

"I can only hope it will be a fatal fall," whispered Death.

She stepped with one foot onto the first step. She released the walker, grabbed the cane and threw it to the bottom of the stairs. With both hands holding the rail on either side of the stairs she slowly, painstakingly descended. At the bottom, with one hand still clutching the rail she stooped to pick up the cane. *Success.*

She moved to the furnace and undid the latches holding the cover plate in place. It fell to the floor. She took care of the pilot light. After staring at the plate, she decided to let it lay. It would require two hands to reinstall. That meant no cane; it was too risky. She turned back toward the stairs and slowly began her ascent. She was surprised at how much harder it was going up. Her legs were already exhausted and she was less than halfway. She paused to rest for a second and her legs buckled, jerking both hands from the rails. She was falling before she knew it. She landed on her right side with a thud on the cold cement floor and let out a scream as a sharp pain ran the length of her body.

She rolled to her back and lay still, praying. She lifted her head and looked down her body. Her left foot was pointing toward the ceiling. Her right foot was pointed toward the wall.

"You've done it now," screeched Discouragement. "You'll definitely live your last days in a nursing home for sure." Sarah began to cry as much from fear as from the pain. There was no getting around it; she knew that her actions would cause major changes in her life.

When she'd agreed to get the necklace, she'd never really planned on using it. It was just part of an agreement to let her stay in her home.

"Sarah, this isn't going to go away," said Malta. "You need help." Reluctantly she pushed the button.

In a few seconds, her phone was ringing; she counted 17 times. Then it stopped. In a few minutes she heard the siren in the distance. Another minute and it was screaming loud. She heard pounding on the front door. Then running feet went past the basement window to the back. There was more knocking, then the sound of splintering wood. At the top of the stairs stood a fireman. "She's down here," he yelled, shoving her walker aside. Seeing that only added to her humiliation. She shook her head at her foolishness and choked back more tears.

In just a few seconds she was surrounded. One intense-looking fireman put a blood pressure cuff on her while another asked an unending string of questions. "What's the president's name? What's the date? What city are you in? What happened? What medicines are you taking? Are you having problems breathing?" They scooped her onto a long, cold plastic board and strapped her down. The movement caused her to cry out in pain, especially the trip up the steep stairs.

As they were carrying her across the kitchen, Malta prompted her to speak her thoughts. Through her tears she managed to say, "All this just so I could blow out the pilot light and save a few dollars."

"Ma'am, did you say 'blow out' the pilot light?"

"Yes."

"Did you turn off the gas?"

"No. I didn't know I was supposed to. George always...." her voice trailed off as she watched him run for the basement door.

She didn't think it was possible to be more embarrassed, more humiliated, than she was already, but when she saw the firemen shaking their heads and smirking at each other, she felt like a chastised, incompetent child.

"Ma'am," said the returning officer, "I don't want to say you're lucky that you fell and hurt yourself, but it's a good thing we're here. You would have blown up yourself, your house, and possibly your closest neighbors."

The ambulance arrived at the hospital within minutes. Nothing in Bradbury was very far from anything else. Sarah was X-rayed in the ER, which confirmed a broken hip. The good news was, instead of needing a hip replacement, the bones could be pinned. They whisked her into surgery late that afternoon.

Her exhaustion and the medication caused her to sleep all through the evening and night. When she opened her eyes she looked up into the face of a smiling nurse.

"Good morning, my name's Jan. How do you feel this morning?"

Sarah assessed the situation; she felt pain, a sharp unrelenting pain in her right hip. She had an IV in her left hand and her right arm was one big bruise. Then the memories of last night all came flooding back. She teared up slightly, "How long will I be here?"

Jan patted her arm gently, "That's partly up to you. We'll keep you on this floor and start rehabilitation therapy. Probably after a week or so you'll be moved to a temporary facility to continue your therapy, all together you can expect rehab to take about six weeks."

She didn't ask the question, but she knew the answer. They wouldn't want her to go back home by herself, and they wouldn't want her to drive.

She took the medicine Jan had brought her and with much embarrassment and excruciating pain, used the bedpan. When Jan left, Sarah started thinking. Suddenly, having Parkinson's and having to use a walker to get around didn't seem so bad compared to the situation she was in now. Waves of discouragement rolled over her as she listened to the spirit of Deception: "You were so ungrateful when you should have been grateful for what you still had left. You were just too stupid to see it then."

"Your life is wasted," lied Depression. "You can't do anything for anyone now. Everyone has to do for you. You'll never go back to the jail to minister. You can bet God is really mad at you." Sarah began to fixate on God being mad at her. This was an open door for the spirit of Guilt, who readily joined

Deception at his gruesome game. "You're such a failure! Your ministry and your prayer walking have come to an end. You just ruined the plans that God had for the rest of your life because of your stupidity."

"Sarah," whispered Joel, "God is not mad at you for your failures, accidents, and weakness. Your sin sometimes surprises you, but it never surprises God. Before He even saved you He knew every sin you'd commit your whole life, and He called you as His daughter anyway."

"No one is a failure by God's standard until they give up and just quit trying. No pun intended, Sarah, but Proverbs says that 'the righteous falls seven times and rises again.'² You can fall, get up, and try again and fall, get up, and try again. As long as you keep getting up after each fall, God never classifies you as a failure. You're not a failure. God always looks at your heart and your intentions."

"God can still use your life even though it looks bleak to you," said Joel. "Romans 8 says He can turn anything for good.³ He is the all-powerful God of the universe; He still wants to use you. Trust Him."

"You have the ability to make bad situations worse by the way you react. The opposite is also true."

The life in Joel and Malta's words imparted hope and faith during one of the most trying times in her life. By an act of her will, Sarah began to sing out loud, "You're all I want. You're all I've ever needed. You're all I want. Help me know You are near."⁴ There was no one in the bed next to hers, but she wouldn't have cared anyway. Joel looked at Malta, who was grinning from ear to ear. He nodded. Joel pulled his sword and split the evil spirits between their yellow eyes. When they vanished, Sarah felt a freedom she hadn't felt for quite awhile.

She was still in significant pain from the surgery, but she called Barbara and asked her to pick up her Bible, devotional book, and other reading material. She also asked her to call Herald to fix her back door. *It could have been worse*, she thought. *I could have not only blown myself up, but also taken some of the neighbors with me. Clarence Harvey would have been only too happy to tell of my stupidity and death in large headlines on the front page of the Gazette.* She shook her head and said sheepishly, *Thank God for the lesser of the two evils. Even though I'm really in a bind, I'm grateful to be alive.*

CHAPTER 30

"Do not be afraid to allow the Holy Spirit to reveal any unforgiveness or bitterness. The longer you hide it, the stronger it will become and the harder your heart will grow. Stay tenderhearted."

John Bevere[1]

Paul hadn't slept well last night. The spirits were influencing his dreams again. He'd tossed and turned so much that Kathy pleaded with him to move to the couch. At 3:50 he finally trudged out of the bedroom. On the way down the hall, he passed the steps to Jordan's room. Saldu was pointing up. Paul took the suggestion. Jordan's door was ajar and his nightlight spilled out into the hall. Paul entered and stood over his crib. He was lying on his back, clutching his favorite blankie in one arm. Winnie the Pooh was sitting by his side like some incompetent night watchman, and it made Paul chuckle.

Hael watched as Paul brushed Jordan's fine, brown hair to the side of his head and pulled his T-shirt down over his belly button. Jordan was so precious to him. Soberly, Paul made a sincere commitment to spend more time with the family.

Every so often, Jordan made little sucking motions with his lips. Paul was so filled with emotion for the little guy he wanted to scoop him in his arms right there, but he knew it would be selfish on his part. Besides, Kathy had an ironclad rule—never wake a sleeping child!

Paul stayed by Jordan's crib admiring his son. His thoughts drifted. He wondered if his dad had ever stood over his crib admiring and appreciating him. *Unlikely*, he thought. He couldn't picture his dad being sentimental over much; it wasn't a side of his dad that he ever saw.

He was probably sentimental for his drinking buddies. I can imagine them crying in their beer together. He must have used it all up before he came home, that's for sure. Whenever he came home drunk, all he did was spew contempt.

Contempt, that was what Paul felt toward his dad now. When he was younger, it was fear; when he became an adolescent, it was hatred. Paul's feelings had mellowed to contempt through the years because his dad was gone and unable to continue sinning against him.

Saldu had been standing by Hael watching Paul's tender side expressing itself toward his son. They were enjoying the intimate scene; Hael pulled his flute and played a lullaby. When Paul's thoughts switched to his childhood wounds, their ministry did, too.

Paul couldn't remember a time in his life when his dad wasn't a drunk. But Saldu and Hael knew it didn't happen until Paul was three and a half, when the family business started to falter. Paul's dad, Wilson, had taken over the family clothing store from his father, who constantly pressured Wilson to perform. Wilson had wanted desperately to be a mechanic. When he was just 16, he saved the money he earned from working in the family store and bought a 1936 two-door Ford coup that wouldn't run. He overhauled the engine, replaced some parts, and proudly drove that car for the next six years. He loved the hands-on aspect; he loved puttering, getting greasy, and figuring things out by trial and error.

When he was a senior in high school, he broached the subject that he might not want to follow his dad in the family business. His dad pitched such a fit that he never brought it up again. He always resented the clothing store. When a new shopping center was built on the town's outskirts, most of the downtown customers were pulled away, and Wilson watched the numbers steadily deteriorate. He hated the fact that he was going to be the one to kill the family business. It would become his legacy. Emotional pain always seeks pleasure, or what it perceives as pleasure. That's when he started going from the business to the bar and then home.

Before that, Wilson had been a caring, involved father. He did indeed stand over Paul's crib admiring his son. It was Wilson who coaxed Paul to take his first steps and Wilson who insisted on having a family portrait taken every year, at least for the first three years.

Saldu placed his hand over Paul's heart. He could feel the anointing surging through his hand into Paul's spirit. He spoke softly, "Receive this, Paul, really receive it: It wasn't you your father was mad at; it was himself, and it was his own father. Unfortunately, it just spilled out on everyone else who was around. Once the spirit of Addiction trapped your dad with alcohol, it was a downhill ride, an open invitation for Anger and Rage and other bad spirits to join in. Your father was ensnared by evil, and it spilled onto everyone he was around, but mostly his family. As a child you were a helpless victim with no protection. But you didn't deserve that. You deserved better. You were a beautiful, wonderful, worthy child created in God's image to run and play and laugh and be loved. Father cried many tears. Every night you cried yourself to sleep, He cried, too. It was not His plan for your father to become a drunk." A murky haze of deception started to lift.

Saldu pulled his flaming sword. "Receive the Love of the Father for you. Feel His unconditional love. He chose you before the foundation of the world, and His thoughts toward you are more than the sand on the seashore.[2] Even in your sin and brokenness, you are a source of joy to Him, just like Jordan, in his immaturity, is a source of joy for you. Receive," said Saldu as he tried to plunge the sword into Paul's heart and spirit. It wouldn't penetrate.

Saldu dropped his head to his chest, *Still the wall of unforgiveness.* "Paul, listen, being in unforgiveness moves you out of the fold. Sheep don't survive well without the shepherd's loving care. You're putting yourself at great peril by being on your own. You're moving into the same territory your dad did."

"If humans only knew how bitterness and unforgiveness cut them off from Father, they wouldn't be able to repent fast enough," said Hael.

The next morning after breakfast, Paul stayed to play with Jordan, giving him a rambunctious piggyback ride. Jordan squealed in delight. Kathy loved watching Paul play with Jordan and threw back her head, laughing at Paul's imitation of a horse's whinny.

As Paul was getting ready to leave, Kathy commented, "It says here in *The Gazette* that Sarah is in the hospital. She apparently fell and broke her hip. What a shame."

"Yes, that's too bad."

"And...."

"And, what?"

"Well, you're her pastor. Aren't you going to go visit her?"

"She hasn't been attending here for a long time. She's probably with the Baptists or somewhere else."

The look that Kathy shot him made him squirm. It was like she could prod his conscience through telepathy or something.

"Maybe I'll stop and see her; that's the best I can say right now. Ever since she came by the church and tried to tell me...." He stopped abruptly. He'd forgotten he purposely didn't share that story with Kathy.

"What?"

"Nothing. Forget I mentioned it. I'm late. Gotta go," he said as he ran out the door, grimacing at his error.

He felt like a creep for ducking out, and he felt bad for not telling Kathy about Sarah stopping by the church. It's just that he knew she would take it seriously enough to pray about it, and he really didn't want that.

He passed the hospital on his way to the church but had no intention of stopping. *The farther away I get from Sarah the better I feel.*

You could be a blessing to her today, whispered Saldu.

"*No way,*" screeched Unforgiveness. "*Keep your distance.*"

210

He put his leather folder down on his desk and plopped into his chair. *How could the day start out so good and in a matter of seconds turn bad? If only I would have left one minute earlier, before Kathy read that paragraph in the paper.*

He picked up the phone to check his voice mail. He flinched. *How can I have 27 messages?* That's more than he usually received in a month. What he didn't know was that the older adults had also organized the "Call the Pastor Phone Protest." The messages ranged from cordial and polite with people leaving their names, to several anonymous, angry callers who even used profanity. Larry McBride rambled on for a full three minutes, or there probably would have been a few more callers before the mailbox had filled up.

His day was taking a fast nosedive. *What else can go wrong?*

Kathy had split her thoughts between Sarah being stuck in the hospital with a broken hip and her curiosity over what sounded like a confrontation she had with Paul. She felt bad for Sarah. She perceived her as a kind of crazy old loner who probably didn't have much of a support group. Kathy toyed with the thought of visiting Sarah herself. Then she dismissed the idea because she felt her ulterior motive might be to try to get information on Sarah's meeting with Paul. All morning she wrestled with whether she should go. Finally she felt like she heard a yes from the Lord. *Lord,* she prayed, *Help me to go with Sarah's best interest at heart and not to satisfy some curiosity of my own.*

She dropped Jordan off at Mary's and then headed to the hospital. She prayed for Sarah all the way. When she entered the hospital room, the first thing she noticed was Sarah reading the Bible and various devotional guides and religious books stacked beside the bed. The second thing she noticed was that there were no flowers. She made a mental note to call the church secretary and have her order some.

"Hello," she said, approaching Sarah's bed. "I'm Kathy Reynolds, Pastor Paul's wife."

Sarah's face brightened immediately. She had prayed for them so much that there was a special place for them in her heart, almost like they were family members she never saw.

"Hello. Please sit down."

"Thanks," said Kathy, scooting the chair toward the front of the bed. "Well, what happened?"

"I'm afraid the details are too embarrassing. Let's just say I fell and broke my hip and leave it at that," said Sarah with a chagrined look.

Kathy relaxed. She immediately felt drawn to Sarah and she had no idea why.

They talked chitchat for a while: therapy, hospital food, hospital gowns, and pain medicine.

Kathy was at first pleased when Sarah asked about Jordan, but then she remembered that Paul had been concerned. *I can't believe she has some kind of fixation on Jordan; she just seems like the grandmotherly type.* Kathy considered herself fairly discerning when it came to people, and she had been immediately at ease around Sarah so she dismissed the thought.

"I notice you have a lot of reading material. I hope the days go fast for you."

"I'm looking forward to catching up on my praying. Especially my prayer walking."

"I'm sorry, I don't understand. It doesn't look like you'll be walking, at least for a while."

"I can prayer walk in my mind. I've done it so much that I can visualize every house. It's even better this way. I used to be worn out after I walked four blocks, but now, when I finish, I can go around again," she said with a smile, pointing to her head.

"Ask her 'How long she's been prayer walking,'" said Valoe.

"I started just about the time that you moved here," replied Sarah. Valoe dropped the revelation into Kathy's mind.

"Did you pray for us, in front of our house?"

"Yes, you were on my regular route. Sometimes I walked morning and evening, and some times just morning. On days that I didn't walk, I always prayed for your family. I received a specific word from the Lord that I was supposed to do that."

Kathy could feel her eyes watering. She was deeply touched and equally grieved by the way Paul had accused Sarah of being a lunatic. *All the time she was fervently praying for us.*

"Sarah, may I pray for you before I go?" She reached out and took her hand.

CHAPTER 31

"I don't have to attend every argument I'm invited to."

Unknown

"Anger is a bad counselor."

French Proverb

Paul was shuffling papers on his desk just to have something to do so he could avoid going home. The secretary was gone; so was the janitor; it was almost 7:30. "I guess if I don't go home soon, she'll have two things to be mad about." He collected his papers and lumbered toward the door.

He pulled up in front of the house and sat in the car for a while. He felt like a kid who had crayoned the walls and now mom had seen it. Why hadn't he just told Kathy about Sarah's word? He already had Sarah pegged as crazy so maybe Kathy wouldn't have taken it too seriously. He was kicking himself now. He slouched into the house and tried to pretend nothing was wrong. *Let her make the first move.*

Kathy had been upset all day that Paul had purposely concealed some sort of information from her. She had been praying that she could share her hurt and frustration in a way that he could understand. She was also praying that she wouldn't fly off the handle. She felt like she was pretty much under control—until she heard the key in the lock, and then she wanted to run to the doorway and unload. She took a few deep breaths and decided to let him make the first move. After all, he was the one who needed to apologize.

"Hi, Hon, sorry I'm a little late."

"No problem. Dinner in five minutes. Get Jordan."

"OK."

Paul was thinking, *She didn't say anything about Sarah, and she seems to be in an OK mood. Maybe I'm off the hook.*

Kathy was thinking, *He didn't say anything about Sarah; he's such a weasel.*

They sat down to dinner, said an obligatory prayer, and started eating. The silverware against the plates was the only noise. Finally Paul broke the silence, "What did you do today honey?"

"Not much," she said nonchalantly, "some laundry, fixed dinner, played with Jordan. Oh, I almost forgot," her tone turned sarcastic, "I visited Sarah in the hospital." That stopped Paul in mid-bite. His defensiveness overtook him, "I can't believe you went all the way to the hospital and pretended to care about a complete stranger, someone you don't even know, just to try to milk information out of her. That's pretty low, disguising your fact-finding trip under the guise of ministry."

Kathy thought, *Ha, I've got him now.* She paused for a moment to compose herself. "For your information, I didn't go to the hospital to try to get information out of Sarah. I went because she is a church member and I doubted that *you* would visit her. I didn't even bring up whatever happened between you two." She was trying not to, but she was feeling smug.

"What happened anyway?"

"She tried to give me a prophetic word," mumbled Paul.

"And what was the word she gave you?"

Paul shrugged, "Nothing really," he said, trying to sound laid-back. "She came to my office one day and tried to tell me that God had shown her that

I was supposed to take a part-time job as chaplain at the new jail and that we were supposed to minister there together." He paused briefly. "See, it's a ridiculous word; the woman is half crazy. She has this fixation about me any-way; she just wants me to go to the jail so I can be with her. I saw through her word immediately."

"Well, I don't think she's crazy, but I can't speak to whether the word is accurate or not. I guess you could always just make a fleece. Ask God to have them offer you the job if it's His will."

"Well, I think she's crazy and," he mumbled the next words, "they al-ready offered me the job."

She jumped to her feet, "THEY WHAT? And you didn't tell me that, either?"

"Hold on. It's not like it seems. They offered me the job before Sarah gave me the word. I didn't even consider it. It would have taken up more family time. It didn't seem like it was from the Lord at all. I didn't purposely hide it from you; it was just a nonissue. I immediately forgot about it."

"Well, now what do you think?"

"The same thing I thought then. I don't take words from crazy ladies about my employment. That I got offered the job was merely a coincidence. I'm one of the local pastors. They probably were calling off a list, and when I said no, they called the next pastor. I'm sure they have someone by now. Can we just give it a rest?"

"No, we can't give it a rest. I have more to say. I visited with Sarah, and I don't think she's crazy at all."

"Oh really? How do you explain her stalking our house—?"

"Will you stop saying that! She wasn't stalking! She was prayer walking. She prayer walks the neighborhood at least once a day, if not twice. She prays for us a lot. She said the Lord put it on her heart when we moved here."

"Right, you can say that the Lord put us on her heart. I still call it an unhealthy fixation."

"I'm telling you, she prayer walks, and that's why she was pacing up and down in front of our house."

"OK, so she was prayer walking. She's still done lots of other crazy things. She sold her land to the jail instead of the church."

"That's her prerogative, and I don't see that that makes her crazy. Maybe they offered her a very good price. I think you should at least see if the job at the jail is still available."

"No, I'm called to the church. I'm not going to go chasing other jobs."

"But can't you at least call and see if it's available? If it's not, then at least you won't have to wonder if you missed God."

"*I'm* not the one who is wondering," he said in a sarcastic tone.

"Well if you call then maybe I won't be wondering."

"You don't have a right to tell me how to run my ministry. I'm not calling and that's final."

"But we used to be partners—"

"I said no, and that's final."

"You're so controlling. Who died and made you king?"

"I'm not controlling. I'm just right. Why aren't you submissive?" At that verbal jab, Valoe rested his hands on Kathy's shoulders. "Don't return evil for evil."

She took a deep breath to control herself. "When you come home, you don't even communicate with me any more. We're like two people living single in the same house. We just don't connect. You don't even have time for Jordan. Where are you, physically and emotionally?"

"I resent it that I have to come home to your badgering cross examinations. Who do you think you are? I need to be able to relax in my own home, and I need to be able to run my ministry the way God tells me."

Paul tossed and turned on the couch that night.

≪≪≪

Sarah had been in the hospital a week, and in her mind that was seven days too long. Therapy was slow, tedious, and painful. The therapist, Janet, came to her bed and helped her work her leg and foot. Once a day she was transported by wheelchair to physical therapy. She was trying to walk, holding on to parallel bars. Janet always encouraged Sarah as she held her up with a belt circling her mid section. Progress was slow. Of course, the Parkinson's made it worse.

The caseworker from social services had come by and discussed temporary facilities with Sarah. She'd need to be totally cared for the next five or six weeks. The only place offering that was the Manor, unless she wanted to be transported to Mt. Peilor, but she didn't know anyone there.

The Manor had three levels of care for their residents. The first was assisted living. This was a small apartment where a person lived independently, but the staff did the laundry, cleaning, and meals. All the residents dined together. The next option was where Sarah would start, the temporary wing. She needed 100 percent care, but most people there were expected to recover and move on or go to the third level, which was skilled nursing. This was the nursing home. Nobody ever wanted to go there; nobody ever went home from there. That was home until the end.

Social services had been very adamant about Sarah's options. First, living at home by herself was not an option. If she recovered fully, they recommended she hire someone to live with her or that she move into the independent living facility at the Manor. If she didn't recover fully, they recommended the skilled unit.

Sarah was praying fervently about her living arrangements and about the prisoners that she was unable to visit. She talked Barbara into going to the jail to explain to the inmates that Sarah hadn't abandoned them. "One more thing, please swing by Jamie's Bakery and pick up eight dozen cookies. I had to give up on Slice 'N' Bake cookies, and these cookies are the best. Get five dozen chocolate chip, and one dozen each of peanut butter, snicker doodles, and oatmeal. And get two of the oatmeal without nuts. Spike loves oatmeal, but is allergic to nuts. Oh, and get a cinnamon roll for Toothless Ed. Thanks."

Barbara hung up the phone chuckling. "What a lover."

Barbara wouldn't have turned down Sarah's request for anything, but she was very anxious when she pulled up in front of the jail by herself. She'd prayed all the way there and didn't slow down as she approached the entrance. She explained to the first guard she met that she had a message from Sarah for the inmates. He immediately led her to the main corridor and shouted, "Listen everyone, this is Barbara and she has a message from Sarah."

Never one for public speaking, especially to a group of male inmates, Barbara stammered and stuttered, all the while looking at her shoes. She finally communicated that Sarah had broken her hip. She added that Sarah missed seeing everyone and she was still praying for each of them and would try to come back as soon as she could, but it might be five or six weeks.

Then she moved from cell to cell offering cookies. *I hope they can't see my heart pounding through my blouse.* When she looked to the left, down the row of cells, all she could see were muscular biceps extended between the steel bars. She had to keep telling herself they were waiting for her cookies, not for her throat.

Most of the inmates sent greetings back to Sarah; many commented that they would pray for her as well. Barbara had a special message for Will. After locating him, she told him, "Sarah said she's praying for you and she hopes to get back soon to see you. She also said that she's suspending the two cookie limit for you today—you're to have three."

Will grabbed three cookies and grunted, but Barbara noticed that just for a second, he looked like he might tear up. Then he turned his back and sat down.

By the time Barbara finished, she was much more at ease. The inmates seemed genuinely concerned about Sarah and overall had been very polite. She surprised herself by walking back to the middle and asking, "Who wants cookies tomorrow?"

It was unanimous.

Barbara couldn't wait to report back to Sarah. After being so discouraged about her limited living options, she knew Sarah would enjoy hearing this good news. She turned onto Old Highway 3 and headed for the hospital.

CHAPTER 32

"At the center of all sin is pride. Self-glorification is the solitary goal of pride. That's the motive and ultimate purpose of pride—to rob God of legitimate glory and to pursue self-glorification, contending for supremacy with Him. The proud person seeks to glorify himself and not God, thereby attempting in effect to deprive God of something only He is worthy to receive."

C.J. Mahaney[1]

In Barbara's excitement, she burst in the door, startling Sarah, who dropped her sippy cup and spilled grape juice down the front of her hospital gown. They both had a good laugh about it. "I just got back from the jail, and I had to tell you about it. I've been a nervous wreck all day, and the closer I drove to the jail the more nervous I got. Do you remember you told me that the first time you left the jail you had sweated so much that your shirt was soaked at the armpits?"

"I sure do," she said chuckling at the memory.

"Well, mine was soaked through before I even got to the bakery." They shared another laugh.

"How'd it go?"

"Great, once I started passing out the cookies. Almost everyone was receptive. Everyone took cookies and Sarah, most of the inmates said *they would pray for you*. They seemed genuinely concerned."

"That's so nice to hear. I sure miss my regular visits there."

"And, I'm going back tomorrow!" Barbara said with enthusiasm.

Nothing could have pleased Sarah more. She gave Barbara a few more messages for specific inmates and filled her in on which inmates were already Christians. "Start off by getting to know them. Then you can have a few encouraging experiences before tackling some of the harder cases."

"Wow, spoken like a pro."

Sarah smiled. "By the way, did you give William my message?"

"Yes, he grunted appreciatively."

"Grunted, eh, well it sounds like you're making more progress than I did. From William, I'd consider a grunt to be a whole conversation."

Paul arrived at the church extra early on Sunday. He knew the day would be grueling, but didn't know exactly what to expect. He went to his office and prayed. *God, would You thwart the opposition to Your plan? Let me have wisdom to say the right things and let my message communicate today.*

The knock on his door made him jump. It was Mike, who had come early to lend moral support. "Well, Mike, what am I up against today?"

"At the very least there will be a petition. I don't know where the plan to withhold the tithes is."

"Mike, I'm going to hit the issue of withholding the tithe in the sermon today. Can we change the order of the service and take up the offering after I preach? I think we'll get a better response financially."

"Sure."

The petition was circulated in the older adult's Sunday school class and everyone signed it. Wilma even made a joke that set everyone laughing.

"Look," she said while writing her name twice as big as the other signatures, "I'm John Hancock."

Paul hadn't dared enter their Sunday school class to confront them about the petition. That was clearly their domain, and a petition didn't mean anything anyway to the government of the church. Anything official required a vote.

Paul was sitting on the front row when they filed in together. He almost laughed; they looked like a retired military unit. Everyone marched together, single file, not looking to the right or the left, and then they all sat together in the center section, filling rows three through seven.

Paul felt like he was on trial, and they were certainly a hanging jury if he ever saw one. No one cracked a smile. Many sat with their arms crossed in front of their chests.

No offering was taken during the special music, and when it was finished, Paul stood behind the lectern.

"How many Pentecostals does it take to change a light bulb?" He paused for effect then answered, "Ten; one to change the bulb and nine to rebuke the spirit of Darkness." He got a few laughs from the younger crowd, but rows three through seven still looked like they were sucking lemons.

He began, "I know that there are concerns among some of the members over the proposed building plan—"

"Amen to that," shouted Floyd Fenley. His wife blushed and elbowed him in the side. His comment got a bigger laugh than Paul's joke.

"—but I'm sure we can come to an agreement that will satisfy the majority of the church. Tonight we will have a meeting to discuss the plan. There will be an open microphone, and I invite all of you to come and make your opinions known. We, the elders and I, want to hear everyone's input. Please come."

Now, put this in your theological pipe and smoke it, thought Paul as he began preaching about the tithe and how it was holy unto God. He didn't come right out and say he was preaching for the benefit of the older member's boycott, but everyone knew. When he ended, he called the ushers forward and sent them up and down the aisles with the golden plates. To his surprise, every person on rows four through seven dropped in their tithe envelopes. *Yes! Yes! They were reachable; they were reasonable. They heard my message and changed their minds.*

Later that afternoon Mike called to tell Paul that inside all those envelopes were tithe checks with a big "VOID" written across the front. Some of them had scrawled notes in the memo or the back saying that when the building campaign was dropped they would resume paying their tithes. And some of the notes were not even Christian in content.

Paul was crushed. He hung up the phone and went to his office. Not only was the boycott still in full swing, but his preaching had failed to sway even one opposing member. This pulled up all his old rejection issues. Kathy was playing with Jordan and hadn't even heard the phone ring. Paul passed the afternoon battling demonic mood swings from anger at Kathy for not being sensitive to his needs, to self-pity at having so many church members who were jerks.

Physical therapy was grueling for Sarah. Not only was it physically painful, but even worse was the psychological pressure. She knew she had to do well if she ever wanted to walk again.

Tomorrow they were transferring her to the temporary wing at the Manor to continue her therapy. She groaned as she pointed her right foot, then flexed. "Eight more, you're doing fine," said Janet, her physical therapist. Sarah looked toward the colorful, encouraging poster on the wall, gritted her teeth, and continued.

So far in the six days that she'd done therapy, she had been unable to stand on her own, even with the assistance of the parallel bars. *When did I get so weak? I'm on a downhill slide.*

It was nearly impossible for Sarah to get comfortable in bed. She didn't have the strength to roll herself over. *If I stretch out, my right side lets up a little, but my leg hurts. If I try to curl up on my side my leg eases some, but the pressure on my side makes the whole thing throb. It seems like there should be one position where everything stops hurting, if only for a moment, but I'll be darned if I can find it.*

The doctors and therapists had all been encouraging, in an effort to help her, they increased her Parkinson's medicine. But inside she constantly wrestled with the fear she wouldn't walk again. *It was hard enough just getting around with my walker before I broke my hip. These constant tremors made it hard to grasp anything. My hands almost seem useless.* And although she hadn't told anyone, she started to notice that swallowing was sometimes a problem.

She was shuttled between her hospital room and physical therapy in a wheelchair. The thought of spending the rest of her life in one of those was almost unbearable. She tried to put on a happy face during the day with the staff, but at night Sarah would pray to the Lord and weep, crying out for mercy and strength until she fitfully dozed.

The next morning, Jan gave her a sponge bath, helped her brush her teeth, fixed her hair, dressed her, and packed her books and belongings. She wheeled her to Barbara's waiting car, where one of the male nurses picked her up and gently placed her inside. Pain shot down her leg and she grimaced. "Sorry," he said. Then Sarah watched as he folded the wheelchair and placed it in the back seat. Just knowing it was following her to the Manor made her cringe. She wondered if it would carry her the rest of her life. She turned her head and stared out the window so Barbara wouldn't see her tears.

Barbara turned on her blinker and pulled into the Manor driveway. She looked at Sarah. "You know, if you continue to do well in therapy this is only temporary. We can find someone to live with you, and you can move back home in a few months. I've been checking with some home health agencies. It's quite expensive, but with the money from the ground, you can certainly afford it."

"The money is…" she bit her lip. *Jesus*, she prayed silently, *Help me to trust You, and help me to have a good attitude. I've never felt so scared and helpless in my life.*

Barbara parked the car outside the glass double doors and disappeared inside. In a few minutes she came out accompanied by two male aides.

"Hi, I'm Wayne."

"And I'm Gary. We're going to lift you from the car and put you in your wheelchair." The phrase *your wheelchair* was almost more than Sarah could bear. She teared up, but managed to nod and put her arms around Wayne and Gary's necks to help with the lift.

Gary grabbed her suitcase and held the door, and Wayne wheeled her inside the lobby. Barbara followed behind. Everything was like she remembered it. There was a lounge to her right, with a television blaring. Four people in wheelchairs were watching television, and there were others on couches, most with walkers parked in front of them. Several were asleep and slouched uncomfortably in their seats.

Wayne pushed Sarah by more patients in wheelchairs. "Hey everybody," shouted Gary. "This is our new resident, Ms. Sarah. Everyone say 'hi.'" Several patients looked up as Sarah passed by.

"It's an hour 'til lunch, but people start gathering early," said Gary pointing to the dining room on the left. Sarah looked toward the long corridor they were approaching. When Wayne turned the corner, she flinched as the smell of urine hit her in the face.

"You're going to be in a double room, but now there's no one else in it," said Wayne. Halfway down the corridor, he turned left into room 120. Sarah's eyes scanned the stark room. Yellow walls, a small sink, a door to the bathroom, and two beds, each with a small dresser. The only things on the walls were a large clock and a bulletin board listing the date and the nurse on duty.

Barbara read Sarah's mind and volunteered, "I'll swing by your house and pick up a few things that we can put up on the walls."

When Barbara returned several hours later, she had to use a cart to transport all the things she'd brought. All Sarah's worship CDs, a CD player, more books and devotional guides, pictures from around her house, the afghan from the couch, her love letters, and the big world map that Sarah covered with pushpins every time she prayed for a different city. She plugged in the CD player, put in five worship CDs, and pushed "repeat all." "I'll change them whenever I come, but I think that having worship music constantly will help your mood," Barbara said.

"Also," she added with excitement, "I saw this in the drugstore the other day, and it made me think of you." She held up a colorful world globe, put it on Sarah's nightstand, and plugged it in. "See, it's a night light and it rotates. If you can't sleep you can pray for the countries as they move past you."

In bed that night Sarah tried to slightly adjust her body to alleviate as much pain as she could. She held the afghan close to her, like a toddler would his blankie. She stroked the wool. *Lord, am I going to spend the rest of my life in the Manor? When I die, will they find my stiff body under this pink chenille bedspread?*

CHAPTER 33

"The proud man counts his newspaper clippings, the humble man his blessings."

Fulton J. Sheen[1]

The tension in the sanctuary was obvious. The older folks sat together again on the center pews. The rest of the members fanned out on the left and right sides. The crowd was mostly older members. Most of the nondisgruntled folks had stayed home, with the exception of the elders.

Paul called the meeting to order with prayer and introduced Mike as tonight's master of ceremonies. They had both agreed that Paul shouldn't lead the meeting, but could surely comment. Mike listed a few ground rules and then opened the microphone to the audience. After a few minutes, Wilma made her way to the front.

"Well, it's no secret where I stand on this church building plan. I'm not in favor of anything that would cause us to leave our building. This church was built in 1907, and most of the older members, including myself, have grown up here. This is home to us. We were baptized here, married here, have seen our kids married here, and many of us have even buried loved ones in the adjoining cemetery. The only way you'll get me to leave is in a box." She wiped a tear from her eye and sat down to applause.

Floyd wanted to know what would happen to the building if a new one was built.

John Williams was concerned about debt. "This church is paid for. If I'm not mistaken, we had the mortgage burnin' in 1950, seven years early. We took a special offering and paid it off. We own it free and clear. If the church goes and gets itself in debt up to its ears and then a recession hits, we'd be in a terrible bind. What would we do then? We'd owe hundreds of thousands of dollars that we wouldn't have. I say we keep the one that's paid for and run two or even three services if needed."

One of the elders stood to defend the plan. "I think the Lord is bringing this increase, and I don't think it's going to stop. We need to be prepared for the future, to take the next step. I understand the sentimental attachment to the building, but we can't let sentiment stand in the way of what the Lord is calling us to."

After going back and forth for the next hour, Mike felt it was about time to bring things to an end. Floyd stood and interrupted him. "If I'm not mistaken, and I know I'm not, we can propose a vote on any topic as long as we give at least three days' notice. So, I propose a vote on Wednesday night."

"That's true Floyd. Do I have a second to Floyd's proposal?" asked Mike.

"You don't know what I'm proposing yet," replied Floyd.

"I assumed it was a vote on the building campaign."

"No. I propose that we vote on whether to keep Pastor Paul. I think I speak for all the older members that we don't want to lose our church, and we would encourage Paul to take those who want to build and leave. That would satisfy everyone."

Mike stammered and stuttered, but nothing intelligent would come out. Finally he asked, "Floyd, are you sure you want to make that proposal?"

"If he doesn't, I will" said Joe Kemper.

Mike knew the church's bylaws, and he knew they were within their rights, as long as there was three days' notice. He was trapped, and he knew it. The frustration in his voice showed when he asked, "Do I have a second on this proposal?" Everyone in the middle section raised his or her hand.

"Let's vote. All in favor of voting on Wednesday night whether to retain Pastor Paul, please raise your right hand." A quick glance at the center section and he knew the motion had passed. "All opposed same sign." Most of the hands on the sides, but not enough. "The motion passes. We'll vote by secret ballot Wednesday night. Only church members, not just attendees, may vote. Meeting adjourned."

Mike glanced at Paul, still seated on the front row. He could tell Paul was fighting back tears. Kathy was seated beside him with her arm around his shoulder. "*Lord*," she silently prayed, *What are You trying to tell us?*

Barbara left the church and drove straight to the Manor. "I've got some news you might want to pray about," she said holding on to Sarah's hand. "The older members at the church want to vote Pastor Paul out."

"They want to vote him out?" repeated Sarah in disbelief. "Why would they want to do that? The church is growing."

"They hate the building campaign. They don't want to leave the church. Too many memories."

"Oh, that poor man! Is being voted out good or bad? If he's not at the church he might take the job as chaplain, or he might just move away. Oh, Lord, give him wisdom."

CHAPTER 34

"Pride is like the veins in our body. Pride is like our blood. It flows from the heart. It is the core and fiber of our being. The only way we can get away from it is to get a transfusion from Jesus. To be mortally wounded by the Cross. Then to rest in the tomb letting the life of Christ flow into our veins, replacing what was once there."

Aaron Pierson[1]

Sarah wasn't making much progress in physical therapy, and although she'd initially been assigned to the main dining room, she'd been reassigned to the dining room in the back where residents require help to feed themselves. The tremors in her hands had increased substantially.

Wretched spirits of Depression and Discouragement had come sniffing around and latched on to Sarah again. With each passing hour, her attitude sank lower.

"How're ya doin' today Ms. Sarah?" said a food service worker, setting her plate down in front of her and pulling a bib over her head. Sarah tried to force a smile, but it just wouldn't come. She looked around the table at the other residents, many who looked on the verge of death at any minute.

Some were unable to talk; they could only grunt. Others were partially paralyzed, the result of a stroke. Some were tied in their wheelchair with restraints so they wouldn't topple out.

At least I have regular food, not that ground-up mush, she thought, groping for something positive. Several aides were already beginning to feed the other residents. Unwilling to admit that she belonged with this group, she picked up her glass of milk, but it slipped from her hand and spilled across the table. The aide frowned, but forced a cheery voice as she jumped to wipe the spill dripping off the table on to another resident's lap.

"Now Ms. Sarah, you know you're here 'cause you can't feed yourself. I have to help you. You just wait till I get over there."

She felt her face flush. She wanted to run, but that was certainly not an option. She tucked her chin and did her best to hide. Finally the aide arrived, "OK Sarah, open your mouth. Doesn't this meatloaf smell good this evening?"

"Umm, meatloaf," mocked Despair. "You get to be patronized and humiliated like this three times a day until you die. You've outlived your usefulness, and now you're just a burden."

Later, lying in bed, physically weak and in pain, a tear trickled down Sarah's cheek. *My life is coming to an end. I can't take care of myself. I don't know if I'll ever walk again or leave this horrid place.*

"Sarah, you must praise Him through your trials and tribulations," said Malta. The music that came forth at creation has never ceased. But like a human's inability to hear a high-pitched dog's whistle, you lack the spiritual senses necessary to hear the rocks, hills, and trees constantly cry out praises to God. When a human sings praises, heavenly residents immediately join in. A full heavenly orchestra accompanies you, once again, unheard by human ears.

At this encouragement, she began by an act of her will to praise Him in song.

"Every blessing You pour out I'll turn back to praise…." Thousands in Heaven joined in. "And when the darkness closes in, Lord, still I will say, 'Blessed be the name of the Lord, Blessed be Your name.'"

Unbeknownst to her, a celestial orchestra was accompanying her praise, and eight other worship angels had joined her in the bedroom. They carried absorbed glory from constant worship around the throne and radiated that brilliant light. Their voices harmonized with hers in other-worldly beauty. The music ascended to the throne room where heavenly residents danced with angels and sang the next line, "Blessed be the name of the Lord, Blessed be Your glorious name."[2]

Sarah stopped singing and massaged her hip under the covers. "Oh, what's the use? What difference does this make anyway? I'm just not into worship today." All the angels abruptly stopped singing and faced her.

"Don't stop. Press through."

"Sing; praise Him!"

"The sacrifice of praise offered from a place of discouragement is the highest and sweetest praise of all," said one of the worshiping angels, bending low over Sarah's bed.

One of the angels started humming the "Hallelujah Chorus." The angels around the bed immediately lifted their hands and faces toward Heaven. Sarah half-heartedly joined in, humming and stumbling over the words.

The heavenly voices gained momentum. She felt energy come over her, which she could not explain. She sang, "And He shall reign for ever and ever...," and tried to flail her feeble arms as if she was directing a choir, bringing in singers, beckoning others to sing softer. The unseen angel choir gathered around her bed and followed her musical cues. Their voices, directed by Sarah, came once again rolling tumultuously into the throne room like a tidal wave of pure joy. Handel, along with thousands of others, bowed low, worshiping and weeping softly in front of the throne.

After singing the song several times, Sarah fell asleep exhausted, as the shining globe rotated quietly on her side table. The angels continue singing, dancing, rejoicing in Jesus, and rejoicing in Sarah's decision to press through in praise.

"They just don't realize that when they praise, they're never alone," Joel said to his heavenly companions.

A huge, glimmering worship angel played his flute by her bed, and Sarah's tense body relaxed slightly. His cohort spoke over her, "Sarah, you don't realize that all of nature constantly sings praises to our God. The roar of the sea, the 'caw, caw, caw' of the crow all ascend to the throne as 'Holy, Holy, Holy.' It resounds in the throne room as praise from creature to Creator. The flowers, the hills, and even the rocks cry out day and night, 'Holy, Holy, Holy.' Your praises ascend to the throne room, filling it, echoing off the walls, vibrating through the crystal river flowing from Father's throne. Your praises are heard in the throne room, and your praises make a difference."

"I wish Sarah could see that whenever she chooses to praise, she's connected to the unending, global-celestial worship cycle," said the flute playing angel, stopping to gently run his large hand across Sarah's cheek.

"Her time on earth is coming to an end," said Malta. This announcement sent the angels back into a fit of frenzied activity—dancing, singing, cheering, leaping, laughing, worshiping—angelic pandemonium!

"I can't wait," said Malta, "to carry her to her eternal home. I wish it were tonight—"

"Yes," interrupted Joel, "the end. It's my favorite part of the job. I love to see the faithful ones when they run into the waiting, open arms of Jesus."

"Sarah will be so astonished when she experiences His unfiltered, unconditional love. Imagine her amazement of His joy over her."

"Make it soon, Lord! Make it soon!" shouted Joel. This petition set off another round of celestial pandemonium.

CHAPTER 35

"If thou desire the love of God and man, be humble, for the proud heart, as it loves none but itself, is beloved of none but itself: the voice of humility is God's music, and the silence of humility is God's rhetoric."

Francis Quarles[1]

Paul also felt like his whole life was coming to an end. He and Kathy had been discussing the vote for three days. His demons of Pride, Respectability, and Selfish Ambition were working overtime. Also, being taunted by Fear and Rejection caused his moods to vary wildly at a moment's notice.

"Like I've said before honey, if you are voted out, then the Lord has something else for you. There is no one on earth who can stop His plans for your life. No one can thwart His plans."

"Even if they vote in my favor" said Paul, jumping up from the chair to pace in front of the mantle, "how can I minister effectively knowing that slightly less than half the congregation is in favor of me leaving? How can I proceed with my five-year plan if they are so dramatically opposed?"

"I'm so sorry that this plan that you're so excited about isn't working out, I know this is emotionally grueling for you. But try to put it in perspective; God is not up in Heaven wringing His hands over tonight's vote." She stood and held out her arms offering a hug, "OK?"

"How can you be so calm? Don't you know what's riding on this vote?" He turned his back to pace again.

"I know what's not riding on it—God's will for our lives. Whatever happens, whichever way it goes, God's hands are not tied."

Paul nodded, running his fingers through his hair, but he remained unconvinced. "It's 6:45, time to go," he said curtly.

While Kathy was protective of her husband and his feelings, she was not as emotionally invested in the church as Paul. As they drove, Kathy prayed silently, *Lord may Your will be done in our lives and for this church. I pray for unity of Spirit, and I ask that the enemy will not be able to use this event for his purposes.*

Paul prayed, *Lord let them keep me.*

As they walked together to the front pew, Paul remembered what Mike had said, "You can expect to see some new faces tonight. They are older members who rarely attend any more, but when something happens that's controversial, they run back and make their opinions known. Since they're still members, there's nothing we can do." Paul scanned the congregation to see how many reinforcements had been brought in. The church was packed. *Oh my gosh, it seems like I've never even met half these people.*

Mike called the meeting to order. He explained the reason for the assembly and what the voting procedure would be.

"The vote will be decided by a simple majority rule." After several questions from the members it was time.

"Paul, I need you to wait in your office please, until I call you." *Dead man walking*, whispered Discouragement to Paul as he self-consciously exited the sanctuary. Of course, Saldu was with him doing his best to encourage Paul in the Lord, but Paul wasn't listening. His ears were tuned to the deceptive spirits that regularly accompanied him.

"Who do these older members think they are? Do they run the church? Why can't they just cooperate?" spouted Self-Righteousness.

"Who will hire you if you get fired from your first church after just a few months?" asked the spirit of Fear.

"What a loser that would make you!" added Criticism.

The baskets were passed and each member took a pre-printed ballot. They merely needed to check the box next to "RETAIN PAUL REYNOLDS AS PASTOR" or "DISMISS PAUL REYNOLDS AS PASTOR." The mood was somber, both sides were convinced that they alone knew the Lord's will on this issue and that those opposed were hypocrites and sinners. The spirits of Faultfinding, Unforgiveness, Self-Righteousness, Selfish Ambition, Judgment, and Treachery were divided equally between both groups and circling the sanctuary like it was a choice buffet.

Sarah was in bed for the evening, but she wasn't sleeping. She knew the vote was starting, and she had purposed in her heart to pray for the Lord's will to be done. In fact, she'd been praying off and on since she heard about it. Her prayer was always the same, *"Jesus, I pray that Your perfect will would be done for the church and for Pastor Paul and his wonderful family. I pray against division, divisiveness, and strife between church members. I pray that You would transition Paul to the position as chaplain and bring the new person that You have for the church."* After praying for 20 minutes, she dozed off. The Parkinson's, plus the demands of physical therapy, had sapped what little energy she had.

The baskets were passed again, the ballots were collected, and the elders retreated to the fellowship hall to count the votes. Kathy had purposed in her heart that whatever happened, God's will for their lives would not be thwarted. She had made a decision that however the vote went, she would praise Him. *"God, our lives are in Your hands, and You may do with them what You want. I will trust You no matter how the decision comes back. God, please comfort Paul and let him have confidence in Your leadership, not his own."* Because of her attitude, she was able to receive the comfort that Valoe was imparting to her. That prayer enabled Valoe to easily dispose of a spirit of Fear trying to infiltrate Kathy's thoughts. Even though she was aware that half the congregation was staring at the back of her head thinking negative thoughts, she was truly experiencing God's peace that passes all understanding.[2]

Saldu was making less progress with his charge. Paul was pacing, sweating, even cursing under his breath, refusing to listen or be comforted. The black, crablike body of Self-Pity clung to Paul's shoulder and hissed, "This is just a conspiracy. This is a bunch of old people who need to die in the wilderness so God can bring the visionaries into the Promised Land." Saldu grimaced. He hated it when the enemy twisted God's precious Word for their benefit.

That's right, thought Paul, this is a great progressive plan for God's Kingdom, and these old people with no faith and no vision for the future are messing it up.

Saldu came close to Paul, and Self-Pity leapt off his shoulder to escape the angel's radiant glory. The oily spirit landed on the floor, baring his yellow fangs and hissing.

"Paul, you've forgotten that nothing can come your way that Father doesn't allow. Even what seems like a defeat to you becomes an opportunity that He can use for your good. You just need to trust Him instead of trying to get what you want by manipulating every situation."

Paul considered the thought, but if he was voted out, his pride couldn't handle it. The anticipation of facing the crowd and the humiliation was more than he thought he could stand. It played on all his insecurities and rejection issues from his past. The dark spirits were drawn to him again, feeding on his fear, and he was giving them his undivided attention. Saldu sighed and took a few steps back.

The vote was finally tallied; it had been recounted several times because it was so close. Paul was back on the front row with Kathy. Mike was behind the lectern with an unpleasant look on his face. "By a vote of 72 to 69 the church has voted to remove Paul as pastor. Meeting is adjourned."

CHAPTER 36

"While grace for salvation is free, building a store-house in Heaven is costly. It will cost us every day, all day long. As we extend ourselves, we run the race here in order to apprehend the prize of Heaven."

Shawn Bolz[1]

Breakfast, lunch, and dinner continued to be humiliating for Sarah. Learning to let others do things for her that she could no longer do for herself was harder than she'd ever imagined. Therapy wasn't progressing like the doctor had hoped, and although the staff hadn't said it yet, Sarah got the impression that unless the Lord healed her, she'd never walk again. She watched jealously as other patients moved slowly up and down the hall with the help of a walker.

The residents who dined at her table were in such poor health they could barely talk or even remember. She also resented how the staff patronized her. It made her feel like a stupid, incompetent child. She declined the offer to help put together a puzzle with some of the other residents. She couldn't work up the motivation to introduce herself or join in the activities, most of which she felt were beneath her. Her mood fluctuated wildly between gritting her teeth in an attempt to praise and outright despair.

"Miss Sarah," said the cheerful voice of the activities director, "We're watching a movie. Can I wheel you out there?"

"No, I think I'll pass."

"We're having popcorn; you'd better think it over."

"I just want to be by myself, thanks; but can you roll me in front of the sliding glass door? I do like the view out the back. Everything is so green. One more thing, can you hand me my glasses and Bible?" She let out a deep sigh of discouragement as she sat in her wheelchair watching the sun sink behind the trees. Joel looked at Malta. "You're the worshiper," he pulled his flaming sword in jest and pointed it at him, "Get something started." Malta played a melody on his flute and without even realizing it, Sarah began humming along.

The spirits of Discouragement, Despair, and Depression hissed toward Malta, then turned their attention to Sarah.

"Why should you praise Him? You're living in this old age home that reeks of urine. Is that how you deserve to end your life?"

The sun was disappearing below the tree line as Sarah stared out the window. A tear ran down her cheek.

"Hasn't He abandoned you?" whispered Despair. "Really, hasn't He?"

"Sarah," said Joel, "the more you praise, even when you don't feel like it, the more you will feel like it. It's a virtuous cycle. What you do as an act of your will, God graces to become a natural part of your life." Sarah stared into the twilight contemplating Joel's suggestion. Slowly she began nodding her head, then with more determination.

Malta was surprised when she blurted out, "As an act of my will, I will praise You. Whether You heal me or not, I will praise You. If I never get out of this wheelchair again, I will praise You. If I die in this horrid facility and never get to go home again, I will praise You." She raised her withered arms and began to sing.

Discouragement, Despair, and Depression were momentarily stunned, then fled the room shrieking. Angelic intervention wasn't needed; Sarah's confession had sent them away.

"That's my little warrior princess," beamed Joel. "Resist the devil and he will flee.[2] Sarah, your weapons are mighty against the enemy's kingdom. He is a defeated foe. He is under your feet. He only has the power you give him."

The three of them had a full-fledged worship service, and by the time Sarah finished singing, she actually felt joyful. *I haven't felt like this for so long. God, You are so good, even if my circumstances aren't what I'd like. Lord, I deserved Hell and only Hell; any goodness that has come this way in my earthly life is a bonus. Help me to have Your mind. You laid down Your deity, left Heaven's riches, and stepped into humanity and humbled yourself unto death on the cross for me. Amazing!*

Barbara called to tell Sarah the news. She prayed for Paul and his family, the church and the jail. Then she forced herself to pray in the Spirit while she read, even though she wondered if her prayers were really accomplishing much.

She had no way of knowing she was praying for the safety of an unsaved motorcycle rider in Tulsa, Oklahoma. Bob was traveling to Muskogee to visit his mother for the weekend. For her birthday he promised her he would attend church with her. It was planned that he would be convicted of his sins and accept the Lord, unless Satan could bring the glorious process to a grinding halt, which he was trying to do with a vengeance.

Under the influence of the monstrous spirit of Death, an inebriated driver was headed south driving a van. Bob was headed east. They were slated to meet at the next intersection. The inebriated driver would run the stop sign, crash into Bob, and take his life. Demons circled over the intersection like hungry buzzards, propelled by their leathery wings. Waiting—hoping— to carry away the soul of one driver, possibly both if they got lucky.

Sarah continues to pray in tongues for God to spare Bob's life, although she didn't know that. When Bob was a mile from the intersection, Sarah's mind begins to drift. She looks at the books on the bed and remembers that they are library books that need to be returned. *Who will I get to take them back for me? I hate to impose on Barbara. She does so much for me already."*

One half mile apart.

Maybe I'll just renew them again. I wonder how many times you can renew books? This will be the third time.

One quarter mile.

Sarah let go of the distraction and starts praying in tongues again. A thought popped into Bob's head: *I'm really thirsty; I should get something to drink…*

One eighth of a mile.

…but I hate to lose the time.

Another thought comes to him, *You've got to get gas anyway, just pull over now.*

Bob glanced at his gas gauge and hit his right-turn indicator. Sarah's weak petitions through the strength of the Holy Spirit were enough to thwart the forces of darkness.

At Maine Street and 22 highway, the van barreled through the stop sign. No one was there to land in the gnarled talons of the waiting demons.

Sarah stopped praying and said to herself, "Maybe I'll just buy the books; there are only three of them, anyway."

Sandy, the aide, came in to put her to bed.

"How are you tonight, Ms. Sarah?" She thought for a moment and knew her attitude was her choice. She decided to be positive.

"Well, now that you mention it, I'm great because I know that God loves me, and more than just loving me, He really likes me, and that makes me very happy."

"I wish I knew He liked me."

"Are you a Christian?"

"Yeah, but no matter how hard I try, I just can't seem to get my act to-gether. I've got too much sin in my life." She looked at Sarah briefly and then glanced away embarrassed. "I know He's always mad at me—with good reason."

As Sandy helped Sarah brush her teeth, use the toilet, get into her pajamas, and then to bed, she got to hear how God loves her too, even in her weakness.

"Sandy, don't let the devil lie to you. There are two kinds of people—the rebellious and the immature. Many times their lives look the same—they are both involved in sin—but the attitude of their heart is very different. And God always looks at the heart. Even when you're totally disgusted with yourself, God never counts you as a failure until you just flat give up and quit. The Bible says that the righteous fall seven times, but they get up each time.[3] God's mercy is new each morning, and His forgiveness is always there for His children who repent. Don't let the devil convince you that God is mad at you. He loves you even in your failure and immaturity. When you are overcome by sin, run to Jesus. He's Your only hope."

Sarah dozed off that night praying for Sandy to receive a revelation of God's love for her.

CHAPTER 37

*"Nothing sets a person so much out of the devil's
reach as humility."*

Jonathan Edwards[1]

Kathy slept well last night, but Paul hadn't slept at all. He'd been in his office, his emotions fluctuating between crying, sadness, rage, and blame. Saldu's efforts to encourage Paul to respond like Jesus were immediately dismissed. *"When He was reviled, did not revile in return; when He suffered, He did not threaten, but committed Himself to Him who judges righteously."*[2]

The fetid spirits were gaining ground. With each belief that Paul invested in their deceitful words, Saldu was hindered more. "Paul, trust God; don't blame man."

When the sun came up, it was not a happy day at the Reynolds' house. After trying for several hours to do everything she could to placate and encourage Paul, Kathy finally decided just to get out of his way. She put Jordan in the stroller and left for the park.

Valoe's help, combined with Kathy's willing spirit, enabled her to retain her peace and belief in God's plan for their lives.

"Paul's not in a good place spiritually," said Valoe. "He's not capable of seeing anyone else's needs but his own. If you expect anything from him, you'll be repeatedly disappointed. But even if things were going great for him, only one man can truly meet your deepest needs, Kathy, and His name is Jesus. You need to be turning to Him more and more for love, comfort, encouragement, and direction. He is truly your knight in shining armor; you are His beloved bride, and He can walk you through any trial or crisis. His mercy endures forever,[3] and He longs to keep you in peace during this tumultuous time."[4]

"Yes, Lord," prayed Kathy, "I know You are the only one who can fill my needs. Fill me from the inside; help me not to look to Paul or anything external for my satisfaction. I know that You are the only one who truly satisfies." A deep feeling of peace settled over her. Kathy prayed Psalm 34:18 for Paul, *"The Lord is close to the brokenhearted...."*

After playing hard at the park for several hours, Jordan tugged on Kathy's blouse and said, "Mommy, I hungry. Go to McRonalds?"

"I hungry too. OK, let's go."

Kathy and Jordan sat at a table next to a husband, wife, and two children. The children finished eating and left to play in the ball pit. "Mommy, I play there," said Jordan pointing.

As Jordan scampered off, Kathy rolled her eyes and commented to the couple, "Look at that, a few minutes ago he was totally exhausted. They must really pump those cows full of steroids," she said laughing.

"I'm Richard Walker and this is my wife Susie."

"My name is Kathy Reynolds."

"Are you by any chance the wife of the pastor at the Victory church?"

Kathy's heart sank. *How do I tactfully answer this?* "No, I mean yes. I am his wife, but he's not the pastor there anymore, as of last night."

"I'm sorry to hear that," said Susie.

"Actually, I'm not sorry to hear that at all," replied Richard. Susie glared at him like he'd lost his mind and like she wanted to give him a swift kick under the table.

"Mrs. Reynolds, I'm director at the jail, and I offered your husband a job as chaplain awhile back, and he turned me down. I have not been able to fill this position no matter how hard I try. There's an elderly lady named Sarah who used to visit inmates all the time, and she said that God specifically showed her that Paul was supposed to be the chaplain. Hearing from God is more your department than mine, but I just know she was really, really convinced."

Kathy was more than a little taken aback. She didn't know quite what to say.

"Have that husband of yours give me a call." He handed her his business card. "We're getting enough inmates now that I could probably even start him out three quarter or maybe even full time."

"Thanks," said Kathy staring at the card. "Thanks so much." *And thank You, Lord.*

CHAPTER 38

"Temper is a weapon that we hold by the blade."

James M. Barrie[1]

"It is an old and common saying, that 'coming events cast their shadows before them....' When destruction walks through the land, it casts its shadow; it is in the shape of pride. When honor visits a man's house, it casts its shadow before it; it is in the fashion of humility. 'Before destruction the heart of man is haughty;' pride is as surely the sign of destruction as the change of mercury in the weather-glass is the sign of rain, and far more infallibly so than that."

C.H. Spurgeon[2]

When Kathy and Jordan arrived home, Paul was gone. He came straggling in several hours later looking like death warmed over. He hadn't shaved or bathed that morning.

"Honey, I've got the best news," said Kathy handing him the card. "It's a total God thing, an answer to our prayers. You haven't even been fired from the church for 24 hours," she winced at her poor choice of words, but continued, "and already God's opened a door for you at the new jail."

Paul looked at the card, crumpled it up, and threw it on the floor. "That's what I think of the jail." He turned abruptly.

"But, I, maybe you don't understand." She bent over and picked up the card. "The director wants to hire you. He has a job for you. He wants you to call him. Sarah even heard from the Lord—"

"I told you before, I don't need any career advice from Sarah."

The elation she had felt just minutes earlier evaporated, and her tone turned serious. "Paul, this is God's blessing; it's His will. You need to learn to do God's will God's way. You're just fooling yourself if you think you can do God's will *your* way."

"I don't need any advice from you, either," he said defiantly.

"I thought you'd be excited. I-I don't understand—"

"You don't need to. You're not out there doing the stuff; I'm the one who has to go to work every day. I have to weigh things out. I have to get a job I feel good about. I am the sole breadwinner in this marriage."

Kathy clenched her teeth and exhaled through them while she held her face between her hands. She finally looked up. "Don't you think it's time you quit worrying about being recognized, about your precious reputation, your incredible future accomplishments?" Her volume was increasing. "You used to be concerned that the Lord's name would be exalted; now it seems like you're the only one you're working to exalt. I'm sick of you feeding your ego. I'm sick of you playing your 'look at me' games, and I'm sick of your five-year plan. You're eaten up with pride, and you don't even know it. You need to repent and do what the Lord has called you to do," she yelled, waving the business card toward him. "When are you going to grow up spiritually? You love having a Savior, but you resist having a Lord."

The truth in her words had hit their mark. Paul glared at her, but remained silent. He was incapable of acknowledging her accuracy. He turned his back to her and swore under his breath.

She continued, her voice more calm this time, "Something bad happened when you became interim. Jesus was no longer your focus; you were the focus. Then it became ten times worse when you were voted in as pastor. You need to repent and get back to where you were. God is offering you a position as chaplain. The least you can do is pray about it."

"You always want me to take the humble route; I'm tired of a poverty spirit. You just don't understand me. I'm the one who will be out there working. It's got to be something I'll enjoy. Bottom line is, it's my job, and I'll be making the decision."

"But we should be a team. We used to pray together, and if we were attacked by warfare, we'd fight it through together. You'd call me on the phone and explain some problem you were facing and then we'd pray. I felt like we were making an impact together. Now we're not united at all. You're off and running, and I'm not part of the decisions. I never even know what you're thinking. Remember, I didn't even know you had an offer," she waved the business card again.

"I don't tell you things because you're always trying to run my life."

"Duh, I am part of your life, remember? You married me. Just because you ran the church for a few months doesn't mean you get to run me and every aspect of my life. You used to be so open to me participating with you, but it's like you shut the Spirit out and now you just want to control everything, and you want me to follow you blindly. You won't even listen to my input. I have no voice, Paul. I have no voice."

"Oh, you have a voice alright—It goes nag, nag, nag. *And* I listen to you just fine. I listen to you ramble on and on and on! I just don't agree with you."

"I feel in my spirit that this jail opportunity is really God. It's too much of a coincidence. This is the second offer. God brought it around again. I've been praying for you for months, Paul, and I don't agree with you, either. I don't think you'd even consider the fact that you might be in error. Why do you have to run everything your way? You're like a one-man show."

"Well, I gave you the position of Sunday school director. If you want to run something, you can run that."

"Well that's a moot point now, isn't it?" As soon as she said it, she regretted it. She took a few steps toward him, her arms outstretched. "Paul, I'm sorry."

He vented a long string of profanity toward her and turning abruptly, slamming the door. Kathy heard the tires squeal away from the driveway.

Why doesn't she understand me? Why doesn't she understand I'm concerned about promotion for me and my family?

"I can't even believe I said that." Kathy held the crumpled business card and sat in the overstuffed chair trying to distract herself by smoothing out the wrinkles. The printing on the card blurred as tears filled her eyes again and ran down her cheeks.

Lord, this isn't how it was supposed to be. This is not the man I married. The man I married was passionate for You. He had a vision to do your will. He used to leave tracts everywhere—gas station restrooms, restaurant tables, and the library. Lord, all my hopes and dreams for our life together serving You are eaten up by his pride and insecurity.

Valoe stood behind her, hands on her shoulders, interceding as she sobbed out months of grief and pent-up anger to the Lord.

Paul's familiar dark spirits fed off of his rage as he headed for Mt. Peilor.

"Working in a jail would sure be a demotion. You'd be working with drug addicts and thieves—the scum of the earth," hissed Pride. "You were destined for bigger things."

"Paul, the jail looks small, but God's plan for it is huge," whispered Saldu. "It looks demeaning, but it will bear so much fruit for God's Kingdom. These prisoners are broken, but they know they're broken and they're hungry for God; they just don't know how to find Him. There's so many good things that Father has planned for you. Trust Him with your life, humble yourself, and serve these hurting men. When your life is over, you'll be amazed at the rewards you receive. Everyone who humbles himself will be exalted![3] Right now the focus of your life is yourself. Your purpose should be God's Kingdom, but you're actually a stumbling block."

"Ha," sneered Deception, smirking at Saldu, "Paul forgot he was put on this earth to bring glory to God's name, not his own!"

Probably the only true words he's ever spoken, thought Saldu, sadly.

"You don't need that jail," scoffed Pride. "You can get a job anywhere. Under your leadership that church was really growing. People were praying and visiting on Wednesday and Thursday. There hadn't been that much action there in years. I can't believe they fired you."

"That's right," whispered Deception wrapping a tentacle around Paul's chest, "you're on the cutting edge. You're a visionary. There was action going on at the church. Now that you're gone, it will probably dwindle back to apathy."

"You need to find another church and get out of this one-horse town. You should go somewhere where the people are a little more sophisticated, where they can appreciate your education, where they can appreciate you as the visionary you are. You've got drive, your five-year plan shows that," added Self-Adulation.

Yeah, I've got drive. I'm not afraid of hard work. I just need a group of people who want to follow the Lord and be progressive. I'm sick of this, "We've-never-done-it-this-way-before" attitude.

"That's exactly right, Paul," croaked Deception wrapping another tentacle around his neck, "you're too good for this backward town. You've got a master's degree from seminary. What do these people know—?"

"Paul, don't you realize you're walking right into the enemy's ambush?" Saldu interjected. "Use your discernment. Resist these flaming darts! Put up the shield of faith. God has great plans for you, but you have to follow His plans in His timing! You also need to turn this car around and go back and apologize to Kathy. You really wounded her. She loves you and really does have your best interest at heart. You need to turn the car around NOW, Paul. TURN AROUND NOW!"

Paul was so used to listening to his demonic cohorts that he could no longer identify the voice of truth. The spirits kept telling Paul exactly what he wanted to hear, and he kept listening all the way to Mt. Peilor.

"You probably shouldn't have said half that stuff, but you need to go cool off, and you can always apologize when you get back," said Manipulation. "You're under a lot of stress. She'll understand."

Saldu's power was useless until Paul repented and asked Father for help. He could only watch in revulsion while he prayed fervently.

Paul had never been to Mt. Peilor before. It was the biggest small town around for miles. He saw the exit for the business district and pulled off. Although he wasn't aware of it, he was following instructions from the demons, and soon he ended up in front of the only business open this time on a Thursday night—a bar.

Paul's dad had been an alcoholic. Growing up, Paul swore he would never touch the stuff. However, when things got stressful in college, he turned to the bottle for relief. When his dad died of cirrhosis of the liver, it was enough to scare Paul into quitting. Although alcohol hadn't been much of a temptation since, he was surprised to feel that old impulse again.

"You just need one drink to help you relax. Your muscles are tight; you're tense. Too much pressure, too much stress," whispered Manipulation.

Paul looked up and down the street. It was pretty much deserted. *Who would know me here anyway? No one.*

Saldu knew the stakes were high tonight. He prayed, he rebuked the warfare, and he cried out for mercy, but he knew in the end it all came down to Paul's choices. Saldu got out and stood between the bar and Paul's car. He pulled his flaming sword and held it with two hands high above his head and listened to his instructions from the open Heaven above. The jewels on the sword's handle glistened, reflecting the flickering flames.

As Paul got out of the car, Saldu plunged the tip of the blade into the street directly in front of Paul. "It's the flaming sword of the Lord, Paul, to divide between what is and isn't Him in your life. Don't walk out of its protective boundary. I can't help you if you do." Saldu's eyes were blazing like fire with a severity that implied it was time to make a serious choice.

"Don't walk away from the protection of Father who loves you so much. Your life and ministry are just beginning. He has wonderful plans for you, Paul. Don't be deceived. Do what you know in your heart is right. DO THE RIGHT THING!"

Although Paul couldn't see the sword or Saldu; he hesitated, sensing in his spirit that a decision needed to be made and that the stakes were extremely high.

What am I doing at a bar? I can find someplace else to let off some steam. He started to turn back toward the car. Immediately he was distracted by a spirit of Addiction that materialized on his shoulder, "One little drink can't hurt anything. It will just help you to relax and see things a little more clearly. Then you can go home and apologize. By then Kathy will have cooled off, too. She probably doesn't want you home right now anyway. When you wake up tomorrow, it's a new day. Then you two can start planning your new future together. What can one drink hurt?"

Yeah, what can one drink hurt? I can get back on the straight and narrow tomorrow. Besides, I had professors in seminary that drank. Paul stepped through the unseen sword, crossed the street, and pushed open the door to the smoky bar. Saldu sheathed his sword and looked toward the heavens, awaiting instructions he knew were coming.

Paul emerged an hour later and walked unsteadily toward the car. One drink "just to relax" had turned into several, which had turned into far too many. His evil alliance had persuaded him he was invincible.

With the help of his spirits, Paul was able to stay between the lines driving back to Bradbury. When he arrived at the city limits, instead of going home, he listened to the spirits' suggestion that he drive by the jail. He parked in the lot and glared at the big building. To him it represented his failures and seemed to taunt him. He felt impotent, weak, and powerless. He squeezed the steering wheel. *This should be my ground for my church. If Sarah weren't so money-hungry it would have been. I can't believe she thinks I should work here. Doesn't she ever give up? I hate this place and everything it represents. I don't want to work with these losers. I didn't earn a seminary degree to work with common criminals at some jail. Anyone who knows John 3:16 can do that! I was meant for bigger and better things. I wouldn't work here if it were the last job on earth. I wouldn't even work here if God Himself told me to.*

Saldu wept.

The powerful, gargoyle-like spirit of Death entered the car and fixed his scaly, dark eyes on Paul. "It's time to head for home, Paul. You'll feel better in the morning." Clutched in Death's embrace, Paul turned the ignition. Death sneered at Saldu and dug one talon firmly into the side of Paul's head. His blood red fangs appeared as he smiled at the other demons. "I've got orders. Tonight is Paul's night!"

The spirits danced, shrieked, and taunted Saldu with their mocking laughter.

"We're going to take him out, and you can't stop us."

"We've won this one. He's as good as dead."

"You can't intervene unless he repents, and his heart is as hard and as cold as a stone."

With no demonic assistance driving this time, Paul veered wildly down the road. When he reached the same stretch of road where Sarah had almost lost her life, the demons sprang into action. The gravel crunched under the right front tire as the car veered onto the shoulder. In his impaired state Paul overcorrected and shot across both lanes. He hadn't buckled up. Saldu would have normally reminded him, but not tonight—by Paul's own choice, he was on his own.

Saldu remained seated as the car headed over the steep bank. Paul screamed out in terror and spread his arms to brace himself. A kaleidoscope of scenes from his life flashed in slow motion through his mind—his mother and father, his wedding day, his ordination, Jordan's birth, and the last ugly words he yelled at Kathy.

"Oh, God," he screamed, but not as a prayer.

"It's too late," roared Death as he grabbed Paul's head and smashed it against the window on the second roll over. The scent of fresh blood caused the demons to salivate.

Saldu gathered Paul's spirit as the car came to its final resting place—on its roof, in the creek. Though the demons could not claim his spirit—it was eternally redeemed by Jesus—they rejoiced over and danced on his bloodied, lifeless body.

"We did it. The proud ones are always the easiest," shouted Self-Adulation.

"We cut his life short by half a century, at least!" said Addiction.

"We don't have to worry about his ministry any more. If he had lived and followed the plan, he would have been major trouble for us," said Manipulation.

Deception grinned, "It was no secret he had a strong calling on his life—"

"They all do," interrupted Death, "they just don't realize it."

The spirits continued celebrating Paul's wasted potential, potential that would never mature and assault their kingdom. They especially rejoiced in the knowledge that they had caused great sorrow in the God-head over the premature death of their loved one.

CHAPTER 39

"The life of every man is a diary in which he means to write one story, and writes another; and his humblest hour is when he compares the volume as it is with what he vowed to make it."

James M. Barrie[1]

"The high calling is not out of reach for anyone that the Lord has called. I will tell you what will keep you on the path of life—love the Savior and seek His glory alone. Everything that you do to exalt yourself will one day bring you the most terrible humiliation. Everything that you do out of true love for the Savior, to glorify His name, will extend the limits of His eternal kingdom, and ultimately will result in a much higher place for yourself. Live for what is recorded here (Heaven). Care nothing for what is recorded on earth."

Rick Joyner[2]

Paul could see his body in the upside-down car and immediately knew what had happened.[3] Although he struggled frantically, he could not escape Saldu's gentle, but strong embrace. Grief and dread flooded his mind and soul. "No, no, wait. I'm too young to die. I have a wife. This can't be happening. Please God, No, NO! I have a son." Panic flooded over him like a tidal wave. "I can't go yet; it's not my time. It can't be my time. I'm too young. Send me back; send me back. I can't go now! This is a nightmare.

I've got to wake up! HELP ME, HELP ME!" Saldu didn't answer; he just followed protocol, turned his face toward the celestial city, and lifted off the earth.

The death of God's committed saints is always a joyful time for the guardian angels who, of course, love their charges very deeply. But as Saldu carried Paul, he shuddered for what he knew was ahead—the test of fire.

Saldu had seen the agony and regret too many times before, and he was aware of Paul's unrepented sin—lack of humility, great ambition, unforgiveness, and his tendency to pass judgment, among other things. Saldu had been working with him for years to develop a Christlike character focused on others' needs.

Rebellion and wasted potential. Wasted opportunities, wasted days, weeks, and months have all added up to a wasted life. There was so much more that God had for him. Saldu knew great regret and emotional pain was ahead. *God's mercy is so great, but at the evaluation, before He wipes away every tear, well, this will be brutal. When he sees the Lord's burning heart of love toward him and His eyes overflowing with affection just for him, he will indeed suffer a tragic type of loss.*

Saldu's strong wings propelled them closer to the celestial city. Paul was fully conscious and could see a bright light, brighter than earthly words could adequately describe. It was brighter than 10,000 suns, and it seemed to be coming toward him at the speed of light. It beckoned to him and welcomed him. Even though he knew it was home, and he longed to be there, already a wave of remorse washed over him and a deep sense of regret consumed him. He was drawn to the city, but the closer they got, the more repulsed he was by his sin.

As they arrived, all Paul could see was brilliant, blinding red. Saldu escorted him to the edge of a massive fountain with thousands of jets shooting columns of crimson liquid high into the air. The massive fountain obscured everything, and it seemed to go for miles high and wide—Paul could see nothing else.

He had lost his robe of humility at seminary, and his robe of righteousness was filthy and torn. He intuitively entered the fountain, and his spirit was clothed with his new heavenly body. As the blood washed over him, it left behind a golden celestial glow, not a red stain. He looked in amazement at his hands, arms, and feet. He felt as light as a feather and was now wearing a dazzling robe of light. But the awe of the incredible spiritual transformation was swallowed up in a very real, overpowering sense of dread unlike anything he'd ever felt.

When Paul stepped out of the other side of the fountain, he saw Jesus, in His indescribable splendor, waiting for him. He was dazzling, holy, and radiant. His beauty was unspeakable. Love emanated from Him and glory swirled around Him. His fiery eyes of love looked directly at Paul, penetrating every cell of his being. Paul had never felt love like this before. His whole body was alive and energized in Jesus' presence. Every cell of Paul's new being loved and adored the beauty of Jesus, yet his first response was to look away—to the side, to the ground, anywhere except into those loving, penetrating eyes. In the midst of this true, true love, he was overcome with sweltering shame. Surrounded by beauty and pure love, for which he was created, all he could think was, *I don't deserve to be here. I wish the ground would open up and swallow me.*

Paul could feel power emanating from Jesus as He ran and embraced him. His deep, tender voice enveloped his whole being. "Oh, Paul, I love you."

Paul felt full of shame over the eternal consequences of his sin. Unable to look into Jesus' eyes, he buried his face into the brilliant robe. "I've got to go back; I've got to go back," whispered Paul as he sobbed, "What about my wife? I can't be here yet!" Jesus' great love overwhelmed him.

"I know, I know," a tear runs down Jesus' cheek. "It's too soon. It's too soon, Paul."

Paul took a step back and looked desperately, pleadingly at Jesus, "Send me back, please, just send me back."

"I can't Paul. I can't." Paul could feel the Lord's grief on top of his own. He was unable to stand under the weight of it. He collapsed again into Jesus' arms. Paul could feel the Lord's heart beating. His heart was not synchronized with it. With each beat, he could feel the Lord's anguish. Paul was crushed by the Lord's grief and great disappointment at his early arrival.

"Oh, Paul," said Jesus, rocking him from side to side, "I had such a great destiny planned, such a great calling for your life. You're here so early. But oh, Paul, I love you."

He felt waves of unconditional love and glory washing over him.

"I had so much ahead for you, but you didn't listen to Me. You felt My promptings. You heard My voice," said Jesus as the tears rolled down His face.

When Paul saw the Lord's tears, he was crushed again; more waves of shame and grief overwhelmed him. "I'm sorry. I'm so sorry," he sobbed repeatedly. "I'm sorry. Can I go back? Can I do it again?"

"No, it's too late Paul. Your earthly life is over." The finality in Jesus' voice wreaked anguish in Paul's heart.

"You can send me back; just raise me from the dead."

"Paul, I'm sorry. Your sinful choices overruled My perfect plan, and your choice is final. Your life on earth is really over. You made room for the enemy to enter. It's a tragedy for you, for My Father's Kingdom, for Me and for those on earth who love you. This was not Our plan."

Paul fell to the Lord's feet sobbing and frantic. With great tenderness Jesus picked him up and embraced him again.

"You freely, willfully chose to operate outside of My Father's will. We had many more years and a great, great destiny for you." At those words, pictures flitted through Paul's mind, pictures of him leading someone to the Lord, pictures of him laying hands on the sick and seeing them recover, pictures of him working with the prisoners.

With His eyes full of love, Jesus took Paul by the hand and led him to a golden altar.

"Now it's time for your evaluation."

With tears in his eyes, Saldu brought out a plain looking, cloth-bound book with Paul's name on the spine and set it on the altar.

"Paul, here is your life's offering to the Lord from your time on earth. These pages recorded your life and the pages will play back your life. You will be evaluated and rewarded based on your daily acts. We'll start with the most joyful day of your life for us," says Saldu opening the book. The page is like a movie, and Paul watched as his college friend led him to the Lord.

"We all rejoiced," said Jesus with a smile. "All the angels rejoiced and especially you, remember Saldu?"

"I could never forget, Lord," he said, smiling through his tears.

Saldu turned the next page, revealing Paul's initial joy over his salvation. Soon he was winning his friends to the Lord through his clumsy witnessing attempts.

"Could you sense the Holy Spirit with you in those early days?" asked Jesus with a smile. "You were so successful in the beginning because you didn't care what anyone thought. You felt the joy of your salvation; you emptied yourself and just let the Holy Spirit lead you. We were all cheering you on when you left tracts around town or tried to witness to your waitress."

"Here's the chapter on Kathy," said Saldu, beaming. "Look more closely at the page." With his spiritual eyes now open, Paul looked deeper into the page. It was his wedding day! Paul smiled when he saw Saldu and Valoe on the platform like members of the wedding party. Feelings of romance and love for his wife flooded over Paul. He felt the tenderness of his emotions he felt for her that day. Then he remembered his cruel argument and the final ugly comment. "I'm so sorry. I'm so sorry, Kathy, that I didn't love you better. You were a wonderful wife and mother," he sobs.

He looked deeper into the page and saw two grim-faced police officers knocking on the parsonage door. "Kathy. Oh Kathy, I'm so sorry." He turned to the Lord and frantically cried out, "Oh, please can you spare her this moment? PLEASE!"

"I'm sorry, Paul. It's going on right now. I can't spare her, but I will comfort her." Dry heaves drove him to the ground. With so much regret bombarding him, he wished he could go insane or just cease to exist, anything to stop the all-consuming agony. Jesus helped him up and put His arm around Paul to support him. "I can't believe my choices hurt so many other people."

He sobbed again. "I'm so sorry, Kathy; I'm so sorry." The intensity of regret and the indescribable agony he felt would have killed a human body.

With great tenderness in His voice Jesus said, "This will be an extremely painful trial for Kathy, but she knows how to come to Me with her needs. When Sarah finds out about your death, she'll double the prayers she already prays for her, and Kathy will find comfort in her distress. I've already dispatched two additional angels who are with her now. I will give her the ability to see things from My perspective, not to be stuck forever in the despair of a worldly view. Valoe will teach her how to wield the sword of the Spirit to defeat the enemy's attacks that will tell her I took you out early. She will wear the armor of a warrior princess. Later, I'll bring a husband into her life. She will love again."

Paul has never felt such gratitude, "Oh, thank You, thank You, Lord, for taking care of her." He couldn't bear to look back at the book as Kathy opens the door.

Saldu flipped the page—Paul's preparation at seminary.

"This is where trouble began," said Jesus, His brow furrowed and His voice disturbed. "Here is where you lost your first love. You traded My simple truth for intellectual success at the halls of academia. You stopped following My will and started striking out on your own. Here, we call that defiant, disloyal, and sinful.

"You looked to the professors for affirmation, trying to fill that ache for a father figure. Your focus switched from contentment at being the son I adored, to trying to take on the role as their son. To please them you entertained their watered-down Gospel, which was a form of religion with no power—a false gospel.

"Graduation day was all about you and your plans for future accomplishments. By then you'd stopped asking for My guidance and you stepped out on your own. Finding prestige through church employment became your idol. Humility was far from you."

A somber-faced Saldu turned the next page—the interim position at Bradbury.

"I did lead you here to Bradbury, Paul. Being interim pastor was the next temporary step in My plan for you. But you were so busy planning to have large crowds at *your* church that you overlooked the needs of the people who were already there. They had wounds that needed to be healed; they were not just numbers to be counted. Why did you want so many more when you weren't shepherding the people I gave you?

"Simple acts of kindness, in My name, performed on a daily basis are what I expect of all My people. As a pastor, My ambassador, My representative to the earth, you should have set the example above everyone else. Let's look at the opportunities you missed during just one day in your life."

Paul stared at the page. Driving to the church that morning, he passed a lady standing beside her car looking at her flat tire.

"This is Tanya Albertson. I had you leave the house 30 minutes early so you would be there when she needed you. She'd been wounded by some Christians at youth camp. She'd harbored a grudge against Me for 30 years. You were supposed to stop and change her tire. That act of kindness was going to challenge her deception. She would have eventually visited the church and rededicated her life, but you just drove by. Now look deeper into the page."

Paul stared and another picture came into view. He was snapping at his secretary, Veronica, for not having his letter ready to mail to everyone in the database.

He was filled with regret and embarrassment as he watched himself throwing a fit, acting like a five-year-old.

"You knew that Veronica's mother was in the hospital, and she was already emotionally distraught. You had even given her permission to cut her work hours that week. Not only did you miss the opportunity to be a blessing by comforting her during this traumatic time, you heaped anxiety and condemnation on top of her. You didn't even visit her mother in the hospital. Worst of all, you said you'd pray and you didn't. Later, you even demanded that she lie for you by telling one of the older church members that you'd already left." Paul watched as he stormed off to his office, and he saw her break down in tears as soon as he was gone.

He looked deeper into the page. He was listening to one of the church members pouring out his heart about how his marriage was unraveling and his wife was ready to leave. Paul was shaking his head, acting sympathetic, but he was looking past the man to the clock on the wall.

"Joe had waited two weeks to get this appointment with you. It took all his courage to admit that he'd made a mess of his marriage. You were his last hope. But Mike had called and invited you to lunch right before Joe arrived. You spent the whole time trying to wrap up the session quickly because you wanted to be with Mike. He was on the search committee that would pick the new pastor. You know that Joe's wife left the next week?" Paul nodded.

The page changed again. Kathy was at home preparing dinner. *I wonder what time he'll be home tonight? You'd think at least he could call when he's going to be late.*

She put some aluminum foil over the pan of lasagna and put it back in the oven to stay warm and then put the salad back in the fridge. She sat in the chair by the fireplace and prayed, "Lord, I'm so lonely. Will You help us to have a nice evening together? I feel so disconnected." Tears welled in her eyes, "I feel like the church has become Paul's mistress, like it's my competition, and I'm losing miserably. Lord, will You let him hear me. God, I need to feel like I'm heard. I need to feel like he at least values my opinions a little." She heard the car door slam and ran to get dinner on the table.

"Look what happened here, Paul. Listen to how you talked about the church and your day, but you didn't ask about hers. Right here she tried to share something with you that's meaningful to her, but you weren't interested."

After a little chit-chat Kathy said, "I've been doing this great study on pride and humility, and I'd like to share it."

"Sure hon, you can start a ladies group any time you like." Paul didn't bother to look up from his plate.

"No, I didn't mean an on-going ladies study; we already have one of those. I thought maybe I could share it some Sunday morning."

He put his fork down and stared at her. "You want to preach a sermon—from the pulpit? You've never preached before, and don't you think that's a little theologically heavy for someone who doesn't have formal training?" *Besides*, he thought, *I'm the one with the Master's in Divinity.*

"Paul, not only did you keep her from delivering her message, you criticized and belittled her. Kathy had been studying diligently, and the Holy Spirit opened up the Scriptures to her. She not only had My Word for the church, but she had the words of life that you desperately needed to hear. Ironically she was your guide back on the straight and narrow path. If you had listened to her, you wouldn't be here now."

"I betrayed her and belittled her in so many ways. She always hung in there and encouraged me toward the right path. I needed her teaching more than anyone. Help me. I'm so sorry. Help me." His depth of regret was unfathomable.

"Paul, this was just one day. You had thousands and thousands of daily opportunities to give a cup of cold water in My name,[5] but you were focused on yourself. You were too shackled by pride to notice anyone else's needs. I wanted to give you good gifts and promote you. I wanted to give you spiritual gifts to touch and heal other people, but I couldn't trust you. Your pride would have caused you to take credit for every good gift I gave you."

Paul hung his head and began sobbing again. Everything was so clear now. Why hadn't he had his priorities straight on earth? "Why was I so rebellious? I had to do everything my way." His new, perfect body felt totally healthy, but inside his mind the pain was so intense that he couldn't endure it, yet he couldn't escape it. He longed for one more chance. He longed for death. Neither would come.

The next page was the proposal for the jail in Bradbury. "Paul, you didn't even pray to see if it was My will. You just went with the flow and even tried to manipulate the situation for your advantage. It wasn't a spiritual decision for you; it was strictly political because you perceived it could benefit you. If you would have followed My leading, the church would have changed their opinion too. I planned for you and the church to advocate the plan for the jail. You would have all been in unity. Instead, Sarah was severely persecuted for carrying the whole plan herself, which was never My will for her. Yet she faithfully endured.

"You even used your spiritual position to manipulate Sarah, and you have no idea how much confusion and pain you caused her. As a teacher you will be judged more strictly because you misused your position and your power. You had potential to use it for good, but you used it to your benefit. If you're not with Me you're against Me."[6]

Paul hung his head again. "I misjudged Sarah. I said and thought terrible things about her. Forgive me; please forgive me. I should have helped disciple her, but she was the more spiritual one."

Saldu turned the next page, which showed Paul, elated on the day he was voted in as pastor. Paul had spent hours thinking and stressing over the vote, but he suddenly realized that he hadn't even prayed to see if he should accept the position. "I just reveled in the fact that they wanted me."

Saldu flipped the rest of the pages, revealing wasted opportunity after wasted opportunity fueled by his manipulation, gossip, criticism, jealousy, and rebellion. Paul wept and wept as he watched. He saw countless daily opportunities that he missed. He saw that many of his decisions were fueled by demonic influences.

How could I have been so blind? I was so disobedient, but I thought I was so spiritual.

"Living in pride is like living in a room with no lights or windows. You can't function in any meaningful way, but you don't realize it. You just get used to it, and it makes you spiritually blind and deaf. Pride opposes truth every time, but humility draws you near to the truth and the cross.[7] You stopped embracing the cross, Paul."

The next to the last page was the fight he had with Kathy. He was shocked at his ugliness toward her. "I was so cruel to her, and she was the one who was hearing well." He put his hands over his ears in a failed attempt to drown out his last profane words shouted at her. Deep, inexpressible remorse bore down on him. "I never got to apologize," he sobbed. "I really didn't mean it. I love her. She was right, and I was wrong...." He watched Saldu plunge the tip of the sword into the street between him and the bar at Mt. Peilor. "It's the flaming sword of the Lord, Paul, to divide between what is and isn't Him in your life. Don't walk out of its protective boundary. I can't help you if you do." He heard the demon's twisted manipulation and his final decision, *Yeah, what can one drink hurt? I can get back on the straight and narrow tomorrow.*

The last page was the car ride. This time Paul was watching the scene from the outside. He could see the holy brilliance shining from Saldu. He heard the eerie sound of shattering glass and twisting metal as the car rolled over. He shuttered. *I never thought I'd throw my life away as a drunk driver.*

"My Word says that I gave you My commandments that it may go well with you.[8] My Word is truth,[9] not just a good suggestion. You failed to listen; you followed your lying demons, and they led you straight to your death—like a sheep unknowingly going to the slaughter."

Paul fell to his knees in anguish and buried his face in his hands while he rocked back and forth. "I can't believe I failed so miserably."

"Paul," said Jesus, kneeling beside him and putting His arm around him, "In order to be great in the eyes of the world, you need to be intelligent, handsome, rich, have a special talent, or a certain family name. Very few have what it takes to be great in the world's eyes. But I designed My Kingdom so everyone can be great because to be great in My Kingdom one only needs to humble himself and be the servant of all. Everyone with desire can do that. Paul, you wasted your life trying to be great in the wrong kingdom. I wanted you to have your eye on the prize, but you had your eye on your pride, on making an earthly name for yourself. You didn't value eternity and didn't think that Heaven's reward was worth paying the earthly price."

Through his tears Paul watched Saldu lay a thick leather-bound book with rich tooling on top of Paul's first book. On it in golden calligraphy was Paul's name. The book was shining, alive with heavenly glory. As Saldu opened the first page, the book released a sweet melody, a symphony of sounds never heard on earth.

"Let Me tell you a little about My perfect plan for your life. I had a great destiny for you as I do for all my beloved children. Father, Holy Spirit, and I took such joy planning your destiny before the foundation of the world." Saldu began to turn the shimmering pages.

"The interim position at Bradbury was never supposed to turn into a full-time position. It was only to move you to Bradbury so you could meet Sarah and take the job as chaplain. That was your life's calling.

"Let's go back to March 12, when you were 6," said Jesus, motioning to Saldu. Paul looked at the page and all the overwhelming feelings from his 6-year-old heart coursed through his veins like he was actually living it for the first time. He was visiting his favorite uncle, Emery, in jail. He was the closest thing Paul ever had to a real father.

His uncle had been hunting and thought the gun's safety was on. When he pulled in his driveway the neighbor kids came running to see the deer in the back of the pickup. While his uncle's back was turned, a 7-year-old opened the door, reached in the pickup, and grabbed the gun by the barrel to pull it out. The shot hit her in the neck and she died in the hospital the next day.

Paul wasn't there when it happened, and he didn't know the little girl who was killed, but he remembered seeing his uncle's downcast face behind those bars. When Paul and his mom stood there, his uncle looked up with tears in his eyes and said, "It was an accident," then sobbed and sobbed. In his child's heart and swayed by his love for his uncle, he felt a tremendous sense of injustice. He vowed one day that he would do something to help people like his uncle.

"You being a chaplain was one of the ways I was going to work your uncle's situation for good.[10] Most men at the jail had no fathers, either. I wanted to heal your heart so you could be a father to them. Jail is full of fatherless men separated from their children. You could have helped them become good fathers and break this horrendous cycle.

"Had you gone to the jail, I would have given you a healing anointing, and I would have used you to heal Sarah and extend her life's ministry at the jail, also. She's My joy, and I delight in her obedience when she hears My voice."

His stern eyes flame with intensity, "Paul, you let yourself be led by your mind, not My Spirit. Of course your disobedience opened you up to deception by demonic spirits. So many times you called good evil and evil good. Your evaluations were in gross error. Your priorities were rarely mine."

As Paul looked into the pages, he saw the jail and the faces of the inmates he would have led to the Lord and those he could have helped to lead productive lives. He saw the lives of the people whom they would have impacted—their wives and girlfriends, children and grandchildren. To his surprise, he felt a deep love for them.

"You would have had an effective, anointed ministry there until your late 70s." Agony and regret bore down on him so that his knees buckled, but the Lord caught him.

The next page was a family portrait. Kathy and Paul along with Jordan in his 30s, next to a pretty brunette who was holding a toddler. "This is Jordan's wife Cynthia, and their son, Caleb; of course those plans won't change." Paul was at first surprised to see that there were other people in the portrait—adults and children. Then waves of indescribable pain overwhelmed him, and he knew their identity before the Lord even said it.

"You and Kathy were going to have two daughters, Susan and Diane; these would have been their husbands, Danny and Larry. And between them, they would have had these five precious grandchildren, Calvin, Canaan, Ashton, Kendra, and Lonny."

More tears flowed as he gently reached to touch the faces of his two daughters and his grandchildren. As he touched the grandchildren, he saw flashes of himself and Kathy, in their fifties, pushing the grandkids on swings, helping them cast a fishing reel, and standing beside them on a merry-go-round.

"I had a rich, full life planned for you Paul, not only in your family life, but in your ministry. You would have touched the lives of hundreds and hundreds of My lost, hurting children, and in turn they would have touched hundreds more, but you would not yield to My leadership. In your rebellion, you walked away from My protective covering and the enemy was able to cut your life short. Everyone who hears My words and doesn't do them I liken him to a foolish man."[11]

"Kathy was right, and Sarah was right, and I was wrong. How could I have been so blind?"

"You were blinded by your pride, Paul. You were so busy trying to build yourself up that the godly opinions of others around you didn't even register. In addition to Saldu, Holy Spirit and I were constantly wooing you. At first you disregarded our voices, but after saying no for so long, you lost all spiritual discernment. You can't even begin to understand the pain I felt when you ignored Us." A tear ran down His face. "I watched you run after your idols of pride and self-promotion. Year after year I called you, Paul, hoping you'd realize that there is no satisfaction in any other. I alone am the Light and the Life. You loved yourself too much and never loved Me enough. There is suffering in earthly sacrifice, but the eternal rewards far outweigh the temporal discomfort."

Paul was literally trembling from head to toe. He felt mentally distraught and tormented by regret. He ran his fingers through his hair on both sides of his head and bent at the waist. He pulled clumps of hair out, but he felt no physical pain and new hair immediately appeared. He began to pummel and scratch his face with his fists while screaming, screeching a primal sound. No blood or bruises appeared. He couldn't injure himself or feel physical pain in his new, eternal, indestructible body. He'd never imagined such regret and torment was even possible. He felt he might pass out or even die.

Jesus placed His hand on Paul's head and spoke, "Peace." Paul didn't stop crying, but he stopped screaming and hitting himself.

Saldu flipped to the last page. There, hovering above the book, was a hologram of a large, elaborate crown made of shimmering gold.

"Each precious jewel represents one life that you should have touched and the lives that they in turn would have touched."

Through his tears, Paul saw the base of the ornate crown was designed with solid gold. Embedded in the gold were precious stones—rubies, emeralds, sapphires, and large white pearls in the shape of crosses. The crown was adorned with several hundred diamonds arranged in a pattern of olive branches. On the top was a large red spinel diamond, which represented Jesus' shed blood. Paul has never seen anything so beautiful. He longed to present this amazing crown to the Lord to thank Him for the overwhelming mercy he had been shown—mercy that he now knows he never deserved and could never earn.

"Now it is time to reveal how your life lines up with My plans and My Word. When you gave your life to Me, I became your foundation and you began building your life's work. Your building choices were gold, silver, precious stones, wood, hay, or straw. Everyone's work will be put through the fire to see whether or not it keeps its value. The fire is impartial; it is the equalizer of every person's work. If the work survives the fire, that builder will receive a heavenly, eternal reward. But if the work is burned up, that builder will suffer great loss. The builders themselves will be saved, but like someone escaping through a wall of flames.[12]

Saldu bent low and blew his breath on the books, and they burst into red and orange flames. Paul hoped against hope that he would have a beautiful crown to present to his wonderful Savior. But when both books were consumed and the flames died down, all that remained was a dull, quarter-sized lump of gold. Paul's last hope was shattered. He fell forward and caught himself on the altar. Devastation overwhelmed him as he saw that the lifetime of selfish choices had culminated in the agonizing scene that now lay before him. With sadness etched on his face, Saldu handed the small lump of gold to Paul.

Jesus approached him. Paul was filled with sorrow. Humiliated, he looked away, remembering the many warnings from Saldu. Jesus said, "Your life was mostly composed of wood, hay, and straw. Your small lump of gold is unrefined because you wouldn't submit to My leadership. You wouldn't go through My refiner's fire. You were so focused on your temporal earthly life that you missed your eternal calling and your many heavenly rewards. Did you not read in My Word? *Don't love the world and what it offers. Those who love the world don't have the Father's love in them. Not everything that the world offers—physical gratification, greed, and extravagant lifestyles—comes from the Father. It comes from the world, and the world and its evil desires are passing away. But the person who does what God wants lives forever.*[13]

"My eternal Word clearly states that the first and greatest commandment is to '*love the Lord your God with all your heart, with all your soul, and with all your mind.*' And the second is equally important, '*Love your neighbor as yourself.*'[14] We were all waiting to help you fulfill those commandments, but you were distracted by so many temporal things."

Paul dropped the gold at His feet, not so much as an offering of thanks, but to rid himself of the wretched reminder of his failure, compromise, and regret. He fell on the floor writhing in agony. In the shadow of the glorious man, Christ Jesus, Paul wept and gnashed his teeth. But all the regret in the world would not buy one more chance or one more day to serve the Lord on earth. His life was squandered, mostly worthless to God's Kingdom, an eternal tribute to his selfishness—unrepairable, and unfixable.

He had never known such torture. He writhed in agony and screamed out, "Can Hell be more painful than this? Forgive me! I'm so sorry! I'm so sorry! I didn't mean to hurt You." He sobbed and wailed, "Even with the Holy Spirit living inside me and angels guiding me and Your living Word, I still wasted my life. I wasted it and through my rebellion, cut it short."

He beat his hands on the ground and wailed, rolling from side to side. "I don't deserve to be here. I never submitted my life to You. I squandered the precious gift of life that you gave me. I only looked out for myself and didn't care about others. How can You even love me? How can You even want me here? I don't deserve to be here. I, more than anyone, deserve Hell. Oh, if I could only do it again."

After what seemed like several eternities to Paul, but was really only several minutes, Jesus knelt before him. "You're My brother, Paul; I love you."

"Oh, Jesus, how can You love me? I'm not worthy to be Your lowliest servant. I'm so sorry I hurt you. My life is a total failure."

"But that's why I died, to forgive your sins and failures. I will never forsake you; you are a member of My precious, blood-bought family."

With great compassion, Jesus took Paul's face into His hands, His fiery eyes flashing. "Paul, I love you, and you trusted in Me for your salvation," His nail-scarred hands wiped the tears from Paul's left cheek. "Though you did not do many works to benefit My Father's Kingdom, you trusted My blood to redeem you." He wiped the tears from Paul's right eye. Waves of grace wash over Paul. "Through My blood sacrifice on your behalf, I pronounce you totally forgiven." The excruciatingly deep pain, shame, and regret disappeared as he felt the Lord's great love wash over him. The agony that he thought would certainly kill him just a few minutes ago was replaced by total peace like he'd never experienced. He reveled in it. Jesus leaned close to his face. "Receive the joy of your salvation." Paul laughed until he doubled up as waves of joy and peace engulfed him.

It was now just an eternal fact, a slice of sad history that Paul's life had been mostly wasted. But by the miracle of God's eternal mercy and the power of Jesus' shed blood, not only were his sins forgiven, the sting of regret was wiped away from Paul's emotions forever. The heavy burden of his failures that had caused him to cry out in anguish was annihilated by Jesus' sacrifice. Although the memories remained, all the shame and pain had been redeemed and turned into ecstatic, overwhelming gratitude to his risen Lord. Paul was passionately in love with Jesus, his wonderful redeemer, whom he now realized, had shown him unfathomable grace when he deserved none at all. For the first time, he had a clear understanding of what he deserved and what the Lord had saved him from.

A celestial dignity was bestowed on Paul that was not there before. He was now secure in the Lord's unconditional love for him, his sins were forever forgiven, and every tear was wiped away.[15]

Jesus took Paul by the hand and pulled him to his feet. With total abandon, Paul flung himself into the waiting arms of his loving Savior and they embraced.

"Now Paul, Heaven is not a barren, sterile place. Everything is alive here; everything is moving and growing. And your spirit will continue to grow. No one stops growing in Heaven; your gifts and destinies are without repentance. Even though you missed out on many of the heavenly rewards I wanted to give you, you're still a part of the great cloud of witnesses cheering on those who still dwell on earth. I have assignments for you regarding the people left behind. They still have unlimited opportunities to follow My Word.

"Even though you're not on earth to nurture and bless your wife, you can still support her. Prayers don't stop when a person dies. Your first assignment is to pray for Kathy and Jordan. Your death didn't thwart My plan for her destiny. You can pray for her healing and for the new husband that I'll eventually bring into her life."

"Oh Lord, You're so good to bring someone else for her so she won't be a single mother long. Thank You, thank You."

"Your second assignment is to pray for the Holy Spirit to empower the new chaplain I'll put in place. Pray for all the prisoners and their families. Pray for the families of their victims who are grieving.

"Pray for Sarah; she'll be joining us soon, but she can still accomplish so much in the short time that she has left. Pray that she will be wholehearted and not give in to Discouragement and Depression at the Manor."

"You're going to learn and grow and see so much more of My glory. There are many chambers in My heart and many rooms to explore in Heaven. You'll be My intercessor before the throne, crying out day and night. There's a great war for souls that never stops; your real life's work is just beginning. Look back at the earth now. It is merely the womb of life, but choices made there cement eternal futures."

Suddenly Paul could see the earth and the second Heaven that overlaid it. He saw the angels warring against demons and the principalities and powers over cities.

"I'll take you into My war room and show you My strategies for the end of the age. Your prayers will help fill the golden bowls before My throne.[16] You can help plunder My enemy's kingdom and usher in My victorious return."

"Oh Jesus, there is no one like You. You are full of love and mercy. You redeemed me when I was your enemy. I only deserve Hell, but even though my sins were great, You have forgiven them all and given me Your righteousness as a gift. I exalt Your name above every name. You are truly King of all kings and Lord of all lords. There is no one like You. Your love and mercy are unfathomable!" This time Saldu's tears were tears of joy.

"Enter into the paradise prepared for those I love," Jesus said with a big smile and His eyes aflame with compassion. Flanked by Jesus and Saldu, Paul turned toward the massive, celestial gate still praising his loving Savior.

"This is why eternity is not too long to bow before His throne and praise Him," said Saldu with a smile, as, arm in arm, they ushered Paul into his eternal home, God's heavenly city of Paradise.

# CHAPTER 40

"The Lord spoke to me about a spiritual Sons of Issachar clock we have been given in this time and showed me that every minute that passes is like money passing through our fingers. It came with directions: value the time you are given as you would value money. Spend time wisely. Time is life. Time can be used to make money, but money can't be used to buy time. Every minute is far more valuable than money."

Joni Ames[1]

"Let me be thankful, first, because he never robbed me before; second, because although he took my purse, he did not take my life; third, because although he took all I possessed, it was not much; and fourth, because it was I who was robbed, not I who robbed."

Matthew Henry[2]

Sarah woke in the middle of the night hurting all over. Pain was nothing new since she had broken her hip.

Self-Pity was crouching on the bed waiting, "Sarah, poor, poor Sarah. You're stuck in this smelly nursing home. What'd you do to deserve this? It must have been bad, really bad. You know that the only way anyone ever leaves this place is horizontal!"

"Your life is over, and what do you have to show for it?" asked Depression. "You failed at having kids. You'll die alone; they'll sell your house and get rid of your possessions at a yard sale. The only thing that will mark your life is a square of granite with your name carved on it. Who will even remember you were here?"

My life is almost over. What difference have I made by being here?

"Sarah, don't buy that lie," whispered Malta, as he pulled out his harp and began to play a sweet melody. "Your efforts make an eternal difference. This life is mostly about preparing you for the age to come. Every day you are rushing closer to eternity, which is your real life. Invest in the right kingdom—no heavenly pavement down here. Give the last of everything you have to glorify Jesus. He is so worthy of all your efforts. In this nursing home you are His mouth and you are His hands; don't waste His precious time here."

That's right, this nursing home is my mission field, at least for a little longer.

"His love for you is so extravagant; just receive it and then give it out to everybody you meet. He wants you to lavish the same love and compassion on others as He does on you," added Joel. "Look at the people around you. In six months, half of them will be living eternally in Heaven or in Hell. You can help them make the right decision. Think how grateful you are that the Lord saved you toward the end of your life."

"If He really loved you, He'd have saved you when you were 12, not when you were old," whispered the slimy voice of Discouragement.

"When you feel discouraged, it's the enemy shooting his fiery darts at you," said Malta. "He hates you, but you can defeat him by quoting or singing the Scripture."

Malta played the harp and sang over Sarah, inserting her name in the Scripture. "Sarah is hard-pressed on every side, yet she is not crushed; Sarah is perplexed, but she is not in despair; Sarah is persecuted, but she is not forsaken; Sarah is struck down, but she is not destroyed."[3]

With her spirit empowered by God's Word, she made up her mind once and for all that Self-Pity and Pride would no longer have a part in her life.

"When the enemy lies to you and when you're feeling low," said Malta, "Go find someone else who is discouraged and do something to help them."

Sarah decided that if she was going to live out the last of her life at the Manor then she would do it with a good attitude. With God's help she would wreak as much havoc on the enemy's kingdom as she could, through praise, prayer, witnessing, and any other way the Lord would show her.

Dear Jesus, help me to live a life that makes sense for eternity. Help me to make an impact in Your Kingdom today. Help me to share with the staff and patients, and especially help me to pray, pray, pray all day long.

She memorized a new Scripture and vowed to quote it frequently. First Thessalonians 5:16-18: *"Be joyful always; pray continually; give thanks in all circumstances, for this is God's will for you in Christ Jesus."* She determined that through God's grace she would have a good attitude so that the staff and patients would see God's love through her.

With Sarah refusing to entertain the negative attitudes that the tormenting spirits fed on, they left for the day. She had resisted and they had fled. This opened the door for more supernatural activity and intimacy with the Holy Spirit.

Nancy was her aide that morning and she entered the room without knocking.

"Good morning," chirped Sarah. "Isn't it a wonderful day?"

"What ever you say, ma'am; that ain't the way I see it."

Well come over here, Nancy, and tell me what's concerning you and then, while you're getting me dressed, I'll pray for you the whole time."

Sarah felt like she had received a picture in her mind from the Lord and decided that this time it would be OK to share it. "Nancy, the Lord just showed me some rosebuds, really tight and unopened. They're in a vase in the dark. As long as the temperature is cool, they're not going to open, but then I saw the sunshine on them and the warmth caused them to open right up. They were the most beautiful apricot colored roses—really large. I think the Lord is telling you that you're like those tight buds and you need to start exposing yourself to the warmth of the Son and then your life will really blossom."

Sarah received more revelation. She felt that Nancy's son was estranged from her, but she was too scared to say it.

"Go on," encouraged Malta, "Tell her. It will help heal her heart."

But what if I'm wrong? thought Sarah. Roses are easy. This is serious.

"You're not wrong, but remember you've committed to give it all you've got while you're still here?"

Sarah took a deep breath, but spoke so quietly that Nancy had to ask her to repeat her statement.

"I wanted to know if you have a son." When Sarah saw the tears start to well in Nancy's eyes, she didn't wait for the reply. "Are you estranged?" Nancy nodded as the tears rolled down her cheeks. Sarah grabbed Nancy's hand. "It'll be OK. The Lord wants you to know that He's working on your son's heart and that within a few months he'll come back home. But you need to forgive him and not keep bringing up the past. That will only drive him away again."

Nancy ran into Sarah's bathroom to compose herself. When she left, she felt genuinely cared for and thrilled about her son. Maybe prayer does work, was the thought flowing through her mind.

≺ ≺ ≺

Barbara visited almost every day and was a constant encouragement to Sarah. "Tell me where to put the push pins on the world map. What countries did you pray for last night?"

"I prayed for Belize, and I prayed for the Cook Islands. I guess I was in a tropical prayer mood last night," laughed Sarah.

"The Cook Islands? Your prayers are sure stretching my poor geography skills. Where, pray tell, are the Cook Islands?"

"They're about halfway between Australia and South America. Or, just look for Hawaii and go south. You can find that, right?"

"I'll have you know I'm not *that* bad," she replied, rolling her eyes. "Well I'll be, here are the Cook Islands."

"Did you make it to the jail this week?" asked Sarah.

"Yes, and I have a special surprise." She pulled something out from behind the chair. "I took pictures of all the inmates and put them on this bulletin board, all the inmates except Will, that is. He wouldn't pose without making an obscene gesture," she said shaking her head.

Sarah laughed, "That sounds like the Will I knew."

"I'll hang it here so you can see their faces. They all say "hi," as always, but Skinner wanted me to tell you that he's getting out in eight weeks. He's still so excited that he doesn't have nightmares any more. He can't wait to come by and visit you."

He better hurry, thought Sarah.

Sarah's deeper revelation of the Lord's love for her consumed her every thought; she even dreamed about it at night. It motivated her to endure daily humiliations and embarrassment with grace. Her attitude continued to improve. She studied the Scriptures about the apostle Paul not considering his present sufferings to be worthy to be compared with the glory to come.[4] Sarah remembered some of the things that Paul went through for the Gospel: beatings, imprisonment, being stoned with rocks, being shipwrecked and floating in the sea, persecutions, false accusations, sleepless nights, hunger and thirst, being cold and naked.[5]

Sarah meditated on that and tried to imagine how she'd hold up under all those tribulations. *I can't believe what Paul went through. I have a warm room and enough food, and not only is my freedom of speech protected, but I have a captive audience.*

With the Holy Spirit convicting her, she was able to let go of the last vestiges of her pride, resentment, and feelings that she was entitled to a better life than this. *If the apostle Paul suffered like that, and Jesus left the perfection of Heaven to suffer here for my salvation, why do I think I should be exempt? The servant is not better than the master.*[6]

When it came time to be spoonfed at the table, she would think of Paul going hungry. *He would think I live in the lap of luxury*, thought Sarah, and she no longer resented wearing a bib and being fed like a toddler.

She was even able to be gracious to the aides who bathed and toileted her, no matter how humiliating it was. As the warm bath water washed over her and the aide scrubbed her sagging, wrinkled body, she was able to release her humiliation by closing her eyes and thinking of Paul, bobbing in the cold, dark sea for a whole night and day. *Yes, compared to Paul, my life is fine.* She began to reframe her thinking. Instead of feeling resentment because of her helplessness she thought, *Every one of my needs is met, and I even have helpers to assist me.*

Joel and Malta were there to constantly remind her that short-term sacrifices would reap long-term rewards. "Only one life, t'will soon be past, only what's done for Christ will last."[7]

The staff was drawn to Sarah's kind words and cheerful attitude—a rarity there among the patients. They welcomed the prophetic words she spoke over their lives, and the more she used this gifting the more it increased.

When Sarah's arms became too weak to propel her wheelchair, she received an electric one. It was like getting a new lease on life. Each day Sarah cruised up and down the halls with ease, looking into rooms for patients who were alone and discouraged. Most days she was able to lead someone into a relationship with the Lord. She also started an informal Bible study five days a week, right after lunch, to disciple her new converts.

Discouragement, Abandonment, Depression, and other demons were fighting to hold their ground with the new believers, but with Sarah's prayers and spiritual warfare these spirits had a hard job.

Sarah was more convinced than ever that her prayers could have an effect since she'd read in her devotional guide about a Chinese pastor who was paralyzed from a stroke. When asked if he was discouraged because he could no longer do much for God's Kingdom he replied, "When I pray from this bed, all of China shakes."[8]

"That's right," said Joel, "Don't underestimate the power of your prayers, especially for those who will die in the next 24 hours. Remember how the Lord saved George at the last minute? You can do that for others."

"The shining sun and the falling rain are given both to those who love God and to those who reject God; the compassion of the Son embraces those who are still living in sin. The Pharisee lurking within many believers shuns sinners. Jesus turns toward them with gracious kindness. He sustains His attention throughout their lives for the sake of their conversion, which is always possible to the very last moment,"[9] said Malta.

She would frequently request, "Lord, I pray that I would always pray." Unbeknownst to Sarah, her prayers were the catalyst for one of the lay leaders at the Christian church to begin arranging a regular visitation program for the Manor. Twelve members would eventually sign up and commit to visiting the Manor once a week to pray with and witness to the patients and staff. This would ensure that a Christian witness would be in place when Sarah was gone.

With more grace given to her, Sarah's prayers, for those inside and outside the Manor, were more consistent and powerful. She prayed for all the staff and patients in the Manor, in addition to prayer walking the four blocks in her mind and praying for the inmates, Victory Church, numerous missionaries, various countries, and those who were going to die in the next 24 hours.

News of Paul's death had hit her hard, but she drew great comfort from the Lord that Paul was with Him. Kathy and Jordan had visited her shortly after his death, and Sarah continued to pray fervently for them.

Kathy was doing as well as could be expected. Many of the women from the church had gathered to support her. The church even offered to let her stay at the parsonage rent-free for several months, but she chose to move back to her hometown to be close to her family and friends. Jordan thrived on spending time with his grandparents, "Papaw" and "Nana," and his many cousins. Kathy was back at her home church, had reconnected with many old friends, and the crisis was causing her to press in to find deeper intimacy with the Lord and His new direction for her life. He was pouring His grace on her liberally.

The search committee at Bradbury Victory Church had just extended a call to pastor Alan Koch and his family, who had been God's first choice to pastor this church when Paul's interim term was up.

Barbara, helped along by Sarah's prayers, fearlessly, and without excessive perspiration, visited the jail at least twice a week. She ferried messages back and forth from Sarah to the inmates. The director had asked Barbara to consider co-leading a Bible study once a week with one of the men from Victory Church who had volunteered to help out. This was their second week, and 17 inmates had attended. The prisoners decided to name their group "Hug a Thug" because they felt so cared for.

CHAPTER 41

"Sometimes I walk through graveyards and speculate how many unfulfilled promises and untapped dreams lie dormant under my feet. I ponder the many lives that fall short of God's intended purpose....Die Empty! My goal is to give the graveyard nothing but a vacant carcass of a used-up life!"

Wayne Cordeiro[1]

Sarah prayed during most of the day and many times during the night. She dozed fitfully, her body's pains not quite letting her reach a restful sleep. On those nights, from her bed in the darkened room in the Manor, the last place on earth she wanted to be, she listened to the continual worship music and watched or laid her hand gently on the rotating globe. Many nights she received visions from the Spirit, pictures flashed through her mind of isolated native villages, modern cities, starving children, or a soldier alone and dying on the battlefield. She prayed for those impressions as she drifted in and out of sleep.

During the dark, still hours when she was wide awake, she also cried out for salvation for people around the world who were going to die in the next 24 hours. She called it her "thief on the cross" prayers because the one thief

crucified next to Jesus had been saved just before he died.[2] She was especially motivated to pray these prayers because George had been saved on his
deathbed and she was full of gratitude.

"Jesus, I pray for those who are going to die, that You would let them see
Your beauty. Let them see You in Your pure love, longing for them to spend
eternity with You. I rebuke demonic influence that would lead them astray.
Lord, strip away deception that would cloud their minds and confuse them.
Let Your truth be known in their hearts and minds. Jesus, in Your great
mercy snatch them from the enemy's grasp even up to their last breath."

The Holy Spirit was busy answering Sarah's prayers all around the world.
Avner, a young rabbinical student in Israel, had been meditating on the
messianic prophecies as he did his homework that evening.

When he went to bed, Avner dreamed he was in the crowd at the temple
the day Jesus unrolled the scroll and read Isaiah 61:1-2:[3]

*The Lord God has put his Spirit in me, because the Lord has appointed
me to tell the good news to the poor. He has sent me to comfort those
whose hearts are broken, to tell the captives they are free, and to tell the
prisoners they are released. He has sent me to announce the time when
the Lord will show his kindness and the time when our God will punish
evil people. He has sent me to comfort all those who are sad.[4]*

The crowd was murmuring, "Isn't this Jesus, the carpenter's son?" As
Avner listened, he knew that he was hearing the truth. He didn't know how
he knew, but even as he actively tried to resist, he knew in his heart that
what he heard was real and true. He awoke immediately and Jesus in all His
splendor and loving kindness was sitting on the side of his bed. He looked
straight into Avner's eyes and said, "Today this Scripture is fulfilled in your
hearing, Avner." Then He was gone.

The next morning Avner boarded the city bus. Three stops later, a suicide bomber reached under his coat and detonated the dynamite strapped
to his body.

≺≺≺

In Pattaya, Thailand, a young woman was dying alone in the back alley. She had contracted AIDS from working in the sex trade. Her immune

system was devastated. For several weeks she had fought a dry cough. When she grew too sick to work, she was discarded. She lay in an alley shivering in the night air, her face flushed, overcome by a very high fever. Most of her hair had fallen out and red patches covered her face. She felt she was suffocating; each breath was more challenging than the one before.

In response to Sarah's prayers, an angel appeared. Although she was unaware of its presence, she suddenly remembered the time, as a little girl, when she went to a meeting and a missionary told of a man named Jesus who loved her. He promised Jesus would respond to those in need who called His name. When she went home that night and told her mother, she was severely beaten and told to never return to that place. With one last effort, she drew in a breath and as it left her body she weakly whispered, "Je—sus." The next second, her spirit was gently cradled in the angel's arms and released from the bonds of earth.

In Haiti, outside a shack with battered wooden walls and a tin roof, an elderly woman lay on a cot moaning. Several Haitians were chanting over her, and she was surrounded by sacred objects: candles, incense, swords, knives, needles, nails, goblets, mirrors, amulets, and masks meant to keep away harmful forces. Women were casting spells for protection and others were holding her head up to help her sip a potion.

The Haitians watched the sky for falling stars that evening. In their folklore, when a star falls someone will die. A star did fall that night and Edwidge did die, but not before an angel was commissioned to drive back the spirits of Voodoo and issue her a clear invitation to trust Jesus to forgive her sins and dwell with Him for all eternity.

Several months passed. Though Sarah's body was progressively weakening, her spirit had grown stronger. She had made an impact on the Manor. Everyone knew who to come to if they needed encouragement and prayer, and many of the workers and patients needed just that. So many people started visiting Sarah for prayer that the staff joked about needing to "take a number."

If Sarah wasn't cruising the halls in her wheelchair looking for others, she made herself available by parking at a table in the game room, starting a puzzle, and praying silently. Before long, several residents would join her. As they worked together, Sarah would share about how the Lord loved each one of them from before the foundation of the world and how He still had a plan for their lives no matter how brief their lives might be. "As long as you have breath, there is a will of God for you today—no exceptions!"

Her love for Jesus was growing each day. She loved Jesus more than she loved the few possessions she had left or her reputation. He had fully captured her heart, and she was totally abandoned to Him. Sometimes that love was so strong that she could only describe it as "an ache of love."

"Jesus, I long to see You face-to-face. I long to look into Your eyes of love and see them looking back at me," she whispered under her breath as a prayer many times each day. Her will had been signed long ago, leaving all her assets to missionaries in the 10/40 window. A "Do Not Resuscitate" sign hung on the end of her bed. She was ready to go home when the Lord was ready to take her.

Sarah woke in the middle of the night. Her body was paralyzed and her speech was slurred, but her thinking was still clear. She could not move to push the call button. She had imagined before that to be a prisoner in her body, unable to communicate, would be terrifying. But as she lay in the darkness, unable to move, she was not afraid. She prayed as she listened to the worship CD.

"You're just one step closer to home, Sarah, one step closer to home," whispered Malta tenderly. "You are perfectly loved and there is no fear in love."[5]

"Your body is failing, but your spirit is strong in the Lord. Fight to the end, oh mighty intercessor," said Joel. "Your prayers are powerful. We will hold up your weak arms[6] as your prayers advance the Kingdom one last time."

I don't even have to be able to talk to do God's will. All I have to be able to do is think.

"That's right," said Joel. "As long as you have a pulse, you have a purpose."

Sarah had prayed for the countries and cities in the 10/40 window so many times she had many of them memorized. *Lord, I pray for India. Let Your Spirit fall there. I pray that Christians there would have great spiritual impact. Lord release angels to Calcutta, to Delhi, to Bangalore, to Mumbai....*

In the Spirit, Joel was watching Sarah's prayers ascend like pleasing incense before the glorious throne on the crystal sea. Thunders and lightenings radiated from the throne[7] and the room was full of worship, brilliance, life, and color. Warring angels, reflecting His glory and fierce in their holiness, lined up before the throne. The first one approached and bowed low before the Lord. When Sarah's prayer for Calcutta ascended, Jesus laid His hands on the angel and commissioned him, "Go." The angel turned, set his fiery gaze on Calcutta, and vanished.

To Delhi, prayed Sarah.

"Go!"

To Bangalore.

"Go!"

To Mumbai.

"Go!"

"So amazing," said Joel smiling. "The prayers of an elderly woman, three quarters of the way dead, are shaking the enemy's kingdom halfway around the world."

"Even after all these eons, I'm still astounded that our glorious, omnipotent God has chosen to partner with frail, broken people and He binds Himself to their prayers."

For the next hour, angels were commissioned to the battle in India. Principalities were defeated, strongholds came down, deception was lifted, and souls were saved.

Somewhere around 4:00 A.M., between Cairo, Egypt, and Amman, Jordan, Sarah's arm dropped from the rotating globe as she slid gently into a coma.

Joel and Malta finally received the news from Father that they had been longing to hear. Before sunrise, they were to bring Sarah home. Celestial light flooded the room. The angels glowed with the anticipation of the swallowing up of temporal, earthly life into an eternity of love and peace.

The angels paused from their celebration. "Another stroke," said Joel, smiling tenderly as he looked at Sarah's face.

"Precious in the sight of the Lord is the death of His saints,"[8] shouted Joel. They resumed their marching, dancing, and praising around Sarah's bed.

Malta blew his shofar, and the heavens opened. The atmosphere was energized with even more glory. The sounds of celestial music wafted into the room along with heavenly colors and fragrances. Angels carrying instruments surrounded Sarah's bed. This heavenly choir followed Malta's worship, and their joyful praise not only filled the room, but flowed back to the throne of grace like a tidal wave of pure joy.

Sarah was wholly protected in her utterly vulnerable state from the yellow-eyed demon spirits huddled together in the corner.

"We've tried unsuccessfully to kill her for 16 months. Let's face it. We can't even steal one second from the life span appointed to her," groused Intimidation.

Joel gazed at the spirits with eyes like blazing fire. He unsheathed his flaming, two-edged sword, and on his next pass by that side of the room, slashed through the gnarled demonic mass. They vaporized into a harmless puff of yellow sulfurous smoke. Joel grinned as he resheathed his sword, "I love my job."

With the sun slightly below the horizon, the angels gathered around the bed in a hushed excitement. Joel and Malta bent over Sarah.

"Soooo—close," whispered Malta, stroking Sarah's forehead and smiling at Joel.

"Get ready," said Joel, gazing into the opened Heaven, awaiting the final word. Malta laid his hand on Sarah's chest to feel her shallow breathing.

"NOW!" shouted Joel, having received orders from God's fiery throne. As her last breath escaped her frail, fleshly shell, the sun's first rays peeked

over the horizon. Surges of light permeated the room as the heavenly corridor of glory touched earth. Sarah's spirit emerged into Malta's waiting arms.
Glancing back, she caught a glimpse of her aged face, ashen-colored and
wrinkled. She was whisked through the portal toward an unseen realm of
eternity by a jubilant Malta, with Joel flying ahead. Escorted by her two
triumphant angels, she was moving faster than the speed of light.

Liquid warmth enveloped Sarah. For the first time ever, she felt the complete absence of pain and the presence of total peace. She was leaving behind all sin and the damning results with which she had lived since birth.
Shielded by her two ecstatic angels, she moved rapidly toward a brilliant
light in the remote distance.

CHAPTER 42

"And the King will answer and say to them, 'Assuredly, I say to you, inasmuch as you did it to one of the least of these My brethren, you did it to Me'"
(Matthew 25:40).

"I have held many things In my hands and I have lost them all. But whatever I have placed in God's hands that I still possess."

Randy Alcorn[1]

Before she even had a chance to wonder or conceive of her experience, she was at her destination. "Thank you, Joel. Thank you, Malta," she cried out in excitement, but wondered where that knowledge came from. The two guardians escorted her to the edge of the fountain which was shooting thousands of crimson streams skyward, obscuring everything else from view.

All she could see was brilliant, illuminated, blinding red. Without hesitation, she ran into the fountain's streams, followed by Joel and Malta, all three laughing and shrieking like children. She felt her "body" changing. Living light radiating from the Lord Himself transformed her. She was aware that He was everywhere, but she could not see Him yet. She was fully alive in His presence.

The mantle of humility slipped from her shoulders to reveal the brilliant robe of Jesus' righteousness, a free gift. As the blood washed over her, it left behind a golden celestial glow, not a red stain. She was enveloped in the golden glory; the horrific remnants of sin's effects were washed away. "I'm alive for the first time!"

Gravity's grasp was not in effect there. She jumped and leapt and floated. She threw her head back and laughed uproariously when she realized that her mobility had more than returned. She spun and twirled and grabbed Malta by the shoulders, looking him eye-to-eye, and shook him, "There are no wheelchairs in Heaven—no wheelchairs!" She heard her voice shout out the wonderful proclamation, but it wasn't her regular voice, the elderly one with the embarrassing tremor, it was her youthful voice, only richer. It was the true melody from which the earthly voice had been a cheap, tinny copy.

She looked at her hands, still on Malta's shoulders. The wrinkled, gnarled, swollen digits were perfectly soft, unblemished. She opened and closed her hands effortlessly; arthritis was a fading memory. She had become a younger, perfected version of herself, clothed in a glowing celestial robe!

If she had looked in a mirror, she would not have seen her sin-crippled elderly face staring back, but a youthful, divine individual in complete perfection, body and spirit. She had become the person she was created to be from the beginning, had not sin rushed in to corrupt the world and to corrupt her.

Joel and Malta were enjoying the celebration as much as Sarah, and she was reveling in it! She laughed and shrieked. Her emotions were lively and unrestrained in a way she had never experienced.

"It's hard for me to believe you were an introvert," said Joel.

This caused Sarah to laugh even more. Then the three friends joined hands together in delight: circling right, then circling left, moving faster and faster like children on a playground. When they finally stopped dancing, the angels surrounded Sarah and she was swallowed up in their enthusiastic embrace of love.

Splashing in the fountain felt like she'd been cold all her life, and for the first time she was warm, like being mentally tormented and finding peace, like being depressed and having delirious happiness overtake her, and like being weak, sick, and terminally ill and being transformed to total, perfect health.

She was experiencing the full manifestation of her salvation, experiencing what it means to be a new creature in Christ, all the old had totally passed away and all things had become new for her.[2] When her physical body died, death died for her, and she had followed her risen Savior into life indeed, finally free from all influence of the bludgeoning presence of evil.

Her earthly past seemed very dim, at least the sinful, broken parts. She had not realized the burden of carrying around her sinful ways until they had been shed in death, until she felt their absence for the first time. It was like she'd been carrying around a 500-pound backpack, which she had never been without. They had constantly battled her new nature once she was saved. What she "lived" on earth now seems like a walking, warmed-over death that held absolutely no allure.

It was truly unrestrained freedom. She was now living in perfect peace and harmony. Indescribable feelings had pushed out bitterness, envy, lust, sadness, shame, anger, and jealously. She was so engulfed in love and good feelings that she wondered why she had ever been a prisoner to those wretched things.

As the warm liquid poured over her, she knew that this was what she had been created for, this was what she had longed for on earth and tried to fill with cheap substitutes that never satisfied. She was no longer an alien passing through a strange land; she had arrived at her home, and it was beckoning to her at every level of her being. Each cell and molecule of her new body was vibrating in happiness and unity. For the very first time, she felt comfortable in her skin.

The concept of time, keeping schedules, and being late was left on earth. She didn't even think, *How long have I been here? Should I go someplace else? What is my responsibility?* She was living in the present, with no shame or regrets about the past or worries and stress about the future.

Between the laughter, she realized she was humming, humming along with the waters, which were vibrating and undulating with "music." But no earthly music had ever sounded so sweet. When she listened, she heard innumerable voices singing, "There is a fountain filled with blood drawn from Emanuel's veins and sinners plunged beneath this blood lose all their guilty stains."[3] It was as if the music passed right through her body and she became one with its message.

Her senses were fully alive for the first time, and she was no longer limited just to five. She felt and experienced things that never existed on earth. She could see and smell the fragrances of music and colors. Everything was alive, even objects that were inanimate on earth were all crying out praises to Him.

The ground was vibrating with the glory of God. If she concentrated on it to the exclusion of the other things, she could hear its sweet voice sing out to her, a rapturous swell of music proclaiming God's eternal, indestructible love. She was amazed to watch the notes float by on their staffs and to smell and taste their sweet fragrance—music sweeter than any earthly rose.

She closed her eyes to concentrate on all the new sounds. She was aware of a melody welling up inside her in response to the music-saturated atmosphere. "The Lord is good and His mercy endures forever…"[4] She sang the phrase again and again, in awe as she watched the multitude of living golden notes praising intensely around her.

With all time restraints and other earthly rules and restrictions lifted, she might have stayed for an earthly year frolicking and rejoicing in the fountain of life, had her attention not been drawn to the light illuminating it from behind. She was fixated on the brilliance. As she walked through the fountain, her excitement heightened and she began to run, faster than she had ever run before. Whatever was on the other side of the fountain was glowing brilliantly, illuminating the red, which was a more intense color than she has ever seen. The closer she came to the fountain's end, the brighter the light became. She burst out of the fountain and came face-to-face with her loving Savior, waiting with outstretched arms. She was not aware that she looked just like Him in His glory. His blood has demolished her sin and washed away all earthly remnants; she was as white as snow and glowing with heavenly glory.

When she saw His glorious presence, His dazzling purity, and His unspeakable holiness, she intuitively fell prostrate before Him. *He is Light and Life itself.* She lay her hands on His beautiful nail-scarred feet and felt an overwhelming love like she'd never felt before, like warm oil pouring over her. It was a love that cannot be experienced on earth; human hearts and bodies lack the capacity to endure love this intense—it is reserved for the new bodies of eternity's elect.

She felt secure and refreshed; she laughed and cried at the same time, which no longer seemed a contradiction. Pleasant emotions bombarded her; being in His presence, actually touching Him, was like being in the fountain multiplied by a thousand. Each experience absorbed into her being, and with each one she felt more alive and energetic.

She didn't know if she'd been at His feet for two minutes or two weeks, and she wasn't concerned either way. Jesus reached down, gently lifting her to her feet, and swept her up into a cheek-to-cheek embrace that left her feet dangling off the floor.

Immediately, with lightening speed, she knew Jesus' thoughts, *Welcome home, Sarah. Welcome to Your heavenly home. We were thinking of you when We planned it.*

She clung to Him as tightly as she could and absorbed wave after wave of His love for her. *Never let me go, please never let me go,* she thought as tears of joy rolled down her cheeks.

He finally set her back on her feet, but kept His right arm securely around her waist. He held out His left hand. "Shall we?" His gentle voice asked. Gazing into His eyes of love, she could not find her voice, but intuitively stepped onto His lovely nail scarred feet, and they danced and danced and danced engulfed in the heavenly music.

Joel and Malta beamed as they watched the beautiful, devoted bride enjoying the first dance with her bridegroom King. The angels waited behind a golden altar holding a huge leather book, richly tooled, with her name in gold calligraphy. The dance concluded in front of the altar.

"Now, My precious Sarah, before you enter into your Heavenly reward that I have prepared for you, we must evaluate your life on earth." She could barely take her eyes off of Him. Finally she forced herself to look at Joel and Malta, who were beaming at her and anticipating the great joy that was ahead. Joel opened the book almost to the very back.

What about those first 71 years I lived just for myself? Look at all the wasted pages. Jesus immediately answered her thoughts. He gave her a wink and nodded to Malta, who flipped backward through the pages. Each golden-edged page was crimson, the same color as the fountain. Sarah gasped and threw herself at the Lord's feet in gratitude and adoration.

"As far as the east is from the west, that's how far I removed your transgressions from you.[5] Over her sobbing, Jesus' gentle voice continued. "Sarah, I knew you wouldn't come into the kingdom until you were 71. I knew that before We created the world. On the day you were born, I rejoiced and counted off each day until Pastor Hall visited you. While it was hurtful to watch you make choices that were not in your best interest or Mine, I still rejoiced over you each day because I looked beyond your present to your future. You see, I knew that once you heard the Truth you would accept it and that you would give your whole self to it. You did more for My Kingdom in 18 months than many people who are saved 71 years! I celebrated your future even while you were still My enemy living in the kingdom of darkness."

Jesus lifted Sarah off the floor, and they stood together again in front of the book with His strong arms supporting her.

The page was like a movie, and she saw Pastor Hall knocking on her door.

"I can't believe that's me! I'm so emaciated. I was on my way to Hell—I was going to kill myself!" When Pastor Hall spoke the Scripture, she saw that it is alive. The Holy Spirit was convicting her, and she saw Joel and Malta standing behind her.

"Were you with me all the time?" she asked, looking lovingly at them. They glance at each other and smiled. "Sarah, we were never more than a prayer away."

The Lord continued to turn pages, commenting on Sarah's prayer walking. He showed her each house and all the residents.

"Sarah, in this house, Sam Wagner was ready to leave his wife, Lisa, for another woman. Your prayers enabled Me to soften his heart. He soon cut off the illicit relationship. Pastor Koch is going to visit them in six months and lead them to salvation. They're going to have a baby 13 months after that. Joshua David will have a strong healing anointing. He will travel the world holding crusades and draw hundreds of thousands of people to Me."

Malta turned the next page. "This is the home of Jason Miller. Jason became a Christian on June 17, 1960. He has battled a pornography addiction for over 10 years. It was destroying his life and his marriage. And worst of all, the condemnation he constantly felt kept him from being able to receive My love for him. Your prayers, added with others', drove away the spirit of Addiction that controlled his life, and the anxiety and constant shame he felt left, too. He feels like a new man, like he has a brand new start on life.

"Nancy Trost lives next door to the Millers; she had several large cancerous uterine tumors. She was terrified to be operated on. I healed her while she slept. When she woke up and the tumors were gone, she found her childhood Bible and started reading it again.

"The Snyder family lives in this white bungalow."

"I remember when I was first prayer walking, for several weeks I felt led to loiter there and pray extra long," said Sarah. She looked at Jesus with a curious smile.

He smiled back, motioning to the page, "Look at this precious little toddler, Mitchell. What do you see?"

"I don't know what You mean, Lord," replied Sarah. "He looks happy and healthy to me."

"He is now. He was born healthy, but at 2 months of age, because of a generational curse, he was developing Dystonia, a rare neurological disorder. If you hadn't prayed, Mitchell would have eventually been unable to walk, sit, or eat. The wonderful part is that you were obedient and prayed extra hard. I was able to heal him before his mother had to go through the anguish of even hearing the diagnosis."

"Oh Lord, You are so good; look at all the people You healed, physically and emotionally." A question popped into her mind, but she refrained from asking it. Then she remembered that He knew her thoughts, and she looked at Him for the answer.

"Well Sarah, My beautiful one," He said, taking her chin in His hand and turning it toward His face. "It was My perfect will for you to be healed of your Parkinson's. It was My perfect plan for Pastor Paul to become the chaplain and receive an increase in the anointing. He was going to lay hands on you on June 12 at the jail, in his office, and I was going to heal you so you could stay a little longer and minister to the inmates. Paul's disobedience affected the lives of many, many people in a negative way. You were one of them. Unfortunately, people's sins have consequences, and not just for them only."

With a mischievous twinkle in His eye He said, "Now Sarah, you've been dead for less than an hour; the staff at the Manor doesn't even know you're gone. If you'd like I can easily—"

"No, no, a thousand times no," she shrieked, throwing her arms around Him. "Now that I've seen Your beauty face-to-face, I never want to leave You, ever, ever. Returning to earth, even in perfect health, would seem like dying a thousand deaths to me."

Thirty pages of explanation later, Sarah was beaming at the way the Lord had used her to touch every person on her prayer walk route. "Over half of your neighbors who didn't know Me will get saved because of your prayers. Also you averted a commercial airline disaster with 237 people *and* seven dogs on board." Jesus and Malta smiled at Joel.

"An airline disaster? But I just—it was such a simple prayer!"

Here you are wearing that colorful blouse and remembering to pray for the women in India. Not only have many of them gotten saved, but they are teaching their children what the missionaries are teaching them.

The next page was the Wednesday prayer meeting. The stinging emotions were gone and Sarah laughed as she watched Joel and Malta holding her up as she walked to the microphone. "Oh, Lord. I was terrified, but the worst one was at the Elk's club." Malta quickly flipped to that page. Sarah was surprised to see Joel and Malta holding her up again. "You two were really on the job. It seems funny now, but it sure wasn't then."

"Every time you obeyed Me, especially when you were scared, it was like sweet incense coming up before My throne. From the incense came your little frightened voice, and do you know what it said?" Sarah nodded no.

"It said, 'I love You, Lord. I love You more than I love my reputation. I love You more than my rank, position, standing in the community, or my status. I love You, Jesus, most of all.' Sacrificial obedience is the sincerest form of worship."[6] A tear trickled down His cheek and Sarah gently wiped it away.

"Sarah," said the Lord, "not only did your prayers bring about many wonderful events, but your prayers were responsible for thwarting many of the enemy's plans." Sarah watched herself praying while she read a magazine. Her prayers stopped a drunken husband from beating his wife and child, averted two auto accidents, and kept the spirit of Suicide away from a former satanist who was still being severely harassed.

Malta turned another page, "Here you are praying in tongues while you drove to the grocery store." Sarah saw a man with an oxygen mask on his face and hooked up to tubes in the back of a speeding ambulance.

"Lord, is he? He looks dead."

"Well, he did die several times on that ride, but he's fine now. This is Micah Burris, a pastor in Pennsylvania. He almost took himself out way too early through stress, workaholism, unhealthy diet, and no exercise. He repeatedly ignored My conviction and his wife's pleas. After his heart attack, I healed his damaged cardiovascular system. The doctors said it was a miracle.

"He's a totally changed man. He spends time with Me each day and has learned to cast his cares on Me. He also makes family time a priority. He's setting appropriate boundaries and learning to delegate. He eats healthy food and exercises regularly and has lost 54½ pounds. He's so excited that he's writing a book that will help thousands of pastors learn the same things. I have so many good things planned for him. Now he won't get here for 23 years, 2 months, 5 days, 6 hours, and 45 seconds—right on schedule."

He flipped the next page. On it, Sarah was praying as she was pushing her cart down the produce aisle. "Your prayers helped conceal an underground church in Albania, saving them from persecution and saving the pastor from prison. Now look here; revival broke out among the villagers of a small Polynesian island. Now here your prayers enabled Me to release finances to pay the rent on the medical building where missionaries were healing physical and spiritual wounds in Uganda. That all happened while you grocery shopped."

Sarah collapsed into His side and buried her face in His robe. Tears poured down her cheeks. "Lord, I've never seen any of these people. I've never been any of these places."

"You didn't have to; you just had to pray."

"Oh, Lord, if I'd known it was so easy, I'd have prayed so much more!"

"Not one has ever stood here, Sarah, that didn't say the same thing."

She couldn't speak; she was too overwhelmed.

The Lord gently held and comforted her while this reality set in; then He turned her back toward the book, "Look at the next page. Here you are at Reverend Templeton's grave. I invited you into the fellowship of My sufferings when I asked that you sell your land. You accepted My invitation.

"Most who profess Christianity want the mountaintops, but they don't want the valleys; they yearn for the power of My anointing, but they won't enter the wilderness voluntarily. They long for a deeper relationship with Me, but they won't take up their cross and die daily. Because they refuse those experiences, they never mature; they remain self-focused. Tested integrity is what I desire. You, Sarah, persevered with right choices. You endured isolation and hostility for My sake. I watched you love Me by making the hard decisions."

"How could I not love You, Lord? You saved me and showed me such great mercy when I deserved Hell."

"Here's another time you had to push through your fears. Here's the first day of visiting inmates at the jail. Your obedience just makes Me smile. You were so scared that your sweat glands were working overtime, but you obeyed anyway because you knew it was My will."

"I wouldn't have been nearly as scared if I could have seen my angels sitting next to me in the car."

"Sarah, My Word clearly states that all believers have a guardian angel with them; unfortunately, very few 'believers' really believe the Bible. If they did, life on earth would be totally different."

"Look at you with your cookies and your sweaty armpits, shuffling up to the jail that first day. I was so proud of you! Even though you were only able to minister there for a short time, you made a bigger impact than you know. Even the men who never seemed responsive wondered what motivated you to keep coming back. During the day they were macho braggarts fighting for dominance among the other inmates, but at night when the lights were off, they were scared little boys looking for answers to make their pain go away."

"Lord, who will be the chaplain now that Paul's gone? And what about William?"

"I'm moving Ricky Beech from Kansas to be the new chaplain. He's a former inmate himself so he understands the men. Most importantly, He understands My love *for* Him so He can effectively share My love *with* them. He will reap the harvest from the good seed you sowed with your cookies and prayers. And yes, William will be saved." This news caused Sarah to let out a big whoop and leap for joy.

As the pages continued to turn, the Lord stopped to comment. "Sarah, here you are at the Manor, in your wheelchair. You were looking out the window, wondering if praying in tongues was having any kind of an impact." She saw Bob riding his motorcycle in Oklahoma.

"Sarah, you thwarted the enemy's plans to take his life. He did receive My salvation that Sunday. Look deeper into the page." Sarah watched as angels appeared behind an elderly woman shuffling down the street, protecting her from a mugging. Sarah was too stunned to speak. "Look deeper. Because you prayed in tongues, a premature baby survived and a grandmother, who was raising her three grandchildren alone, was healed of cancer."

"Lord, did that all happen in that one day?"

"Praying in the Spirit is powerful; all that happened in that one 20-minute session in your wheelchair by the door."

The last few pages concluded Sarah's time at the nursing home. "Sarah, having a good attitude during adversity is something you can only do when you totally submit to Me. Many of My faithful servants descend into anger toward Me at the end of their lives. They accuse Me and fall right into the enemy's trap."

"It took me a little while to understand that, didn't it?"

With a huge smile on His face, He grasped her around her waist and threw her up in the air like a father with a toddler. He shouted with joy, "It's all forgiven, Sarah; everything you confessed is forgiven. I have unlimited mercy, and I love, I LOVE, to lavish it on My children." Sarah's mind no longer rejected truth, but absorbed it immediately. She celebrated this revelation.

"Now look at you on the day you said yes to the Holy Spirit and surrendered the last of your pride and resentment. The impact of your life and your prayers exponentially increased. You started stepping out into your prophetic gifting again, in spite of past hurts. I was so proud of you. You encouraged so many at the Manor with My loving words flowing through your mouth."

She looked into the page and saw herself reaching out to lay a shaky hand on the shoulder of the woman at the breakfast table beside her. "Sarah, every breakfast, lunch, and dinner, when the aide was rolling you back to your room, you reached out and patted Ethel. Her disease would not even allow her to respond with a smile. Since she was so nonresponsive, all the staff and patients totally tuned her out, but she still hungered for and needed love and companionship. The only thing she looked forward to each day was those three pats from you after meals. You were truly My hands reaching out to her."

"Lord that was such a little thing. It took absolutely no effort."

"Did you read in My Word that God is not so unjust as to overlook your work and the love which you showed for His sake?[7] You fulfilled all the works I had for you to do while you were there. You encouraged patients and staff alike. You led many patients to Me who will soon be joining us, and your prayers ensured that a witness will continue at the Manor for years to come.

"And look here," He said, His voice climbing in excitement. "This is My faithful, but discouraged Bible translator, Lori Garcia; your prayers gave her the stamina she needed to continue translating the New Testament for a northeastern Iranian minority tribe. Up until this time, the Jamshidi had never had a copy of the Scriptures. You'll share in the reward for the transformation of that village."

Malta turned the next page. "Look at you in bed at night, unable to sleep because of the pain. You turned those times into sweet intercession instead of complaining. You could have been angry with Me because I didn't respond the way you wanted, or you could have easily worked yourself into a severe depression. Instead, as you prayed by your rotating globe, the flames of Holy Spirit fire settled onto the different countries you prayed for."

"Sarah, you still don't really realize that your prayers had an impact not just in Bradbury, not just in Missouri, not just in North America, but all around the world. In some way, sometimes little and sometimes big, your diligent intercession touched every continent. And the best news is that your impact is still being felt even though you aren't on earth anymore. People who accepted My gift of salvation will lead others into a relationship with Me. The benefits and blessings of your prayers will just keep going until I return to earth."

"Now let's see how you spent your money. Most of my children don't realize that I prosper them to raise their standard of giving, not their standard of living. You altered your spending to live a simple lifestyle and sent most of your money to the poor. I know you toyed with having the inside of your house painted and purchasing new kitchen appliances. Instead you sent the money to organizations that helped orphans, child soldiers, widows, the persecuted, and the poor—the very ones who weigh so heavily on my heart."

"Oh Lord, I'm so glad I made that decision. What difference does it make that my refrigerator wasn't stainless steel or that the oven light didn't work? I left it all back on earth."

"As you can see now, it makes no difference. You did well when you chose to love people, not things. Here you are ready to buy a beautiful peach-colored orchid. You decided instead to send the $30 to India where it established a healing room. Because I will heal their bodies, many Hindus will find true healing of their souls."

Matla was still grinning ear to ear. He flipped to the next page.

"Here you are at the department store putting back all the clothes you just tried on. You went to the Salvation Army instead and found what you needed for much less and sent $100 to an orphanage in Myanmar. They rescued this precious nine-year-old, Titux. His parents gave him to the army where he was taught to be tough, to hate, to kill. He will be loved well by my faithful workers at the orphanage.

"This page is interesting," said Jesus pointing to Sarah sitting on her couch holding her check.

"Now that was tough. Fifty thousand dollars was more money than I'd ever had in my life! It was pretty easy to give the tithe, but the more I gave the less I had and the harder it got."

"Where is that money now?"

"You're going to show me aren't you?"

"Let's see how it was used." Sarah leaned over the page, "Bancock, this elderly woman has rescued 18 women and children. They all live together in her two-room house. She's not a missionary; she is a widow who lives by faith caring for those discarded by traffickers to die on the streets. She just keeps bringing them home. She was discovered by a missionary who will move this group to a dormitory-style facility built by your money. They and others will be rescued and restored through My love."

"I meant for my children to run and play and be totally carefree, instead they are abused and exploited in the most horrendous way. Your money will provide everything needed to restore these beautiful ones to wholeness."

"Oh, Lord, I can't wait for them to get here. I love them already."

"Sarah, when you prayed in tongues you didn't know you were an inter-cessory abolitionists, partnering with Me to free my children trapped in the web of human trafficking. Some day soon the little children will rest in my arms. I am appreciative of your obedience."

"Jesus you took my money and used it to help the most destitute, dis-couraged, and downcast on earth. Thank you for sticking with me until I gave it all."

"To look after orphans and widows in their distress is what I call 'true religion.'"[8] You invested your money well, Sarah. Your treasure is now in Heaven, not rusting away on earth. I'm so proud of you."

He winked at Joel and Malta as He closed the back cover on the book, skipping the last page with the picture of the crown.

"Now it's time to reveal your life's work." Joel's fiery sword ignited her book. After the flames died out, the book was gone and in its place was a large, glistening, golden, jewel-encrusted crown. Sarah gasped; she could not comprehend its beauty. "I've never seen anything so beautiful on earth!"

The lower circlet of the crown was lined with fur and composed of six gold segments joined together by hinges and set with precious stones that formed crosses and flowers. Four smaller plates showed detailed pictures in cloisonné enamel of the crucifixion, the keys of death and Hell, the resurrection, and His ascension. From the circlet, eight half-arches met at the top completely covered with 142 rose-cut diamonds, 18 brilliant rubies, and 8 large pearls. Behind the arches was the finest quality red velvet, on which hundreds of gems were set. On top, where the arches met, was a large sapphire, supporting a diamond-studded cross.

Sarah was astonished. She was so taken aback that she lost her footing and Jesus steadied her. "This must be a mistake!" This comment caused Joel and Malta to dissolve into gales of laughter.

"Sarah, the first 71 years of your life were washed under My blood when you trusted Me to forgive your sins. Then I gave you My righteousness as a gift. The sins you committed the last 16 months of your life—you repented of them all. We have no record of any sin in your life.

"We do have a record of the many daily acts you did in secret that so pleased Me. Not only did you prayer walk, Sarah, but your life was a walking prayer. Intercession was the tool you used to set many people free from the enemy's clutches.

"Sarah, there are a few Christians who truly give themselves to intercession and service, but of those, there are very few who do their good works in secret, being content that I alone know what they do. You were one of those. You truly performed for an audience of One. And as much as you performed kindnesses to the least, you performed those kindnesses unto Me. This is your crown, the crown of life referred to in My living Word."[9]

With her heart overflowing with inexpressible gratitude, Sarah, through tears of joy, looked at the glorious, jewel-encrusted crown, the representation of her life on earth. She was ready to lift the crown to cast it at His beautiful nail-scarred feet. Instead, she stepped closer to Him, brushed His hair to the side, and looked at the scars of love on his forehead left from the crown of thorns. As she touched a scar, she saw a vision of the soldier jamming the crown onto His head[10] and the blood running down His face. "Oh Lord, look what You endured for me," she said, gently rubbing her fingers across the many scars. "Nothing I did, no sacrifice I made, is anything. I did nothing, and You did everything. You left this glorious Paradise and died for me."

"Sarah, you were the joy that was set before Me for which I endured the cross.[11] Love hung Me on the cross; desire for you kept Me there. You are My beautiful bride. You are the pearl of great price."[12]

"Thank You, Lord. I'm so grateful that You suffered for me and snatched me from eternal torment and gave me eternal life. I wish I had more to give You. I wish this crown was a million times bigger, a million times more glorious than it is. It pales next to Your great glory. Its worth is nothing compared to knowing You."

In the background she heard and felt sweet music radiating from all directions, penetrating every cell in her body, "All hail the power of Jesus' name! Let angels prostrate fall; bring forth the royal diadem, and crown Him Lord of all."[13] She gently lifted the crown from its place on the altar and, on tiptoes, placed it on Jesus' head. "I crown You King of kings and Lord of all." She, Joel, and Malta all bowed before Him.

"Well done, Sarah, My good and faithful servant. Well done, indeed. You may enter into the joy prepared for those who love Me," He said, pointing to an ornate pearl gate that went higher and farther than she could see. "Let Me show you the mansion that I have carefully and joyfully prepared for you.[14] I've been longing for this day when I could finally give it to you."

Malta and Joel went before them and pushed open the massive gates. Jesus offered Sarah His arm and, staring deeply into His eyes of love, she grasped it. Together they walked under the massive arch. Jesus pointed down to the pure gold, transparent as glass. Sarah laughed, "It's the heavenly pavement. What a revelation that was!"

Then her attention was drawn away from the beautiful walkway by voices—the happiest, most excited and ecstatic she has ever heard. Hundreds of people from every tongue, tribe, and nation run over the top of a grassy knoll, celebrating. They were jubilant—waving, leaping, laughing— and some were holding hands. Every face was a reflection of pure joy.

They must be angels coming to greet the Lord, but they don't have wings. Sarah was in awe, staring at their beauty and grace and especially their overwhelming, contagious joy. She immediately laughed, finding it impossible not to be swept up into their delight.

"No, Sarah, they're not angels; they're part of My beautiful bride, and they're not coming to see Me right now; they're coming to see you," He said as He and the angels stepped aside.

"Me, but Lord—" and then the jubilant group swarmed around her. The first three to reach her were a young Jewish man, a woman from Thailand, and a grandmotherly looking Haitian named Edwidge, who all threw their arms around her. The whole crowd was excitedly speaking over the top of each other in their own languages, yet she could simultaneously hear and understand even those at the back and the hundreds in-between.

With fervent gratitude and intense passion, they all said the same thing, "You don't know me, Sarah, but on the day I died, you prayed, and the Lord's great mercy saved me from the enemy's kingdom!" They clamored to thank her with exuberant hugs and kisses through their laughter and their tears. From the center of the throng, embracing a woman from the Cook Islands, Sarah thought, *I love each of these dear ones more than I ever thought possible.*

Jesus nodded to three remaining figures waiting on the knoll. With elbows linked, George, Pastor Paul, and Reverend Templeton hurried down the hill to welcome Sarah.

Malta and Joel stood on either side of Jesus, all three with their arms around each other's waists, reveling in the first glorious moment of Sarah's many eternal rewards. They look on like proud parents, tears running down all of their cheeks. Jesus' sweet voice sang out again, "Well done, Sarah, My good and faithful friend. Well done!"

Endnotes

Epigraph

1. William Cowper, quoted on www.wholesomewords.org/devotion2.html (accessed August 23, 2010).

Chapter 1

1. Pierre Teilhard De Chardin, quoted on http://quotationsbook.com/quote/19635/ (accessed August 3, 2010).

2. See Psalm 116:15.

Chapter 2

1. John MacArthur, quoted on http://www.biblebb.com/files/mac/sg2198.htm, (accessed July 30, 2010.

2. See Romans 3:23.

3. See Romans 6:23.

4. See Matthew 18:14.

5. See John 3:16.

6. See Romans 6:23.

7. See Hebrews 7:26-28.

8. See Isaiah 64:6.

9. See Proverbs 16:18.

10. See James 4:6.

11. See Philippians 2:8; Matthew 20:28; John 15:13.

12. See Luke 15:10.

13. See Revelation 5:9.

14. Zephaniah 3:17

15. See Luke 5:16.

16. See John 5:19.

17. See James 4:6.

18. See Luke 14:11.

19. 1 Corinthians 3:15

20. See Revelation 22:12; Matthew 25:1-30.

21. Lambert Dolphin, "Description of the Spiritual Gifts," http://ldolphin.org/Spgifts.html (accessed July 26, 2010).

Chapter 3

1. Saint Augustine, quoted on http://www.tentmaker.org/Quotes/humilityquotes1.htm (accessed August 21, 2010).

Chapter 4

1. Frank Bartleman, unknown.

2. See Proverbs 18:6-8.

3. See Proverbs 25:22-23.

4. See Proverbs 25:17-18.

5. See James 1:26.

6. See Matthew 6:18.

7. Maria Robin, quoted on http://www.blogcatalog.com/blogs/orthopaedic-residency-the-attending-perspective.html (accessed August 23, 2010).

8. See Revelation 1:1-3; John 1:47-51; 4:6-30, 39-42; Matthew 8:14-17.

9. See 2 Corinthians 14:3.

10. See 1 Corinthians 14:1.

11. See Genesis 37:5.

Chapter 5

1. Kenneth Cope, Heaven Don't Miss it for the World, (Lightwave, 1988).

2. Randy Alcorn, *The Treasure Principle*, (Sisters, OR: Multnomah Publishers, Inc., 2001), 17.

3. Randy Alcorn, *The Treasure Principle*, (Sisters, OR: Multinoma Publishers, Inc., 2001), 17.

Chapter 6

1. F.B. Meyer, quoted on http://twitter.com/venablethree (accessed August 19, 2010).

2. John Flavel, quoted on http://www.seegod.org/humility.htm, (accessed August 20, 2010).

3. See Romans 8:37.

4. See Hosea 4:6.

Chapter 7

1. C.S. Lewis, quoted on http://www.pbs.org/wgbh/questionofgod/ transcript/spirits.html, (accessed August 19, 2010).

2. See 1 Corinthians 13:4-7.

3. Michael Sullivant, prophetic dream, Metro Vineyard Fellowship, 2001.

Chapter 8

1. F.B. Meyer, quoted on http://www.seegod.org/humility.htm. (accessed August 23, 2010).

2. See Matthew 25:34-36.

3. See Hebrews 6:10.

4. See Matthew 25:37-40.

Chapter 9

1. Bobby Conner, sermon, Christ Triumphant Church, 2002.

2. See Galatians 5:16.

3. Aaron Pierson, *Humility, What We Lack! What The Lord Is, The True Treasure* (self published), 7.

4. Joyce Meyer, Enjoying Everyday Life broadcast, 2007.

Chapter 10

1. Bernard of Clairvaux, quoted on http://catholicexchange. com/2010/08/02/132941/ (accessed August 20, 2010).

2. See Mark 16:17.

3. See 1 Corinthians 14:18; 1 Corinthians 14:4-5.

4. See Acts 2:1-4.

5. If you don't speak in tongues, stop and ask for this extraordinary gift now. The Holy Spirit will provide the words, but you must provide the mechanics of speech. Don't just open your mouth and wait silently. You must use your lips and tongue and push the air through your voice box. Ask the Holy Spirit to give you this gift; then begin praising the Lord in your own language and this wonderful gift will come.

Chapter 11

1. St. Augustine, unknown.

2. See Matthew 9:38.

3. See 1 Kings 18:41-45.

4. See Daniel 10:10-14.

5. See 2 Kings 20:2-6.

6. See Exodus 33:2-3, 12-17.

7. See Genesis 18:20-33.

8. See 1 Peter 5:7.

Chapter 12

1. Joseph Addison, quoted on http://www.icelebz.com/quotes/joseph_addison/ (accessed August 20, 2010).

2. Isaac Watts, "When I Survey the Wondrous Cross," published 1707, public domain.

3. See 2 Timothy 2:2-3.

4. See Psalm 23:5.

Chapter 13

1. Frank Bartleman, http://lighthouse-of-hope.org/Pages/Articles/ordinary.htm) (accessed August 22, 2010).

Chapter 14

1. Adam Clarke, quoted on http://www.freequotesomg.com/famous_quotes_topics/Pride_Quotes/ (accessed August 22, 2010).

2. James M. Barrie, quoted on http://www.worldofquotes.com/topic/sacrifice/index.html, (accessed August 22, 2010).

3. See Esther 4:14.

Chapter 15

1. Bill Treasurer, http://www.eonetwork.org/knowledgebase/specialfeatures/Pages/CourageistheKeytoGreatLeadership.aspx, (accessed on August 23, 2010).

2. Malachy McCourt, quoted on http://www.quotegarden.com/anger.html, (accessed August 22, 2010).

3. See Romans 8:11.

4. See Matthew 18:23-34.

Chapter 16

1. David Mallet, quoted on http://www.quotesdaddy.com/author/David+Mallet (accessed on August 22, 2010).

2. Joyce Meyer, http://www.cbn.com/spirituallife/devotions/Meyer_ChoosetobeChanged.aspx (accessed August 22, 2010).

3. See Isaiah 53:3.

4. See Isaiah 53:4.

5. John Marquez, "Phase 3 Turbo," Christ Triumphant Church, 2008.

Chapter 17

1. Andrew Murray, quoted on http://www.tentmaker.org/Quotes/humilityquotes1.htm (accessed August 21, 2010).

Chapter 18

1. Bobby Conner, sermon, Christ Triumphant, 2005.

2. John Paul Jackson, unknown.

3. Terri Sullivant, prophetic word, Home Group, 2005.

4. See Luke 10:38-42.

5. Shawn Bolz, *The Throne Room Company* (North Sutton, NH: Streams Publishing House, 2004), 13.

Chapter 19

1. Andrew Murray, quoted on http://www.worldinvisible.com/library/murray/5f00.0565/5f00.0565.10.htm (accessed August 20, 2010).

2. Mignon McLaughlin, quoted on http://www.quotegarden.com/anger.html (accessed August 20, 2010).

3. See John 15:16.

4. See Matthew 11:30.

5. See 2 Corinthians 12:9.

6. See John 5:19.

7. See Matthew 5:9.

8. 2 Corinthians 10:5

9. See Philippians 4:8.

10. *New Living Translation* (Carol Stream, IL: Tyndale House, 2008).

11. See 2 Chronicles 16:9.

12. See Romans 8:38-39.

Chapter 20

1. A Missouri Western University Organization, http://www.michaelppowers.com/path/humility.html (accessed August 18, 2010).

2. Contact *Voice of the Martyrs*, USA, by phone, (918) 337-8015, or email, thevoice@vom-usa.org, or visit them on the Web at www.persecution.com.

3. Visit www.1040window.org for more information.

4. See Colossians 1:13.

5. See 2 Corinthians 5:17.

6. Jim Elliott, quoted by Randy Alcorn; *The Treasure Principle* (Sisters, OR: Multinomah Publishers), 6.

7. C.T. Studd, quoted on http://www.eaec.org/faithhallfame/ct-studd.htm (accessed August 23, 2010).

8. See Revelation 2:2-4.

Chapter 21

1. John Eagan, "We Are Ordinary—Devotional," http://mk-mk.facebook.com/topic.php?uid=33874450515&topic=5408 (accessed August 22, 2010).

2. Joyce Meyer, Enjoying Everyday Life broadcast, 2010.

3. See Lamentations 3:22-24.

4. See Matthew 18:12-14.

5. Bob Yandian, Enjoying Everyday Life broadcast, March 19, 2008.

6. See 2 Corinthians 12:9-10.

7. See 2 Samuel 11:3-5, 14-15.

8. See Acts 22:7; 26:14.

9. See Exodus 2:12-15.

Chapter 22

1. Mother Theresa, unknown.

2. Mother Theresa, quoted on http://www.quotedb.com/quotes/ 309, (accessed August 23, 2010).

3. See Ephesians 2:1-2.

4. See Proverbs 16:18.

Chapter 23

1. Andrew Murray, *Humility: The Beauty of Holiness*, http://www. unveiling.org/Articles/humility6.htm, chapter 6.

2. Michael Sullivant, prophetic word, Metro Christian Fellowship, 2001.

Chapter 24

1. Elizabeth Kenny, quoted on http://www.quotegarden.com/anger. html (accessed August 22, 2010).

2. See Philippians 2:3.

Chapter 25

1. Luke 22:27 NIRV.

2. See Matthew 13:18-19.

3. See 1 Peter 5:8.

4. Paul Billheimer, *Destined for the Throne* (Fort Washington, PA: Christian Literature Crusade, 1988).

5. See James 4:7.

Chapter 26

1. C.J. Mahaney, *Humility: True Greatness* (Sisters, OR: Multnomah Publishers, 2005). 21.

2. Wayne Cordeiro, *The Final Challenge*.

3. See Proverbs 16:25.

4. See 1 Peter 2:24.

5. See Romans 3:23.

6. See 2 Corinthians 5:19.

7. See James 1:27.

8. See Hebrews 11:6.

9. See Matthew 12:15.

10. See Romans 10:17.

Chapter 27

1. Walter Buettler, unknown.

2. John Bunyan (The Shepherd Boy Sings in the Valley of Humiliation) quoted on http://www.wholesomewords.org/devotion2.html (accessed August 23, 2010).

3. See Psalm 64:3-5, *New Living Translation* (Carol Stream, IL: Tyndale House, 2008).

Chapter 28

1. Andrew Murray "Humility" e-book. Chapter 6. http://www.worldinvisible.com/library/murray/5f00.0565/5f00.0565.06.htm.

2. Thomas Aquinas, quoted on http://www.the-orb.net/encyclop/culture/philos/abelard3.html (accessed August 22, 2010).

3. See Romans 8:32.

4. See Luke 11:11.

5. See Luke 6:19; Matthew 12:15.

6. Proverbs 17:22

Chapter 29

1. Mike Bickle with Deborah Hiebert, *The Seven Longings of the Human Heart* (Kansas City, MO: Forerunner Books, 2006), 19.

2. See Proverbs 24:16, English Standard Version.

3. See Romans 8:28.

4. Kelly Carpenter, "Draw Me Close," Song.

Chapter 30

1. John Bevere, quoted on http://chfweb.net/articles/quote092298.html (accessed August 22, 2010).

2. See Psalm 139:15.

Chapter 32

1. C.J. Mahaney, *Humility: True Greatness* (Sisters, OR, Multnomah Publishers, 2005), 32.

Chapter 33

1. Fulton J. Sheen, quoted on http://www.quotecatholic.com/index.php/category/humility/ (accessed August 22, 2010).

Chapter 34

1. Aaron Pierson, *Humility, What We Lack! What The Lord Is, The True Treasure* (Self published), 2.

2. Matt Redman, "Blessed be the Name of the Lord," Survivor Records (UK), 2002.

Chapter 35

1. Frances Quarles, quoted on http://quotationsbook.comquote/15527/ (accessed on August 23, 2010).

2. See Philippians 4:7.

Chapter 36

1. Shawn Bolz, *The Throne Room Company* (North Sutton, NH: Streams Publishing House, 2004), 27.

2. See James 4:7.

3. See Proverbs 24:16.

Chapter 37

1. Jonathan Edwards, quoted on http://dailychristianquote.com/dcqedwards.html (accessed August 23, 2010).

2. See 1 Peter 2:23 *New King James* (Nashville, TN: Thomas Nelson, 1995).

3. See Psalm 136:26.

4. See Isaiah 26:3.

Chapter 38

1. James M. Barrie, quoted on http://www.brainyquote.com/quotes/quotes/j/jamesmbar149337.html (accessed August 20, 2010).

2. C.H. Spurgeon, quoted on http://www.spurgeon.org/sermons/0097.htm (accessed August 23, 2001).

3. See Matthew 23:12.

Chapter 39

1. James M. Barrie, quoted on http://www.worldofquotes.com/topic/Life/2/index.html (accessed August 22, 2010).

2. Rick Joyner, *The Final Quest* (Fort Mills, SC; MorningStar Publications, 2006).

3. Many details of the judgment are not given in the Scriptures. I used extra-biblical experiences to make my point. I do not claim that this is how the judgment will be. Don't miss this chapter's message by getting bogged down in whether the judgment will look exactly like this.

4. 1 Corinthians 3:12-15

5. See Matthew 10:42.

6. See Luke 11:23.

7. Aaron Pierson, *Humility, What We Lack! What The Lord Is, The True Treasure* (Self published), 23.

8. See Deuteronomy 12:28.

9. See John 17:17.

10. See Romans 8:28.

11. See Matthew 7:26.

12. See 1 Corinthians 3:10-15.

13. See 1 John 2:15-17, *GOD'S WORD Translation* (Grand Rapids, MI: Baker Publishing Group, 2007).

14. See Matthew 22:37-39.

15. See Revelation 21:4.

16. See Revelation 5:8.

Chapter 40

1. Joni Ames, quoted on http://www.elijahlist.com/words/display_word/3549 (assessed August 23, 2010).

2. Matthew Henry, quoted on http://www.wholesomewords.org/devotion1.html.

3. See 2 Corinthians 4:8.

44444444444444

444

444

4. See 2 Corinthians 4:17.

5. See 2 Corinthians 11:23.

6. See Matthew 10:24.

7. C.T. Studd, quoted by Randy Alcorn, *The Treasure Principle* (Sisters, OR: Multinomah Publishers), 79.

8. Alan Hood, *The Excellencies of Christ* class, International House of Prayer, 2001.

9. Brennan Manning, *Abba's Child* (Colorado Springs, CO: NavPress, 2002), 66.

Chapter 41

1. Wayne Cordeiro, *The Final Challenge.*

2. See Luke 23:32-33; 39-43.

3. See Luke 4:16-18.

4. Isaiah 61:1-2, *New Century Version* (Nashville, TN: Thomas Nelson, 2005).

5. See 1 John 4:18.

6. See Exodus 17:12.

7. See Revelation 4:5.

8. See Psalm 116:15.

Chapter 42

1. (Randy Alcorn, The Treasure Principle, (Sisters, OR: Multnomah Publishers, 2001) 59.

2. See 2 Corinthians 5:17.

3. William Cowper, "There is a Fountain," in Conyer's *Collection of Psalms and Hymns*, 1772. *Music:* Cleansing Fountain, 19th Century American camp meeting.

4. See 1 Chronicles 16:34.

5. See Psalm 103:12.

6. Beverly Bartlett, sermon, Hernhut Club House, 2009.

7. See Hebrews 6:10.

8. See James 1:27.

9. See 2 Timothy 4:8.

10. See Mark 15:17.

11. See Hebrews 12:2.

12. See Matthew 13:46.

13. "All Hail the Power of Jesus' Name," Edward Perronet (words) and Oliver Holden (music), 1780, public domain.

14. See John 14:2.

ABOUT JACKIE MACGIRVIN

She welcomes your feedback on *Angels of Humility*, invites you to join her blog, and encourages you to sign up for free daily email reminders to pray for those who will die in the next 24 hours. Visit http://jackiemacgirvin. com. She is available for speaking engagements, humorous or regular.

Recommended by Jackie Macgirvin

WEBSITES:

Jackiemacgirvin.com—sign up for daily email reminders to pray for those who will die in the next 24 hours.

Joshua Project (joshuaproject.net)—highlights the ethnic people groups of the world with the fewest followers of Jesus; sign up to receive a daily email.

Voice of the Martyrs (persecution.com)—sign up for weekly prayer requests and request the free book, *Tortured for Christ*.

10-40 Window (1040window.org)—the area of the world that contains the largest population of non-Christians.

Mikebickle.org—free teachings about eternal rewards, prayer, and humility and everything else; click on Kingdom Life, then on Eternal Perspective or Humility.

ExodusCry.com—the prayer movement to end slavery. (More people are slaves today than at any other time in history—27 million. Nearly one third of trafficked prostitutes are children.)

BOOKS:

Light the Window, a prayer manual for the unreached, available at ywampublishing.com for $3.99.

Dancing with Angels by Kevin Basconi. Fascinating testimonies of modern-day angelic encounters, available at http://www.kingofglory ministries.org/store/books/dancing-with-angels.html.

Driven by Eternity by John Bevere, available at messengerinternational. org.

Humility by C. Peter Wagner, available at regalbooks.com.

Humility: True Greatness by C. J. Mahaney, available at waterbrook-multnomah.com.

Rees Howells: Intercessor by Norman Grubb, available at clcpublications.com.

The Final Quest by Rick Joyner (this is the author's favorite book), A panoramic vision of the greatest and last battle between light and darkness. Available at morningstarministries.org. To hear this audio book free (PDF, TXT, and more), archive.org/details/AudiobookTheFinalQuest-RickJoyner.

"Only one life, t'will soon be past, only what's done for Christ will last."
C.T. Studd

"And Satan trembles when he sees, The weakest saint upon his knees."
William Cowper

"He is no fool who gives up what he cannot keep to gain what he cannot lose." Jim Elliott

Jesus, I pray for those who are going to die today, that You would let them see Your pure love, longing for them to spend eternity with You. Lord, strip away demonic influence, wounds, deception, and strongholds that would keep them from accepting You. Let them see your eyes of love looking into theirs. Let Your truth be known in their hearts and minds. Jesus, in Your great mercy snatch them from the enemy's grasp even until their last breath.

Made in the USA
Las Vegas, NV
08 February 2021